The Aspen Grove

JANE FULKERSON

"Well, it *coulda* happened…"
– Shorty Timmerman

Dedicated to:
David,
David Eugene,
Jess, Sarah and Eva

"Civilization is hideously fragile......there's not much between us and the Horrors underneath, just about a coat of varnish."

—C.P. Snow

PROLOGUE
PRESENT DAY

CURRENTLY IF YOU DRIVE THROUGH the valley where the O'Neals, the Sullivans, and their friends and neighbors once lived, you will find that it looks like much of the rest of this country. The ribbon of freeway which runs north and south is lined with oil tank farms, industrial parks, malls, housing developments, churches, bars, baseball diamonds, and all of the other amenities we commonly refer to as "civilization." The valley looks nothing like it did in the 1800's, when it was first settled by people who came from points east on this continent or from across the Atlantic.

There are a few landmarks that haven't changed. Ridge lines that haven't been altered by bulldozers or covered with clusters of microwave and cellphone towers standing tall against the skyline. On occasion, the sky is the same brilliant blue and at night the same constellations are visible. And there is the river. It is intent on running its course from northwest to southeast, merging with other tributaries and ultimately becoming part of the Mississippi River.

Running through the valley, the river is alive and constantly moving. The large rocks and boulders which form the riverbed give the water its voice as it collides with them, rushes around or over them, sometimes creating a roar and sometimes a gurgling chuckle.

At a particular bend of the river, on the southern bank, stands a large grove of Aspen trees. It has been there for centuries. The older parent trees periodically die, fall to the ground, and decay into the earth. The younger sprouts, responding to the light and water which nourish them, take the responsibility of keeping the grove alive and thriving.

On an autumn day, when the breeze is brisk, if you stand in the center of the grove and close your eyes, you will hear a sound that will make the hair on the back of your neck stand on end and give you goose bumps. The crisp yellow leaves make a sound that is primal, like the sound of birds in a meadow, suddenly startled to flight. It's a sound that has been heard by humans and animals for eons.

The trees in the grove have been silent witnesses to all that has happened around them. If they could speak, and were so inclined, they could tell stories that would break your heart or give you hope. Since they cannot speak, I will attempt to tell you part of the story of the O'Neals, the Sullivans and some of the others who lived here. Part of the story is all I know. No one ever knows the whole story about anything.

CHAPTER 1

COLORADO, 1883

READY FOR THE DRIVE

WHERE THE EARTH MEETS THE sky, a sliver of light appeared. It was the beginning of another new day, and in the trees and along the barn roof the birds were beginning a weak chorus of chirping, which would grow stronger as the morning wore on.

Daniel could hear them. He'd been dozing for the last couple of hours, not asleep, not really awake, inhabiting that in between world before real dawn.

He normally got up early, but this day would start even earlier than usual. This was a day he had long planned for, anticipated and even dreaded somewhat, all at the same time. He and several other men from three area ranches were going to begin an eighty mile cattle drive. They were herding several hundred head of cattle they had pooled for the drive to the nearest rail head. Daniel, though not the oldest participant in this venture, had the largest number of cattle and therefore felt somewhat responsible for the success of the drive. The last drive they had made, two years before, had been nothing less than an ordeal, largely because of adverse weather. They were starting this one in mid August, a month later than the previous one, so everyone was hopeful that it would be a much better experience for all concerned.

Johanna, Daniel's wife, was already up and in the kitchen downstairs. She and their cook and housekeeper, Rosa, would be gathering eggs from the henhouse, slicing slabs of bacon and making biscuits to feed the men who would be arriving in another hour or so. They would have a large breakfast, mount up and ride out. The two youngest riders participating in the drive, the Hanson boys, Ben and Jack, had camped out the night before, keeping a watch on the cattle that had been gathered during the two previous weeks. The cattle had been counted by brand and were now mingled together, grazing and drinking from the nearby river. The upcoming drive would be long and arduous.

In the two rooms across the hall from Daniel and Johanna's bedroom slept Sarah, their five year old daughter, and James, Johanna's sixteen year old brother. James had lived with them for the past four years since their father, William Sullivan, had died. Daniel wondered if James would get up to see them off or not, as he was very disappointed not to be going on the drive. He had asked Daniel many times during the summer to be included, and his arguments were legitimate. He was a very accomplished rider, a hard worker and knew how to handle cattle as well as the Hanson brothers, who were eighteen and nineteen years of age. Daniel had nearly relented at one point, but remembering the struggles of the previous drive, where they had lost cattle during thunderstorms and nearly lost a rider in a treacherous river crossing, he had refused James' request.

There had been no loud arguments and no misbehavior, as James respected Daniel too much for that. Daniel had spent quite a bit of time reasoning with James. He told the boy that where he was really needed was at the ranch. There were horses and the remaining cattle to tend to. Johanna, Rosa and her ranch hand husband Hernando would undoubtedly need help with something every day.

As the time for the drive had drawn closer, James had grown very quiet and the last three days had found him spending a lot of time away from the house: fishing, riding until late in the evening, and taking his supper on the front porch while the rest of the family ate at the kitchen table. James knew it would be at least two years before another drive when he would be allowed to participate, and that seemed like a long time away.

Knowing it was time to get up, Daniel rose from the bed and dressed in near darkness. As he left the room, he glanced back at the bed and remembered the previous night with Johanna. They had made love in an especially tender way, knowing it would be the last time they would be together for eight to ten days. They were seldom apart for that length of time.

Stepping across the hall, Daniel quietly entered Sarah's room. He could hear her gentle breathing, and leaning down he touched her hair and kissed her on the forehead. She made no movement. Daniel whispered, "Love you, Sarah Girl" and left the room. Back in the hallway, he listened to see if there was any sound coming from James' room. There was not, so he moved quietly down the hallway and then down the stairs.

Johanna had risen earlier than usual and had gone downstairs to start the fire in the wood burning stove which took up a large part of the kitchen. It was used for both heating the house in winter and cooking meals for her family. In the ten years she had been married to Daniel, she had finally learned most of the secrets of using the stove.

This was not the house she had grown up in. Rather, it was the second house built by Daniel's parents and had become her home at the time of her marriage. She and Daniel had lived with his mother, Mary O'Neal, for the first four very difficult years of their marriage. Mary had died quite suddenly one very warm August afternoon while harvesting vegetables in her garden. To everyone who knew her it seemed a very appropriate way for her to leave this earth. Johanna had learned a great many of her life skills from both her own mother and Daniel's and she counted herself very fortunate to have known and been loved by both of these remarkable women.

Today would be an important day in their lives. Cattle that they'd spent two years raising, branding, caring for and swearing at, would be moving eastward, under the care of Daniel and their neighbors. She hoped it would go well, because the sale of the cattle would bring much needed cash income to their household and give them a greater sense of security. Johanna generally didn't spend a lot of time thinking about this because her family lived as well as most of their surrounding neighbors. They all worked very hard for everything they had and everyone seemed more or less content with the lives they had forged in the valley. But now that there would be additional income, Johanna had begun thinking about things she would like to have, not just about what they needed to stay alive.

She had made a short list of things for Daniel to look for in Culver, the rail head destination, once the cattle had been sold. She and Sarah needed new dresses and Daniel and James definitely needed some new shirts and she had carefully thought out how many yards of various material she would need. Also, items like thread, buttons and some lace for the garments she would make for Sarah. Last night she had sat at the kitchen table with Daniel going over the list in detail, explaining to him what he should ask the mercantile store clerk. She'd gone over the list a couple of times and then noticed that Daniel was smiling at her, so she'd stopped and said, "Daniel, do you understand all of what I'm saying?" His smile had grown even wider as he'd replied, "I think I can handle it." He'd then picked up the list, put it into his shirt pocket, picked up the kerosene lamp and they'd walked upstairs to bed.

Now, Johanna was busily measuring flour into her mother's worn but treasured blue mixing bowl, concentrating on making a double batch of biscuits. She and Rosa had been hoarding the eggs they'd collected that week from under the hens in the henhouse. They'd kept them in the cool of the back porch, knowing they'd need every egg they could gather for this large breakfast meal. Rosa was slicing bacon and counting the pieces, trying to calculate how many slices the men would eat. Johanna finally said, "Rosa slice both of the slabs from the smokehouse, because I'm sure they'll eat all of it." Rosa knew she was right.

Rosa and her husband Hernando had come north to this valley over twenty years ago as a very young, newly married couple. They left an area over 100 miles south that had been plagued by drought and lack of work opportunity. Their encounter with the Sullivan and O'Neal families had been very positive and the couple had worked for both families alternately ever since. Many of their years in the valley had been plentiful and others had been desperately lean. Rosa and Hernando had always been paid and housed, even when cash was short. After a few years they were regarded as part of both families. They had never been able to have children of their own but had helped care for and raise both Daniel and Johanna and their siblings and loved them all very much. They lived in the small house that stood about fifty yards from the current O'Neal home. It was the first structured home John and Mary O'Neal, Daniel's parents, had built and lived in after a more primitive sod house.

The evening before, Johanna had set the dining room table. Both additional leaves had been placed in the table to comfortably accommodate the anticipated number of men. Ordinarily, the table was kept at its smallest seating capacity to maximize the living space and the family ate their daily meals around the rough wooden table in the kitchen.

Johanna had carefully spread the dining table with her second finest tablecloth and had laid out her good china. It had been brought to this valley by her grandmother after being carefully packed and shipped from Ireland on the same ship that had brought her grandparents to America. Her father had carefully crafted the china cupboard which now stood in her dining room. Her mother had used the china on rare special occasions, and until recently, so had Johanna. But, in the last couple of years, she had decided to use it whenever guests graced their table. She reasoned that, should all of the china be chipped or broken by the end of her life, then so be it. She secretly hoped some of it would survive to be inherited by her daughter, but she wanted people they regarded as their friends to feel special whenever they came to their home and shared a meal.

She now busied herself in the preparation of biscuits and coffee while she and Rosa chatted about how they would serve the meal. Daniel had come downstairs and gone to the barn and saddled his horse, Zeb. He ventured out to the pasture where the cattle had bedded down the night before to see how the herd and the two young cattle-men were doing. A little while later, Daniel returned and said that all was well and everything was in order. Johanna hoped the drive would begin without any problems.

Upstairs, James had awakened about an hour earlier and was listening to the sounds in the house. He had decided the night before that he would not go downstairs until the riders had left the house and began moving cattle off the premises. He could not bear the thought of having the Hanson boys making remarks to him about the fact that he wasn't going, or simply smirking at him, saying nothing. He was sure they would, because they'd already taunted him a couple of times when he'd helped round up and count the cattle for the drive. He didn't trust his ability to resist making some remark in return that would upset his sister. He knew how important this day was to his family and didn't want to do anything to mar its memory. He'd brought some bread and jerky into his room the evening before so he wouldn't have to be tortured by the smell of bacon and eggs cooking below him. He wasn't that much of a martyr to his feelings for his family.

Outside he could hear the sounds of men arriving at the house and soon he could hear conversation coming through the heat grate that was near the head of his bed. The most clearly audible voice was that of Calvin Syme, who was their nearest neighbor to the south. Calvin was five years older than Daniel, had a wife, Emma, and two sons younger than James. He was a man of great humor and had hunted and fished with Daniel and James for many years. It was knowing that he wouldn't be along on the drive to listen to Calvin tell stories of his youth and jokes he'd remembered from years ago, that made James the most sad about missing the drive.

Below in the kitchen, Johanna and Rosa began frying bacon and scrambling eggs. The biscuits were coming out of the oven and more were going in, coffee was being poured and there were sounds of eating and eager talk of how many miles they'd make that day.

From the kitchen, Johanna watched the men eat the meal she and Rosa had prepared. She noticed how carefully they ate, not spilling coffee or losing food from their plates onto the tablecloth. These were not refined men, but they were men who knew good manners. They appreciated the care with which this meal had been prepared and served on good china, and they had no intention of making a mess if they could avoid it.

Daniel sat at the head of the rectangular dining room table. He was, in Johanna's opinion, the most good-looking man in the room. He was just over six feet tall, with sandy, brown hair that had been blond in earlier years. His blue-green eyes were as quick to smile as his lips. The hint of freckles across his face darkened during the summer months when he spent most of his time outside. At thirty years of age, he was strong because of constant physical labor and Johanna couldn't remember the last time he'd been ill. He looked a lot like his father. Daniel had inherited his father's calm nature and his mother's intelligence and good humor.

The other men seated at the table along with their good friend Calvin Syme were the Hanson boys, Ben and Jack, Jonathan Ellis, known by all simply as "Ellis", Swifty Rhodes, Rosa's husband Hernando, and the cattle drive's cook, Sam. Ellis and Swifty were the hired men who worked part time, as they were needed, for both Calvin and Daniel. They lived alternately in the bunk house on the O'Neal ranch or at a boarding house in the town of Fergus, which was eight miles from the O'Neal homestead.

They did "odd jobs" to supplement their ranching income and many utilized their talents. Ellis, in his early 40s had served in the Union Army in the last year of the war. He was an excellent tracker and a valuable asset to his ranch employers as he kept them supplied with venison and an occasional elk. He made it a point of keeping the wolves and coyotes at bay during calving season and gave all of the hides of predators he shot to James for tanning. He had always been a single man, saved little money, enjoyed visiting the saloons in Fergus and had a "lady friend" who worked at one of them. He wasn't a man who said much, but his loyalty to the O'Neal and Syme households was unquestioned.

Sam had come to the drive late, as the cook originally hired had broken his leg just the week before. Sam was an unknown element; he had appeared at the O'Neal ranch and told them that he knew they needed a cook for the cattle drive and would like the job. He was very vague about his experience as a cook or where he had come from, but after Daniel consulted with Calvin, they had decided to hire him… more out of desperation than anything else.

At the table Daniel was conversing with Hernando, giving him last minute instructions about things that needed to be done while they were gone. Ben and Jack were exuberant and showed no signs of lack of sleep from their previous night of watching the herd. They finished their breakfasts quickly and seemed impatient with the older men at the table who were taking their time, having second helpings of eggs and bacon and additional cups of coffee. This was the first real adventure for these boys. Their father, Robert Hanson, who was unable to make the trip, seemed to have no apprehension about their ability to accomplish their task as drivers. He had strictly instructed Daniel that the money received for the Hanson cattle should not be entrusted to them, but paid to him directly once the men returned home. He had given Daniel permission to give his boys a few dollars of spending money once the cattle were sold, because he knew they would want to explore the larger town of Culver. He also knew the boys would spend the money unwisely, and he had no desire to hear how they'd spent it once they returned.

Johanna and Rosa busied themselves pouring extra cups of coffee and asking the men if they wanted more food. Ben and Jack, wearing big grins, each made a point of asking where James was and Johanna simply said that he was busy doing other things at the moment. She knew her brother could hear the commotion in the house and felt a twinge of sympathy for him.

When it was time to leave, Daniel stood. One by one the men graciously thanked Johanna and Rosa for the wonderful breakfast as they too rose and began to leave the table. Calvin lifted his plate as he thought to help clear the table, but Johanna assured the men that all would be taken care of after they left. As careful as the men had been with the china, Johanna didn't want to take any more chances than necessary with its survival.

Gradually the house cleared and Daniel hesitated at the door until everyone was gone. He turned to his wife and allowed her time to put her arms around his chest and say the things she always said, when he left to go for an extended time or even to check cattle in bad weather.

"Daniel, promise me you'll be careful."

"You know I will."

"You won't take any unnecessary chances?"

"You know I won't."

"You know I love you."

"Yes I do. And you know I love you, Jo." It was the name he'd called her since they were children and now used only in private moments.

She hesitated and then asked, "You have the list for the shopping?"

"Put it in my saddle bag and tied the saddle bag on Zeb this morning," he replied, smiling.

"I love you, Daniel," she repeated.

He answered by kissing her and holding her close for a long moment.

"We'll be back in a few days, Johanna, and tell Sarah I will bring her a present."

With that, he broke loose from her grasp, picked up his hat and gloves from the sofa in the living room, turned and walked out the door. Just before closing it, he turned, smiled broadly and said, "I love you."

Then he was gone.

Johanna went to the window and watched the men mount their horses, which were all tied to the front yard hitching rail. She heard Ben yell loudly, "So long James, see you when we get back." He was looking up at the front of the house, because he knew that was where James' room was located.

Johanna frowned and thought to herself, "Too bad your parents never taught you any manners." She heard Jack laugh and she shook her head. She watched a bit longer and listened to the men ride out of the yard, towards the cattle who were peacefully grazing near the river.

Shortly, she heard the animals mooing and milling and then gradually she could tell they were beginning to move east. She sighed and went back towards the kitchen to begin cleaning up after the meal. Rosa was well into the task and Hernando had gone out the back door to tend the chickens and begin his day of chores.

It would be at least another hour before Sarah woke up

and she had no idea when James would come downstairs to eat some breakfast, but she inventoried the remaining bacon and eggs and determined she would make him a large breakfast.

CHAPTER 2

DAY ONE OF THE DRIVE

AT THE END OF THE first day's trek, Daniel was very happy with how the day had gone. Mostly that was due to the fact that the previous winter had been a relatively easy one with the snow coming in late and leaving early. The cattle had come into the spring as stress-free as they could possibly be in this harsh country. There had been an abundance of rain in the spring, bringing good grass in the summer, which meant the cattle were healthy and carried extra weight. They could walk additional miles each day without becoming unduly tired or having to stop and graze along the way, as the men pushed them toward their destination.

It wasn't overly hot, and the flies seemed at a minimum. Even though there was a great deal of dust generated by the movement of the herd, a breeze from the northwest kept the dust moving in a direction that didn't overwhelm the men who were riding at the rear.

Because of his years of experience with both horses and cattle, Ellis was the most valuable rider they had, and he did the work of at least two men and never seemed to tire. The Hanson boys were in the height of their glory and eager to prove they were grown men and as good as anyone else on the drive, so they would never be caught "slacking off."

Swifty, in his mid 20's, was a young man who had drifted into the lives of the O'Neal and Syme families when they had been preparing for the drive two years ago. He'd hired on as a temporary drover, but hadn't left after the drive was over and both Daniel and Calvin were glad to have him working for them. When anyone asked Swifty where he was from, he'd reply, "Oh, just all over."

Daniel rather suspected he'd had a run in with the law at some point, but didn't ask him a lot of questions about his past. Swifty was a hard worker, but both years he'd worked for them, he'd disappeared for several weeks during the fall. When he'd returned, he'd offered no explanation as to where he'd been. Occasionally Swifty would go fishing with James on the river, but even then, when it was just the two of them fishing together, he offered no information about his life. Now on this trail, Daniel noticed the young man had an especially keen eye for spotting cattle that were drifting or falling behind and he took it upon himself to keep those animals in line.

Daniel and Calvin together served as the "ramrods" of the outfit, who watched where they were going and kept everyone moving in the right direction. Following the lay of the land and making sure the cattle would be in a place they could water and graze at some point every day was their major task. It meant generally following the route of the river, but staying south of it most of the time.

They'd have to cross the river twice, as it crisscrossed in front of them, ideally on day two, and again on day four, as they neared the end of the drive. They hoped to be on the north side of the river, approaching Culver at the end of day four. There, they'd rest and water the cattle and then drive them into the railroad stockyard on day five.

The riders would have part of that day to rest and recuperate, and then a day to buy whatever they intended to take home with them. The plan was to leave Culver on the seventh day. The time it would take to get home would depend on weather and how hard they pushed the horses. Each man had two spare mounts, which were being herded along with the cattle. The men would trade out horses every other day or so to keep their mounts as fresh as possible.

The "chuck wagon" driven by Sam and pulled by four mules belonged to Calvin. It was a sturdy vehicle that could handle the rough terrain, and there were two spare wheels, one attached to each side. A box of tools rode under the seat and Daniel and Johanna had put together what they referred to as the medical kit; which contained straight, slender boards that could be used as splints, bandages, iodine, a heavy needle and thread for stitches and other basic essentials to be used in minor injuries. They could only hope that no one would be seriously hurt.

Before leaving, all of the households represented, the Symes, O'Neals and Hansons, had provided food for the trip. It consisted mostly of ham, venison and beef that had been smoked or turned to jerky. In addition there were cans of beans, fruit and plenty of flour and lard to make biscuits. The only fresh food they had was a half bushel of apples, harvested a week earlier from the Sullivan orchard, which would be used as part of their lunches and in the evening. The menu was going to be simple but there would have to be plenty of whatever was going to be fixed, because the men would be working from before dawn until after dusk.

As the first day ended and the Hanson boys were sent to find wood for a cook fire, it became apparent that Sam the cook was the weak link of the outfit. As Daniel and Calvin helped unhitch the mules and led them to a place where they could be hobbled to graze, Daniel mentioned to Calvin that he thought he'd smelled whiskey on Sam's breath when he'd been close to him. They decided that after supper while Sam was cleaning up after the meal, the two of them would search the wagon together and try to locate the bottle and dispose of it.

They could not tolerate anyone drinking on this trip, especially the man driving the wagon which could be driven into a hole or over the edge of a draw. It was simply too dangerous. When Sam had been hired, "no drinking on the trip" had been emphasized to the man and he'd agreed. Daniel was now visibly aggravated and Calvin tried to calm him down as they tended to the mules.

"Damn it Calvin, we cannot afford for anything to go wrong on this drive."

"I know, Daniel, but it's going to be alright. We'll work this out with him," Calvin said, as he finished wrestling with the hobbles on the last mule. "Don't worry so much; we've had a good first day." The older man stood up and took hold of Daniel's left shoulder. "Remember two years ago? *That* was a real bitch of a first day - pouring down rain that didn't quit for the next two and a half days. We nearly drowned our asses." He was chuckling as he reminded Daniel of their earlier adventure.

Daniel couldn't help but smile at Calvin's good nature and he took a deep breath and said, "Okay, we'll tend to this after supper."

Camp was made. Saddles had been pulled from the horses and were positioned near the wagon, as the men would use them to rest their heads as they slept in their bedrolls. Ben and Jack had brought in enough firewood to last through supper and into the evening. They had each tied their saddle ropes to small dead trees and had drug them into camp as firewood. They dismounted and untied their ropes from the dead trees.

"Found these layin' down by the river" Jack said proudly and Ben added quickly, "Yeah, they were pretty easy to round up. Didn't give us any trouble at all."

Swifty and Ellis each grabbed the tools from the wagon needed to accomplish the task of converting the dead trees to firewood: a very sharp axe and a bowsaw. The wood was brittle and quickly came apart. It wasn't ideal wood for a long burning fire, but they needed coals to cook over and time to enjoy one another's company for a short time, not heat for the night.

Sam began lugging supplies from the wagon and stumbling around the campsight. Calvin and Daniel looked at each other apprehensively, and together pitched in and helped with the cooking skillets and utensils. All of the men on the drive had lived outdoors, had been on hunting trips, or had cooked over open fires during the war for their own survival. The job of the cook was to do that job for them, so they could rest after a long day of hard work.

That evening, Sam did some of the cooking, but the beans were burned and he needed help with the clean up. No one outwardly complained, but the crew was not happy with the cook.

As the sun began to set into a beautiful display of deep gold and yellow, Daniel and Calvin took Sam aside and began to discuss their arrangement as his employers. Calvin took the lead by clearing his throat.

"Sam, as you remember, Daniel told you there would be no liquor on this trip." Calvin, who was just slightly shorter than Daniel, a little bit heavier, with a short beard that was starting to show some gray, was an imposing figure. His eyebrows furrowed as he spoke seriously to Sam and he tried to make his soft brown, humor loving eyes, as stern as possible.

"What you talkin' about?" Sam replied shakily, "I ain't had no liquor!" He seemed indignant and the fact that he was denying the obvious made Daniel angry.

He stood directly over Sam, who was about four inches shorter than he was and said very matter of factly, "Listen Sam, we're going through that wagon and when we find your bottle, we're going to empty it into the ground, do you understand that?"

Now Sam was more than indignant, he became surly and snarled, "I ain't got no damned bottle, so you can hunt that wagon all you want."

With that Calvin and Daniel went through the wagon front to back and when they were finished, had found no whiskey bottle. As they climbed out of the back of the wagon, Calvin remarked, "Well, hell, maybe he drank it all and that's the end of the problem."

"I sure hope so," Daniel replied, "I don't want to have to put up with this all the way to the railhead."

Calvin sighed and said, "Let's go check on the cows, Daniel. We're first up."

Daniel and Calvin had volunteered to take the first shift of watching the cattle during the night. This was an around-the-clock endeavor and the men would have to take turns during the night, in two shifts, to make sure the cattle and horses didn't stampede or wander off. In addition, they would have to keep their eyes open for predators who might be in the area. Adult cattle and horses were not likely to be attacked, but prowling animals could spook the cattle into a stampede or scatter them. Two sets of human eyes watching the herd at all times was an absolute necessity.

They walked back to the campfire where the men were settling in, joking and just relaxing. The Hanson boys, who had not slept at all the night before were fading rapidly and were already laying out their blanket rolls and getting ready to sleep.

"You get that sorry excuse of a cook straightened out?" Jack asked.

"It's gonna be fine," Calvin replied, "Now get some sleep, we've got a long day tomorrow."

"Swifty are you and Ellis set for the second shift?" Daniel asked.

"Yup, we'll be waiting for you to wake us up." Ellis replied, as he added a couple of more pieces of wood to the fire and stacked some additional logs within reach. He wanted to keep the fire burning awhile longer, because he had learned over the years that the smell and sound of a good campfire would put him to sleep within an hour.

Daniel and Calvin re-saddled their horses quietly, having given both their mounts a rest from carrying the saddles and all that was attached to them, their ropes, rifles in their scabbards and saddlebags. Daniel spoke to Zeb, his very dependable, four year old roan gelding: "You did a good job today Zeb. Now just gotta' put in a few more hours, then you can rest." He patted the horse's neck affectionately, and received a friendly snort in return.

He put his left boot into the stirrup and pulled himself up into the saddle and turned Zeb to the left. As he did so, he glanced right, toward the campsite. He noticed that Sam was bedding down beneath the wagon and he hoped all would go well and be quiet during this night.

Daniel and Calvin decided to generally ride in a circle, one man going left the other right, keeping the herd contained between where they were and the river. Riding very slowly and stopping often, so as not to agitate the animals, it would take nearly an hour to make a complete circuit. Daniel knew the moon would be three-quarters full when it came up. With no cloud cover, once their eyes adjusted to the darkness, they would be able to see well enough to make out the outlines of the animals in the herd.

"Okay, Calvin, meet you back here in awhile." Daniel took out his father's pocket watch and held it close to his face. There was still just enough light to make out the time.

"Nice night," he commented to Calvin.

"It's perfect," Calvin replied.

The two men rode off in opposite directions into the growing darkness.

CHAPTER 3

DANIEL REMEMBERS

RIDING SLOWLY AROUND THE PERIMETER of the herd, Daniel would occasionally stand up in his stirrups, just to change positions and relieve the pressure put on his back. When he came up on a small rise, overlooking the herd, he dismounted and stood beside Zeb who put his head down and pulled off the tops of some grass beneath his feet.

Daniel was tired, but it was a good tired and he was very thankful things had gone so well that day. As always, when he was away from the ranch, on hunting trips in the high hills to the west of his home or on a cattle drive, his mind turned to the ranch and his family.

He wondered what Johanna's first day with him away had been like. How was she doing? Was James being helpful and not giving his sister a bad time? How was Sarah, his only child? Was she missing him, as she usually did when he was away? He smiled at the thought of her.

After a few minutes, he remounted Zeb and slowly found his way off the rise and back down to the level of the herd and worked his way to the river, which was so much lower than it had been on their last trip. He let his horse take his time and drink the cool water. Zeb let him know when he was finished by lifting his head, shaking it and then heading back to the low bank.

Much of the herd was now bedded down and very quiet after their long walk during the day. They were settled in and Daniel headed away from the water where the mosquitoes were thickest, and found a place where he could just watch everything out in front of him for awhile. He heard no coyotes howling and figured they might start their chorus later, when the moon had fully risen.

Once again, his mind returned to the ranch and Johanna. He thought about the lifetime he'd spent with her, because although they had only been married ten years, since the time he was 20 and she 19, they had known each other all of their lives.

Johanna had grown up on the Sullivan Ranch, a few miles west of where he'd lived since he was born. They were both third generation residents of this land that had at one time been totally unsettled and very hard. Both sets of their grandparents had come to this valley at about the same time, when there was nothing from horizon to horizon but grass, water, and trees. Their grandfathers had both had a dream of creating a place to raise their families and establish viable ranches which would be inherited by their children and grandchildren. And they had done that, living first in sod shacks, gradually building a herd of cattle. They feuded with the local Indians, enduring years when they honestly did not know if they would survive. Eventually, they'd been able to build houses and barns and had "become respectable" as their Grandfathers had liked to put it.

Johanna's family had come from Ireland and they were not poor. They had owned land and property, but her grandfather, Thomas Sullivan, had been restless. In the early 1820s when he was still a young man, he had decided to move to St. Louis, a place he knew nothing about, except what his brother who had immigrated there had written and told him. He had taken his share of wealth from their father's estate and headed to the new world, bringing his young wife, who was expecting their first child.

They crossed an ocean and nearly half a continent. It had been quite a journey and they had settled in with the brother's family in St. Louis. The families jointly operated a large mercantile store which helped supply the growing number of inhabitants of St. Louis with everything they needed from clothing, furniture, hardware, and building materials. St. Louis was beginning to boom in the 1820s and things were going well. However, Thomas Sullivan wanted more: land of his own, away from the thousands of people all living like ants on a hill.

And so, after a couple of years he'd packed up his wife Mary and young son William, and struck out west with everything important they owned, including the trunk full of china which had survived the journey from Ireland. They had driven their wagon west over a trail, until there was no more trail, and beyond that until there were no other people in sight. Finally, after weeks of westward travel, they had found the valley and decided to call it home.

Daniel's grandparents, Patrick and Catherine O'Neal, had a totally different early life. They were quite poor and looking to better themselves when they came to New York. Things had not gone well for them there and they kept moving west as they could work and earn money to travel onwards. Both of them had been very hard workers, laborers who worked for minimum pay because they were Irish.

Catherine had worked as a domestic, and her husband had worked in sawmills and as a farm hand or carpenter. They saved every penny they possibly could, as they too gradually made their way to St. Louis. Work was easy to find and they dug in to earn enough money to continue their westward trek. And so it was that eventually they took that same trail west and met up with the Sullivans and had formed a partnership that had endured for decades and generations.

Luckily, the claims their grandfathers had made on the land had held fast, when the area had become part of the territory and then state of Colorado.

Johanna's parents had brought three children into the world. Johanna was the oldest, then Thomas who had died at the age of four of a fever and then James, the youngest.

Daniel's parents had four sons: Daniel the oldest, Maxwell "Max" who had been thrown by a horse at age 13 and died of a broken neck. Jesse left the ranch at age 20 and had gone west to California to work in the lumber industry, and finally Richard, who as soon as he'd turned 18 had left the ranch and headed for Denver. They seldom heard from either Richard or Jesse - just an occasional letter, letting them know they were still alive and that their lives were going well. Both were happy to be well away from the very hard life on the ranch.

All of the children in both families had been schooled by their parents and grandparents and the importance of learning to read and write and do basic mathematics had been stressed emphatically. Now there was a school, the Cole School, between the ranch and Fergus and Daniel was glad that their children would be able to receive an education from someone other than he and Johanna.

Their "children" - Daniel thought of those words. The first four years of their marriage, Johanna had become pregnant twice. Both times the pregnancies had ended in stillbirths and both times they had been boys. She had carried the babies five and six months, respectively. Nearly six years ago, when she had become pregnant the third time, the doctor in Fergus had insisted that she spend most of her time resting in bed. Daniel had been insistent that she obey his recommendation.

It had been difficult for Johanna to do this because she was such a good homemaker, but both Daniel and Johanna knew it was the only way she would safely deliver the child. There were times in the last three months when she was carrying Sarah when Daniel would come home in the evening tired from his work. Still, he would spend the evening with his wife, rubbing her back, which hurt constantly from lying in bed. He would hold her in his arms and they'd talk softly to one another about memories they'd shared as children or what this child they would be having soon would be like. When the baby would kick, he'd touch the place she'd indicate where she could feel it and leave his hand there until the baby would kick again. Feeling the life inside her and fearing the loss of another child terrified him and would continue to do so until the child was born alive.

He was delighted to have a daughter, he loved her more than he had ever imagined it possible that a father could love a child. But, he knew that unless they had a son, the fate of the ranch was in a precarious situation. He knew from personal experience that only a son who wanted more than anything to continue the history of ownership of the land would do so. He was the only one who had kept it going into his generation.

Johanna and James still owned the Sullivan homestead, and the land was used to graze the O'Neal cattle, but the house was now boarded up and abandoned. James insisted that when he was a bit older he would live in "his own house" as he called it and raise horses. It was his dream. He wasn't much for cows, but he loved horses. Daniel didn't know how that was going to turn out, but he knew that only incoming revenue could keep either place going.

He knew the railroad was coming. The last time they'd been to Culver the buyer who had purchased their herd told Daniel that within five years there would be a rail spur line into Fergus. The railroad saw it as a gateway to produce that could be very profitably shipped East, to markets like St. Louis and Chicago.

Daniel knew this would be both good and bad for his family. It would make shipping cattle east a lot easier, but it would bring more people who were eager to farm and break up the land. There would be small landowners who would want to see the larger parcels of privately owned land divided into smaller portions, used to raise crops, support large gardens and smaller herds of animals. Without a continued line of O'Neals and Sullivans, the two ranches would not survive this influx of population and change of direction.

The next wave of settlers was already beginning to arrive in their area. Two years ago the Johanson family had moved onto land that was unclaimed by any of the other ranchers. It was not prime property but to the Johansons, who had come from a rocky, forlorn part of Norway, it looked very good indeed. They were raising a few cows, pigs, goats, and were determined to farm the land. The property had a good well, like all of the ranches, but it was just a very small place and how long they could hold on, was anyone's guess.

While getting ready for the drive, Ove Johanson had approached Daniel to ask if he could put twenty cows in the drive and Daniel had said yes because he liked this family. He knew it was the only way the Johanson cattle could be sold this year. Ove had offered to go along as a drover, but Daniel knew he didn't have the knowledge or the horse for the job.

He'd told Ove that they had all the drovers they needed, but asked if he would be willing to look in on his and Calvin's families during the drive, just to make sure they were doing alright. Ove's face had lit up and he'd replied that he would be most honored to do that. It was a gracious gesture on Daniel's part and a grateful one in return. Daniel had later discussed the deal with Calvin and Calvin had agreed to take the cattle into the herd as well, but he had laughed and said to Daniel, "I don't think Ove knows my wife very well."

Daniel replied, "Well, maybe he'll get to know her, while we're gone."

"Brave man," Calvin had snorted.

With that, they had both laughed heartily.

The moon had risen fully now and in the distance Daniel heard the wail of coyotes. He hoped they would stay at a distance. By the light of the moon, he could see by looking at his watch that he'd been out among the cattle for over two hours. He continued moving quietly around the herd until he met up with Calvin.

"How's it going, Calvin, are you staying awake?" Daniel asked quietly.

"Well, I could use some strong coffee right about now, but that's not likely to happen," Calvin quipped.

"Things seem pretty quiet out here tonight, and in another hour we can get some shut eye." Daniel yawned, just thinking about it.

"Let's take one more circle around the herd and call it a night." Calvin suggested.

Daniel agreed.

CHAPTER 4

DAY ONE AT HOME

THE FIRST DAY DANIEL WAS away, things had gone very well, beginning with James coming down for breakfast. He had ambled downstairs and into the kitchen as Rosa and his sister were finishing the clean up after feeding the drovers and he immediately went to his sister and gave her a hug. Johanna was delighted, as she hadn't known exactly how her brother would behave after the men left. Johanna and her brother had always been close; now more than ever, for they both knew they were the only remaining survivors of their "tribe," although they never spoke about it.

"Oh Jamie, what would you like for breakfast?" she asked him, using her pet name for him as they broke their embrace.

"I think I would like some fancy eggs and bacon, and some bread and jelly," he replied. "Fancy eggs" was his way of saying he would prefer them scrambled.

"Coming up!" Johanna exclaimed, smiling, as she reheated the skillet and began preparing breakfast for her brother. She didn't mention anything about the leaving of the drovers, because she knew he'd heard it all, from his perch above.

She worked quickly, and soon she placed his breakfast plate in front of him and poured him a cup of coffee. With one for herself she sat down to his right, so he wouldn't have to eat alone.

Johanna and her brother looked very much alike. Both had blond hair and fair skin, which burned quickly in the summer if they didn't keep their arms covered and faces shaded with wide brimmed hats. Both had large, rich blue eyes, with thick, soft brown lashes. Johanna kept both her husband's and James' hair cut fairly short for them, but hers was long, well past her shoulders and she kept it tied back and out of the way, especially while cooking.

"What are your plans today, Jamie?" Johanna asked, taking a sip of the coffee, which now had gone a bit strong from sitting on the stove for so long.

"Ummm, well I plan to spend some time taking care of the *pigs*." He said the word with definite disdain, shoveling eggs into his mouth. "Pen and pig house are kind of in a mess," he added, just to emphasize to his sister how much he would be enjoying his morning. He took a bite of bread, licking his lips, savoring Johanna's chokecherry jelly. Thoughtfully he added, "Hernando needs some help with the chicken coop - roof repair, I think. *"Then,"* he paused, chewing on some bacon, "Red and I are going out to check cows. That should just about take care of the day, unless you have something you want to add to the list." He added this last part, just to tease her.

"That sounds good," she replied, glad that her brother

was going to dig right into the pig situation. "Rosa and I are going to have a laundry day because it looks clear and not like rain, and tomorrow we plan to make applesauce most of the day," she added.

Late in the week before the drive, Johanna, James, and Hernando had taken their wagon and had gone over to the Sullivan ranch to harvest some apples from the small orchard. Rosa had stayed home to care for Sarah.

Year by year the apple trees were falling into disrepair because they were not receiving the proper care an orchard requires. There were many trees with dead branches that hadn't been pruned for years and there had been no cultivation since the house had been boarded up and James had moved to the O'Neal ranch. But the small determined trees kept producing fruit. At least once in late summer every year, Johanna made a point of harvesting some of the apples. She continued the tradition of applesauce and apple pie made from apples picked from her father's orchard. William Sullivan, up until the year of his death, had lovingly cared for the trees and his favorite product from them had been tart cider, which he'd shared with family and friends for many years. It had become one of his trademarks.

The day of this year's harvest had been beautiful and the three pickers had harvested several bushels of the small but deliciously juicy apples. Because of the abundance of rain in the spring and early summer, the trees had been laden with fruit. Johanna had felt it was such a shame that so many apples would go to waste. She had mentioned to the Symes and the Johansons that they were welcome to come and pick, but the day they were there, they saw evidence that only the birds had been there to harvest.

Now the apples on the back porch were ready to be converted to applesauce.

"Will there be apples left for pie?" James had asked hopefully, finishing up on the last of the eggs and munching on a slice of bacon.

"Oh, I think there will be a pie or two made tomorrow," Johanna had replied, laughing and tousling her brothers hair.

"You need a haircut Jamie."

"Not this week," James replied, taking the last bite of bread and rising from the table. "Got too much to do sister and thanks for breakfast." He hit the back porch door and rounded the house headed for the barn and pig pen at a trot.

Johanna joined Rosa in the process of boiling water and preparing to do some laundry.

Once James made it to the pig pen, which had been built on the far side of the barn, due to the unpleasant smell of pig manure, he gathered the tools he needed to clean out the pig house and dug into the job. Because the pigs were vulnerable to attack by wild animals, each night they had to be herded into their house to keep them safe. During the day, however, they roamed the outside pen where they were fed, watered and allowed to wallow and root about.

James hated this job more than any other because he had so little regard for pigs. They were loud, dirty and seemed to have no gratitude towards the people who fed or cleaned up after them. Every time he thought he'd had it with pigs and was about to tell Daniel he would no longer be responsible for their care, he would think about how much he loved bacon and ham. Then, he would just get back to work with a smile and when a particular pig would start to get on his nerves, he'd tell the animal in a very congenial tone of voice, just how much he was looking forward to seeing both of its hindquarters hanging in the smokehouse.

Hernando joined him in a bit and they worked together, raking out the pig house and throwing the manure over the fence into a pile which would later be hauled out to the pasture to green up a spot that was overgrazed. Nothing on the ranch was ever wasted.

Hernando noticed while shoveling manure that a piece of the fence was coming apart because of the constant rooting of the pigs and the fact that they liked to lay right up against the fence. Hernando and James decided to fix it now rather than later. Procrastination might result in escaped pigs, which were difficult to round up. The fence project took longer than they thought because it involved sawing lumber from a stack in the barn and then another loose board was discovered, so they spent most of the morning with the pigs.

After finishing this job, James and Hernando moved on to repairing the roof of the chicken house. The windstorm two weeks before had done some damage. The chickens were alarmed with the human intrusion into the chicken yard. The hammering and sawing set the birds into a frenzy with many of them running in circles below them, flapping their near useless wings, clucking loudly. Chickens were about as annoying to James as pigs, but they didn't smell as bad and they made eggs, which went together well with bacon.

And so it went all that first day, one job leading to another until the workday was over. James hadn't gotten to the cow checking part of his planned day, but he mentally put that at the top of his list for tomorrow. By late afternoon, Johanna and Rosa were taking laundry off the two clothes lines that ran from one crossed pole to another, folding it into the large laundry basket and hauling it back into the house.

A little later, when Johanna called them in for supper, Hernando and James cleaned their boots away from the back door and left them just outside, because they still smelled of pig manure. They washed their hands, up to their elbows by the pump behind the house and dried themselves off with the worn but clean towels Johanna brought out to them.

"You two have had quite a day," Johanna said as she handed them each a towel. Hernando affirmed they had gotten a lot done and expressed his gratitude to James for his help. "You are a good worker, James," he said smiling. "I'm sure the pigs will be much happier in their clean house tonight." James and Hernando shared a laugh at that, as they were both convinced that the dirtier the house and pen, the happier the pigs were.

Just before coming up to the house, they had herded the six large, non-cooperative pigs into the pig shed and closed and bolted the door for the night. "Till morning then!" James had yelled at them through the door and had turned and dramatically brushed his battered work gloves together, saying to Hernando, "*Well*, that job's done. They had both laughed tiredly and headed for the house.

Everyone was hungry and they gathered into the kitchen for supper. Sarah greeted James with open arms; she wanted her uncle to tickle her - and he did. James was the only uncle she knew and she openly demonstrated her affection with hugs and demands for his attention, which he gladly gave. After supper, the two of them took their places on the sofa and James read to her for awhile from a book of children's bedtime stories which she had totally memorized by the time she was three years old. Normally, this was Daniel's time with his daughter and Sarah obviously missed him. After they'd finished reading, Sarah questioned James about where her father was. Just as she had questioned her mother during the day. She had followed Johanna and Rosa all over the yard, as they washed clothes and then hung them on the line, with Sarah picking up dropped pins and handing them back to the women.

Now, sitting on the sofa next to James, she asked him, "Uncle James, where is Daddy tonight?" James looked down at his niece as she twirled a strand of her golden hair around her small right index finger while looking up at him.

"Your Father is bedding down the cows on a trail east of here and probably eating beans for supper." James replied, trying very hard not to think too much about what he was missing.

"Where is east?" Sarah asked, now climbing up into his lap and resting her head on his shoulder.

"East is pretty much in that direction," James replied,

pointing his left hand and arm towards the wall nearest them.

"What's there and what does it look like?" Sarah was now chewing on the hair she was twirling.

"I don't know, because I've never been there."

"Will he be home soon?" Sarah asked, now looking like she might burst into tears at any moment.

James, seeing that the little girl was quite sad about her father's absence and realizing he was not helping the situation by being morose about not being out there with him, said, "Yup, he'll be home before you know it ...*and*...I'd be willing to bet he is going to bring you something very *special*. Isn't that right sister, out there in the kitchen drying dishes?"

Johanna stuck her head around the corner and said, "I think that's right. At least that's what he said this morning before he left."

Sarah's entire countenance changed. Her face lit up and she jumped off James' lap and ran to her mother. "A surprise? What is it, what's he bringing me, Mommy?"

Johanna put on her most mysterious face and said, "I don't know, it could be anything. He didn't say."

Sarah jumped up and down clapping her hands with delight and it reminded Johanna so much of when Sarah was barely one year old and first learning to walk. The little girl would spend the entire day with her mother and Rosa and when she heard her father's footsteps on the porch, she would suddenly begin to prance and clap her hands. She would squeal with joy when Daniel came through the front door. The first recognizable word she'd said was the word "up" and she would say it, indicating that she wanted Daniel to lift her into his arms and then over his head. Sarah was very fond of her mother and James, but she loved her daddy with all of her heart.

Soon after the storytelling, Sarah was upstairs in bed, Rosa and Hernando retired to their own house and James and Johanna were left in the living room. Johanna was darning a pair of Daniel's socks that he hadn't taken along on the drive because they were in such poor condition. James sat cross legged on the floor doing an inventory of his hooks and material used to tie fishing flies.

He was looking at the open box of flies his father had tied over the years which James had inherited after his father died. "I'll never be as good at it as he was," James said, meaning tying flies and fishing. In a deeper sense, he guessed he also meant he'd never be as good as his father at anything.

Johanna had looked many times at the flies her father had tied and then at the more colorful and inventive ones tied by her brother. "Jamie," she said seriously, stopping what she was doing and looking him directly in the eyes, "You are a better fly tier and fisherman now, than our father ever was, and that's the truth, my sweet. You have a natural talent for both."

"But he did it so easily," James reflected, remembering fishing with his father from the time he was quite small, until the age of twelve, when his father had died, "He could lay a line to water like nobody else.

"Did he catch more fish than you do?" Johanna asked, smiling.

"No," James replied. But in his father's defense, he said, "But he enjoyed it more than anything else and it was so easy for him. And everything I do, I have to work so hard at."

"What he enjoyed," Johanna said to her brother softly, "was watching you catch fish and learning to tie flies. Passing that on to you meant so much to him."

James nodded and said, "I remember the first time I lost one of his flies after he died." He picked up one of the treasured flies from the box in front of him, and turned it around carefully between his fingers. It was a small brown fly with just a touch of reddish brown bird feather, one of his father's favorites. "I knew these were the last ones of his I would ever see or use, and I was determined never to lose one. Didn't fish with them until I was fourteen.

Then the first time I went fishing and used one, the water was high and my first cast...my *first* cast, the fly caught on something under the water. I couldn't retrieve it. I even went back to that spot, after the water went down and I couldn't find it. I didn't think I could ever use another one of his flies, because it felt so bad to lose that one."

"But you did, didn't you?" Johanna said, picking up the darning again and fishing the needle back and forth through the thread. "It's just like Mother's china," she mused, realizing for the first time that it was all part of the same thing. "Things that we treasure are no good unless we use them. They are like some meaningless thing to pass from one generation to another, with no life to them at all."

James nodded and put the fly back in the small wooden box with the sliding lid that his father had crafted so many years ago as a young man. This too was a treasure and it housed not only his father's meticulously tied flies, but some of his own. Someday, he thought when he was too old to fish, maybe someone else would use the flies and maybe they wouldn't be able to tell them apart. Maybe they wouldn't even know for sure who had tied any of them. Somehow knowing this was comforting to James. He decided that sometime in the next few days, he was going fishing. He would use one of his father's perfectly tied flies - and he wouldn't worry at all about losing it. "I'm going to bed sister," he said, picking up everything in front of him on the floor and standing up. He leaned over her and kissed her lightly on the cheek.

"Night Jamie," she said, "I'm going to finish this and then I'll be up too. Quiet on the stairs, don't wake Sarah."

He didn't need a lamp to find his way to his room. By feel, he put the fly box and tying supplies back into the large wooden box that fit under his bed. He slid it easily back into its place and then went to the window which faced south. He turned his head and tried to look eastward. They were out there, he knew... Daniel and the others. Jamie looked for a long time at the moon which was rising and the landscape he could see by its light. After awhile, he sighed, took off his clothes and went to bed. Tomorrow was another day.

CHAPTER 5

RIVER CROSSING

EVERYONE IN THE CAMP WAS up early. Sam the cook tried hard to fix a good breakfast and lunch for the riders, but it ended up that Calvin and Daniel did a lot of the work. It was discouraging, but "doable," as Calvin always said. Once years ago, when a complicated situation arose, Calvin came up with the phrase, "It's okay Daniel, it's doable." It had gotten to the point that when a difficulty came up they would look at each other and in unison say the words together.

Once the mules were hitched to the wagon and horses saddled, the next task was to get everyone and all of the animals across the river. Swifty's back up mount did not want to be saddled that morning but with some help from Ellis, the animal was brought into line and soon everyone was mounted and ready to go.

The men began rounding up strays and moving the cattle and horses along the riverbank. Within the first hour, they found a place where the river widened and the banks on either side gently sloped to the water. It was an easy crossing site.

Ben and Jack swung wide and began slowly herding the animals into the river. Once they started across, the two young men doubled back and kept the herd moving. Calvin and Daniel assisted Sam in getting the wagon across, which was much easier than Daniel could have hoped for. Sam was then told the general direction to take for night camp and he headed out, loudly cursing the mules. Daniel and Calvin both shook their heads as they watched the wagon lurch away, then turned their attention back to the herd.

The animals were allowed to cross slowly, so they could pause either on the leaving side or destination side to drink deeply and take the crossing at a leisurely pace. The river was shallow, with only one spot a few feet wide in which the animals actually had to swim. Once on the other side, the men spread the cattle out on the wide, flat open area and let them graze for awhile. This was a place for the cattle to get ready for the next big push, which would mean covering as much ground as possible over the next two days.

Calvin and Daniel, along with Swifty went back to the south side of the river and backtracked looking for any animals they might have left behind. Swifty found three in a draw, walking westward at a pretty good clip. He turned them around and soon joined up with the two older men.

"Look who I found," Swifty said, grinning as he rode up.

"Looks like three of Johanson herd," Daniel said, swatting the backside of the last of the trio to pass him to move them toward the river.

Calvin joined the conversation by saying, "Probably lonesome for Little Norway," which is how he referred to the Johanson place.

All three of the men shared a laugh at that, and Daniel added, "Good job, Swifty, we want to leave as few behind as possible."

"Right," replied Swifty, pushing his horse into a canter to keep the three delinquent cows in line for the river. "That's what I'm here for."

Once more at the river, Daniel, Calvin and Swifty let their animals drink. Calvin instructed Ben to gather everyone's canteens and go back upriver to a spring he'd noticed from the other side as they'd passed it. "Fill everyone's canteens, Ben and get back as soon as you can." The young man did as he was told and within half an hour was back, redistributing the much needed water to the riders. Daniel took a long drink. The water tasted very good and was extremely cold.

"That is a deep spring. Glad you spotted it, Calvin" Daniel said to his friend as the two men sat enjoying the moment. Calvin agreed.

"I think it's time we got them moving," Daniel commented.

"Yup. We've got a lot of miles to make yet today and tomorrow before we cross the river again," Calvin said, as he hung his canteen back on his saddle, "Need to get goin'."

With that, the riders began pushing the cattle up over the rise and headed straight east.

Daniel had chosen to ride Zeb a second day. He was the most dependable and surefooted of the mounts Daniel had chosen to bring along. He wanted those qualities for the river crossing, walking among he rocks and going up and down the riverbank. Tomorrow, he'd switch out to Socks, a three year old sorrel gelding whose greatest attribute was he loved to chase cows.

Daniel checked the extra mounts for all of the riders later that day. Ellis was keeping them bunched together and all of them seemed to be doing well. The unsaddled horses had nothing to do or worry about but to keep up with the herd and graze along, which was easy work for them.

Late in the afternoon, the herd caught up with Sam and remarkably the cook had unhitched the mules, hobbled them, had a fire going and was starting to cook supper. Calvin and Daniel gratefully pitched in and helped. Supper was not too bad that evening.

Ben and Jack took first watch, followed by Calvin and Daniel. The night was quiet with no problems. Daniel was beginning to think that this was probably the easiest thing associated with cattle he'd ever done in his life and he began to regret not letting James come along for the drive.

CHAPTER 6

APPLESAUCE AND DREAMS

DAY TWO AT THE RANCH passed quickly with each hour filled with activities that were routinely done in late summer, in anticipation of winter. During July and August, produce from the garden was harvested and put in the root cellar, which was located next to the smoke house, or canned in mason jars, then neatly stored in what they called the downstairs bedroom. It was a bedroom only in a sense that there was a small narrow bed in the middle of the room that could be used by an overnight visitor. The rest of the room was filled floor to ceiling and wall to wall with shelves that Daniel and Hernando had built to hold the mason jars filled with everything from corn to applesauce. Some of the shelves were filled three jars deep and all were marked with the date they had been filled. There were empty jars along the bottom shelf and by the end of the summer most of them would be filled. By the beginning of next summer the empty jars would outnumber the full ones and the process of filling them would begin again.

Johanna and Rosa were now working on replenishing the supply of applesauce, which was a precious commodity and carefully rationed during the winter. Making it was labor intensive. Both women knew that by the end of the day, they would be wringing wet with sweat and moisture from the boiling pots would be dripping from the ceiling. They had opened all of the ground floor windows, so that an occasional breeze might bring a breath of fresh air into the kitchen. Johanna was nearly out of sugar and what they planned to use in the applesauce and a couple of pies would be the last of it until she could get to Fergus again to buy supplies. They began the process of peeling and coring, dropping peels and cores into a couple of large buckets, which Hernando would carry to the waiting pigs.

James came down early and after a quick breakfast headed out the door to saddle his horse to make the cattle check he hadn't been able to get to the day before. During breakfast he had spoken only briefly to Johanna and Rosa, as he was preoccupied with thinking about his task for the day. He knew it would extend into the afternoon and he didn't want to be questioned too closely by his sister about his plans for the day. He didn't like telling her half truths.

"Be careful out there today, Jamie," his sister had called after him as he had left the house and he had assured her that he would.

Red, his primary riding horse was in the fenced lower horse pasture and came quickly to the fence when she saw James approach. The filly was smaller than most of the O'Neal horses, even though she was now over three years old. James was sure she would never fill out to the size of what was considered a desirable cattle working horse.

Red eagerly accepted the halter and lead rope and James led her through the gate, to the barn hitching post where she was quickly saddled and bridled. The boy mounted the horse and gave her a nudge which took her from a walk to a gallop in just a few seconds. He let her run as they rounded the barn and headed for the upper pastures to check on the remaining O'Neal cattle herd. After several minutes, James pulled her back down to a walk and the horse settled into her normal brisk walking stride.

Red had been purchased two years ago, when she was only a yearling. Daniel had let James go with him into Fergus for the annual horse sale, which was always held in June. That day Daniel had been looking for another stallion to diversify his herd and he was hoping to acquire one by using cash and trading two of his mares, which were both excellent cattle horses. He didn't intend to let them go, unless he could bring something home that would be worth the trade. Daniel had taken Ellis as well as James to the sale with him. Daniel and Ellis each led a mare on a lead rope, following along behind the horses they were riding.

James had a plan of his own that day, which he had not disclosed to either of the men he was with. At a very early age, he had decided that one day he would buy and raise his own horses. Over the years as a young child he had listened to and watched his father quietly, as *he* bought, sold and traded horses. James remembered once when he was ten, he had accompanied his father to the Fergus horse sale. On the way there, James had listened as his father had said to him, "You should never act cocky when you are buying a horse, because if you do, the horse trader will make it his goal from that moment on to make a fool of you and take you for anything he can." James regarded it as one of the gems his father had given him.

Two years ago in June, as he'd stood outside the corral of horses to be sold, James had spotted the red, yearling filly. It was very unusual for a yearling to be sold at a horse sale and James, then fourteen years old, had boldly approached the horse trader to ask about the yearling. "She's a little bit wild, son," was all the trader would say.

When the small, red horse had been literally pushed into the sales ring, she'd lived up to her reputation. She reared at the fence and spooked at anything that moved and raced around the ring, and then stopped to paw the ground and shake her head wildly. Several men could be heard making remarks such as, "Someone should just shoot that animal and get it over with."

James looked at the small horse closely. While everyone else there saw only a wild creature, James saw how she was built. She had long legs, strong hind quarters and a long neck, which to James meant speed. He pulled on Daniel's arm to get his full attention and said, "I want that horse."

Daniel had turned to James in surprise and replied, "You can't be serious."

"I am serious and I have money." Out of his pocket James pulled the silver money clip that had belonged to his grandfather and then his father. It contained the few dollars that had come with the clip and the money he had made from running his trap line the previous winter.

Daniel was caught completely off guard because he

had no idea James had any intention of buying a horse that day. He decided he must dissuade James from making a disastrous mistake.

"James," he whispered quietly, so as not to let the men around them know this conversation was even taking place, "That horse is no good! You don't want a horse like *that*. They end up hurting people or themselves."

"I want to buy her," James had said emphatically and a couple of men nearby overheard him and snorted audibly.

"James, I can't let you do that," Daniel had put his mouth close to James' ear and whispered the words as quietly as possible.

With that, James did the only defiant thing he'd ever done in his life. He climbed up onto the top rail of the fence and answered the auctioneer's opening call for a bid of eight dollars.

"Here" shouted James, raising his right hand. His voice, which was changing at that time broke in the middle of the word and several men laughed openly. Daniel felt embarrassed for James and lowered his head and looked at the ground. He prayed that someone would outbid the boy.

Suddenly the mood of the sale had changed, a charge of energy was felt around the fence. Everyone there was paying attention. Horse trading moments like this created stories that a community like Fergus could talk about for a long time...sometimes for years. "Remember the time the Sullivan boy bought that crazy horse that later went through a fence and killed somebody." Daniel could just hear it.

The auctioneer called out for a higher bid and none

came. Daniel was mortified and James was elated. "Sold for eight dollars," the auctioneer had shouted, followed by "You got quite a horse there, son." Everyone but Daniel, James and Ellis had laughed and it proved to be the moment of the day.

Later that afternoon, Daniel had been able to trade his two mares and put up a minimum amount of cash for a gray stallion that was everything the red filly was not. Daniel, a very good judge of horseflesh, had felt that the day for him was a great success. He was, however, not happy at all with what James had done.

The trip home from the horse sale that day had been a very disagreeable adventure. Merely getting a halter and lead rope on the filly had been nearly impossible. Once the task had been completed, getting her to follow on the lead rope was exhausting, both for James and the horse he was riding.

Daniel had been stern with the boy, which was an unusual occurrence, because James was usually compliant with whatever Daniel asked him to do.

"James, you are going to have to take full responsibility for this horse, and if one of you doesn't get killed in the process, I'll be very surprised," he'd said in a frustrated tone of voice.

Daniel, leading the gray stallion, who quickly acquired the name "Shadow" led off towards home. He was followed by Ellis, who kept looking back, keeping an eye on James and the wild horse he'd bought. Daniel refused to pay any attention to the boy, who quickly fell behind the other two riders.

James was riding "Molly", a buckskin mare Daniel had broken. She was a gentle horse James had ridden since he was twelve when he'd first moved over to live with his sister and Daniel. The horse was confused about what was happening on the road back to the ranch. She kept turning her head to look at the horse she was pulling at the other end of the lead rope and sometimes had to turn completely sideways to even see the animal behind her.

James tried everything to get the filly to properly follow on the lead rope. The young horse did everything but turn herself inside out. She ran from side to side, got herself tangled in the rope, and frequently would plant all four feet suddenly into the road. At one point she sat down, jolting James and the buckskin to a sudden stop. This went on every step of the way back to the ranch.

Ellis had been told by Daniel to offer no assistance to James. During the trip back to the ranch, Ellis had to turn his face away from looking at James numerous times, just to keep from laughing. It was the most entertaining show he'd seen for a long time. All he could do for the boy was keep him in sight, in case he got into some real trouble.

Daniel had not stopped or looked back towards James the entire trip home and he arrived at the ranch well before either Ellis or James. He put Shadow in the smallest pasture near the corral, which was occupied by "Rascal," the other stallion on the ranch. Daniel looked his newly acquired horse over again carefully, very happy with his choice in the trade. He wanted to get the horse branded tomorrow, to help insure his ownership.

Daniel wasn't sure if it would ever be possible to brand the horse James might eventually come home with and he wasn't sure he wanted the O'Neal Sullivan brand *on* the horse. After unsaddling his mount and putting away both his horse and saddle, he had leisurely strolled up to the house and had sat down in the porch swing. Johanna had come out onto the porch and after looking around for her brother and their hired hand had inquired, "Where are Ellis and James?"

"You'll see," was all Daniel would say in reply. Johanna had sat down on the swing next to him and asked, "Daniel where are they?"

Daniel shrugged, "You'll *see*," was his reply a second time and he'd given his wife a look that said, "Don't ask me again."

Near sunset, Ellis had come riding into the yard, followed within minutes by James, dragging the yearling that he had named "Red". It was pretty obvious that James and Molly were exhausted, while the crazy yearling, showed no signs of slowing down, continually pulling on the rope and running side to side, just as she had when they'd left town.

"What on earth?" Johanna had exclaimed standing up, when she saw James come riding into the yard.

"Exactly!" Daniel had replied and then added, "Please take a big plate of food down to Ellis in the bunk house, because he deserves it." The grateful hired hand profusely thanked Johanna when she'd done so.

As Johanna had turned to leave the bunkhouse, Ellis had remarked, "Your brother has a tiger by the tail, Mrs. O'Neal, and that's the truth."

That's how it had begun two years ago. For the first six

months after arriving at the ranch, Red had required just about all of James' time. For a while that became a bone of contention between Daniel and James: Daniel was constantly reminding James of the chores he was responsible for and James was hurriedly doing them, so he could get back to the corral to work with the filly.

The young horse had no trust in anybody and that was the problem. It took many long months before they developed that basic element that is needed between any rider and horse if they are to accomplish anything together.

Finally, it had begun to happen. The little horse who had eaten voraciously, when she'd first come to the ranch, began to fill out and grow up. Gradually, she'd begun to trust James, and then she had developed a dependency on the boy, anxious when he didn't appear when he usually did. Eventually, during the last year, she had calmed down considerably, letting not only James, but Daniel and Ellis and finally even Swifty and Sarah approach her. Daniel insisted that Sarah not go near the horse unless James went with her.

James had been right about the speed. Red could outrun any horse in the area. The boy made a point of riding Red to town once in awhile, with Daniel or Ellis driving the wagon so they could buy supplies. James wanted the people in town who thought he'd made an unwise decision see just how fine a mount he'd ended up with. The story about the Sullivan boy who'd bought the crazy horse was not told anymore.

The morning Johanna and Rosa were making applesauce, James and Red arrived in the upper pasture, where the cattle herd would graze until the weather forced them down closer to the ranch. On this open range, cattle and horses alike had to learn quickly to forage for themselves.

James was encouraged by how much grass was still available and he noticed how the green had paled and turned light brown, as it did in late summer and early fall. Riding the upper meadows he encountered a number of the O'Neal cattle and saw that these animals, like the ones now headed for Culver, were well fed and healthy. The cattle were all shorthorns, a hearty breed and they acted skittish when James approached them. They too had been part of the round up earlier in the month and then had been driven back up into the hills. Now the cattle acted as if they expected to be rounded up again and they eyed James suspiciously.

"Don't worry, I'm not here to take you to market," James had called out to them. "That'll be awhile." He watched the cattle for some time as they grazed and then turned and headed toward the Sullivan place, which he still regarded as his home.

He and Red made quick time to the house he'd grown up in. When he had accompanied Johanna and Hernando to the homestead to pick apples, they had stayed in the orchard and had not gone near the house. It upset Johanna too much to see how the place she'd called home all of her early life had begun to deteriorate, so she avoided it. James never mentioned the house to his sister, but periodically, he felt a need to come back to it.

He rode up to the barn and dismounted at the hitching post. The door no longer opened easily and he could only open it a bit to squeeze inside. It still smelled of horses to him and birds flitted around in the rafters, startled at his entrance. He noticed that some of the roofing had been blown away, probably the same wind that had damaged the chicken coop they had repaired yesterday. He knew that once the roof began to give way and allow in rain and snow, the building below would begin to rot and crumble. He quickly exited and closed the heavy door.

James untied Red from the hitching rail and walked toward the house squinting his eyes, imagining his mother in the garden, just east of the house and his father coming through the front door to greet him. Walking up the front steps, his eyes were no longer squinted and he saw the house as it actually was. He noticed that some of the boards on the porch were no longer even, but pitched at odd angles. The door and all of the windows were securely boarded over with strong planks and heavy nails. Daniel and Ellis had spent most of a day four years ago hauling the lumber from the O'Neal ranch and carefully covering each opening. It was an effort to prevent windows from being broken by hail, someone throwing stones or the house being vandalized.

Now, James noticed, even those boards were starting to look weathered and the house itself looked like an aging person, whose face carried creases and wrinkles that hadn't been there just a few years before. James went down the steps and slowly walked around the house looking for visible damage. He saw nothing major, just an overall decline from what he'd seen the last time he'd made this pilgrimage a little less than a year ago. Walking around the yard, he began to understand why Johanna could no longer come here. Because she'd lived in the house longer than he had, she would naturally see changes that he didn't.

He'd made a complete circle around the house and then looked at the other outbuildings on the property; the smokehouse, the special toolshed his father had built early in the history of this place, where he'd kept his carpentry tools and fishing gear, and the small building where James had learned to tan hides of animals he and his father had caught in their winter trap line. It was all in the same state of disrepair. After a while, James knew it was time to go. He mounted Red and turned her toward the O'Neal ranch. He wondered if he would someday be able to resurrect his home from the state he'd seen it in today. He wasn't sure. The thing he was sure of was that he wanted to raise horses and somehow he had to find a way to do that.

His plan to begin this venture was to have Red breed with Shadow within the next year. He felt in his own mind it would be a good combination. With Shadow's steadiness and strength and Red's speed and spirit, he felt he would have a strong beginning to what would eventually become his own herd. He wondered what a horse from Red and Shadow might look like. He wasn't sure, but he was eager to find out. James glanced at the angle of the sun in the sky. It was now afternoon and he had to get back. There were chores he needed to help Hernando with and he was looking forward to apple pie.

CHAPTER 7

AT HOME AND AWAY

THE THIRD DAY OF THE drive proved to be difficult and frustrating. Traveling on the north side of the river, the herd was making good time. They had started very early in the morning at Calvin and Daniel's insistence and were moving faster than they had since the beginning of the trip. The herd was strung out in a long wide line. Daniel was bringing up the rear with Swifty, urging the few stragglers of the herd to keep up, and they couldn't see the lead cows and drovers. Suddenly Daniel realized the herd was slowing down dramatically and ahead through the dust he saw Calvin, who had been out in the lead position with Jack, come riding back towards him at a brisk trot. "We've got a problem ahead, Daniel," Calvin announced as he rode up on Daniel's right and stopped, still facing him.

"What's up, Calvin?" Daniel took off his wide brimmed hat that was covered with dust and wiped his sweaty face on the sleeve of his shirt.

"Fence. Fence up ahead that goes from as far as I can see up off the river, right down to the river bank."

"Damn," Daniel breathed the word softly and then added, "Well, let's go take a look." He gathered his reins and turned to Swifty, "Get Ben to help you circle them up here, Swifty, and just hold tight till we get back."

Swifty nodded and rode to the right to pick up Ben to help circle the herd in. The last thing they needed was for their cattle to go crashing through some landowner's fence.

Calvin and Daniel rode forward quickly and soon were at the fence. It was new, well constructed and the wire was still shiny. As Calvin had said, it trailed off into the distance to their left and disappeared into a tree line hundreds of yards off in the distance. To their right the fence led down to the water line. Obviously, they would have to recross the river and continue on the south side for the rest of the trip, or until they could find the twin fence to this one that would mark the end of this particular landowner's claim.

"We knew this was coming," Calvin said grimly, commenting on the situation in general. "Yup," Daniel replied, "We've been lucky up to this point."

"Wonder how many more of these we'll run into between here and Culver?" Calvin wondered aloud.

"Don't know Calvin, but we have to figure out a way to get back across the river. Let's take a look at the riverbank here."

With that the two men rode along the fence until they reached the bank. It was lined with scrubby brush and tall cottonwoods. This was not a good place to cross for the cattle or the wagon.

A couple of cows wearing the O'Neal Sullivan brand had approached the fence and were using the fence posts to rub up against. Daniel ran them off commenting, "Well it didn't take them long to figure out what a fencepost was for, anyway."

Jack came riding up in a flurry and announced they were getting the cattle under control and wanted to know what else he could do to help.

"Just try to keep the cows off the fence and circled in here, Jack, until Daniel and I get back," Calvin ordered "Hopefully, that won't be too long."

They backtracked at least half a mile until they came to a place that had obviously served as a crossing for an earlier herd.

"Sorry I didn't see this when we went past it, Daniel," Calvin said, "Dust was pretty thick and I was watching ahead."

"It's doable," Daniel replied, grinning. "I'm going to cross and see what the terrain on the other side looks like. Find the chuck wagon and get Sam ready to cross when I get back."

"Will do," Calvin replied and turned his horse to go find Sam.

Daniel crossed the river, taking extra care to watch where he was going as Socks didn't have the agility or the horse sense that Zeb did. His mount was tentative around water, whereas Zeb had no hesitation whatsoever about charging in.

Once on the other side, Daniel could see where the earlier herd had turned and followed the river. The terrain on this side was far less desirable than on the other side. It was rocky, had less vegetation and about a hundred yards in, there was a steep cliff made of soft dirt that would be difficult if not impossible to drive the cows over. By the tracks along the river, Daniel could tell that the earlier herd had been fairly large, but it had been some time since they had made the crossing, as the tracks were visibly old.

He couldn't see too far ahead, so he had no idea how long they would have to stay on this side of the river, but they simply had no choice. He recrossed the river, his horse wading shallow water for a bit and then swimming ten yards of deep water that wasn't moving too swiftly. Once clear of that, Socks lunged up into the more shallow water and then the remaining yards to the river bank. Once on the other side, Daniel's first task was to round up Zeb and saddle him up for the upcoming task of getting the cattle across the river. He could see Zeb in the distance; so took off his right glove, and using his thumb and second finger, gave a loud whistle. Zeb came running.

They took the wagon across first, the mules protesting the slightly steep bank to the water, and Sam swearing a blue streak. That done, they began bringing cattle across and immediately turned them eastward again. Now Daniel and Calvin watched for the other fence they knew would be coming up on the north side of the river. It was several miles before they found it, just as shiny and forbidding as the first one.

Daniel sent Swifty across to scout ahead to see if there was another fence in their path for the last leg of their journey for the day. The terrain on their side of the river was becoming more and more difficult. Crossing back to the north side of the river again was arduous because of the height of the river bank and now the cattle were tired from the additional work of negotiating the rougher terrain.

Getting the wagon back across was difficult and Daniel thought at one point it might tip over as it slid and skidded down the bank into the river. Jack and Ben took the herd across, while Daniel and Calvin backtracked for strays. They found none, which was a relief and then they too crossed the river to the north side.

Swifty had ridden hard east along the river looking for an additional fence and then rode back to tell them that at least for the next several miles, they were clear. Daniel and Calvin decided they would keep going until darkness nearly overtook them and then stop for the night.

Everyone was exhausted from the unexpected difficulties of the day and camp was very quiet that night. They had lost time, but at least they were once again on the right side of the river and would hopefully be able to reach Culver the next afternoon.

The Hanson boys agreed to take the first shift and Ellis and Swifty volunteered to do the second. That meant that Daniel and Calvin would be able to sleep all night, if they could still their minds and not worry about what was going to impede them tomorrow. Daniel felt too tired to eat, as the fatigue of the trip and very little sleep was finally starting to catch up to him. Calvin brought him a plate of food as he sat by the fire, just watching the flames dance in the darkness.

"Gotta eat, partner," Calvin said as he sat down beside him.

"Yeah, I know," Daniel said, thanking Calvin for bringing him some ham and beans, with a couple of biscuits on the side. Daniel picked at it with his fork and then picked up his canteen and drank deeply.

"I'll be glad when tomorrow is over, Calvin," Daniel stated tiredly.

"Know what you mean. Think I'm getting too old for this kinda' deal."

Daniel laughed and said, "We are going to be chasin' cows till they bury us, and you know it."

"Well, in a few more years, I'm hoping my boys will be old enough to step up and give me some slack," he replied, realizing too late that this would be a sore spot for Daniel. He quickly went on, "But yeah, I'm sure you're right, I'll keep doing this one way or another, till I fall off my horse."

Daniel smiled over at his friend, overlooking the mention of his boys and said quietly, "Well, I hope you get to see your sons work your land Calvin, I really do."

After a moment of silence he said, "You know these beans aren't half bad. I think Sam is getting the hang of this." Both men laughed and a short time later, after helping Sam clean up the dishes, they unrolled their blanket rolls and within a short time, both were sleeping, with Calvin snoring loudly.

The third day at the ranch found Hernando and James cleaning chimneys. The dirty job required the use of some long brushes that had belonged to Daniel's father. He was a great believer that "clean chimneys saved fuel and helped prevent houses from being burned down." That was reason enough to clean them thoroughly in preparation for winter when a fire would have to be burning nearly all of the time.

It made a mess both inside and on the roofs. By the time James and Hernando were finished they were covered with soot. They had to strip down to their waists and lather up with soap, using hot water that Rosa placed in a large wash tub in the yard. They washed their hair, scrubbed thoroughly and then Rosa dumped the water and they did it again. After two washings they were starting to look human again and Johanna came out into the yard with a straight backed chair and towel and ordered James to sit down so she could cut his hair

At first, James begged off, saying he had other chores to do, but his sister won out. Giving up and sitting down in the chair, he allowed his sister to wrap the towel around his bare shoulders and begin to cut his wet hair. He closed his eyes and felt the warm sun on his face.

Sarah had come outside to join them and she asked her mother if she could cut James' hair, too.

"No, I think we'd better let your Mommy cut it," James said, looking up at his sister and smiling. "Might be better."

Sarah wandered off a bit to the chicken coop, talking to the chickens through the fence and picking up stray feathers. James watched her, wondering if she would remember moments like this, when she grew older.

"I'm going fishing tomorrow, sister, want to come with

me?" he asked. "Rosa could watch Sarah. It might be fun. You haven't fished the river with me for a long time."

"I'd love to Jamie, but I'm baking bread tomorrow and I kind of expect Mr. Johanson will be stopping by to check on us. I'm a little surprised he didn't come by today. Daniel said he was going to stop at Symes and our house, while they were gone." Johanna paused, gathering a bunch of James' hair between her fingers and snipping off a significant length of it. "I want to be here, if he stops by. It would be rude, if I weren't."

James replied, "Well if he comes tomorrow and Hank is with him, send him down to the river with Daniel's old flyrod and he can fish with me. I'm going to try my luck by the Aspen grove." Johanna said that she would do that.

Hank was Ove and Hilda Johanson's thirteen year old son. Henry was his actual name, but he liked to be called Hank, which everyone on the ranch obligingly did. He was a kid you couldn't help but like. He was quick to learn and it was largely because of him that his parents and younger sister were learning English at the rate they were. He thrived on school and while he had been teased at first for his accent, he knew how to play marbles better than any of the other boys. When he first appeared at the school, he'd had only a handful of the colorful orbs, but now he was in possession of a major portion of several of the boys' marble collections. They were trying at every opportunity to win them back.

Last summer he had made the trip to the O'Neal ranch several times, sometimes with his father and sometimes alone. He wanted to learn to fly fish and James' was more than happy to teach him. As far as James was concerned, anyone who wanted to learn to fish was a human being worth knowing. Hank learned the rhythm of the cast quickly and was soon catching fish, which delighted him more than anything else he'd learned so far in this country. He'd only been able to get to the ranch once earlier this summer as everyone had been preoccupied with getting the cattle ready for the drive.

Johanna was finishing up with the haircut and several times, James reached up to check and make sure she wasn't cutting it too short. "When it's too short, my hat doesn't fit right," he had informed her several haircuts ago and his sister had made a note of that and was careful not to cut too much off.

"How is that?" she asked and handed the mirror she'd brought into the yard to James. The mirror was about six inches square and James held it up and circled it around his face, trying to observe the haircut from as many angles as possible.

"Looks good," he replied, standing up to shake out the towel and brush himself off. "Thanks sister," he said. "I'm going to get a clean shirt and go check on the horses."

Johanna finished shaking out the towel and brought out some hot water to soak the two very dirty shirts Hernando and James had worn while they had cleaned the chimneys. She was glad that job was done, because she agreed with Daniel's father; the fire did burn more efficiently, when the chimney was clean.

"Sarah come over here, sweetheart, I want to trim your hair a bit."

Sarah wrinkled her nose and asked, "Do I have to?"

"Yes you do. I want to trim it back from your face, it keeps falling in your eyes."

"Okay Mommy," the little girl said and came over and climbed up onto the chair, let her mother put the towel around her and carefully trim the hair around her face. Johanna hummed a tune and Sarah, not knowing what the tune was, joined in, humming random notes, which amused her mother.

Johanna treasured simple moments like these. Although she didn't know it she was a rare person indeed, because she had what she wanted and she wanted what she had.

James came out of the house, buttoning his clean shirt and headed for the horse pasture. Hernando came out of the house he and Rosa shared, tucking his shirt into his pants, ready to move to the last chores of the day.

Later, after the now-washed shirts were hanging on the line to dry during the night, the pigs were in their house, the chickens were settling in for the evening, the family trooped into the house for supper, not realizing that during the entire afternoon they had been watched.

CHAPTER 8

THE INTERLOPERS

THEY HAD ARRIVED A LITTLE after noon and had settled in on the low sloping ridge above the large horse pasture. They had tethered their horses well back into the tree line, hoping the horses below would not catch their scent and give warning of their presence. There were three of them and they were hunkered down, with only their faces showing over the ridge.

"No dogs down there," observed the man using the field glasses, "That's a good thing." "Only see one grown man so far. Just two women, a little girl and a kid, besides him."

"We should just go down there after dark and take the horses," the youngest of the three, said nervously.

"Not so fast… not so fast," the one with the field glasses countered, speaking quietly, "We want to take our time on this one."

"Yeah, I know what you want to take your time with

and I say we get the horses and get the hell out of here," the younger man said.

"Shut up and listen to what I'm tellin' you Nelson," the older man said, this time turning around and facing the younger man directly. "You're not runnin' this outfit, I am, and I say we take our time, make sure there ain't no other men around and when we go down there, we go through that house. get their money and valuables and *then* we take the horses and get the hell out of here. Is that clear?"

Nelson had been riding with the other two men long enough now to know that arguing with Stiles was dangerous. He'd seen what could happen, so he backed off, went and sat down under a tree and let the other two plan out what they were going to do.

Stiles turned around and once again looked through the glasses. The left lens worked well enough, but the other one was cracked, making the image seen through the right lens blurry. He'd stolen the glasses from a man he'd robbed months ago and he hoped some day he'd find a better pair, but for now these would have to do. He closed his right eye and studied the house and yard area again and then moved the glasses so he could see the horses.

"Some mighty fine horses down there, uh huh," he commented and added, "Gotta have money to own horses like that."

The third man asked to use the glasses so he could take a look. "When I'm done with them, then you'll get a look," Stiles had said, with every intention of just taking his time.

The most significant thing that distinguished the three

men on the ridgeline from one another was the number of crimes they had committed.

Edward Stiles had been born in Michigan to poor farmer parents. His father drank heavily and had regularly beaten both his wife and son. Edward's mother had finally left both of them when the boy was twelve, and three years later Edward had left his father's house in the middle of the night, never looking back.

On his own, he had quickly became a thief, sometimes working as a farm hand or laborer for short periods of time, always taking something of his employer's with him when he left; money, a horse, or something else of value. He was now twenty-five years old and hadn't worked for some time, finding it easier to rob others. He had committed violence against both men and women. Once in Chicago he had beaten a prostitute nearly to death, "just for the hell of it," as he told the story later. Stiles was nearly six feet tall, slender, but extremely strong and easily provoked to anger. His eyes were more black than brown and he wore his dark brown hair down past his shoulders, tied with a piece of leather at the back of his neckline. He had a long, badly healed scar on his left forearm and hand, made by a man who had slashed him with a knife during a bar fight years ago. The knife had ended up in the chest of the man who'd owned it.

Joseph Deem, known to the other two simply as "Joe," had grown up in Chicago and had been homeless for most of his life. He was tough and had no formal education whatsoever. One night in a Chicago tavern he had met up with Stiles and the two had been a dangerous team ever since. Joe had lethal ability with a knife or a gun and had killed two men in Chicago when he robbed them of their very thick wallets. These events had taken place over a year ago when he and Stiles were on a spree of robberies gathering money to make their exit from the city. Joe was short and had unruly reddish blond hair and although he was two years older than Stiles, he was a follower and the quietest of the three. Joe was quite willing to let Stiles figure out where they were going and what they were going to do next.

Frederick Nelson, who went by "Nelson," grew up in western Ohio. His father had been a veteran of the war between the states and had come home a changed man. He had moved his family around from town to town and had been very strict with his children. Nelson had received some education and was the only one of the three men who could read or write. That was one of the reasons the other two let him stay on as they sometimes needed to utilize that ability. Like Stiles, he had occasionally worked as a farm hand and laborer, but found it difficult to take orders.

Unlike Stiles or Joe he had never killed anyone, or even beaten or robbed anyone at knife or gunpoint. He was merely a petty thief who had gradually drifted westward. When he was twenty one, he had met Stiles and Joe on a riverboat going south on the Kankakee River and while on the boat, the three of them had decided they would strike out further westward. They reasoned there would be little law to govern them and they could take what they needed as they made their way to Denver or possibly even California.

So far, with only few exceptions their plan had been successful. They had stolen horses and other property and had managed to find ways to sell these stolen items miles away from the scene of the theft and had even figured out how to rustle a few cattle and sell them to unscrupulous buyers, although they were now being sought in two states for that crime. The main strategy of their plan, such as it was, had been to keep moving and keep ahead of the law.

Now, as evening drew near, Stiles outlined the plan for the morning. They would watch the ranch house for awhile and see if any other men arrived. With the one-eyed field glasses Stiles could see a bunk house and the number of horses in the pastures indicated that there were other men living there who were working this ranch.

At an opportune moment, providing no other men showed up, they would go down to the ranch, rob the people there of any cash they had and replace their worn horses with the better mounts in view below. After that, they would head west again, perhaps finding a place to "lay low" for awhile.

One last time, Nelson had advocated they go down under cover of night, steal the horses and leave.

"You know the country west of here, huh?" Stiles had hissed angrily "You want to just ride off in the dark, through God knows what out there and run your horse off a cliff and break your neck? Not *me*, dumb shit, now be quiet and do as I say."

Nelson had stayed quiet after that.

Joe had finally managed to get a turn at looking through the glasses and had made the comment, "I see which horse *I'm* takin'."

"Don't even *think* about the big gray," Stiles had replied empathically, "That one is mine."

"No problem," Joe had replied, "I'm takin' the red horse. It's mine."

Nelson remained quiet and didn't ask to look through the glasses. He knew he'd take whatever horse the other two didn't want.

CHAPTER 9

WITHIN STRIKING DISTANCE

DANIEL WOKE UP BEFORE DAWN on day four, got up, built a fire and began making coffee, trying to be as quiet as possible. He had slept well last night and now felt rested and filled with new energy. He knew he'd need it on this final push to Culver. With the smell of coffee, the other men were soon up and by full dawn everyone was ready to go. Daniel saddled his third horse, "Babe," a tall rangy dark brown mare, who was tireless. Daniel was sure that whatever they encountered today and tomorrow, Babe would be able to handle it. He was now trying to save Zeb for the trip home.

The cattle were sluggish as they headed out. They too had been worn down by yesterday's trek and were starting to show some wear and tear from their long walk.

"Well here we go," Calvin said, riding up alongside Daniel as they again headed east. "You feelin' better this morning?"

"Oh yeah," Daniel said, smiling at his friend. "Get a little shut eye and I'm like new."

The two pushed off, one to the right, the other left, with Swifty and Ellis bringing up the rear. Ben and Jack guided the leading edges of the herd. Sam and the wagon were upwind from the dust and the mules were trudging along at their usual stride. The drovers gradually picked up the pace and soon the cattle were moving well, being urged on by the riders who whistled and occasionally yelled at them.

Just before mid morning, Daniel began to feel uneasy. A feeling that something was wrong crept into his mind and wouldn't leave. He pulled back from the herd and turned and watched the trail behind them, thinking perhaps they were being followed. Moving forward again, he watched the long ridgeline to his left and occasionally just stopped and looked around, not knowing what he was looking for. Calvin noticed Daniel's behavior and rode over to him

"What's up?" he asked riding in and turning to ride to Daniel's right.

"I don't know, Calvin, I just have a strange feeling we're being followed or watched. You feelin' anything like that?"

"No," Calvin replied, "Do you want me to fall back and check to see if anyone's back there?" he said, indicating with a backward nod of his head.

Daniel hesitated a moment and then said, "No, let it go. It's probably nothing. I think maybe I just got spooked by that whole fence thing yesterday."

Calvin silently rode on beside Daniel for awhile. Over the years of hunting, and running cattle with the man beside him, he'd learned that his instincts and intuition were good. Better than good. It had led them to game, when no trail was evident and had helped them find lost cattle, when Calvin didn't know they were lost. Daniel could read the weather better than anyone Calvin knew and he had learned that when, for example, Daniel said it was time to get out of the open and head home, it was.

"You sure you don't want me to circle back a ways?" Calvin asked one more time.

Daniel smiled and turned to Calvin and said, "No, let's just ride it out and see how it goes. I'm sure everything is okay."

Calvin nodded and said, "Okay," and turned his horse back to the track he'd been following earlier.

"Everything's gonna' be okay, today Babe," Daniel said to his horse, patting her on the neck. "Everything is going to go just fine."

And it did. They didn't encounter any more fences. They stopped about straight-up noon to water the cattle in the river, letting them get a leisurely drink, and then headed east again.

By mid afternoon they were getting to a place Daniel remembered. "We'll be just outside Culver by sundown," he told Swifty in a voice not even trying to disguise how relieved he was to know that. He smiled at the thought of his own uneasiness earlier in the day. All was going to be well, he thought.

CHAPTER 10

DAY FOUR AT THE RIVER

JAMES SLEPT A LITTLE LATER than he'd intended to, so dressed hurriedly and ran down the stairs as quickly as possible. "I'm late, gotta' go, sister," he said, grabbing a quick breakfast. On the back porch the night before he had laid out everything he was going to take with him. His fishing rod, the satchel containing his fishing flies and creel were ready to pick up and go. His loaded Winchester in its scabbard lay on the shelf above, safely out of Sarah's reach.

As James picked up the rifle, Johanna taunted him by saying, "You going to shoot the fish you can't catch?" She was adding wood to the firebox of the stove, as she spoke.

James rolled his eyes at his older sister and said, "No, I'm thinking I might get a chance to shoot a couple of rabbits and then you and Rosa can decide if we have fish or rabbit for supper," he said

James noticed his sister already had dough in their mother's mixing bowl and it was covered and rising.

Sarah was rolling small balls of dough on the table with her floured hands and James said, "You're up early little girl, whatcha' making there?"

"I'm making little loaves of bread and we're going to have them for supper," Sarah said this without even looking up, totally focused on what she was doing.

"Okay, that sounds good," James said, pulling the strap of the satchel over his head and picking up his flyrod with his right hand. He turned and exited hurriedly through the back porch door.

Johanna, realizing suddenly that her brother had left without a proper good-bye, wiped her hands on her apron and headed through the living room and out the front door as James trotted past the house.

"Jamie, you be careful out there," she called out.

The boy didn't answer, but raised his right arm holding the flyrod into the air over his head to indicate that he'd heard her.

Rosa was out by the clothes line beating the circular woven rag rug from the living room, trying to get as much dirt out of it as possible. Dust was flying in every direction and Johanna called out to her, "Rosa, James is either going to bring rabbit or fish home for supper tonight."

"Maybe both," Rosa laughed, "Maybe we'll have rabbit and fish stew."

"Well, that would be different," Johanna said, and turned and went back into the house.

James trotted to the barn hitching post, propped up the rifle and rod and quickly took the lead rope and halter from the hook just inside the door. He headed to the large horse pasture to find Red already pressed up against the gate of the fence. She had seen him coming around the house and had known he was headed in her direction.

At the barn, he quickly saddled and bridled the horse. He wrapped a lead rope around the horn of the saddle, tied on the scabbard, creel and satchel, picked up his fly rod, mounted and rode out as quickly as possible. He wanted to spend as much time on the river today as he could.

Holding the fishing rod across the saddle horn with his right hand and reins in his left he urged Red into a light canter. It was a beautiful day and above him in the warm morning sunlight, he watched two eagles riding a column of air upward. He was always amazed that these large birds could rise high into the air, with only a rare wingbeat. He wondered what the earth looked like from that height. He watched them for a few seconds and then turned his attention to the trail he was following. A mile and a half later, he reached the Aspen grove and quickly dismounted. As he rode up to the grove, he noticed that at the top of the tallest trees some yellow was appearing, reminding him that autumn would soon be here, then winter.

He carefully put his satchel on the ground near a large rock, laying his rod across its flat top. He led Red to a sapling surrounded by tall grass and clipped the lead rope to her bridle and tied the rope to a small tree. He loosened her saddle girth to make her more comfortable for the time he would be fishing. James pulled the rifle out of its scabbard and leaned it up against a tree, near the rock where he had rested the rod. He wanted the rifle available in case he needed it. A few weeks earlier he and Daniel had seen a female bear with young cubs along this stretch of river and he was taking no chances.

Eager to get a line in the water, he quickly ran line from the reel through the line guides attached to the rod and then reached inside the satchel and brought out the box of flies; he opened it carefully and then paused. Remembering the promise he'd made to himself earlier in the week, he lifted out the fly he regarded as the most treasured one in his possession. It was a fly his father had used to catch many fish, but one James had never dared tie to his own line. Carefully he tied it on and then spoke to the fly, as though it were alive. "Go catch a fish," he said and then cautiously stepped into the water.

The river at this point was much narrower than it was miles downstream where Daniel and the herd were crossing it. The volume of water going past James was much more confined and swift and was still deep enough to fish, though late in the summer. During the spring runoff, the river at this point was sometimes out of its banks and early to mid summer was the best time to fish it. The water felt chilly through his trouser legs, but not cold, as it had earlier in the year.

Walking to his favorite casting point, James faced upstream and made his first cast. He was pleased with how the fly felt at the end of his line and after it lit upon the water, he let it ride along the current near a rock that had produced many a strike. On his second cast, the fly rode the current in almost exactly the same path and James saw a swirl of water as a fish rose to take it. James set the hook and a few minutes later, had the fish on shore and was taking the hook out of its mouth.

He placed the fish, a beautiful trout, into his creel and attached the strap of the woven basket to a familiar branch of a nearby tree that grew horizontally out into the water. It was a perfect place to keep the fish alive and fresh for its trip back to the ranch later that afternoon. He glanced up at the sky for a brief moment and somehow knew his father was proud of him. He checked the fly, making sure the hook wasn't bent, and smoothed the lines of the fly straight back along the shank of the hook. "Okay," James said aloud, "let's do that again."

Striding back out into the current he readied to cast just as Red whinnied sharply. He turned his head to look in her direction and noticed that she was facing downstream. He started to speak to the horse saying, "What is it girl, what do..." and then he heard the sound, the crack of a rifle shot as he felt something hit the right side of his upper back. He stumbled, but caught himself, realizing quickly in confusion, that he'd been shot.

Lifting his feet felt difficult, but he made the few steps needed to reach the bank of the river. Red whinnied again, this time more loudly and frantically. He looked in her direction and saw she was pulling hard against the lead rope, shaking the sapling wildly.

James carefully put his rod down on top of the large rock and reached for his rifle which was just a little over three feet away. Another shot was fired and he heard the bullet rip through the air past his head, missing him by inches. His fingers touched the rifle and he picked it up, racked it and then turned to face the direction from which the two shots had come. He could see no one but heard the third shot and felt the bullet hit his left chest with such force that it knocked him backwards and caused him to fall. As he did so, he felt the rifle slip from his grasp and then felt his back meet the earth. The impact sounded loudly in his ears, and he lay there struggling to take a breath but could not. Looking up, far above he saw yellow leaves, quivering in the breeze and he noticed how the sky above the tree seemed to have become a much darker blue, almost black.

For a brief moment he wondered where the eagles were now. Were they watching this from above? Once more he struggled to take a breath but his wounded body would not allow it. From somewhere far away he heard Red whinny again and then darkness began to close in around him. The boy's last conscious thought was, "Don't take my horse."

The three men cautiously rode up to where James lay on the ground. Joe dismounted and went over to check to see if the boy was dead. He prodded the body with his right foot and when there was no answering movement he announced, "He's dead alright, Stiles, you hit him where it counts." Since Stiles had fired the three shots Nelson had been very upset, saying over and over to nobody in particular "There was no need to go and do that. Wasn't nobody suppose to get killed." About the third time he'd said it, Stiles had loudly told him to shut up.

Now the younger man just sat on his horse about twenty yards away from the others, looking about nervously, as though he expected someone else to ride up.

Joe was going through the small satchel he'd picked up from the ground and discovered there was nothing but a small wooden box inside that he opened roughly and dumped on the ground. "Nothin' in here but fish hooks," he'd observed, flipping the box aside, and then started going through James' pockets. He'd found only a small, worn pocket knife, which he'd put into one of his own pockets.

He picked up the Winchester, turning it over in his hands. "Nice piece," he said, "Mind if I keep it?" He had directed the question to Stiles who replied casually, "No, I don't mind. Why don't you round up that horse you want so much and let's get on over to the house."

That had proven easier said than done and Joe quickly realized he had his hands full. He'd gone over to the red horse who was still thrashing about against the rope and attempted to get close enough to unsaddle her. Red's saddle had begun to slip off the center of her back and hung awkwardly to one side.

Red reared every time Joe got near her and the man had finally gotten up on the lead rope, and had boxed the horse severely with his right fist around the horse's eyes and ears. Red had suddenly stopped moving and stood in stunned silence, as Joe undid the saddle girth and dropped Red's saddle to the ground. "Okay, so now you know who's boss, right?" he said loudly, as he remounted his own horse and pulled the lead rope in tight and wrapped it around his saddle horn. "Ready to go," he announced to the other two, "Got myself one hell of a nice horse here."

Stiles and Nelson said nothing as they turned to leave the scene. None of the three men even glanced backward as they rode away from the river.

CHAPTER 11

DAY FOUR AT THE HOUSE

JOHANNA HAD HEARD THE DISTANT shots and smiled, "Maybe we *will* have rabbit fish stew for supper tonight, Sarah," she'd said to the little girl who was working beside her in the kitchen.

"I don't think that sounds very good," Sarah had replied wrinkling up her nose. She had gone into the living room to find her cloth doll to show her the tiny loaves of bread she was making. After bringing her doll into the kitchen, the two had quite a conversation about bread making. Johanna listened, amused by her daughter's vocabulary and imagination.

A little while later, Johanna was greasing a bread pan when she heard a shot, quickly followed by another, alarmingly close to the house. The next thing she heard was a scream that unmistakably had come from Rosa.

Johanna dropped the bread pan on the sideboard next to the stove and ran to the front door, not taking time to wipe her hands. She was horrified by what she saw when she opened the door. Two men on horses were galloping toward the house, one of them leading a horse she recognized immediately. Looking right, she saw Rosa running toward Hernando, who was lying on the grass a few feet from the front porch railing. She saw Rosa kneel beside her husband and immediately begin screaming uncontrollably in her native Spanish.

Her heart in her throat, Johanna quickly turned from the door and ran to her daughter, grabbed her around the waist and thrust her onto the fourth step leading to the upstairs. "Sarah," she said with all the voice she could muster, "You go upstairs and you hide. You *Hide,* and don't you come out until I tell you."

"Mommy what….."

With difficulty, Johanna took a deep breath and shouted at her daughter, "Never mind Sarah, you go *NOW*!"

The little girl, seeing her mother behave in a manner she never had before, clutched her small cloth doll, scrambled up the steps and around the corner, into the upstairs hallway. Johanna waited only until she saw that her daughter was complying with her command and then turned and ran for the door leading into the back porch, where a loaded shotgun hung on the wall just above the doorway leading to the kitchen.

Just as she reached the middle of the kitchen a man came through the doorway and she stopped short and took a step backward. He took a step toward her and she lunged toward the drawer under the sideboard, where she kept two butcher knives. The man grabbed her from behind and before Johanna realized what was happening he threw her across the kitchen with such force, that when she hit the storage cupboard across the room, she heard and felt the bone in her upper left arm snap like a twig.

Johanna gasped, slid to the floor, rolled to her right side and pushed herself back up to her feet, using her right arm and right knee. The man was immediately upon her again, this time grabbing her hair, holding her up against him yelling loudly, "Where do you keep your money?"

"Money?" Johanna asked incredulously "What do you mean money? We have no money."

The man, tall with dark hair that was pulled tight back behind his head, was not taking this for an answer. "I want you to tell me where the money is right now," he shouted again and he bodily picked Johanna up and threw her completely across the kitchen table.

As she flew through the air, the back of her right shoe caught on the edge of the table, and the mixing bowl full of bread dough wobbled over onto its side. As she fell down onto the floor, she saw the bowl come off the top of the table and begin its descent to the floor. A feeling of desperation filled Johanna and she reached out with her right hand to break the fall of the bowl. It brushed past the end of her fingertips and crashed onto the floor, spilling the dough. As the bowl that had always been so precious to her broke into several large pieces, Johanna felt a rush of anguish and anger.

Lying on the floor, Johanna tried desperately to think of how she might defend herself against the man who was coming around the table to stand over her. He spoke in a threatening voice, "I want your money and I'm not leaving this house till I get it."

Johanna knew that Jamie had money in his upstairs bedroom that he would use to buy additional horses in another year. It was his, and somehow she must keep these men from searching for it.

"It's there" she said, struggling to stand, wincing at the intense pain in her left arm. "Let me show you," her trembling words barely louder than a whisper.

Stiles reached down and roughly pulled Johanna to her feet. The pain in her left upper arm and shoulder was excruciating, and she tried not to cry out, as she did not want to alarm Sarah.

She was conscious of the fact that the two other men, the ones she'd seen riding in only moments ago, were now inside her house. She could hear Rosa, much closer now, wailing in pain. What had they done to Rosa, she wondered to herself as she walked shakily around the table, back to the cupboard she'd just collided with and reached for the small knob on the door.

"No you don't," Stiles said, coming in from behind and reaching around her. "You got a gun in there or somethin'?"

"No," replied Johanna quietly, "It's what you're looking for; it's the money."

Stiles opened the small cupboard door and said, "Where? Where is it?"

"Inside the green tea tin. It's all the money we have in the house." Johanna stepped aside so he could reach inside the cupboard, where he found the only green tin, grabbed it and tore the lid off. Inside, he saw a small collection of bills, and when he pulled them out, he counted six dollars.

"This is it?" he asked her rudely. "This is ALL the money you have in the house."

"Yes," Johanna said, lying, hoping that the man could not read her eyes and that all three men would now leave her house.

She turned her gaze to the other two men who were now standing in the kitchen as well. She noticed that one was short and had reddish hair, and that the other one, who was perhaps a bit younger, looked as if he would rather be anywhere but here.

"Search the house," Stiles ordered and Joe immediately turned and marched toward the stairs, taking them two at a time. "I'll look up here," he announced.

"Nelson," Stiles ordered, "you look around down here and see if you can find anything we might be able to sell down the road."

Nelson, glad to have something to do, turned and headed for the china closet, as it was the only thing on the first floor that looked as though it might contain anything of value. At the china closet he discovered that the glass door was locked. Johanna, reaching out with her right hand, opened her mouth to tell him that locking the door was only a formality and that the small key was inside the top drawer, where the tablecloths were stored.

Before she could say anything, Nelson smashed his gloved right hand through the thin, brittle glass and ripped the door off its hinges. Again, Johanna felt a great sadness, as the image of her father crafting the closet flashed through her mind. The impact of the man's hand through the glass caused some of the china to fall and shatter on the dining room floor. China that had survived an ocean voyage and long rides in rough wagons was being broken.

With no warning, Johanna felt the tall man who had come through her back porch door grab her roughly by her broken arm and turn her around towards him. Instinctively she knew what he meant to do and she began to resist. Her left arm was useless to her, as it was painful even to try and move it. She brought her right arm up and tried to push him away from her and she kicked at him. Once again, using tremendous force, he threw her, this time toward the cast iron stove.

Johanna tumbled downwards and the left side of her head met the massive immovable object. Her ears rang sharply, her peripheral vision shrank inward and she felt warm liquid running down onto her face. For a moment she thought she might lose consciousness. She reached back, up over her head with her right hand, trying to grasp the handle of the warm oven door to help her stand upright. Stiles pulled her partway to her feet dragged her into the area between the living room and dining room, and dropped her to the floor.

Johanna was dazed, but she rolled onto her right elbow, trying to stand. Using the toe of his right boot, the man above her kicked her arm, causing her head to fall back against the floor boards. He stepped around her and kicked her savagely twice in her left rib cage. Johanna felt immeasurable pain. She rolled her head to the left, and through the open curtained front window saw Rosa twirling around on the porch. It looked almost as though she were dancing on the porch rail and Johanna could not imagine why she might be doing that. She strained to listen for any noise coming from the upper floor and heard none. Where was her daughter? Where was she hiding and what would the man searching the upper floor do to her, should he find her?

Upstairs, Joe was ransacking the bedrooms. First was the bedroom shared by Johanna and Daniel. He quickly went through the standing dresser. Each of the four drawers were full of clothing, which he tore through, looking for any jewelry or additional money. Turning his attention to the trunk at the foot of the bed, he found only warm clothing, blankets, and extra sheets for the bed. In the corner he saw a small table with a large porcelain basin and pitcher nested together. Some clean, worn towels hung on a rack beside the table. "How cozy," he said bitterly, secretly envying the people who lived here.

Quickly he went to the room across the hall. It was a child's room and he briefly wondered where the child might be. He glanced under the bed. In the small closet, he found only a few toys, arranged on the floor in a way a child might place them while playing. On the closet shelves he saw nothing but neatly folded clothing for a child, extra blankets and other bedding.

Re-entering the hallway, Joe moved to the only remaining upstairs room. Obviously, this was where the boy who had been shot by the river slept. He stood in the doorway before entering and surveyed the contents of the room. Under the window that faced south he saw two shelves filled with a motley collection of odd things including deer antlers, a turtle shell, arrowheads, rocks of various sizes and shapes, and the skull of a small animal.

From just inside the door, looking down at the end of

the bed, he noticed a fairly large wooden box underneath. He knelt down and pulled the box out and quickly opened it. Immediately inside he found the pelt of a fox. He pulled it out and held it up. He'd never seen anything quite like it. It was beautiful and he ran his fingers through the hair of the pelt, temporarily mesmerized by the feel of it against the skin of his fingers. The tail of the pelt was completely black, with only a few stark white hairs at the very end.

Joe knew for sure he was going to take the pelt with him, so laid it carefully on the floor next to him. Below where the pelt had been, he found clothing for colder weather which he quickly tore out of the box and threw onto the bed. Digging deeper he found ammunition for the rifle he'd taken at the river. He would take this with him as well, so he dropped it on the fox pelt, and moved on through the contents of the box. At the very bottom he found a silver money clip engraved with a letter. Slipping the bills out of the clip, he counted them. Forty-seven dollars.

It wasn't much, but it was all they were going to find in the house and he knew he was not going to share it. He re-clipped the bills and put them into the pocket inside his leather vest, thinking the money clip might be worth something to someone down the road. He'd find out if the clip was real silver and maybe he could hock it for some additional money.

Downstairs, lying on the floor, Johanna fought to stay conscious. She felt she dared not lose touch with what was happening in the house. She had to keep track of where her daughter was at every moment. The dark eyed man straddled her body and began tearing at her clothing. Once more she tried to use her right hand and arm to resist his attack but in her injured condition, she was quickly overwhelmed and realized that resistance was futile.

Johanna felt her underclothing being ripped and the man unfastened his belt and pulled down his trousers. Now panic stricken, Johanna closed her eyes and tried not to think about what she knew was coming next. She could feel herself trembling uncontrollably. The man roughly spread her legs apart and his mouth was on her neck and breasts. She felt the weight of him against her body and within moments she could feel him forcing himself inside of her. She heard herself cry out, even though she tried hard not to. "No" was the word that escaped her lips and she said it twice more, before she became silent and simply let him finish.

Johanna felt the man get off of her and rise to his feet, pulling up his trousers and fastening his belt. He immediately began yelling at the other two men to finish what they were doing and get ready to leave. Johanna opened her eyes and using her right hand, tried to bring the torn material of her dress together across her body. She could hear the other man who had stayed downstairs rummaging in the back porch area.

He'd exited the house and had re-entered, carrying the last ham hanging in the smoke house. On the back porch he'd found the large canvas satchel that Daniel had long used to carry supplies on hunting trips. The younger man started throwing things into it. He'd unloaded and disassembled the shotgun into two pieces before he threw it into the tote along with all of the extra shotgun shells he could find. Again, Johanna heard someone rummaging through the china closet, and again she heard china breaking.

The man who had been upstairs soon came down and Johanna was thankful that Sarah wasn't with him and that she'd heard no sound from her daughter. "Just be quiet a while longer Sarah girl," she thought " and I'll come and get you."

As Joe came downstairs he held up the fox pelt and said, "You guys ever see anything like this?" His companions looked in his direction and Joe immediately said, "It's mine!" He threw the pelt over his shoulder and that is where it stayed until he walked out the door.

"Find any money upstairs, Joe?" Stiles asked.

"Nope, the only thing of any value is right here," he said, indicating the pelt.

Things were happening quickly now. Johanna looked back over her head and saw the short red haired man go into the back bedroom pantry and come out exclaiming, "You should see all of the food in that room." He was carrying two mason jars of Johanna's newly made applesauce and stepping over Johanna, he went out onto the back porch and wrapped the jars in some heavy rags kept in a basket in the corner. "These are going in my saddle bag," he announced and headed for the front door to stash them.

A moment later he could be heard yelling from the front porch. "God damn, son of a bitch, God damn it." Stiles quickly ran out onto the porch to see what he was yelling at, thinking someone might be approaching the house. When he got outside, he saw what Joe was so upset about. The bridle and lead rope Joe had used to get the red horse to the house were lying on the ground. The horse was gone.

When Joe and Nelson had ridden up to the house, Joe had untied the rope from his saddle horn and had firmly tied it to the hitching post. He had fully intended to unsaddle his current mount, saddle and ride the red horse away from the ranch when they left. Now, the red horse had disappeared.

"I know where that horse is goin' and I'm goin' after it," he'd announced.

"No you're not," Stiles had countered, "We're out of time and need to get out of here. Go round up fresh mounts for you and Nelson. I'm going to get the gray over there," he indicated the gray stallion, who, along with several of the other horses were gathered along the fence, looking in the direction of the house. They sensed that something was wrong.

"Shit," Joe shouted. Hurriedly now he began to pack the things they would be taking from the house. The money in his vest was some consolation, but it was all he had. What he'd really wanted was over a mile and a half away by now.

When the men had entered the house, Red stood quietly by the hitching rail for a few minutes. One of the people she sometime saw near the house who seldom came to the barn or pasture was hanging by her wrists on the porch. Red didn't understand what this meant, of course, but the sound that was coming from this person sent a message to the horse's brain that was unmistakable. It was about pain and to Red it meant that she must get away from this place.

The small horse began pulling backwards on the lead rope. It was attached to the left side of her bridle, so the pull was uneven. The leather straps under her jaw and over her ears were tight, but she kept pulling back keeping her head down. Shaking her head side to side she exerted as much backward pull as she could. Suddenly the bridle began slipping off her head and when she was free of it, she stumbled backwards then quickly regained her balance. Turning quietly, she cantered away from the house and when she reached the corner of the barn, she leapt forward into a full gallop. Without anyone to hold her back and without the weight of saddle and rider, she ran as fast as she had ever run in her life. She rapidly made her way back to the only person she would ever let ride her.

Johanna was now going into shock…she saw the last minutes of the men's stay at the house, as if in a fog. She could feel herself trembling again and she suddenly felt very cold. Two of the men, the younger one and the one with reddish hair, left the house together while the man with the dark hair and eyes stayed behind for a moment. He walked back towards her, stopped and looked down, just feet away. Johanna was filled with the fear that he might shoot her or set the house on fire or do something that would take the lives of everyone in the house. But he merely smiled at her, a smirk really, and he said as he left, "You'll remember this day for a long time girl."

He slammed the door as he left and Johanna painfully struggled to sit upright, but the room began spinning wildly and she was overcome with a wave of nausea. Laying back down, she turned her head to one side so that if she got sick she wouldn't choke. Lying perfectly still, gradually the spinning and nausea went away but she knew she dared not try to get up again. She had to stay on the floor until someone found her and she didn't want it to be her daughter. She began to drift in and around the edge of unconsciousness and in her more lucid moments, she could hear Rosa on the porch. Several times, she heard Rosa call her name and twice Johanna had tried to respond but could not gather enough air into her lungs to project a reply. Her friend and cook was no longer screaming or crying, but by the cadence of the softly spoken Spanish words that were reaching her ears, Johanna knew she was praying.

Johanna prayed as well. Mostly, she prayed her daughter would not come downstairs and see her like this. She also prayed for Jamie, because even in the hazy world she was now in, she could remember the shots she'd heard earlier in the morning and seeing Red on the lead rope.

She was fearful about what those two things together meant and she wondered if Jamie was lying wounded by the river. She tried not to think of anything worse. Mostly her mind wandered to Daniel. She knew that Daniel was every bit as strong as the man who had violated her today, yet in all the years she had known him, he had never struck her, had never shouted at her. Daniel had never forced himself upon her and she had never had to fear him. Until today, she had not fully realized how fortunate she was to live with such a man.

Johanna could feel the left side of her face swelling, until she could no longer see out of her left eye. She felt an intense pain in the left side of her head and it increased as she lay there. She began to feel she couldn't bear it much longer and bit her tongue to keep from crying out until mercifully she drifted off into unconsciousness and felt nothing at all.

Upstairs in James' room under the bed, Sarah lay as close to the wall as possible. She had known immediately where she was going when she got to the upper hallway. The little girl and her mother had played many games of hide-and-seek and there was only one place where her mother seemed to have difficulty finding her. Reaching her uncle's room, she had crawled under the bed, squeezing herself between the wooden box and the wall. Then she had pulled herself along the floor until she was tight in the corner where the two walls met.

Through the heat grate in the floor she had heard all of the sounds coming up from below; Rosa's screaming and wailing, shouting men, and angry muffled voices. Only a couple of times had she heard her mother's voice. She had heard footsteps in the hallway and in each of the rooms and when the box had been pulled from beneath the bed, she'd been afraid she would be found. She had held her doll up against her face and closed her eyes. When she had allowed an eye to peek open, she had seen an unfamiliar boot. She'd glimpsed the tail of the fox pelt that her uncle James had been unable to part with.

Above all was a smell that was very familiar. When

their hired man, Ellis would sometimes sit on the porch with her father, he would roll and light up a cigarette and the smoke would carry the scent the strange man had brought into her uncle's room. After he'd left and gone downstairs, there had been cursing on the porch and then the sound of horses riding away. Now, the only sound she could hear was Rosa, on the porch below her, speaking in the language she spoke only to Hernando sometimes.

Sarah waited for her mother to come and get her. When she didn't, a new fear began to creep into her mind. Maybe her mother *wouldn't* come and get her. This had caused her to involuntarily wet her clothing and she hoped no one would be mad at her for that, as she hadn't done this for a long time. She began chewing on the end of the arm of her small doll and after awhile, the entire arm of the doll was covered with Sarah's saliva. It was the only comfort she had.

CHAPTER 12

DAY FOUR

THE VISITORS

HANK JOHANSON AWAKENED EARLY AND quickly got out of bed and did all of his chores before either of his parents had even had breakfast. He scurried about, milked the cow, gathered eggs and went to the woodpile. He brought enough wood to fill his mother's kitchen wood box until it was overflowing. He hurriedly lit a match to ignite the fire in the stove, filled the tea kettle with water, and set it on the stove to heat. Hank cut a slice of bread and put a spoonful of jam on it and slowly ate his breakfast. By that time both of his parents and his sister were up and his father was looking at him with an amused smile. "You don't always get your chores done this early, Henry. Could there be some reason for that?"

Hank smiled and answered, "You know the reason, Papa. Today is the day I go fishing with James."

"Now wait Henry, you don't ask James to take you

fishing when we get to the O'Neal place. You wait to be invited."

Hank agreed and then pestered his father to get an early start.

"We don't want to get there before they've had breakfast, Henry, because it will look like we expect them to feed us."

His mother, who had come into the kitchen braiding her hair and coiling the braid onto the top of her head agreed with her husband.

Ove was so glad that his son was making friends in this new place and he wanted to accommodate that process in any way he could. "We'll get there early enough for you to go fishing, Henry, don't worry about that."

Hank went out to the small barn and saddled the two horses they would be riding that day. He tried to eliminate anything that would delay their departure. After doing everything he could think of, he simply paced around in the front yard until his father came out of the house and said it was time to go. He ran and gave his mother and sister a good-bye kiss and his mother, whose English was the least fluent of anyone in the family, spoke to her son in Norwegian. She told him to be a good boy for his father and to mind his manners at the O'Neals. She wanted her son to understand her perfectly on those two sets of instructions.

The two had ridden off and Hank's mother and sister turned to go back in the house to begin their tasks for the day.

Covering the three miles to the O'Neal ranch, Hank

rode ahead and often found himself waiting for his father to catch up.

The day before they had ridden over to the Syme ranch, although Hank didn't get up early to hurry that departure. He had drug his feet because he hadn't wanted to go to the Syme ranch at all. Upon their arrival, Emma Syme had greeted them at the door, but had not allowed either of them to enter her house. She had not been rude, but had been very close to the borderline of that territory. She'd told them that everything on the ranch was being taken care of by their hired man, Herbert, and that her two sons Matthew and Luke were helping out nicely.

In truth, Herbert, along with the two boys were doing the chores in a very lax manner and spending as much time afterwards just staying as far away from Emma as possible.

Emma in her younger years had been a lot more cordial. As a matter of fact, when she and Calvin were courting, she made her sweet nature very apparent and many would say she had bewitched the man.

A few years after their marriage this meticulous housekeeper who was an unrivaled seamstress and kept her family dressed in the finest clothes they could afford, and who had seemed so enamored by Calvin at one time, let it be gradually known that she found her husband's personal habits, and that was anything that had to do with breathing, moving, eating, or any bodily noises or functions totally distasteful. Calvin had gotten the message, and he, like his sons and hired man, spent as little time as possible in the house. This was fine with Emma because it made her job of keeping her house neat and orderly a lot less difficult.

Calvin's compensation in all of this was his sons, who were now nine and seven. The boys followed him around constantly like exuberant puppies and together it was as if at some secret moment in time when the moon was full, they had made a pact among themselves: they would never be tamed or domesticated by Emma. Strangely enough, Calvin still loved his wife very much and wouldn't have traded her for anyone. She had given him the greatest gift he could have possibly received, two sons who loved him completely.

Calvin had forewarned Emma that Ove, and possibly his son, would be coming to the ranch during his absence. The day of Calvin's departure Emma had placed two of her oldest chairs on the front porch in anticipation of their arrival.

Yesterday morning at the Symes', Emma had invited the two foreigners to sit on the chairs provided, and without her company they had ingested the hardest cookies Hank had ever eaten, accompanied by two glasses of tepid water.

After that, Ove had gone to the barn to visit Herbert, who'd asked the strong Norwegian to help him rehang a corral gate on which he'd installed a new hinge. Then the two men had sat for awhile and visited about the weather past and present, had spent some time wondering where the cattle drive was by now, and discussed how loudly the coyotes had howled on recent nights, and a few other topics. Soon, there was nothing more to talk about and Ove called for Hank to rejoin him. Hank and the two younger boys had gone back behind the barn to a small pond, which was nearly dry this late in the summer. They had entertained themselves by catching frogs. The boys drew two lines about ten feet apart in the dirt near the pond and tried to get the frogs to race from one line to the other. After a few attempts the frogs seemed to actually understand what the game was and it quickly became difficult to judge who was having more fun, the boys or the slippery amphibians.

"It's time to go home Henry," his father had called and though Hank hated to say good-bye to the two good natured boys and the frogs, he'd mounted up with his father and they'd gone home. On the ride back to their farm, Ove had mentioned that Henry was lucky to have the mother he did, and Hank had absently agreed, because he was already thinking about the next day's trip to the O'Neals.

Now, a day later, they were nearing the O'Neal ranch and Hank had finally persuaded his father to increase the pace a bit. About 100 yards from the house, the two riders could see that something was wrong. Rosa, suspended above the porch floor began calling out to them frantically. They could not make out what she was saying, but it was obvious she was in great distress.

Ove cautioned Hank to wait where he was and quickly rode up to the front hitching rail and dismounted. From a distance, Hank could see that his father and Rosa were in conversation and then Ove quickly turned and beckoned his son to ride in.

By the time Hank got to the hitching rail, Ove had unsheathed his knife and instructed his son to immediately dismount and help him cut Rosa down. Realizing that simply cutting Rosa down would cause her to fall, Ove instructed Hank to climb up on the porch rail and cut the rope. Ove wrapped his arms around the lower body of the woman and when the rope was cut, he carefully lowered her to the floor of the porch next to the swing. Kneeling over her, Ove carefully cut the remaining rope from her hands, freeing her wrists. Her hands were an ugly purple color and she couldn't clasp or unclasp her fingers.

"Miss Rosa," Ove began, "What has happened here?" In a hurried description of the morning's events, she told Ove that three men had come to the house, had shot her husband and hung her from the porch. That was all she could say at first.

"Where are these men now?" Ove had asked her.

"They went west," Rosa indicated, pointing the direction the men had last been seen.

Rosa looked up at him with tears streaming from her eyes and then in a very plaintive voice had asked him to help her get to her husband. Ove obliged, with Hank trailing behind him. The boy was totally stunned by what was happening.

Rosa knelt on the dry grass next to her husband and began to wail and cry again. She brought her hands to his face, but couldn't cup her hands to hold it. Her fingers were totally numb and she could not feel his skin next to hers. Ove, standing above them noticed that Hernando had been shot once in his chest, just left of center and it was apparent the man had died where he'd fallen.

"Miss Rosa," Ove knelt down and touched the woman's shoulder, "Where is Miss Johanna?"

At that, Rosa turned to him and answered, "I don't know, still in the house, I think. She and Sarah, they are still in the house but they have not come out. I don't know," she answered confusedly.

She awkwardly reached for his arm to help her up and together the three of them walked toward the front door. As they mounted the steps once more, Ove turned to his son and put his hand out to block him from entering. "You stay here, Henry. Wait on the porch for me."

Hank simply nodded and sat down on the swing and looked around, trying not to let his eyes go back to the place where Hernando had fallen. His mind raced. What could possibly be happening here? Where was James and the rest of his family? Any thought of fishing had left his mind and now he felt only a desperate hope that his friend was still alive.

Inside the house, Ove and Rosa immediately found Johanna on the floor between the living and dining rooms. "Oh dear God, Oh dear God," whispered Rosa as they quickly crossed the distance between themselves and the injured woman.

She lay before them, the front of her body completely naked. The injuries to her face made her almost unrecognizable. Ove could see by the strange angle of her upper left arm that it was broken. They could see that she was breathing, however, very shallowly. Ove knelt down and placed his fingers on her neck and felt a weak pulse that was more like a flutter than a beat. His next concern was to cover her.

"Where is a blanket, Miss Rosa?" He said softly "Can you show me?" Rosa led him into the downstairs back bedroom and pointed to the bed with her swollen hand. Ove quickly took the blanket off the bed and carried it into the living room. He carefully straightened Johanna's legs and brought her right arm in next to her body. He didn't touch her left arm. Then he gently laid the blanket over her, seeing that she was completely covered up to her neck.

Rosa knelt beside the woman she cared so much for, putting the back of her hand next to the less injured side of her face. There was no response.

"Where is the little girl?" was Ove's next question. Rosa started at the question and it was as though she was really hearing Ove for the first time. She looked quickly around the visible area of the house and said, "Maybe upstairs." The two of them went to the second floor and began looking for Sarah. Rosa calling out, "Sarah, Sarah can you hear me?" There was no reply.

Like the man who had been there earlier, the two of them reached James' room last. They entered the room and saw the results of the ransacking, as they had in the other rooms. Rosa speculated that perhaps the little girl had managed to get out the back door before the men entered the house. They stood there a moment and then Ove heard a sound. It was more like a stirring than anything else.

He moved the wooden box out of the way and got down on his knees and looked under the bed. He looked back at Rosa and said, "She is here."

Ove reached his hand under the bed and tried encourage the little girl to come out. "Come to me little one, you may come out."

Rosa added an imploring, "Yes, Sarah come out to Rosa."

The two hours of hiding under the bed had caused the little girl to doubt that help was coming. Now that it was here, she had only one thing to say about it, and it came in the form of a loud, high pitched scream, "I want my *mommy!*" Ove rose from the floor and spoke to Rosa quietly, "She must not see her mama like that. We must keep her upstairs until the doctor can come."

Rosa agreed. She told Ove that once they had the little girl out from under the bed, she would keep her in her parent's bedroom and try to settle her down. It was agreed.

Ove got down on his knees again and crawled beneath the bed as far as he could, grasped the little girl in his embrace and brought her out from under the bed. The resulting screams caused Hank downstairs on the porch swing to cover his ears.

Sarah cried hysterically for some time and when the sobs subsided, sporadic gasps punctuated her breathing. "You stay with me for awhile, Sarah, your Mommy can't come to you right now. I will take care of you." Rosa soothed her. Gradually, once she was in Rosa's familiar arms, the little girl began to calm.

After Sarah and Rosa were in the larger bedroom and Sarah had agreed to curl up next to Rosa on the bed, Ove felt he could go back downstairs to take care of what must be done next.

He went out onto the porch and sat down next to Hank, who looked at his father questioningly, not sure he wanted to know the answers that might be coming.

"Henry, I need you go to town. You must ride quickly to the sheriff and tell him to come quick, something bad has happened. Also, you must tell the doctor to come. Tell the sheriff that Rosa's husband is dead. Mrs. O'Neal is hurt. Do you understand, Henry? Tell me back what I have said." Hank dutifully repeated almost word for word what his father had just told him.

Hank now knew that everyone they had expected to see that morning was accounted for except James. He wondered if his father was withholding information from him. Swallowing with difficulty, he asked the question he most dreaded being answered, "Papa, is James inside the house?"

"No," his father answered, "he is not here."

For the first time since they arrived, Hank felt more confident that his friend was alive and unharmed.

"Go now quickly," his father said. They both stood up from the swing and Ove embraced his son, admonishing him to be careful.

Hank went down the steps to the hitching rail and mounted his horse. For the first time he noticed the lead rope and bridle lying on the ground next to where he'd tied his mount. He paused momentarily, wondering what it meant and then turned his horse, kicking him hard. By the time Hank reached the edge of the yard, he was riding at a headlong gallop.

Ove turned and walked back into the house. He must try to do something for Mrs. O'Neal before the doctor arrived. He knew it might be another two hours or more before help arrived from town. He knelt beside Johanna again and carefully observed her face. It was obvious that there was extreme swelling and he knew from experience that cold could help reduce it. He'd seen it in his native country. There was no ice available here, so he must do the best he could with what he had. He went out onto the back porch and found a basin. He walked outside to the well and pumped until extremely cold water came. It was the same at his house.

Catching some of the coldest water he could, he took several clean rags that were folded in a corner basket on the back porch and took these things back into the living room. He washed some of the blood from Johanna's face and then formed a cold compress, which he placed on the left side of her head. It wasn't much, he knew.

Lifting the upper portion of the blanket that covered Johanna's body, Ove could see that the skin over Johanna's left rib cage was starting to bruise and he knew this was another area of major injury. He tried to think ahead to what the doctor might need once he arrived. Certainly, it would be easier for the doctor to treat her if she were off the floor. He imagined that at first it would be impossible to just move her upstairs to her bed. There would have to be some intermediate place.

Ove stood and looked at the dining room table. It was small but there was a crack across the table that indicated it had at least one leaf. "Where do they keep that leaf," he wondered aloud. He stood up and began to explore.

He felt terribly uncomfortable doing this, but he went into the room where they had found the blanket earlier. He looked under the bed, but there was nothing. It was the only place in the room that would hide the needed leaf.

Coming out of the room, he noticed a small cut out door on the wall under the stairway. He went to it and opened the nearly hidden door. Inside the cramped closet he found brooms and cleaning items and the two leaves for the table which he carried one by one into the dining room.

It took a great deal of careful effort, working alone to install the two leaves. When finished, it considerably lengthened the table and would be long enough to accommodate Johanna. He brought the sheet from the bed in the back bedroom and placed it carefully over the table.

He pumped more cold water and changed the compress on Johanna's head and then decided that rather than walk over the broken pieces of bowl and ruined dough on the kitchen floor, he would clean up the mess. Carefully, he placed the broken bowl pieces up on the sideboard, next to the buttered bread pans. The dough he cleaned up and carried outside, and dumped it into the chicken coop.

Ove knew the sheriff would probably want to see the damage as it was when whoever did it was in the house, so he left the rest of the kitchen as he'd found it. In the dining room he noticed broken china and many shards of glass on the floor. He retrieved a broom and swept all of the shards and china pieces into one pile in the corner of the dining room. It would now be out of the way and not underfoot.

Next, Ove found a glass in the kitchen and filled it with cold water. He looked through the cupboard and found some cookies in a small jar that he imagined had been baked sometime earlier in the week. He took two out and placed them on a small, chipped saucer he found on a shelf below.

Carefully carrying the saucer and glass up the stairs,

he gently opened the bedroom door which was standing slightly ajar. Rosa, lying on the bed with the little girl, was humming softly and she turned and acknowledged that she saw him. It was obvious that Rosa had been crying, but the little girl lying next to her was near sleep, exhausted from her ordeal. Ove gently placed the saucer and glass on the small table next to the bed, which held only an oil lamp. Ove could read the words formed by Rosa's lips, "Thank you," she said and smiled. Ove nodded and left the room.

He went downstairs and again changed the compress on Johanna's injured head and sat on the floor beside her for awhile, watching her breathing, looking for some change. Her pulse seemed a little more steady, but there was no sign that she was any more conscious than she had been when he and his son had first arrived.

After a while, Ove got up from the floor and walked out onto the porch. Looking into the distance toward town he suddenly remembered he had forgotten to tell Henry to contact the priest. This bothered him, because he knew that the O'Neal household was Catholic. It momentarily irritated him that he could have forgotten such an important detail, but after a few minutes of thinking about it, he knew that it wouldn't be long, once Henry reached the town that everyone would hear about what had happened. Perhaps the priest would just come.

Ove realized that Rosa's husband needed his attention as well. He went back into the house and again went upstairs. This time he went to the room where they had found Sarah and took the top blanket from the bed and went quietly back downstairs.

Leaving the blanket on the swing, he descended the

steps and tried to decide the best way to move this man to the front porch, which was the place he thought most appropriate. Flies were gathering over the area where the bullet had entered Hernando's chest. They were also circling his nose and mouth; Ove could not stand to watch this happen. The tall, determined Norwegian knelt down and reached beneath Hernando, one of his arms beneath Hernando's chest and the other under his knees. By sheer force of will Ove lifted the man up from the ground and carried him onto the front porch.

After carefully laying him down, Ove tucked the blanket around him, making sure that all the flies had been shooed away. He made sure there was no place the persistent insects could enter under the blanket.

Ove now had blood on his shirt and right arm, so he again went to the pump and cleaned himself up as best he could. Once more he changed the cold compress and then just sat on the floor beside the woman, keeping her quiet company. He knew they still had a long wait ahead of them.

His mind strayed to a place he had kept it from going since they had arrived at the ranch. He worried about where the men who had done this damage had headed after they left here. Rosa had said they had ridden west, but he wondered if they could have changed direction once they'd left the immediate area. He prayed that his wife and daughter were safe.

CHAPTER 13

NATHAN AND WILF

IF YOU'D NEVER MET SHERIFF Nathan Westphal before and were just casually watching him go about his business, you would have deduced very quickly that he'd spent time in the Army. It wasn't so much what he did, it was the precise way in which he did it. He was a man who did everything thoroughly.

He'd grown up in Montgomery County, Pennsylvania, the son of a moderately wealthy farmer who believed that with hard work you could accomplish anything, and he had preached that sermon on a regular basis to Nathan and his two younger brothers and one younger sister.

Nathan had grown up believing that he would one day marry and make his living as a farmer, never leaving Montgomery County for anywhere else. He was quite content with the life in that rural, quiet place.

At the outbreak of the war between the states, Nathan had joined the Union Army, largely because of the urging of his father, who believed fervently that the Union must be preserved and was also an ardent abolitionist. Nathan obliged his father, believing, based on what was being said by those who were older, and he considered to be wiser than himself, that the war would be over quickly. Should they decide to persist in this matter the Confederate States surely would begin to realize that they were facing a much superior force and back down. A compromise between the North and the South would be reached, although Nathan could not fathom what that compromise might be.

Entering the Army he had hoped for the cavalry and had seen that hope come to fruition, being assigned to the Sixth Pennsylvania Cavalry Regiment. Almost immediately, Nathan found himself being promoted and by the midpoint of the war he had a number of stripes on his sleeve. What Nathan had not realized growing up was that he was a natural leader. With his father around, he'd never been given much of an opportunity to exercise these inborn qualities. Nathan quickly learned that in the Army, many of the officers had gained their rank because of social position or educational level, two qualities that didn't necessarily equal leadership. These officers depended very heavily on men like Nathan. The young Sergeant became a master at subtle suggestion and he learned that the more subtle the suggestion, the more likely it would be incorporated into orders from his superior officers. Liaison between officers and men of lesser rank was an easy fit for Nathan. He felt comfortable in the company of both.

Three times during the war, Nathan had horses shot out from under him and each time he had walked away without a serious injury or wound. He'd been creased by a minie-ball on his upper right arm, but nothing more. Men around him had fallen, victims of tremendous carnage, but somehow Nathan had remained unscathed. He had mixed feelings about this phenomenon - feelings that vacillated from almost euphoric relief to a guilt that weighed heavily upon his soul.

The war, of course, had gone on much longer than anyone could have possibly imagined, with consequences that were realized only much later. At the end of it, Nathan, now 24 years of age, had come back to his home, somehow expecting that he would pick up his life where he'd left off. Infrequent letters from home had informed him of the death of one brother, a casualty of war, and the sudden death of his mother, both occurring just weeks apart during the first year he'd been away.

He'd also been informed by his sister that their remaining brother had left home and gone west to escape conscription. This had occurred in the second year of the war. Nathan found all of this extremely distressful especially since he could not return home and help do anything about it. He'd yearned for home as the war dragged on and he saw more and more men die around him. Men who would never return to a life of any kind.

What Nathan hadn't learned by letter, he learned once he returned to Montgomery County when the war was finally over. The woman that Nathan had hoped to one day marry and had corresponded with on a regular basis in the early part of the war, had married someone else and had left Pennsylvania.

The most unsettling news was that during the last year of the war his father had sold the land his family had farmed for three generations, and was now living with Nathan's younger sister and her husband in Philadelphia.

Nathan found this unbelievable and had traveled to his sister's home to confront his father. When he got there, he found an old man he hardly recognized who seemed not to know Nathan at all. His father was paralyzed on one side of his body and had to be fed like a small child. He had been like this for the previous four months, his sister informed him.

At first, Nathan was extremely upset about the sale of the farm and had taken his anger out on his sister and her husband. Her husband was a very successful businessman who had become quite wealthy during the war, selling and hauling supplies for the Union Army. His sister had quietly produced written documents that had been prepared when his father was still of sound mind and body, stating that he wished to sell. His signature, firm and strong rested on the papers his sister had handed him. While Nathan was forced to accept this, he could not understand it.

His sister told him that after the death of their mother and brother, and especially after the departure of their youngest brother, their father had become very despondent. He had said over and over that everything that had happened was his fault. Nathan was left wondering why his father could not have waited to see what his oldest son's preference might have been regarding the family's land.

Nathan had been given his share of the money from the sale of the farm and he had thought initially he would buy land of his own and start over. But weeks had turned into months and he'd spent this time living at his sister's home. Day after day, Nathan listlessly wandered around Philadelphia, wondering what he should do. He found himself surrounded by men using crutches to walk, or with empty sleeves pinned up to their shoulders. Others bore horrific scars, walked with a limp or stared off into the distance. Nathan had been very disturbed by their constant presence and it tore at his mind.

One morning, after a night of fitful sleep and a reoccurring nightmare, Nathan had announced to his sister that he was leaving. A few days later, after buying a horse and travel provisions, he had gone into his father's room to say good-bye. He'd knelt beside his father's rocking chair, took his hand and tried to get the man's attention. He knew it would be the last time he would see his father alive, and he had no idea what to say to him. Nathan told his father he was leaving and would be gone for some time, that he loved him and would miss him.

His father briefly seemed to know him, but then had called him by his dead brother's name. Quickly his attention wandered and he began talking about a picnic he'd been on one time with Nathan's mother, an event of which Nathan had no knowledge. A bit later, after his father had become quiet, Nathan had stood, kissed his father on the top of his head, turned and walked out of the room. He embraced his sister, shook her husband's hand, got on his horse and rode west.

That had been nearly twenty years ago and in that time Nathan had been many places. Ten years ago he had drifted into Fergus and had been offered the job of Deputy Sheriff. A year later, after Nathan and the Sheriff had spent several days tracking down a horse thief, they returned home in a cold rainstorm. The Sheriff had taken ill and days later had died of pneumonia. Nathan had been offered the job of Sheriff, had accepted it and since that time had become a fixture in the growing town.

Not long after arriving in Fergus, Nathan had met his future wife, Emily Paulson, who had been previously married to the owner of the mercantile store. She'd become a widow very suddenly several years before and had found herself raising two children, a boy, Jackson, and a girl, Roxanne, while continuing to run the store alone, something she had never intended.

Nathan had noticed Emily within days after arriving in Fergus, but it had taken some time to get beyond casual conversation with her. As the only deputy, he'd been given the task of "making the rounds" of the town, twice daily. This simply meant being out among the citizens, checking to make sure everything was all right and making the presence of the law felt.

He'd stop in each business every morning and afternoon to visit for a few moments, shoot the breeze, and move on. People came to look forward to his visits, because he brought news of what was happening in the rest of the town. Paulson Mercantile Store was his favorite stop, especially in the afternoon when there were fewer customers and he was less likely to be interrupted in his visit with its proprietor.

For her part, Emily was at first taken aback by this man. They were both in their mid thirties at that time, but to her, he seemed older somehow, more serious. Certainly more serious than her husband had been. It wasn't until she'd gotten to know Nathan much better that she'd learned that he had a very good sense of humor. At first, his light green eyes that never looked away from hers while he was talking to her un-nerved her. He was direct, she more shy. Although he knew immediately that she was the one he was looking for, it took her more time to develop feelings for him.

But, Nathan was a patient man. After a number of weeks, she had finally consented to occasionally let him walk her home in the evening, "to see her safely home." Her children, who were taken care of by Emily's mother-in-law when they were not in school, gravitated toward Nathan immediately. They liked him and that was a big plus, Nathan thought, but still Emily kept him at a distance.

Emily, who had never been in an intimate relationship with anyone other than her husband, was wary of his motives. Who in their right mind, she wondered, would take on the job of raising someone else's children? Perhaps, she thought, he wanted her because she owned a business. Finding it difficult to sometimes get all of her bills paid, she knew she was anything but wealthy. What she did not understand was that Nathan would have taken on anything that Emily brought with her. He was genuinely attracted to this tall, dark haired, dark eyed woman who was to him unquestionably the beauty of Fergus. To him, she was not only beautiful but more importantly, courageous.

The moment of realization of what she meant to him had come quite unexpectedly. The children of Fergus were performing in an evening pageant, which was to be presented in the community hall just a few days before Christmas. Emily was one of the mothers in charge of costumes. She'd spent many evenings leading up to the event, sewing, hemming, and adjusting the costumes to fit the children who stopped by her house for final touches.

The night of the pageant Emily had reserved a chair for herself at the end of the first row, far right. She'd been so busy at the store and wrestling with this project, she had neglected to mention to Nathan where she would be or even to invite him to the production. Secretly, she could hardly wait for it to be over. Last minute preparations had been completed, and the kerosene lamps adjusted in the hall so that only the stage area was fully lit. Emily had stumbled in the dim light to her chair and sat down.

The play had begun, and just a few minutes into it, although Emily was not aware of it, Nathan had entered the hall. He had found an empty chair near the back and had boldly carried it to the front and had quietly set the chair down next to hers. That was the first she was aware of his presence. She'd looked up, rather startled and exchanged smiles with him as he'd sat down.

A few minutes later, she had glanced over at him and in the muted light had seen how intently he was watching the pageant, smiling slightly. He'd looked at her then and the look he'd given her had made her heart race. Without breaking his gaze, he had reached down and taken her hand and then had casually turned his attention back to the play. None of the rest of the pageant had registered on Emily's consciousness. She had spent the entire time feeling the strength of the hand holding hers. In all of the evenings he'd been walking her home, he'd never once touched her.

After the play, Emily assisted the children with removing their costumes and putting them away. They were nearly the last people to leave the hall and Nathan had walked Emily and her children home. The ten and eight year old siblings had tripped ahead of them still excited about the play, laughing and exchanging occasional shoves. On the walk home, it was Emily who had taken Nathan's hand and had told him how glad she was he had attended. Nathan had talked about the parts of the play he had enjoyed the most and Emily smiled, thinking about the fact that she hadn't seen the play at all that evening.

Once home, the children had gone inside and Emily had asked them quietly to get ready for bed and told them she'd be in shortly. With that, she had turned to Nathan, who was standing behind her on the porch. She'd gone to him, and there in the darkness he had taken her into his arms and had kissed her like she'd never been kissed before. After breaking their embrace, Emily had asked him if he'd like to join them for Christmas dinner and Nathan had told her that he'd like that very much. Four months later, they had been married.

Now ten years later, Jackson, 20 was pretty much running the store on his own, with help and guidance from his mother and Roxanne was soon to marry a young rancher. Together, Nathan and Emily had never had children, but from the first time he'd met them, Nathan had treated Emily's children as his own.

Nathan had gone through a couple of deputies early in his career as Sheriff; men who hadn't taken the job seriously and who had quickly moved on when Nathan had demanded more of them. One had been caught drinking on the job and the other had turned out to be a bully, who felt that being a deputy gave him permission to order people about, for the hell of it. Nathan wouldn't have it and had fired them both.

Five years into his tenure as Sheriff, Nathan was working without help. After an especially frustrating day he had made a rare stop at one of Fergus' two saloons. The bartender, who liked Nathan but rarely saw him as a customer, had generously poured him a double shot of his best whiskey and told Nathan that the drink was on him.

"Tough day?" The bartender inquired.

"Don't ask," Nathan replied, smiling, shaking his head and thanking the bartender for the much needed drink. He took a couple of sips and then turned his attention to the room around him.

The saloon was busy that evening and after his eyes had adjusted to the dim light, he'd noticed that two stools down from him, sat a man he'd never seen in town before. Nathan was always taking note of those who were not locals so looked the man over carefully. Nathan estimated that, like himself, the man was in his early 40s and had obviously been on the road for quite awhile. His hat, lying on the bar was dusty, as was his worn clothing. His hair, dark brown and peppered with gray, was long, near shoulder length, and looked as though it had not been washed or combed for some time. Nathan also noticed the man was wearing a gun belt and had his rifle, a Sharps, propped up against the bar, next to his left leg.

"Heading through?" Nathan asked the man who had turned his head towards Nathan when he had sensed he was being observed. The man had soft brown eyes, the color of caramel and a beard that had grown three inches below his chin.

"Actually, I'm looking for work. Need to stay in one

place for awhile." the man answered in a soft drawl that Nathan recognized instantly as an accent that said Virginia.

Nathan looked down at his own whiskey glass and began turning it slowing with the ends of his fingers. He looked back at the man, met his eyes directly and asked quietly, "What's your name?"

"Bennington," the man had replied, "Wilf Bennington." He did not add that his full name was James Wilfred Bennington III, as he thought it might sound pretentious. For this place and time, he thought "Wilf" would do.

"Did you serve?" Nathan asked, knowing the man would know what he meant.

"Yes, I did." Wilf answered, determined to not add any details, unless pressed, and then, only reluctantly.

"Infantry, Artillery or Cavalry?

"Cavalry," Wilf had answered, not adding that he'd ridden most of the war in the company of the well known Confederate General, Jeb Stewart.

"Officer or enlisted?"

"Officer," Wilf had replied, wondering how that would influence Nathan's initial impression of him. He realized that the last thing he currently looked like was an officer in the Confederate Army… or any army, for that matter.

Finally Nathan had asked him, not quite knowing why, "Were you at Gettysburg?"

"Yup," Wilf replied. "Hell of a place." He realized too late that he'd done more than just answer in the affirmative.

"Yes it was," Nathan said nodding his head.

There was a long pause, as Nathan went back to slowly turning his glass on the bar and then he raised it to his lips, finishing the amber liquid. He turned on his stool so that he could look at the man more directly, bringing the star he wore on his left chest into view.

"I'm looking for a deputy, would you be interested in the job?" Nathan asked, fully aware that he was taking a chance on someone he knew absolutely nothing about, but trusting his first instincts.

The man next to him didn't move, but his eyes took in the badge and the colt revolver which Nathan wore high on his right hip. He sat there for a few moments as though weighing every word Nathan had spoken. At just the moment Nathan was sure he was going to hear the man say that he was not interested, Wilf nodded his head and said, "Alright. When would I start?"

Nathan had asked him to come to his office in the morning around nine o'clock and they would discuss wages and duties. He was afraid if he told the man too much, by morning he might change his mind. Wilf had agreed and the two men had shaken hands and Nathan departed. Wilf then ordered another drink and when it came he'd tossed it back quickly, asking himself aloud, "What the hell have I just done?" He'd picked up his Sharps and had walked out the door heading in the direction the bartender had said he would find the boarding house.

The next morning, at eight o'clock Nathan was in the office behind his desk, sharpening the two pencils that lived in his desk drawer with his pen knife. Nathan found nothing more frustrating than to find a dull pencil when he quickly needed to write something down. His full attention was given to the task at hand, when the office door opened and a man walked in.

Nathan had merely glanced up and said he'd be with him in a moment. The man removed his hat and sat down on the old horsehair bench against the wall next to the door. He placed his hat next to him, saying nothing. Nathan finally finished the tedious job and put the pencils back in the drawer. Then he looked up while folding his pen knife and asked the man what he could do for him.

The man who had sat patiently on the bench cleared his throat and said in a voice that Nathan instantly recognized, "Well I know I'm early but last evening you offered me a job and I'm here to start."

Nathan was nothing less than stunned, because the man sitting in front of him looked nothing like the one he'd seen in the saloon twelve hours ago. He was closely shaven, except for a moustache which looked to be mostly gray. His dark brown hair now looked lighter, had been washed, and was cut short. He wore a clean pair of trousers and a white shirt, which had spent a long time in a saddle bag, but had been washed last evening, dried overnight and perfectly pressed by the woman who owned the boarding house. His boots were worn, but there had been an obvious effort to polish them.

"I'm sorry," Nathan said, quickly rising to his feet, "I didn't recognize you."

"Well neither would anyone else who's seen me the last couple of years," the man had chuckled good-naturedly.

That was how the first day of the partnership of Nathan and Wilf had begun and it had continued in the same vein for the last four years. The two cavalrymen from opposite sides of the Mason-Dixon line worked well together.

Wilf was quiet and offered no information about his past, though Nathan had asked him many leading questions over time. Wilf had supper with Nathan and Emily and their grown children nearly every Friday night. The talk was about things that were happening in current time, nothing about where Wilf had been or what he'd done. Nathan wondered if he would ever know anything about Wilf's past, except he'd been a Confederate cavalry officer who had fought at Gettysburg. There was a sadness in Wilf's eyes which Nathan knew stemmed from the war... and a lot more.

CHAPTER 14

DAY FOUR IN TOWN

THE DAY HAD BEGUN SLOWLY for Nathan and Wilf, with just routine chores around the office. Wilf headed out a little before 9:00 to do his morning rounds. Nathan knew he'd be back in an hour or so and they'd go get some coffee at the hotel café, unless something else unexpected happened.

Nathan had obtained a copy of a St. Louis newspaper left behind by a guest who'd stayed at the hotel. The proprietor had handed it off to Wilf on his afternoon rounds yesterday and now Nathan intended to take a look at it. He went outside on the board sidewalk, dragging his wooden desk chair along behind him. No use wasting the sunshine, he'd reasoned. He sat down in the chair and opened the newspaper that was over a month old.

Reading some of the headline stories about the madness and mayhem that was going on in St. Louis made Nathan glad he hadn't stayed there. In his journey to Fergus, he had spent over a year and a half living in St. Louis and had been glad to leave it. Within the newspaper were advertisements for plays and other entertainment and social events. Such things were not available in this small town and Nathan knew that it was part of the price of living in a place he preferred.

He thought that someday, maybe he'd take Emily to St. Louis, as she'd never been there and had expressed to him that someday it would be nice to visit the big city. He still had most of the money he'd inherited from the family farm sale years ago, and it was safely tucked away in the bank. Maybe they could use some of that to make the trip someday. He'd have to think about that.

Reading the newspaper cover to cover had taken quite a bit of time and he didn't realize how late it was until he saw Wilf coming up the street on the other side. He called out to him, "Ready to go get some coffee, Wilf?" He stood up and folded the paper, about to take it back inside.

Wilf's attention was focused down the street and he crossed over quickly and came up on the sidewalk, "Rider coming in Nathan - fast."

Nathan turned his attention in the direction of Wilf's gaze and could see that indeed a rider was coming into town, at full gallop.

"Looks like a kid," Wilf commented

The two men stood there together as the rider came down the street towards them. He didn't slow down, but rode full tilt right up to the hitching post in front of them. The horse was totally winded and lathered, and once stopped, dropped his head and panted heavily for breath.

The rider practically launched himself out of the saddle and began talking as soon as he hit the ground.

"Sheriff Westphal you must come quick to the O'Neal ranch. Something very bad has happened. A doctor is needed. "

Wilf and Nathan exchanged looks and Nathan invited the boy to come inside, as there were people on the street, staring in their direction. Nathan drug his chair inside behind him. Before going through the door, he noticed that Curtis Taylor, the man who owned the livery stable across the way, had come out onto the street when he heard the rider coming, and was still standing there.

"Curtis, take care of this horse please," Nathan had called out to him and Curtis had moved to do that.

Once inside the office, Nathan had asked the boy to sit down on the bench and had placed his chair in front of him, so that he could speak to the boy at eye level. Wilf walked over and sat down on top of the desk at a distance, to give Nathan and the boy room.

"Now," Nathan said, "What's your name?"

Hank was sweating heavily from the exertion of the long ride, and was taking deep breaths, trying to catch his wind. "Hank…Henry Johanson, I'm Ove Johanson's son and we live on a ranch near O'Neals."

Nathan instantly put the two together and nodded. "What happened, and start from the beginning, Henry."

Hank looked from Nathan to Wilf and then began. "My father and I went to the O'Neal ranch this morning to check on them. Mr. O'Neal is gone on a cattle drive."

Nathan nodded, as he knew this. "What happened when you got to the ranch?"

Hank stopped and swallowed, his face contorted in

a frown as he thought his way through this, because he wanted to get it right. "Rosa, the cook, was hanging from the porch and her husband was dead on the ground in front of the house. But Rosa wasn't dead, she was just hanging there. They tied her by a rope on her arms." Hank stopped and put his hands over his head to demonstrate and then pointed to his wrists, "The rope was here," he indicated.

"Okay, go on."

"We cut Rosa down and she and my father went inside the house…I didn't go in, my father made me wait on the porch. But when he came out, he said I should come here and get you and the doctor, because Mrs. O'Neal is badly injured."

"Is that all?"

"Only that the little girl was in the house and she was crying a lot…and James wasn't at the house and we don't know where he is. He wasn't in the house."

"Did your father say how badly Mrs. O'Neal is injured?"

"No, only that it was very bad. Rosa said three men came to the house and they are the ones who hurt them. And she said they went west when they left."

"Three men came to the house? Rosa said three men came to the house, was that this morning?"

"Yes."

"Is your father still at the ranch. Did he stay there?"

The boy nodded yes.

"Henry can you think of anything else your father or Rosa said to you?"

Hank thought hard. Then he suddenly thought of something that had just registered in his mind. "There were different horses in the corral by the barn."

"Different horses?"

"Yes, while I was sitting on the porch, I remember there were three horses in the corral. Usually the horses are in the pasture, but these were in the corral. Horses I've never seen before."

"They took O'Neal horses when they left," Wilf said quietly. "Came to the house, did damage, then left on O'Neal horses."

"Sounds like," Nathan agreed.

Nathan stood up and turned toward Wilf, trying to think of all the things they needed to do very quickly. "Wilf, I want you to go to the doc's and get him started toward the O'Neal place. We're going to need a posse and I'd just as soon take it with us on our way - without having to double back to put one together."

"I agree. After I get the doc headed for O'Neals, I'll swing by the boarding house, collect what I need and meet you back here."

Nathan turned his attention to the boy. "You did well, Henry, I'm proud of you. Your horse needs to rest. I want you to wait for your father at my house and I'll have him come and get you later today, or possibly in the morning. I don't want you riding alone anywhere, there's no guarantee the men aren't still in the area."

Hank nodded, knowing he must do as he was told, even though what he wanted to do was go back to the ranch and look for James. "Yes sir," he said quietly.

"Come with me, I'll take you to my house."

The two men and the boy left the office and Wilf went to the livery stable to saddle and mount his horse and head to the doctor's house and then the boarding house.

Nathan walked the boy quickly to his house two blocks away to the south, and went through the front door calling to his wife. "Emily, we've got company."

Emily came out of the kitchen, wearing her apron, flour on her hands, with surprised look on her face. She rarely if ever saw Nathan this time of day.

"Emily this is Henry Johanson and he needs to stay here until his father comes to get him. It might be later today or tomorrow morning, so he may be with you overnight." He turned to Hank and said, "And if you have a chair there at the table, young man, in a little while my wife will feed you some of whatever she's baking.

Emily looked at Henry and noticed that the boy's face was quite pale, and his eyes were large and vacant as he gazed around her kitchen. She wasn't sure what was happening, but Nathan's next request was directed to her and she began to respond immediately.

"Em, I need you to help me get some provisions together, enough for two or three days at least. I need some smoked ham, jerky, dried fruit, and anything else that will keep, canned meat"…his voice trailed off. "Also get both of my hunting canteens down and fill them with water."

With that he turned and went into their bedroom. He reached into the closet, pulled out his Winchester, began checking it and dug for ammunition in the bottom drawer of the dresser. His large hunting and posse saddle bags hung in the closet as well. He took them out and put them on the bed. Next he pulled out his always-made bedroll and started organizing things for the saddle bags; a couple pair of warm socks, a cold weather shirt, and a jacket.

He made sure his can opener, field glasses and flint box were still in the saddle bags from a previous trip, as well as his best pair of heavy leather gloves and sheath knife. He tucked the gloves into his belt. He pulled his slicker out of the closet and then he started hauling things out the back door. He left the saddle bags on the kitchen table for Emily to fill.

Nathan went out to the small stable behind the house and brought out his horse. " Okay Jake, we're going for a ride," he said to the tall honey colored four year old gelding who was about the finest horse he'd ever owned. He saddled and bridled the horse and tied on the scabbard that would soon hold his Winchester.

Then he went back into the house as Emily finished loading the saddle bags and recited to Nathan what all she'd packed for him. "Sounds wonderful," he said going through the house for the second time with the next load. She helped him carry the remaining items out the back door and watched as he went back into the house, got his wide brimmed brown hat and put on his good leather gloves.

"Nathan, what's happened?" Emily asked, as he came back out through the back door. Her voice was shaking which it seldom did, but with the appearance of the boy and Nathan's preparations for being away, she knew whatever was going on was very serious.

Nathan said nothing until the horse was completely loaded and ready to go and then he turned to her and told her what little he knew. He asked that she not share the information with anyone, knowing that distorted stories would be everywhere soon. He hoped to keep the lid on a while longer.

"How badly is Johanna hurt Nathan?"

"Sweetheart, I don't know and I won't till I get there. I don't know how many days it will be before I get back. We'll be going after these men."

Emily swallowed hard, tried not to cry, and quietly embraced her husband. "Please be careful Nathan, please be careful." He held her close and then kissed her and touched her face with his right gloved hand. "I will, Em. Promise." With that he mounted the horse and quickly rode out of the yard. Before gathering a posse, Nathan had one other stop to make: The MacKenzie Hardware Store.

Emily started to lose control but quickly regained herself, turned and walked back into the house. She had a scared boy to take care of.

Once mounted, Wilf raced along the main street, taking the second side street north, all the way to the end to the last house on the right. He dismounted, quickly walked to the door and knocked. A plaque to the left of the door read, David H. Messinger, M.D. Ellen, the doctor's wife, came to the door and greeted him by name. Wilf had helped bring numerous injured people to their residence, both day and night over the years. "Why, Hello Wilf, how are you today?"

"Afraid I have bad news Ma'am, is your husband at home?

Ellen could see by the expression on his face that something of a serious nature had brought the deputy to her door.

"Yes he is Wilf, please come inside."

Wilf removed his hat and stepped inside the house. The front parlor of the residence had been turned into a room where patients could wait to see the doctor, and the room to the right was the doctor's treatment room. In fact, the entire lower floor of the house had pretty much been turned over to the doctor's practice of medicine. The downstairs bedroom was a place where injured patients could spend hours or even days recovering. The place smelled of iodine, alcohol, and herbs that were used in various poultices and teas.

"My husband is with a patient right now, but should be out very shortly," Ellen said and then asked him if he would like a cup of coffee.

"No thank you Ma'am, I need to see the doctor just as soon as possible. His help is needed immediately in the country. Would it be alright with you if I began hitching up the carriage, as we need to leave soon."

Ellen gave her consent and then stepped into the treatment room to speak with her husband. Wilf went outside and began hitching the doctor's horse to the black covered carriage. By the time he was finished and went back into the house, the patient was exiting the treatment room and quickly left by the front door.

Dr. Messinger, a man in his late thirties, had just finished washing his hands and was rolling down his sleeves when Wilf entered the treatment room to speak to him.

"What's happened, Wilf?"

Wilf gave him all the details he had, which caused the doctor to purse his lips and shake his head. He quickly began gathering things he would need to take with him, instructing his wife he would need her help at the ranch, as well. He knew from what Wilf said, that attention would have to be given to at least two people at the ranch. He picked up his black bag and a bulky kit that carried everything from splint material to numerous sizes of rolled bandages and extra vials of various kinds of medicine.

As the three of them walked out the front door, Ellen put a sign that read THE DOCTOR IS OUT under the plaque near the door. Wilf assisted Ellen into the carriage, while the doctor put the things he would need in the back and tied a thick gray tarp over them for protection. Wilf hadn't bothered to admonish them to travel armed, because he knew the doctor never carried a weapon and the warning would be a waste of breath.

"Sheriff Westphal and I will see you at the O'Neal's," Wilf said as he mounted, turned, and headed for the boarding house. He was nearly there, when he thought of something, and turned his horse toward the small Catholic Church. Wilf, a terribly lapsed Methodist himself, had sometimes seen the O'Neals and their hired help come to town for Mass while he was patrolling the streets of Fergus on Sundays.

Stopping at the church, and finding no one inside, he had gone to the door of the neat and freshly painted rectory next to the Church. The priest came to the door and as soon as he saw Wilf, who always wore his metal star on his vest, he knew there was trouble.

Father James MacLeod, Boston born, short, thin, balding and in his late forties, listened intently as Wilf explained why he was needed at the O'Neal's. Responding to Wilf's request he said he would get the things he needed and be along as quickly as possible. He knew well where the O'Neal ranch was, having been there for burials at the family cemetery and visits when there had been sickness and the stillbirths of the O'Neal babies. He had now been in this parish for nearly fifteen years, so knew the hardships and heartbreaks of all of its members. He was a man of strict adherence to the Catholic faith, but one who had great compassion and ready forgiveness in the name of God. Wilf excused himself and said he must get ready for the trip himself and the priest shooed him away saying, "Go, go, go, I can take care of getting myself there. No need to concern yourself with me." The deputy turned and left.

Wilf's time at the boarding house, readying himself for the ride, was much like Nathan's at his home, only the person helping him pack was less calm. Mrs. Hazel Montgomery, a woman in her early 60s who had been a widow since her early 40s, owned the boarding house. She ran the place like a military boarding school with rules and regulations that didn't bother Wilf, but caused consternation among some of the other single men and women who lived there. Hours for meals were strictly enforced as well, and the fact that she was in all probability the best cook in town was the only reason that several of the people living there stayed.

Wilf hit the back door and flew upstairs to ready his saddle bags and put together his field glasses, Sharps rifle, ammunition, and everything else he'd need. Hazel, like Emily, was not used to seeing Wilf in her domain during the day and she was waiting for him when he quickly descended the stairs. He had his saddlebags over his shoulder and said to her, "Hazel, let's go into the kitchen."

She was the only woman in town he addressed by her first name and it was only because she would not have it any other way. Wilf was her favorite, best behaved boarder, and the most reliable in his monthly payment. His room had the best view; his bed her best sheets, and she tried to see he got the best cut of meat at dinner whenever possible. The fact that he never got any mail and never went out to call on any eligible women in the town both broke her heart and at the same time brought out the most protective side of her. She looked after him.

There were times when he would come home after some late night call for help from the townspeople, that she would be sitting in the kitchen waiting for him. She would pour them both a shot of *very* fine whiskey and they would sit at the kitchen table and quietly have a drink together. Wilf found this both amusing and touching and never tried to discourage her behavior, because simply stated, he enjoyed the woman's company.

Now, this morning, he explained what he needed and she was in the pantry gathering items to put into the saddlebags. The pile of provisions she was accumulating on the kitchen table would have overfilled the saddlebags, so he was selecting items that would be the most useful.

"I'll pay you for all of this later, Hazel," he began - but she cut him off, "You most certainly will not, Wilf."

When she asked where he was going, Wilf replied only that there were three dangerous men that he and Nathan must pursue until they were caught. They were an endangerment to the community. He knew that by nightfall she would know at least part of the truth and there was no need to give her any additional details here and now.

Once he had all of the supplies together it was more than he could carry all at once, so she helped him carry everything out the back door. He quickly loaded things onto his horse, mounted and turned to leave.

"Wilf," Hazel said in her "listen to me" voice, "you *will* be careful!"

"I'll do my best Hazel and thank you for your help."

With that he was gone, quickly going around the boarding house and out to the street. Hazel sat down on the back steps and prayed to God he would return safely.

When Wilf rode up in front of the Sheriff's office, he saw that a small crowd had gathered. People were standing on the sidewalks, on both sides of the street and in both directions from the office.

After collecting his own provisions, Nathan had quickly begun the selection of a posse. Curtis Taylor, the liveryman was walking a saddled horse out of the stable when Wilf tied his horse to the hitching post. Wilf could tell by the saddle bags and other gear tied on the back of Taylor's horse that he would be one of the men in the posse. "Good choice," thought Wilf. Taylor, like Nathan, had served in the Union Army, although as an infantryman, and was a very capable man.

Frank Bassett, a man in his mid-twenties, was a carpenter. Earlier in the day on his rounds, Wilf had noticed him shingling a roof on one of the businesses on Main Street. Now, he was leading his horse down the street toward the assembling posse. He too looked loaded for bear. Wilf knew nothing of his survival abilities, but knew Nathan had reason to trust him, or he wouldn't be there.

Another man Wilf was glad Nathan had chosen was William Larson. He was quiet and lived on little or nothing, but owned the second fastest horse in the county, a chocolate colored mare who would just as soon run over you as around you. Larson, when he had first heard Wilf's accent, had confided that he had been a Confederate sniper, doing as much damage as possible from church belfries throughout the war. Wilf had simply nodded, offering no response. Larson had not spoken again to Wilf about his war experience, but the two would exchange nods, when they saw each other on the street in Fergus.

Once the posse was gathered, Nathan called the men into the office where he could talk to them privately and explained what they would be doing for an unknown length of time. He then added quietly, "If any of you have second thoughts, you can leave now and no one will think the lesser of you." No one stirred. "Alright then." Nathan said, moving toward the door, "Let's go."

The men went out, unhitched their horses and headed out of town toward the O'Neal ranch, riding hard. They quickly overtook and passed the doctor's carriage. It was nearly eight miles to the ranch, so there were a couple of times they stopped to rest their mounts and let them catch their breath. At one of their brief rests, while Wilf was looking around at the other posse members, he realized that Nathan was the only man there who was married.

Once at the ranch, Wilf and Nathan hitched their horses at the house and sent the others to the bunk house to await further instructions. The men stood outside, apprehensive about what might happen next. Ove Johanson was waiting on the porch, as he had heard the horses approaching. Nathan, remembering what Hank had said about the death of Hernando, expected to see the man lying on the grass, but instead saw a patch of dried blood.

As they climbed the porch steps Ove pointed out that Hernando was now on the porch, in some limited shade and protected from insects. Nathan went to the covered man and pulled back the blanket to observe the wound. It was the first person killed in cold blood he had seen for quite some time and he felt a flash of anger go through him. He gently tucked the blanket around the body again and then stood and turned. Shaking his head, he headed for the front door, followed in by Wilf and Ove.

Once inside the house Wilf and Nathan both removed their hats and gloves and dropped them on the sofa in the living room and went quickly to Johanna. Nathan knelt beside her while Wilf remained standing a few steps back. Nathan quickly checked her pulse and breathing and Ove explained that both were about the same as they had been since he'd arrived. He had just recently changed the cold compress.

Ove suggested his concern for Johanna's current place on the floor and wanted to know if she could be moved onto the table before the doctor came. Nathan said that he thought that was a good idea and called Curtis into the house to help them.

Ove had another blanket ready in anticipation of this, and the four men carefully got her onto the blanket. They placed it under her one side at a time and rolled it up tight from each edge until they could grasp it, two men on a side. They lifted Johanna to the table and Curtis quickly left the house, greatly disturbed by the battered condition of her face.

Nathan asked to speak to Rosa and Ove pointed him upstairs. Rosa was still in the large bedroom with Sarah and the little girl was awake now. Earlier Rosa had helped Sarah clean up and change into a nightgown. She had given her the cookies and water, which Sarah had nibbled from the edges very slowly in her usual style of cookie eating, and had even offered her doll part of one of them, which made Rosa smile sadly.

Nathan asked Rosa to step into the hallway to tell him everything she could remember about that morning. This time, Rosa had begun the story with James going fishing and the shots they had heard, the men riding in, and everything she could remember that had transpired during the stay of the three men that she had been able to see or hear.

Nathan quietly asked her followup questions about where James might have gone fishing, the description of the men and the horses they had stolen.

The most helpful information Rosa had given him was the direction James had ridden when he left that morning. Nathan had been fishing with Daniel and James at the Aspen grove, so he thought that was where James had most likely headed. Rosa knew the men had tried to steal Red, but the horse had run away. When the men left the ranch, she related, they were riding Daniel's gray stallion, a tall roan colored horse and a buckskin mare. One man had very long dark hair, Rosa had told Nathan, one had reddish brown hair and the other one Rosa could remember nothing about, except he had ridden the buckskin.

All of this was extremely helpful and Nathan thanked her. As he turned to walk away, Rosa had asked when the doctor would be there for Johanna and was the priest coming for her husband? Nathan was able to tell her that Wilf had summoned both of them and they would be along soon.

Nathan continued, "Rosa, I am so sorry this happened. We will do our best to catch the men who did this." Rosa nodded and turned to go back into the bedroom with Sarah. "Rosa, one more thing,"…he paused, not sure how to continue. "Where do you want your husband buried? I am going to instruct someone about digging a grave for him." Rosa paused, unsure of how to answer, but then said, "I had always thought one of Daniel's family would make that decision, but I think inside the family cemetery, but not next to the family." She thought a moment and then finished, "Perhaps over in the corner, the south corner, that would be a good place." Nathan nodded and patted her shoulder and then turned to go downstairs.

As Nathan went down the stairs, he noticed that Wilf was standing next to the dining room table bending close to Johanna. Nathan crossed the floor into the dining room where he could see more clearly. Wilf was oblivious to the presence of the other two men in the room.

The deputy had found a pair of scissors and had begun to cut Johanna's torn dress from her body. He had pulled the blanket down from her shoulder area and had carefully cut up the short sleeve and over her shoulder to the collar. He had finished the left side and was now working on the right, doing the same thing. He pulled the blanket down somewhat further until he could see that the under garment which covered her upper body had been completely torn bottom to top, except for the material which joined the two sides near her throat. At the center, there was a tiny pink bow that was very worn, but still visible.

Wilf gently cut through to the right of the bow. He then very discreetly looked under the blanket to see if Johanna was encumbered by any other clothing and saw that part of her underwear was still wrapped around her right leg. Everything else had been torn away. Wilf carefully continued to cut, freeing Johanna of all of her clothing. He quietly asked Ove and Nathan to help him roll her onto her right side, which was less injured. They complied and Wilf rolled all of the remnants of her clothing as far under her as he could. She was then rolled back flat onto the table. Once this was accomplished it was fairly easy for Wilf to slip all of the clothing parts from beneath her, while keeping the blanket over her. He gathered the clothing remnants hastily, and without comment walked to the stove in the kitchen and put the clothing into the fire box. He noticed there were still a few live wood coals from the fire Johanna had built that morning to do her baking. The coals were barely viable but instantly jumped to life once the clothing remnants touched them. Immediately there was the smell of burning cotton in the room.

Wilf stepped back from the stove knowing that before the posse left this place, he would come back to the stove to finish what he'd started. He then walked back to the dining room table and lifted the blanket covering Johanna's feet and very gently began removing her shoes and socks. He loosened the laces and carefully removed the worn ankle-high brown shoes one at a time, then removed Johanna's socks and put them inside the shoes. He covered her feet with the blanket again, and placed the shoes on the floor under the table.

Wilf stood and stepped back, took a deep breath, and then suddenly lurched sideways and all but ran to the front door. He barely made it to the porch rail in front of the swing before vomiting over the railing. He stood there for a couple of minutes, making sure he was finished, spitting food residue from his mouth onto the grass, not caring that he was being observed by the posse standing and sitting in front of the bunkhouse.

Nathan came through the door with a glass of water and handed it to him, saying nothing. Wilf took the glass from him, rinsed his mouth out and then took a long drink. "God damn it Nathan, God damn the bastards who did this." Wilf spoke softly, but the force behind the words was unmistakable.

"Wilf," Nathan said, after a moment, "We need to go to the river to find James, are you up for it?"

Wilf nodded and said, " We can leave any time you're ready."

Nathan asked Ove if he could wait until the doctor and the priest arrived before leaving. Then he could go and would find his son in town with Emily. "Henry did a good job today, Ove. He's a fine young man." Ove thanked him and said he would remain at the ranch as long as he was needed, but that he was worried about his wife and daughter, and was sure they would be worried as well.

Nathan asked Curtis and Bassett to wait at the porch for the doctor and the priest. He was afraid that curious neighbors or towns people would begin to arrive soon and he suggested that if anyone showed up and wanted something to do, they could begin to dig a grave in the southwest corner of the O'Neal/Sullivan Cemetery.

His stop at the Hardware Store had involved a conversation with Ian MacKenzie, who not only sold hardware, but was also a fair carpenter and always had at least one adult sized and one child coffin in the shed behind the store. He didn't advertise this fact and didn't need to. Everyone just knew.

Nathan had feared that one way or another, they were probably going to need two coffins, one for Hernando and one for either Johanna or James. Ian said that he had two adult sized coffins on hand and Nathan had asked him to load them into his largest wagon and head for the O'Neal ranch. If they were lucky and only needed one, there would be no harm done. It was possible, he knew, they might end up needing three, but Nathan hoped not. Ian, a normally very jovial man, had told Nathan in a sober voice that he would load the coffins and head for the O'Neal's immediately.

Nathan, Wilf and William Larson mounted up and headed for the trail that led to the river. The feeling of dread that Nathan felt was unmatched by anything he had felt since the war. His heart was beating rapidly and his mouth was very dry and he knew no amount of water would help. The men rode silently.

When they got to the Aspen grove they were greeted by the sight Nathan had most feared. They saw James' body lying beneath a tree, a few feet from the edge of the river. Red was standing next to the boy and as they approached, she whinnied and pawed at the ground. They dismounted and Nathan approached the horse slowly, speaking softly to her. Red's eyes were wide and rolled back and her ears were laid back against her head.

"Whoa girl, it's all right, we're here to help him. We won't hurt him. Easy girl."

Red knew these were not the men who had been there earlier. She put her nose down to James' chest, as she had dozens of times in the last couple of hours. James' shirt was covered with blood and there was blood on Red's muzzle and face, where she had rubbed against the boy's chest.

Nathan kept advancing until he could gently touch the horse on the flank and neck and then her face. Gradually, she relaxed and stepped back so Nathan could kneel beside James. He put his fingers to the boy's neck but knew it was futile. He'd seen enough dead men to know what death looked like. Lowering his head for a moment, Nathan struggled to control his anger and then rose and turned.

Wilf had dismounted and walked the few feet to the river where he saw the creel bobbing in the water. "Look at this," he said quietly, "it seems James caught something this morning." He leaned down and unfastened the creel from the branch and lifted it out of the river. Opening the lid, he was greeted by a thrashing fish. Wilf bent back towards the water and aided the fish in its escape. The fish paused before swimming away and then disappeared beneath the surface. Wilf stared at the spot for a moment and then stood. Without a word, he again bent over and carefully began gathering the scattered fishing flies and put them into the fly box. He put the box in the small satchel and hung both the satchel and wet creel over his saddle horn. Nathan in the meantime was re-saddling Red, speaking softly to her.

Finally, Nathan spoke, "We have to get James back to the house and I'm wondering what you think would be the best way to do that, Wilf?"

Wilf thought for a moment and said, "Let's wrap him up in my blankets and you and Larson hand him up to me. I don't want to hang him over his saddle. That would be wrong." Nathan nodded in agreement.

William Larson held back while Nathan and Wilf tightly wrapped the young man in Wilf's blankets, then Wilf mounted his horse and Larson and Nathan, with some difficulty, handed the boy up to him. "You'll have to take my reins and lead my horse, because I'll need both hands to hold him," Wilf commented.

"I'll do that, Wilf," Nathan said as he made ready to mount. He handed James' fly rod to Larson, wanting to get everything at the river back to the house.

As Nathan took the reins and mounted up, Larson suggested maybe they needed a lead rope on the red horse. "I think she'll follow us, no problem," Nathan offered.

She did. Once they began moving toward the house,

Red followed immediately behind them. Occasionally, she would come up beside Wilf and put her nose out to the boy's wrapped body. Wilf cradled James in his arms tightly, so he would not slip off to the ground. They couldn't travel at any speed and moved slowly single file along the trail. Nathan occasionally looked back to see how Wilf was doing and each time saw the look on Wilf's face that he'd seen earlier as he had attended Johanna.

Soon they came in sight of the house and the other posse members rose from the porch when they saw them coming. There were a couple of other men who had ridden to the ranch as well, their horses tied to the hitching post. The doctor's carriage and the horse the priest had ridden were also at the house.

Once they arrived, Larson, Nathan, Curtis and one of the other men, a neighbor, helped lower James and carry him up on to the porch and placed his blanket-wrapped body next to Hernando's.

Frank Bassett reported that two other neighbors and a man from town had showed up and he'd sent them to the cemetery to start digging a grave for the deceased ranch hand.

"Well, we'll need another one," Nathan said, his voice tight in his throat.

Wilf dismounted. His trousers, right sleeve and front of his shirt were blood stained where James' wounds had seeped through the blankets. He flexed his cramped arms, examining the sky, noting it was now into afternoon. He approached Nathan saying, "We're wastin' daylight here, we need to find the trail and get moving."

Nathan pulled off his gloves and put his hands on his hips, looking down at the ground, his weight shifted to one leg. He looked up at Wilf and said in a deliberate voice, having thought about this all the way back from the river, "Wilf, we're not leaving until we have these two men buried."

Wilf was not happy to hear this, as he wanted to begin the hunt for the men who had caused the carnage at the ranch. "Nathan," he began, "Nathan, they have a lot of time on us. I could go. I could go and follow them, maybe take Larson, and if we ride as fast as we can track them, we could possibly catch them early tomorrow."

"No, this posse will stay together and we'll leave when the burying is done."

"Well then," Wilf said, the words tinged in frustration, but no anger, " I'm heading for the cemetery, because the sooner we get this done, the sooner we leave."

"Wilf, thank you for carrying James back. I know that was difficult."

Wilf sighed deeply and then said, "Not as difficult as it's going to be for Mrs. O'Neal and Daniel, when they find out he's dead, Nathan. *That's* going to be difficult." He turned and walked toward the barn, leading his horse, hoping he would find a pick ax or a shovel. "I'm assuming I'll dig the grave next to one of the boy's parents?" He had stopped, turned and was addressing Nathan from several yards away.

"Yes, it should be fairly clear, once you are there. He was a Sullivan, you know. The cemetery's just a bit west of here…there's a trail."

Wilf merely nodded and then turned and went to the barn where he found a pick ax and a shovel, both quite old. Obviously the neighbors who had been here earlier had taken the better tools. "Hope these handles will hold up," he said turning them over in his hands.

Mounting his horse and carrying the tools across the saddle, he rode to the bunkhouse where a couple of the neighbors had gathered and were talking quietly. "Mount up, we're headed for the cemetery." With no argument, they mounted their horses and followed Wilf out of the yard.

Nathan watched until they were gone, knowing that his deputy was not pleased with his decision. Nathan would rather be on the trail as well, beginning the pursuit, rather than taking care of these details, but his conscience told him this was what he had to do. He went into the house to see how the doctor was faring.

Ove, who had seen the men returning from the river, had gone into the house and was sitting on the sofa when Nathan entered. The man was pale and tears were running down his face, and he made no attempt to wipe them away. He had no idea how he could possibly break the news of James' death to his son.

Nathan sat down next to him and touched his shoulder. "Mr. Johanson," he said clearing his throat, "I think it would be good if you returned to your family now." Ove nodded and asked the Sheriff the only question he must hear answered, before he left for town. "Did the boy suffer, if you can tell me?"

"No," Nathan answered, remembering the wounds he'd seen. "James died very quickly and probably with very little pain, if that's any comfort." Ove nodded and rose to go. "I wish...I wish we had come sooner."

Nathan shook his head. "No, if you'd come sooner, the men who did this would have killed you and your son as well. I have no doubt. You did everything you could have possibly done here to help and you did it well. Now go to your boy and take him home. Tell my wife we are safe here and will probably stay the night." Ove nodded, picked up his hat, went out and mounted his horse, who had stood patiently at the hitching rail for hours, then turned and headed for town.

Dr. Messinger and his wife were in the process of splinting Johanna's left arm. Not wanting to interrupt, but wondering what the doctor's assessment of Johanna's condition was, Nathan spoke in a low tone about four feet from the table. "Doctor, can you tell me how she is?"

Dr. Messinger looked up and nodded in Nathan's direction. "Well, the break in her arm is a clean one, so I've been able to set it. It will be painful for some time, but it should heal well. I think she has at least two broken ribs which will heal eventually. She has a head injury and I am uncertain what the outcome will be with that. I am hoping the swelling will go down in a day or two, and we'll know much more about how she's faring then. Until then, we simply have to keep her as comfortable as possible. I am hoping she will regain consciousness." The doctor hesitated and then went on. "Sheriff Westphal... she was raped, but I suppose you surmised that already."

Nathan looked down at the floor, sighed and looked up, "Yes, by the condition we found her in, we figured as much."

The doctor continued, "In a while, I'm hoping I can get some men to help move her upstairs to her bed, where we can make her more comfortable. Probably within an hour. We want to bathe her and I am going to suture a laceration on her head. I wonder if you would be able to keep everyone out of here until we finish with all of that?"

"Yes, Doctor, I'll keep everyone out. You just come to the door and let us know when you want us. Where is the priest?"

"He's upstairs, with…is it Rosa…the housekeeper?"

"Yes. When he comes down, will you please tell him I want to speak to him outside?"

The doctor said that he would and then turned his full attention back to Johanna. Nathan spent some time methodically going from room to room assessing the damage. He then went outside to join the rest of the posse. He would confer with the priest about the burials when the clergyman finished visiting with Rosa.

When Wilf and the other men reached the cemetery they noticed that the diggers in the south corner were making good progress with the grave for Hernando. The soil was dry but there had been enough rain during the summer to keep it from becoming extremely hard. Taking turns with the digging, they worked without stopping.

Wilf located the graves of James' parents, marked by engraved wooden crosses: William and Sarah Sullivan. Moving to the next plot of unused soil, Wilf marked the grave in his mind and with the other men who'd come with him, they began digging. Like the other team, they switched off, with no pause. Wilf made sure the sides of the grave were kept straight, and this job was made easier, as there were not a lot of large rocks beneath the surface.

Riding out to the cemetery, the men with him had at first speculated about who might have done this, where they might have gone, and what they might have done to Johanna. But after Wilf made no comment and only rode silently, the other men had also fallen silent. Now, digging, their only comments were about the task at hand.

Three hours later both graves were dug, the men were all covered with sweat and a thick layer of dirt and all the canteens that had been brought to the cemetery were empty. "Well, that should about do it," Wilf said, from the bottom of the grave that would be used for James. He hoisted himself out and stood looking down into the hole, glad that it was as he had pictured it from the beginning. "Let's ride back to the ranch and see how things are going there." The men left the tools near the piles of earth beside each grave, mounted and rode back to the buildings in the afternoon light.

Upon their arrival, they found that the two six-sided pine coffins were sitting on the ground near the porch. The bodies of James and Hernando had been washed, their wounds tightly wrapped with padded bandages and they were dressed in their best clothing. Wilf and the others dismounted respectfully and stood quietly while several men carried the bodies to the coffins and the lids were nailed tightly shut. The shock of the sound of the nails being driven was jarring, a sound of harsh reality and finality.

Ellen Messinger stood on the porch next to Rosa, her arm around the grieving woman's shoulders. Doctor Messinger remained upstairs with Johanna and Sarah.

The sound of the nailing ended abruptly and men gathered around one coffin and then the other and placed them in the back of MacKenzie's large wagon. A number of townspeople and neighbors had gathered in the front yard. The news that "something" had happened at the O'Neal ranch had spread like wildfire, bringing people by wagon and horseback. After the coffins were loaded into the wagon, a very quiet procession, led by the priest, mounted on his sad looking white horse, began its trip to the cemetery.

Wilf watched them begin to trail away and walked into the house, seeing that Johanna was no longer on the table, but had been taken upstairs. He walked to the wood burning stove in the kitchen, which was now cold, no embers remaining in the firebox. He opened the ash bin door and using the poker that hung on the back of the stove he worked all of the ashes down into the ash bin, pulled it out and poked through them with his fingers, the ashes cold to his touch. He found the buttons, coated with gray ash, scattered in the bin. Using one of the few remaining rags on the back porch, he took the dress buttons out of the bin, one by one, placed them on the cloth and then carried the gathered rag and the nearly full ash bin out the back door.

The ashes he dumped on the ash pile near the smokehouse, and the buttons, as he had planned, went down the hole in the outhouse. Neither Johanna or Daniel would ever see any evidence of the clothing Johanna had worn this day.

Wilf then went onto the back porch and found a metal basin, a towel and soap, walked to the pump and filled the basin with water. Taking off his shirt, he washed himself, his hair and then the shirt in the basin, watching the blood coming out of the cotton material into the cold soapy water. He emptied the basin, refilled it with cold water, rinsing the shirt to take as much blood out of it as possible. He then wrung out the shirt and put it back on. It would have to do. The trousers would remain bloody until this whole thing was over, he knew. He'd have to get clean blankets from the house when Rosa returned. He'd leave the bloody ones with her to wash and retrieve at some later time.

Walking around to the front of the house he noticed that the last of the neighbors had disappeared into the distance toward the cemetery. He climbed the front steps and sat on the porch swing. He'd not go to the cemetery. He'd been there already and he had no desire to watch the man and the boy buried. In his lifetime, he'd seen enough of that and he knew these two people could be committed to God without him.

CHAPTER 15

DAY FOUR - EVENING

HANK SPENT THE DAY WITH Emily Westphal and she was a most gracious hostess. She had come back into the house from saying good-bye to her husband, obviously shaken. She busied herself making tea for them, asking him first if he liked tea. The only tea Hank had ever tasted was herbal tea that his mother made and it was not his favorite beverage. But to be polite, he said "Yes, he liked tea."

Black English Tea was a luxury Emily afforded herself, since she had access to it from the Paulson Mercantile Store that was now run by her son. She justified her extravagance by using each infuser full of tea leaves over and over again, until the liquid brewed in her cup could hardly be called tea. The current leaves in the infuser were due to be used a number of more times, but without hesitation Emily emptied the small metal container and refilled it with fresh tea leaves. If ever there was a time for a strong brew, this was it. She put the kettle on the stove and began heating the water and then turned her attention to Hank.

The boy gazed about the kitchen, admiring the place. He'd never been inside a house in town and this was without a doubt the finest home he'd ever been in, anywhere. Emily's touch with curtains, paint, shelves of books and family treasures, made him realize how humble his own home was, but he didn't feel uncomfortable here.

"Now Henry," Emily said, sitting down at the table next to him, "I have an apple pie in the oven, which will take some time to bake, but once it is done and cooled we'll sample it. Do you like apple pie?" Hank nodded and said that he did.

"Tell me a bit about your family, Henry."

"Hank...I like to be called Hank, please," he began. He then proceeded to tell Emily about his family, his father, mother, and younger sister; all the while his mind was back at the ranch with his father, wondering what was happening there.

Emily listened to what the boy said, all the while thinking about her husband and Wilf riding toward God only knew what. Emily made comments and asked questions, but both of them knew well that neither of them was actually conversing seriously. Emily was attempting to distract and calm the boy and Hank was obliging the very kind woman, whose job it was to care for him until his father arrived. After the teakettle sounded, Emily prepared two cups of tea and placed them on the kitchen table. Hank brought the cup in front of him to his lips, not knowing what to expect. The hot liquid met his taste buds and he was pleasantly surprised and he took his time sipping the finest beverage he'd ever tasted.

"Do you like it?"

"Umm, yes I do, it's very good, thank you."

After emptying the cup, Hank realized quite suddenly that he was extremely tired. His arms felt like lead and he was having trouble keeping his eyes open. Emily immediately understood. "Hank, would you like to lie down for a bit and rest? I'm sure you must be very tired." The boy said that he would. Emily showed him into the front living room, and had him take off his shoes and lie down on the sofa, which was just long enough for him to stretch out. She covered the boy with a light blanket and told him that if he happened to go to sleep, she would wake him up when the pie was ready. Hank nodded, closed his eyes and within minutes was fast asleep, his body exhausted from the extreme stress of the day's events.

It was nearly an hour and a half later, when Emily woke him to the smell of apples and cinnamon which filled the house. He came to the table and even though he tried to eat slowly, found himself inhaling the warm pie in front of him. Afterward, there was more tea and this time the conversation was sparse, although Hank still didn't feel uncomfortable. Emma Syme could learn a lot from this woman, Hank thought to himself!

It was late afternoon when his father came to the Westphal house. Ove gently knocked on the door and Emily asked him in with an invitation to tea and pie. Ove declined politely and said that he'd simply come to retrieve his son and go home. He relayed Nathan's message to her and Emily was visibly relieved.

It was then time for Ove to face his son, something he had been in agonizing dread of every mile he'd ridden from the ranch. Hank knew, without asking, the news his father carried and when their eyes met, Hank simply walked to his father and the two embraced, without a word. "I'm so sorry, Henry," was all Ove could gently say to his son. Emily knew to simply say nothing, and could only imagine what this embrace and the words might be conveying. Ove and Hank stood in the kitchen, their arms around each other for some time, Ove patted his son on the back and when Hank broke away from his father, he simply said, "Can we go home now Papa?" Ove nodded and both of them thanked Emily for her hospitality and for letting Hank stay with her. Emily invited them to come back and see her, and to bring the rest of the family when-ever they were in town. She meant it.

Once out of the house, Ove led his horse, walking be-side Hank to the livery stable, where they retrieved Hank's horse from Curtis Taylor's nephew, who had been left in charge. Once mounted, they quickly left town so that Ove could avoid being questioned by anyone there. About a mile out of town, Hank pulled up his horse and asked his father where they'd found James. He'd been down by the river fishing, his father answered. Hank found some com-fort in that, as he knew it was the thing James most loved doing. Hank wanted no further details.

When they reached home, Hilda Johanson, deeply concerned about the length of time they'd been away, was relieved to see them come riding into the yard. She had expected her son to come bounding into the house with stories of the day's adventures with James and when she saw the expressions on the faces of her son and husband, she knew something was terribly wrong. It was only when Ove told her what had transpired that day that Hank was moved to tears. Hearing it told made it more real to him. He excused himself and went out behind their small barn and cried his heart out.

Wilf was standing on the porch when Nathan and the rest of the posse returned from the cemetery. The sun would soon be gone and it made no sense to leave now to begin tracking the three men who had come to the ranch hours ago. The townspeople and neighbors didn't linger long in the yard, but rather quickly began to disperse toward their homes in town or to the neighboring ranches. They wanted to be home with their families before dark. Some would have to hurry to do that.

The doctor and his wife would stay with Johanna and Rosa at the house overnight and see how Johanna was in the morning. Nathan spoke to the posse members and told them to bed down in the bunk house and be ready to leave early in the morning. Wilf said nothing until the other men had departed and it was just he and Nathan on the porch.

Nathan spoke first. "Wilf, I know you aren't happy about this situation, but it is what it is." He sat down heavily on the swing, very tired and glad this day was nearing an end.

Wilf sighed and sat down on the porch railing, his shirt still wet, his hands on the porch rail on either side of his body, legs crossed at the ankles out in front of him, his eyes averted from Nathan's. Looking into the distance to the west, he spoke slowly and quietly, his Virginia accent more discernable than usual. "Nathan, you called it like you saw it and I respect your judgement. You're the boss on this ride and I'll do whatever you say. You know that. I just want you to understand that I'm going to have no reservations about killing these men, once we catch them and if I get a chance, I'm going to do just that, even if it costs me my job."

Nathan waited some time before speaking and when he did speak it was with the purpose of learning something about the man he'd worked with for the past four years. Watching him today had been a partial revelation.

"Who was she?" Nathan asked, his head cocked to one side and his voice inquisitive but not intrusive.

Wilf turned his face toward Nathan and looked him directly in the eyes, knowing full well where Nathan was going.

"Who was who?" It was his intention to dodge Nathan's questions, as he'd done since he'd first met him.

"Who was she? The one you miss so much, Wilf?"

Wilf sensed that Nathan was not going to settle for evasive half answers. There was something about the events of the day that had exhausted Wilf's reservoir of resistance. He felt as if something was being stripped from him – a layer of armor that he'd worn for a long time that was now just too heavy to carry. He sat there for a long time, wondering how he could possibly answer Nathan's question. His shoulders slowly sank in resignation and he looked at the floor of the porch and then once again met Nathan's eyes.

"She was my wife."

"What was her name?"

This time there was an even longer pause and Wilf again looked away into the distance. He hadn't spoken her name aloud for nearly twenty years and when he answered Nathan's question, the answer was spoken so softly that Nathan barely heard it.

"Her name was Kathryn… and I loved her very much."

Another long pause.

"What happened?

The light from the sun hit an angle that came through all of the dust that had been stirred by the leaving mourners and suddenly everything in the yard went golden and still.

"She was killed in a house fire, Nathan, while I was away during the war. My wife, our two year old daughter, and my mother all died in the fire. I didn't get a letter telling me until four months later. They *all* died… my whole family. My two brothers died at Chancellorsville and Gettysburg and my father shot himself after that. I came home to nothing. I lost the land that had been in my family for four generations…the bank foreclosed. My life ended when I came home. Since then…" Wilf shrugged and went on … "I'm not who I was, Nathan. I'm not sure who I am now…but I'm not who I was."

The similarity of their two stories struck Nathan hard. He remembered vividly how he felt when he came back to Pennsylvania to nothing. Both men had somehow miraculously survived the war only to come home to find that what they were supposedly fighting for was gone.

Nathan spoke firmly but quietly. "I understand, Wilf.

I'm not the person I was either. And I'm sorry you lost your wife and your child and your whole family, I really am. I'm sorry about what happened here today. And when we find these…the bastards who did this, you have my permission to kill them…without any fear of losing your job. And taking care of Hernando, James, Rosa, and Mrs. O'Neal…I think *that's* who we are now." He paused and then added, "Does that make any sense?"

Wilf looked at Nathan and smiled for the first time all day and said, "Well, it makes as much sense as anything I've heard lately." He paused for a long moment and then continued "I appreciate you Nathan and how you have treated me all these years. I seriously don't know where I'd have ended up, if you hadn't given me this job." Wilf paused again and took a deep breath, "I'd be dead in some alley or a snowdrift somewhere. Drunk, I suppose. So, all the time I have left I pretty much owe to you."

The two men sat motionless for several minutes, letting their words settle as the last full rays of the sun cast shadows that would soon fade to darkness.

Finally, Wilf stood up and said, "Now…I think I'll try to round up some clean blankets and get some sleep. I'm dead on my feet."

Nathan said he was going to head to the barn to unsaddle his horse and find a stall for him and maybe some oats, if there were any. "You want me to bed down your horse?"

"That would be good," Wilf said, stretching his back, stiff and sore from the exertion of digging the grave. After Nathan left the porch Wilf went into the house and spoke to Rosa who had lit the downstairs lamp and was sitting with Sarah at the kitchen table, feeding the little girl some ham and bread that had been brought by neighbors.

Even though her hands were still painfully swollen, Rosa offered to fix Wilf and the posse sandwiches, an offer which Wilf gladly accepted. He sat down next to Sarah, whom he was seeing for the first time that day. The little girl looked at him warily and asked him if he knew her daddy.

"I've seen him in town, but don't know him well," Wilf replied, trying to turn in such a way that the little girl would not see the blood on his pant legs.

"Do you know my Mommy?"

"I met her today," Wilf replied, thinking of his only-ever encounter with Johanna as she'd lain on the floor and the dining room table.

"Will she get well soon?" Sarah asked, looking up at Wilf with eyes that longed to be given some good news.

Wilf didn't know how to truthfully answer, but said, "I think she will and we'll know more tomorrow."

"Will Hernando and James come for supper?"

Wilf looked up at Rosa who was slicing bread and ham on the sideboard and he reached out and touched the little girl's hair, thinking that this was how his daughter might have looked and acted at this age. "No darlin,'" he said softly, "they won't be coming for supper. They won't be coming back to us."

"Are they with God now in Heaven?" She was looking

Wilf directly in the eyes and he didn't blink or look away as he answered, "Yes they are with God now in Heaven."

She looked away then and went back to eating her bread, holding her doll with the badly chewed arm. For the first time that day, she seemed satisfied that her questions had been answered.

Wilf turned to Rosa, explaining his need for clean blankets, saying that his were folded and on the porch in need of washing at some point in time. Rosa understood and went upstairs to find two blankets suitable for Wilf to take with him when he left the next day.

When she returned he took the blankets and gathered up the sandwiches on a plate, thanked her and headed for the bunk house. "Rosa," he said pausing at the door, "If you or the doctor need anything in the night, we are just outside."

She nodded and thanked him. Wilf turned and went out the door, taking welcome food to some hungry men. After delivering it, he went into the barn, found a rag and wet it in a water bucket in one of the stalls and went to the pasture fence, where he'd noticed the red horse that belonged to James standing by the gate, looking toward the house.

"Come here girl," he said to Red, as she backed away from the gate. Red raised her head and sniffed the air. She could smell her rider on this man. She came to the gate and reached her head over it. Wilf used the wet cloth to gently scrub the blood off the horse's face and then stood for awhile rubbing her muzzle and neck.

Red sniffed his shirt and tried to reach her face to his bloodied trousers. "It's okay girl, you are going to be okay," he said, knowing that was a lie. He knew that personally. The horse would never be okay again.

On the trail at the end of the fourth day, Calvin and Daniel rode a slow circle around the herd. They were within sight of Culver, lights from the town punctuating the growing darkness. Calvin had ridden into town earlier to notify the cattle company of their arrival and to tell their representative who they were and where they were from. Calvin had received directions about which pens they should use for their herd. The large complex of receiving pens had grown since the last time they'd been there. He'd learned they were the only drive in town, which would make things less complicated the next day.

Calvin had relayed this information to Daniel saying, "This will be our last cow camp, Daniel, we're going to get paid tomorrow," Calvin was laughing as he said this.

"Yes, and I'm really glad of that, Calvin. Ready to get done and get home."

"We going to take first watch tonight?"

"Yes we are, that way we'll get a little sleep and be sharp tomorrow when we go in to deal with the buyer. What time will he accept the herd?"

"Man said mid morning, just bring 'em on in."

Calvin and Daniel had supper, rode herd on the cows until after midnight, then bedded down near the fire which Daniel built up again before lying down. It was getting cooler at night and Daniel knew that when he got home he would have to start preparing the ranch for the long months of winter. He wrapped himself in his blanket roll and soon dozed off. That night he dreamed vividly about Shadow. The horse was running away from the ranch, racing across open country and Daniel was chasing him, riding a horse that had no chance of catching up. Shadow disappeared over a ridge and in his dream, Daniel felt sad, believing he would never see the horse again.

CHAPTER 16

DAY FIVE IN CULVER

EVERYONE IN CAMP WAS UP very early the next day and excitement reigned. The night before the cattle had been given time to drink from the river and rest and now they were milling about. About ten o'clock in the morning the drovers began moving the cattle slowly into the stockyards. Calvin and Daniel met with the heavy set cigar-smoking cattle buyer who was actually glad to see them. Slaughterhouses east needed beef; a severe winter north of them and drought to the south had put pressure on the outlying buyers to produce some beef for consumers. He was authorized to give top dollar which was tremendous news to Calvin and Daniel. There was no need to dicker with the buyer, which was a relief to both men.

The cattle buyer surveyed the herd and was surprised and pleased with the condition of the animals. He ordered the yard workers to begin running them through the chute and count them into a much larger pen. Sitting on the fence beside the official yard counter were Ellis, Ben and Jack, who were doing their own counts, to make sure they were not cheated by the yard counter.

When the yard man yelled the final number to the buyer, Ellis, Ben and Jack all nodded to Calvin and Daniel, indicating they agreed with his count. Calvin had his pencil and small notebook out and informed Daniel they had only lost two head of cattle on the drive, which seemed unbelievable to the two men. Daniel laughed out loud, relief flooding him. "It was worth it Calvin, every damned mile." The two men decided to deduct the two missing cattle from their personal tallies, as they knew Robert Hanson would have a fit if he had to take a loss of even one, and they weren't going to count either against Ove, as he had so few in the herd to begin with.

"Come on into the office and we'll settle up," the buyer suggested. Calvin and Daniel followed him into the small wooden building, noticing there were three armed guards outside. The businessman paid them in cash from his safe, the largest amount of money either Calvin or Daniel had ever seen in one place. Then the two men asked for envelopes to divide the money. The cattle buyer was used to this request and indicated a desk in the corner, where they could divide up the payment. Calvin and Daniel rose and shook the man's hand and the cattleman thanked them for doing business with his company.

He added, "The railroad has informed me that in another year you will have rail access in Fergus. If there are enough cattle in that area, we might establish a small stockyard there."

Calvin nodded, saying, "We'll do our part for sure."

The buyer continued, "Sheep are going big too; there's

a market for lamb and wool back east. Something you might want to think about."

The ranchers mentioned the number of predators in their area and the buyer shrugged, "Just thought you should know, markets are changing."

They assured him they would keep it in mind.

With that, Calvin and Daniel sat at the small table and meticulously made the calculations that would determine how much money went into each envelope. The two ram-rods had decided earlier in the week that everyone working the drive should get a bonus, even Sam. He had managed to improve in his role as cook as the drive had progressed and was responsible for getting the wagon back to Calvin's ranch. Ellis and Swifty certainly deserved a bonus, as they had worked tirelessly every day to make the drive a success and it was largely due to their efforts that all but two of the cattle were accounted for.

After a brief discussion it was settled and everyone involved in the drive had their share in sealed envelopes with their names on them. Calvin insisted Daniel take care of all of the money not distributed in Culver. Daniel reluctantly agreed, knowing he would be uneasy until it was safely delivered to Robert Hanson and Ove. Daniel put the money he was responsible for, including his own, in his saddle bag, which he had brought into the office with him. Calvin put his share inside his vest pocket and patted it smiling. "Gonna' make the Mrs. happy." The two men got up and left, noticing the cattleman had already left to begin directing the next step of processing his newly acquired beef.

Once outside, Ellis, Swifty and Sam were given their

pay, which they each quickly counted, smiled and thanked their trail bosses. The Hanson boys received much thinner envelopes, but even they seemed happy to have cash in hand. Sam drove the wagon into town and Calvin helped him get the mules into the livery corral along with all of their now unsaddled horses, and arranged for the wagon to be parked nearby. Sam then quickly walked toward town, obviously a thirsty man.

The Hanson boys disappeared quickly. Calvin, Ellis, and Swifty all headed for the best saloon in town but Daniel begged off, saying he would join them later. They had all agreed to stay in the nicest boarding house in Culver for the next two nights. Before he did anything else, Daniel wanted to take a bath and put on some clean clothing he had packed in the wagon. He felt like he'd been dragged the entire distance from home through the dirt behind a horse, and wanted to remedy that. Calvin and Daniel agreed to meet later for a drink and perhaps talk about the next day's activities.

Once at the boarding house, Daniel made sure there were enough rooms for all of the men. He next asked when and where he could take a bath and was directed to the bathhouse and into a room with a large metal tub that was soon filled with fairly hot water where he could just soak for awhile. While the water was still warm he washed his hair, which was crusted with dirt, and then his body. He could feel grit accumulating beneath his buttocks and legs, as the dirt settled to the bottom of the tub. Enjoying the last of the warmth of the water, he just allowed himself to relax and let the ache of constantly being in the saddle for four days ease away somewhat.

Putting on clean clothes felt good and he bundled up his dirty clothing, which he could smell, now that it was removed from him. He took it to the wagon and stowed it in the back and headed for the saloon. Daniel was ready for a drink.

By the time he got to the saloon, Calvin was on his third whiskey and he, Ellis, and Swifty, were sharing stories about everything from hunting elk to chasing women they'd known in another lifetime. Daniel decided that he'd have to keep his wits about him to insure the money he was responsible for was constantly accounted for. He'd go easy on the whiskey and turn in early since he had a lot to do the following day. He took a good deal of razzing from the other men about smelling better than they did and having to bathe before getting drunk, but he didn't care. Everyone was in a good mood.

Later Daniel left the other men and took a turn around town on foot to look at places he might visit the next day to complete his mission of buying items to take home. Culver had grown in the previous two years so there were more choices. He was actually looking forward to exploring the town. Daniel wanted to impress Johanna with the choices he'd make in fulfilling her shopping instructions and finding something special for Sarah. Now, he was just very tired and wanted to get something to eat, rest, and get an early start in the morning. Walking back towards the boarding house, he encountered Calvin who was stumbling a bit on his way to a bath, dinner and bed.

"Can't drink like I used to Daniel. Probably going to have a headache in the morning."

"I'd say you've earned it Calvin. You'll feel better once

you get cleaned up. Just don't drown in the tub. Wouldn't want to have to explain that to Emma."

In his inebriated state, Calvin thought this was extremely funny and laughed heartily. The two men parted company and Daniel headed for an early dinner and hopefully a soft bed, which after sleeping on the ground several nights in a row was going to feel good.

That night he had no dreams, but slept soundly, like he hadn't since he he'd left home. The saddlebags rested next to his pillow, a chair was propped up against the door knob of the door leading to the hallway and his colt revolver was on the small bedside table, well within reach.

CHAPTER 17

THE HUNT

THE MORNING CAME EARLY AND there had been little sleep for any of the posse members, especially Nathan and Wilf. The men quietly readied themselves for what they knew would probably be a difficult time ahead, although only Nathan and Wilf had ever pursued human beings for wrongdoing. Nathan checked with the doctor before leaving to find out if Johanna was any improved.

Dr. Messinger reported that he and his wife had taken turns sitting up with her during the night and twice she had opened her right eye and seemed to be somewhat conscious, but had not spoken. She was breathing more evenly and her heart rate seemed stronger. The doctor seemed somewhat encouraged and said that they would stay through the day, unless he was called away to some other emergency. In that case, Ellen would remain. Nathan was able to tell Rosa, who was up very early cooking for the departing posse, that there would be neighbors stopping by to help with chores and anything else she might need until Daniel and his men returned. At the grave side the day before it was one of the details that Nathan made sure to take care of. He felt personally responsible to see that the O'Neal property was taken care of until Daniel's return.

The posse left as soon as there was enough daylight to see a trail, with Wilf serving as lead tracker. Finding the trail was fairly easy, once the tracks of the incoming and departing neighbors were sorted out. Wilf rode a large circle and soon raised his arm over his head and circled his hand in the air to signal Nathan and the others that he'd found the trail of the departing marauders. Those men had left the ranch in a hurry and Wilf quickly could distinguish between the three horses. The largest horse with the longest stride was leading the other two. The men had ridden flat out for a long distance - straight west, so the posse was able to move at a fast clip.

There came a point after about an hour of pursuit where it was obvious the men ahead of them had stopped and there had been a circling of the horses…turning, looking back, and then once again, moving quickly away. Wilf pushed the posse, not resting, barely pausing throughout the morning and afternoon. Nathan let him set the pace and there was little conversation, only total concentration upon the task at hand.

The pursuit continued the first day until there was not enough light to see the trail, even though Wilf was now on foot to be closer to the trail leaning over, nearly on all fours like a hound dog sniffing the ground. Stopping for the night was like a punishment for him but there was nothing else to do. They had no fire that night, fearful the men ahead of them might circle back to ambush them and a fire would have been like a beacon.

The next day began the same way, the men eating dried fruit and jerky in the saddle, moving forward without stopping. They came to a spring of clear cold water and watered their horses and filled canteens, as the men ahead of them had done. An hour afterward, Wilf, who was staying about 40 yards ahead of the rest of the posse suddenly stopped, dismounted and could be seen on one knee, touching the ground, examining it closely. He circled his arm, to quietly signal the others forward. When Nathan and the rest reached him, Wilf, who was taking a long drink from his canteen, pointed to the ground and then explained the stop.

"Some sort of altercation here, I think, Nathan."

Nathan looked at the tracks and could see what he meant. There was a scuffling of tracks, sometimes very close together, especially the two largest horses, tracks overlapping and pulling away from each other. Wilf pointed out that the hoof marks leading away showed that the largest horse was quite a ways to the left of the others, as though following and watching the other two leading to the right.

"Another thing, Nathan, one of the two horses to the right is having some problems. Left rear hoof gets lifted when they stop. Could be coming up lame. They've been pushing these horses hard. Also, looks like the shoe might be a bit loose on that hoof."

"Think this might slow them down a bit?" Frank Bassett asked.

"Hope so, we need all the help we can get here. Let's push on and see if we can gain on them."

Nathan agreed, not wanting to fall behind any more than they already were.

"Nathan, another thing, we have to try and catch them as soon as possible. It's going to rain ...later today or tomorrow, I think."

Nathan scanned the sky, seeing nothing but blue sky and small puffy, non-threatening clouds. He turned and looked quizzically at Wilf.

"My knee's talking to me Nathan, not bad, but weather is changing. We'll lose this trail, if it rains any kind of hard."

They pushed on and found where the men ahead of them had camped and had a fire.

"Pretty brazen," was all Wilf had to say about it as he felt the cold remains of what had been a small campfire. The posse pushed onward.

Later in the day, past noon, Wilf came to a place where the ground was so hard and covered with a shale-like rock that was so loose there was no sign of any kind of imprint. Sadly, he could see that this terrain went on for some distance ahead. His only hope was that the men would continue in a westerly direction and he could pick the trail up on the other side of it.

"We're following Yankees here, Champ," he said to his horse quietly, "I'll bet a month's pay on it." The horse snorted and Wilf said, "Yup, you got it." He continued on foot, leading the horse and letting his eyes race ahead, looking for anything.

About a half a mile ahead, he picked up the trail again and was alarmed to see only two sets of tracks. He halted and looked around apprehensively. Somewhere in the shale, the three men had split up, two continuing west and the other one going in an unknown direction. He signaled in Nathan and the rest.

"Problem here." He pointed westward and said, "Two of our three are going on in that direction. Somewhere behind me I lost the other one, the largest horse. We can split up, with some of us following the two. I could double back and see if I can pick up the third, and follow him, if you want, Nathan."

Nathan looked in all directions and said, "No, we're staying together and we'll stay with these two. We know they are still heading west. My concern is that the third man is going to circle around and double back on us with an ambush from behind."

All of the men agreed that was a risk and once they headed west again, everyone was constantly looking at every rise and cluster of trees. Nathan had Curtis fall behind them about two miles and ride from side to side, seeing if he could pick up a trail coming in behind them. None was found.

Wilf pushed hard for another hour and then pulled up and stared at the ground, puzzled. The outlaw's pace was slowing drastically. He could tell by the tracks that the horse ahead of him with the loose shoe and lame leg was now in real discomfort. There hadn't been any human prints on the ground for several miles so Wilf knew the rider of the horse that was going lame wasn't checking on his mount's worsening condition. It was a mystery to Wilf how this could be.

Again he came to a place where the trail disappeared on ground covered with small loose gravel and shale. Wilf dismounted and knelt down, straining to see any imprint, any disturbance and saw none. "Damn it," he said softly.

Once again he mounted Champ and was about to call Nathan and the others forward, when he saw something ahead on the ground that did not belong there. He eagerly pushed forward and again dismounted. Lying on the ground was an unfired shotgun shell. It had not been there long, as there was no dirt on the piece of ammunition. Quickly, he signaled Nathan and the posse forward.

After reaching Wilf, Nathan and the others dismounted to see what Wilf was holding in his hand. Just as Wilf handed him the shell, they heard two shots. Nathan instinctively crouched to the ground and reached for his colt. Wilf and Curtis reached for their weapons, as well.

"It's a ways out," Nathan said standing up, "I don't think we are within range. The shots were too far away."

"Signal shots? To the third man, you think? asked Curtis."

"Don't know." Nathan was obviously very concerned about their situation.

Looking ahead on the ground, Wilf saw another shotgun shell. The men walked to it.

Curtis again spoke, "Do you think they are putting these out to lead us into an ambush?"

"Why would they fire shots, if they are hoping we'll ride into an ambush?" Nathan was puzzled about what he was seeing and hearing. "Maybe there is a hole in a bag holding the ammunition, rather than a trail being deliberately laid." He said this, talking to himself, trying to figure out which line of reasoning made sense.

Nathan pulled his field glasses out of his saddlebag, mounted his horse and scoured the area ahead. He saw nothing that looked like a human or a horse. The area ahead was scattered with clusters of trees and large rock outcroppings. "A lot of cover ahead," he noted to anyone listening.

"What do you think, Nathan?" Wilf was remounting his horse waiting for his next instructions.

"Let's push on cautiously," Nathan replied, "We're closing in, and hopefully we can come up on them as a surprise. Let's get as close as we can."

Wilf agreed and began moving forward immediately. His biggest concern was the third man he couldn't account for, out there somewhere.

About half an hour later, they came to a place where the men they were trailing had obviously dismounted. Frank Bassett, who had been very quiet, listening and watching, found shattered glass mason jars, which obviously had been used as targets, explaining the shots they'd heard.

There was residue of applesauce on the glass shards which had attracted a swarm of feasting flies. "Look at this," Bassett noted, "They took time to have lunch and shoot at these jars, so don't seem concerned about being followed."

"This is good news," Nathan said. "If they feel confident enough to be shooting at mason jars, they're either not aware of the fact that we're here, or not very smart."

"Hopefully, both," Wilf added. "We need a plan Nathan, look at the sky." He was distressed by the changing weather.

To the west, Nathan could see dark clouds gathering. His heart sank and he knew that Wilf's prediction of rain was in all likelihood going to come true within a couple of hours. He again took out his glasses and strained to look ahead. In the far distance, he could see a notch between two large ridges of rock. It was, he noted to himself, a perfect place for an ambush. If the men ahead of them got to it first and had any inkling they were being followed, it would be where they could turn and lethally ambush the posse.

To the south a long row of heavy trees ran from about a quarter of a mile from where they were all the way to the south edge of the ridge forming that side of the notch.

"Wilf, if we could use that cover and get to that notch ahead of them, *we* could ambush *them*."

Wilf agreed saying, "If just two of us do the approach, we can keep the dust down and have less risk of being spotted. Can't make any noise, because if we spook them, they'll get the drop on us. We can only hope they keep going toward the notch and reach it after we get there."

It was quickly agreed upon. Nathan and Wilf removed their canteens and anything from their saddles and persons that would rattle or make any unnecessary noise. The other three men took their extra equipment and Wilf and Nathan pushed off, quickly reached the tree line of cover and began to urge their horses forward as quickly and quietly as possible. They knew this was their only chance to catch these two men and Wilf had a feeling that bordered on desperation as he felt personally responsible for finding the men they were tracking.

Once they came in behind the rock formations south of the notch they dismounted as far away from the opening as possible, hoping nothing would alert the two outlaws. Each man took his rifle from its scabbard: Wilf his Sharps and Nathan his Winchester. Nathan's Winchester held 15 rounds and he quickly racked one into the chamber. Wilf's Sharps held only one cartridge in the chamber and he put two additional cartridges in his right pants pocket and two more between the knuckles of his right hand for a rapid reload. They hurried to the notch and from behind cover Wilf could examine the trail coming between the two rock formations. He could see that it was a well used game trail, and observed deer and elk tracks, most of them old. He could also see that at one time recently a large cat had come through as well as a number of coyotes. No horses or humans, though, which was a relief.

It was quickly agreed that they should each take a side of the notch which was about ten yards wide. Nathan whispered that he had to "take a piss" and promptly did that... something he'd needed to do for about an hour and couldn't put off any longer! Afterward he said quietly, "Ahhhhhh, that's better." Wilf couldn't help but smile, glad for the release of tension that had been building since they'd left the other men of the posse.

On Nathan's side of the notch there was an opening between the rocks that had tree cover, where he could watch the incoming trail without revealing his presence. On the other side Wilf climbed up on top of the rock and had the cover of small bushes and thick grass that would keep him out of sight, and give him the advantage of observation from above.

Now it was just a matter of waiting. Time passed and then more time. Nathan began to worry that the fugitives had changed direction and weren't coming through the notch at all. Every few minutes he would look behind him to the west to gauge the progress of the advancing storm. If they'd miscalculated, there would be no time to backtrack and re-find the trail once it started to rain. They would lose them, for today and probably forever. Thirst began to work on Nathan and his mouth was so dry, it was impossible to spit and rid his mouth of dust. He glanced up at Wilf and the man was lying motionless where he'd laid down nearly an hour ago. What was he thinking, Nathan wondered. Was he having the same misgivings?

Suddenly, Wilf turned his hatless head in Nathan's direction and signaled Nathan, using nothing but his facial expression. It was dead serious and Nathan knew immediately the men were coming. Soundlessly, he went to the opening in the rock and looked through. Within a few moments, the two men came into his view. Nathan realized his heart was pounding, and he could feel the sweat that had begun to accumulate on his forehead. He took several deep breaths to calm himself and then brought the rifle to his shoulder, careful not to move any of the greenery on the thick juniper, which was his cover.

Nathan noticed that the two men approaching were young, in their mid twenties and looked rough. The tall roan horse was limping noticeably and this was obviously why it had taken them so long to get to where they were now. The two men were having an argument, but Nathan couldn't discern what they were talking about, only that they were both speaking angrily.

Nathan glanced up again at Wilf and his deputy was looking right at him and nodding. The outlaws were now about twenty yards from the notch when Nathan took a deep breath and shouted, "Stop where you are and put your hands up." They jerked their horses to a stop and looked at the notch with stunned expressions.

"You heard me. Put your hands up. Now."

To let the men know Nathan was not alone, Wilf added, "Do as he says. Hands up."

Suddenly the man with the reddish-blond hair pulled his Winchester from its scabbard under his right leg. He brought it up, and swung towards where Wilf was positioned and there was a shot, but not from his rifle. At the roar of the Sharps the man with the Winchester fell out of his saddle with a thud. As Wilf reloaded, the man on the buckskin drew his revolver and fired; his shot took a piece of rock off an outcropping about six feet from where Wilf lay. Nathan fired one shot and the buckskin backed up several feet and then the rider slid out of his saddle and rolled into a sitting position on the ground, his legs spread in front of him, still holding the pistol.

"Throw the pistol, now!" Wilf shouted. The man's response was slow, but he complied, flipping the weapon about four feet from where he was sitting.

"Hands on your head," Nathan ordered. The man tried, but could only raise his right hand.

Wilf slid down the backside of the rock, and stepped into the notch. As Nathan stepped out from behind his cover, Wilf quickly walked to the sitting man and checked to see if he had any remaining weapon that might be a threat. There was none. He picked up the thrown pistol, unloaded it and heaved it as far as he could and then walked to the man he'd shot to verify that he was dead. The large hole that was leaking dark blood was right over his heart.

Nathan knelt in front of the sitting man and looked to see where he was hit. He had hoped to disable the man, so that he could be questioned. The bullet hole in his left chest was bleeding heavily.

"Now," Nathan began with forced calm. "Tell me your name."

The man looked at him in an expression that could only be described as total surprise. "Where did you come from?" The man asked.

"From behind you," Nathan answered, "Only we decided to get ahead of you. That's how it works. Now again, what is your name?"

"Nelson," the man replied, reaching for breath, "Frederick Nelson."

"What's his name?" Nathan asked, nodding his head toward the dead man.

"Joe."

"Joe what?"

"Joe Deem, I think he said one time." The wounded

man was obviously struggling to breathe and he added, "I need a doctor."

"We'll see to that later," Nathan commented tersely, thinking of how Rosa had been hung on the porch. He dared not think about the others at the ranch, or he'd possibly not be able to question this man in a civil manner.

"There were three of you. And the one who left you, what's his name?"

"Stiles," the man answered, adding, "Can I put my hand down now? I can't keep this up."

"Yeah," Nathan granted him this and then continued, "Stiles? Did you say Stiles?"

"Yes."

"Stiles what? Was that his first name, his last name? "

"I don't know, I never heard him called nothin' but Stiles."

"I see. Where'd he go?"

"He got shitty, as always. Took Joe's pelt and wanted some other things that we had… pulled a gun on us, crazy bastard."

"I got that," Nathan replied, "Now *where* did he go?" Wilf had come over and was standing behind Nathan, listening intently to the conversation.

"Who the Hell knows. He'll go wherever he damn well pleases and God help anyone who gets in his way." The man coughed, bringing up bright red blood which spewed out onto his trousers and alarmed him. "I need a doctor, you hear me. I need a doctor."

Wilf knelt down, bringing his face close to the wounded man's and said, "Where are you from?"

"Ohio."

"Ohio? Where's he from, the man you called Joe, where's he from?"

"Don't know, Chicago I think. He and Stiles met up in Chicago. Met them on a riverboat. Don't know anything else."

Wilf nodded, confirming something he already knew. He got up and walked over to the roan mare. He ran his fingers down the back of the lower left leg where there was obvious tenderness. He raised the hoof and saw that the shoe was loose. He could at least remove that with a prybar he kept in his saddle bag.

"I'm going for the horses, Nathan," he said, and walked back through the notch to their mounts, untied them and brought them through. By the time he returned, the sitting man was now lying on his back gasping for breath.

Wilf knew the man was near death. Nathan, still kneeling beside him, asked if there was anyone he should notify when he died. The man shook his head.

Wilf could feel a boiling in his chest. He could no longer contain himself. He went over and stood over the man, refusing to kneel down to his level.

"Who shot the boy?" Wilf asked, trying to control his anger.

"Stiles."

"Who shot Hernando, the man at the ranch?"

"Joe." Nelson looked in Joe's direction when he said his name.

"Whose idea was it to hang his wife on the porch?" Again Nelson nodded in Joe's direction.

Wilf lowered his voice and tried to keep it level. "And who beat and raped Mrs. O'Neal?"

"Stiles. He's the only one who touched her, I swear. The only one." Nelson was struggling to speak now, his voice barely a whisper.

"And what did *you* do, Nelson?"

"Nothin', I didn't shoot nobody, didn't hurt nobody."

"You're wrong, Nelson. You stole a horse, you watched what the others did and you didn't try to stop it. That's what you did. And if it weren't for the fact that you're going to die right here, you'd hang for it." Wilf walked away leading his horse, dropping the reins of Nathan's and headed for the lame roan. Taking the small prybar out of his saddlebag he quickly removed the loose horseshoe.

"And another thing," Wilf was shouting now. "You rode this horse lame for miles with a loose shoe and didn't give a damn. Nobody does that."

He was finished now and went back to taking care of the horse. The roan was so lame that getting it back to the O'Neal's was going to be a problem. Wilf rubbed the horse's neck, talking to her soothingly, not looking in the direction of Nathan and the dying man. He noticed the large satchel hooked over the saddle horn and he pulled it off to examine the contents. The disassembled shotgun and remaining food items were still in it. Wilf spotted the hole in one corner, barely large enough for the loose shotgun shells to fall through. That explained the shells he'd found on the trail. He put the rest of the loose ammunition into his saddlebag. Wilf pulled the saddle off the roan, as he knew it didn't belong to the O'Neals and dropped it to the ground.

"Leavin' this here Nathan, the mare doesn't need to carry the weight." He had detached the saddle bags and carried them over to the buckskin and tied them on to the back of the saddle with the other gear on the horse.

Within minutes, Nathan said, "He's dead, Wilf." The deputy simply nodded, saying nothing.

Before leaving the others in the posse, they had agreed that three quick shots would be the signal to advance. So they knew the others would be arriving before long. As they waited, Wilf and Nathan went through the dead men's clothing, looking for anything that might have been taken from the O'Neal ranch. Nathan found the cash in the clip, with the letter "S". He was pretty sure it stood for Sullivan. He also retrieved a small knife, which he put in his own pocket with the money. There were a few loose coins in Joe's pocket which Nathan simply dropped beside his body.

A scrap of paper in Nelson's pocket had an address in Chicago written on it. "Probably a whore house," Nathan commented, but he put it into his pocket anyway. Hopefully, sometime in the future, he could check with other authorities to see how this man was connected to the piece of paper, or if it led to nothing.

Once the rest of the posse rode in, it was only a matter of minutes before the rain began, lightly at first. Nathan, Wilf and the others scrambled for their slickers, which were not going to be much good against what was coming… a full fledged deluge.

The only decision left to make was about what to do with the dead outlaws. Wilf was adamant that these men not be taken back to the Fergus cemetery. It would be cruel he advocated, if the O'Neal family would know that the men who had hurt them so badly were buried with the other citizens of the town. Something Wilf didn't mention was that *HE* didn't want to ever encounter the graves, as well. The other men were nodding in agreement. Nathan directed that the dead men be laid out on the ground next to each other and covered with rocks to discourage predators from getting to them. Wilf agreed, and everyone set to work. It took over half an hour to cover the men to the degree Nathan thought necessary, and by that time the wind was howling and the rain was coming in sideways.

The men quickly mounted and headed east, leading the O'Neal horses. They traveled at a hurried pace and Wilf quickly fell behind, leading the roan, who was limping badly. Nathan dropped back several times to make sure he was alright. "Doing fine, Nathan. Just don't want to push this girl. We could use some shelter. Any ideas?"

"There is a draw ahead, a little to the north of us. Hoping to make it by dark. Will get us out of the wind, anyway. Not going to quit raining anytime soon."

They did make the large draw by nightfall and found some thick trees that gave them some overhead shelter. Bassett and Larson got a small fire started, but hampered by the rain, it was mostly smoke. The posse hunkered down under their slickers and tried to stay as dry as possible for the night.

At daylight it was still raining, but had let up some. The tired, rain soaked men mounted and rode silently.

Everyone was cold and Nathan was glad he'd brought the warm shirt and jacket, which he'd put on before it started to rain hard. He'd managed to keep his upper body warm, but felt chilled from the waist down. He thought of the Sheriff he'd worked for who had died of pneumonia and hoped it wouldn't be his fate or the fate of any of the men in this posse.

About noon it stopped raining and the wind died down. The posse stopped and gathered some wet firewood, which they finally got burning well enough to get some warmth. It was the first real fire they had been able to have since leaving the O'Neal ranch and it did a lot for their morale.

They kept the fire going until they were somewhat dried out, and were able to make coffee which brought some color back to their faces. They didn't want to spend another night outside, so pushed hard and just before sundown saw smoke from the O'Neal chimney. Nathan made the decision that they would stay the night in the bunkhouse, which had a good stove.

The doctor's carriage was not at the ranch, but Ellen Messinger came out onto the porch as they rode in. She was glad to see that all of the men who'd left were accounted for. They waved to her as they rode by and then got their horses unsaddled and taken care of.

Rosa was the one who came to the bunkhouse and invited the men into the house for a late supper, which they gladly accepted. The warmth of the house was welcome, and they ate hungrily and consumed an entire pot of hot coffee. Rosa was very quiet and asked no questions.

After the three other posse members left for the bunk house, Nathan and Wilf explained to Rosa that they had found and killed two of the three men who had invaded the ranch just days ago. This is the part Wilf had been dreading; having to tell the people at the ranch that the mission had not been completed. But Rosa was grateful for their efforts and tears came to her eyes as she thanked them for all they had done. She reported that Johanna was able to drink water and had been able to take some broth that afternoon and seemed to know who and where she was. Soon after this, Wilf asked to be excused and hastily left, thanking Rosa for the meal.

Nathan stayed and talked to Rosa about how it was going with the neighbors and Rosa told him that people had come every day to take care of the livestock and do the many daily chores. Several neighbors were going to come back tomorrow and harvest the potato crop and get it put into the root cellar. Ove had been back and had been a big help gathering and cutting wood for the woodpile. Nathan was glad that at least this much had gone smoothly for the woman who was holding the fort down alone, without any men to help her.

Nathan had brought in the saddlebags they had acquired at the ambush and left them in the living room for Rosa to go through to identify any O'Neal belongings. He produced the moneyclip and the small knife and Rosa said she knew they both belonged to James. She cried hard at this point, crossing herself, speaking in Spanish. Nathan tried to comfort her and suggested she wait till tomorrow to go through the saddlebags. He offered to help her with that in the morning. She nodded in agreement.

Nathan was determined that the posse would take the remaining outlaw saddle and both sets of saddlebags back to town to be destroyed. No one would ever use these items again.

Rosa asked that Nathan take Wilf his blankets, which she had washed in his absence. Nathan took them and left for the bunkhouse. As he left, he asked that Rosa express their best wishes to Mrs. O'Neal when she next woke.

At the bunkhouse Larson, Curtis and Basset had built a fire in the stove and were absorbing the warmth coming from it. Wilf was nowhere in sight and Nathan dropped the blankets on one of the bunks and found his deputy in the barn attending to the roan. He'd found some liniment and was gently rubbing it into the swollen leg of the horse, talking to her quietly.

"You okay, Wilf?"

"Yup, I'm doing okay, Nathan. Just wish we could have gotten all three. The job isn't done and I want a chance to go back out there."

"No Wilf, I can't let you do that. God knows where that man is now and you are the Deputy Sheriff of Fergus. There are issues of jurisdiction. You'll have to let it go. I know that's hard but that's how it is. I'll send word the best I can and we can only hope that Stiles will be brought to justice."

"Did we do justice, Nathan?" Wilf asked quietly, "Do you really think that what we did brought any justice for Hernando and James, or Rosa and Johanna?"

"Wilf, I don't know." Nathan said with a sigh… "We can only do the best we can. At least that's all *I* can do. All I know for sure is, the men we killed out there will never hurt anyone else. That's the closest thing to justice you'll ever get in a situation like this."

Wilf nodded, standing up and wiping his hands with a cloth he'd found in the barn. "Will that be enough for Johanna and Daniel, I wonder? I can't talk to them about justice."

"I'll talk to them Wilf, you don't have to do that. I'll take care of it."

Wilf nodded and patted the roan before leaving the barn. The last thing he wanted to do was face Johanna and Daniel and tell them he'd lost the trail of the most dangerous of the three men who'd brutally invaded their home.

CHAPTER 18

THE DAY IN CULVER

DANIEL WOKE UP AROUND 7:00 in the morning and headed for breakfast, Johanna's list tucked into his clean shirt pocket. The boarding house served steak and eggs with coffee, and while Daniel was putting away breakfast, Calvin came downstairs, looking like he might not want to eat anything for awhile. He sat and drank coffee with Daniel, trying not to let the smell of the food get to him. "Ohhhh, don't think I'm going to do that again for awhile," he lamented. Daniel laughed and said, "Sure you won't have some steak and eggs, Calvin? It's pretty good."

"Shut up Daniel."

"It's going to be awhile before the stores open. Want to walk around town with me, kind of get your legs under you?"

"Nope, gonna' just sit out in the sun for awhile and try to sober up." Calvin noticed that Daniel had his gun belt on and was keeping the saddle bags close. "Seen anything of the others?"

"No, I have a feeling they slept elsewhere last night, or at least part of the night anyway."

"Well, hope they don't get into any trouble. Would hate to have to bail them out of jail, or something like that. Just hope some *ladies of the night* don't rob them blind."

Daniel shrugged and said, "Well, Calvin, we can only pay them, can't tell them how to spend it. Besides, we're leaving early in the morning. How much trouble can they get into?"

"Oh hell, Daniel, I used to be able to get into all kinds of trouble in twenty-four hours…didn't take me long. In my early twenties, I was a hell raiser. Ended up in jail overnight a couple of times in Denver."

Daniel looked at his friend and smiled, "Calvin, I just can't picture you as a hell raiser, but if you say so, I guess I believe it. We'll just have to hope the Hanson boys are God fearing men who won't go down that path." Both men laughed.

Calvin sighed and looked into the distance saying, "Those were the days… yes sir. You ever raise any hell, Daniel?"

"Nope, never needed to…never wanted to. Been together with Johanna since I was just a little older than James is now. Been blind-assed drunk a few times, but never raised any real hell. Pretty tame, Calvin."

The waitress came and took Daniel's plate away and offered him more coffee, but he told her he'd had enough. "Going to get on with my day, Calvin. If you see any of the men, tell them we are leaving a little after sun up in the morning. I want to cover as much ground tomorrow as we can, so they should plan on starting out reasonably sober."

Calvin nodded in agreement and told Daniel he would relay the message.

Daniel rose from the table. "I'll see you later, Calvin. Take it easy today and let's eat a couple of large steaks tonight. That is if you'll be up to it."

"Oh, I'll be human by noon," Calvin said laughing, and indicated to the waitress he was ready to try some food now. Calvin had time on his hands. He had a wife who wouldn't trust him to buy anything for her, especially not material, buttons or lace, God forbid. Any shopping he did would be for himself or his sons. He was thinking about some new tools, when the waitress brought his breakfast.

Daniel walked out onto the wooden sidewalk and headed east. He wanted to get a new pair of boots, but had decided last night that he'd just get his old ones resoled one more time. He found a cobbler's shop and got that accomplished while he waited in his socks, reading a newspaper which was published weekly in Culver.

By the time he walked out of the cobbler's shop he was telling himself this was almost as good as getting a new pair of boots. He headed for the town's largest mercantile store, looking for Johanna's material and other sewing items.

The mercantile store in Fergus, owned by the Paulson family was where Johanna purchased just about every store-bought thing her family needed, including items like material for the family clothing. She wanted something different, something that not everyone else had and she knew at the railhead town it should be less expensive.

The store had just opened and Daniel went in and explained to the clerk, who was younger than Johanna and very helpful, what he needed. She showed Daniel a variety of material and Daniel at first tried to decide what Johanna would choose for herself. Not being able to make that decision he decided to pick the material he would most like to see his wife wearing. That made it a lot easier and the clerk praised his choices, saying she was sure his wife would like them. The same was true for the material for two dresses for Sarah. He picked a pale yellow and a light blue material and let the clerk decide on the thread, lace and buttons, because he had no idea how to do that. When it came to shirt material for himself and James, he was at a total loss and went by what felt good to the touch and was not terribly expensive.

After that he decided to look for his surprise for Sarah. Daniel thought of the doll Sarah carried everywhere: it was more than a toy, it was her companion and after five years of going everywhere with the little girl, the doll was threadbare. The clerk directed him to the aisle where dolls could be found and Daniel found it a bit overwhelming. He looked at dolls made of porcelain, with their fine clothes and delicate features and knew the trip home alone would possibly cause breakage. He settled on another cloth doll, but one that was a bit larger and more finely made, with a blue checked dress and a friendly embroidered smile. Sarah would like her, Daniel was certain.

Daniel had the clerk wrap everything carefully, with an extra layer of heavy brown paper and tied up tightly with coarse string, to protect the purchases from dust as the package would be riding in the wagon. He thanked the clerk again for all of her help and asked her where he might find used books for sale. She directed him to another store down the street, which specialized in selling used household items, including books.

Daniel made his way to the store as directed and stopped along the way to look in store windows that were kept perfectly clean to display such items as hats, watches, furniture, and dresses and coats on humanlike forms. Daniel knew that Johanna would enjoy this immensely and wished she could be here with him.

He reached the store, which inside smelled distinctly different from the mercantile store he'd just been in. There, everything had smelled new and fresh; here there was a smell of dust, human use and habitation. Daniel actually preferred this place.

The proprietor came from the back, wearing spectacles and carrying a small wooden box that smelled of tobacco. Daniel asked if he had any used books and the man asked what kind of books in particular. Daniel paused and explained that he had a five year old daughter who had memorized the three books they had for her and he was looking for something more challenging.

Smiling the man led him to a long aisle containing the store's book collection. Looking from floor to ceiling, Daniel saw a maze of confusion. Books stacked on shelves and in piles. The man pointed down the aisle and said, "The children's books...they are somewhere in there." Daniel put down his package and saddlebags and waded in.

Other customers were coming into the store needing help and Daniel realized he was on his own. He began going through the books and stacking them in piles of what he'd looked through and what he hadn't. He kept finding books he would have liked to buy for himself and browsed through many of them, but finally decided to stay with his plan to buy only for Sarah.

After nearly two hours of looking and stacking, he'd found two that he thought might be of interest to his daughter for some time: "The Prince and The Pauper" and "Heidi". He sat down on the floor and read several pages of each book and made sure there were no pages missing. The bindings were good and he reasoned that perhaps they'd been owned by only one person, as they were both in very good condition.

Pleased with his finds, he gathered up his things and took the books to the owner of the store who wrapped them up and asked Daniel if there was anything else he would like to purchase. Daniel looked longingly around the store. He said he thought there was probably something else he could use but the two books were all he would take today.

Entering the street again, he found it much busier than earlier. It was now after noon and there were pedestrians, wagons and riders in the street bustling about the town. He headed back toward the boarding house and on the way there encountered Calvin, excited to show Daniel a new saw and set of chisels he'd purchased. When he asked Daniel what he'd bought, Daniel said simply, "Some things for Johanna and Sarah." He didn't want to go into details about the purchase of sewing material and children's books. Instead, he went into the boarding house and admired Calvin's new chisels and saw.

Evening brought the drovers together for steaks and some whiskey and an admonition from Daniel about an early start in the morning. All were in agreement, even Sam, who looked like a sailor who'd been on a bender. It was time to head home. Daniel suspected the Hanson boys were about out of money anyway, so staying in Culver any longer would be a boring proposition.

Daniel turned in early in the evening and not long after, heard the others in the hallway heading to their rooms. Daniel dozed off, pleased he wouldn't have to scour the town in the morning looking for wayward men.

CHAPTER 19

JOHANNA

JOHANNA CAME BACK TO THE conscious world very slowly. Her first reaches toward it were tentative. She was aware of intense pain all over her body. Every part of her that had come in violent contact with the boot of her attacker, the cabinet, floor, or the stove in her kitchen ached. The headache persisted and each time she tried to change her position or lift her head, she was overcome by dizziness and nausea. She could see very little and while she could hear voices around her, she wasn't sure who was speaking much of the time. The world around her was blurry and confusing. She slept for hours on end.

At one point she awoke and realized she was in her own bed and her most prominent sensation was thirst. A woman she vaguely recognized but couldn't put a name to helped her drink some water, which tasted very good and she swallowed eagerly. More sleep followed.

Gradually, things around her began to take familiar form and she was awake for longer periods of time. The doctor, the woman she now could recall as his wife, and

Rosa, helped her to a more upright position in bed. The pain was intense but she was quickly given a spoonful of thick, smooth liquid which eased the pain somewhat. She was then given more water and Rosa brought her broth. Johanna drank it a spoonful at a time and then slept again. When she awakened, the doctor was sitting beside her bed and he asked her several questions:

"Mrs. O'Neal do you know where you are?"

Johanna looked around the room and answered, "My bedroom."

"What is your first name?"

"Johanna."

"Who is this?" He asked, pointing to Rosa

"Rosa," she answered."

"That's very good," the doctor had said, smiling.

Again, Johanna had dozed off, letting the medicine take her away.

Each time she woke, Johanna seemed more and more aware of what was happening around her. She heard voices downstairs and heard Sarah in the hallway. Hearing Sarah's voice had triggered an urgent need within her to see her daughter.

"Rosa, where is Sarah? I want to see her."

Rosa, who had just opened the door to see if Johanna was awake, nodded and said, "Very soon." In just a few minutes, Rosa, Ellen Messinger, and Sarah entered the room.

The little girl's expression was one of apprehension and worry. She had been instructed by Ellen Messinger that she must be very gentle with her mother and not sit down on the bed, because it would cause her mother pain. She must stand by the bed and just touch her mother's right hand and arm. This Sarah did with a plaintive voice asking, "Mommy are you going to get better soon?"

Johanna nodded and tried to smile, and even that caused pain in the left side of her face. "Yes I am, sweetheart. Are you alright?"

"Yes, I was scared under the bed, but Mr. Johanson and Rosa found me."

The mention of this brought a wave of memory to Johanna and she looked at Rosa and said the word, "James?"

Rosa shook her head and said sadly, "James and Hernando are gone, Johanna."

"They're in heaven," Sarah added emphatically, "A man who came to help us said that."

Tears came then, and Johanna reached her right arm out to Sarah and despite Ellen's warning, Sarah very carefully climbed onto the bed and allowed her mother to hug her. The two of them sat there, the small girl and the mother with their cheeks touching, Johanna's tears running onto her daughter's face.

"I'm so glad you are safe, my sweetheart. I'm so glad you're safe."

Sarah released her mother and sat back. "I helped dig potatoes today," she said softly but proudly. "We put them all in the cellar."

"You did? I'm so proud of you." Johanna tried to gain control of her tears and wiped her face with the bed sheet. "I'm just so proud of you."

"Hank was here with his Dad and he helped me gather

eggs and I'm not afraid of the chickens anymore because Hank told me I'm bigger than they are so I'm the boss."

At this, the three women in the room laughed softly and Johanna gave her daughter another hug and said, "I think I'd better rest some more now and I need to talk to Rosa. Can you go downstairs?"

"Yes I can." The little girl gave her mother another gentle hug and carefully climbed off the bed and left the room with Ellen.

Rosa picked up a straight back chair that had been brought from downstairs days ago and placed it next to the bed and sat down.

"Rosa, I remember seeing Hernando in the yard when the men came. I remember the shots. Is he really gone?"

Rosa took her hand and said, "Yes, Hernando died in the yard."

"And James? What happened to him?"

"He was fishing, when they killed him. The Sheriff and his deputy and one other man went to the river and found him and brought him home." She paused for a moment and then continued through tears, " They were both buried that afternoon." Again she paused and then finished, her voice trembling, "I am so sorry they killed James, he was such a good boy."

Johanna looked towards the window. A light breeze was moving the curtains gently. Hearing that James was dead filled her heart with such sorrow. It was impossible to believe that her brother was gone. The boy with so much energy and tenacity, who had been her companion for years and that she had thought would be part of her life for years to come was now gone. How could that be true?

"Johanna, two of the men who came to the ranch that day are dead. The Sheriff and his men chased them and killed them."

Johanna was suddenly jolted back to the room. "Which two, do you know?"

"I don't know, but one escaped. They couldn't find him."

Johanna was lost in thought for a moment and then said, "Rosa, I want to talk to the Sheriff. I must talk to him, can we get him here?"

"He said he would be back tomorrow. He is … he is waiting to talk to Daniel, when he returns."

There was a long silence in the room as Johanna thought about Daniel's return. She knew it would be so difficult for her husband to accept all that had happened.

"Rosa," Johanna said softly, turning to look directly at her friend, "What were you doing on the porch that day? I could see you through the window. It looked like you were dancing on the porch railing. I couldn't understand how you were doing that."

"They hung me by my wrists above the swing." Rosa put her arms out so Johanna could see the angrily bruised and still swollen ligature marks.

"Oh my God, Rosa." Johanna again began to cry.

"Mr. Johanson and his son came and found us. The boy went for help. The posse came, the doctor and the priest came, and neighbors came, and people from town. They all came to help us."

"And you found Sarah under the bed?"

"Yes, In James' room."

It fit together now in Johanna's head, the sequence of events. She was overwhelmed with a myriad of jumbled feelings she could not sort out. There was a numbness there, but also an edge of anger as sharp as a knife. She felt like weeping and howling and being silent, all at the same time. She felt so tired and knew she must rest again. Rosa gave her some more water and she slept and woke sometime later, feeling that she must relieve herself. Rosa helped her use the chamber pot, each movement of each limb and her torso was incredibly painful. She lay back in the bed exhausted. Rosa gave her some more of the pain medicine that Dr. Messinger had left and very soon after that, Johanna drifted back to sleep.

When she woke, it was morning and Rosa helped her out of bed to sit in the chair while her bed was remade. Rosa carefully combed her hair and washed her face and helped her put on a clean sleeping gown, with her left arm kept inside. It helped Johanna feel more like herself and once back in bed, Rosa fed her more broth and a bit of bread with jam, her first solid food.

While she was finishing, she heard voices downstairs and Rosa informed her that Sheriff Westphal had arrived. "Will you please ask him to come up and see me." Rosa went downstairs and within a couple of minutes, Johanna heard boots on the stairway. The Sheriff gently tapped on the bedroom door and Johanna told him to come in.

"Good morning, Mrs. O'Neal," Nathan greeted the woman who looked much better than she had the last time he'd seen her, although her face still looked swollen and was extremely bruised. He sat down beside the bed on the chair and met her eyes in a kindly way. He was not looking forward to this conversation, but knew it was necessary.

"Sheriff Westphal, thank you so much for coming to see me and thank you for all you have done for me and my family."

Nathan was always uncomfortable with thanks or praise, so said simply, "I am just doing my job, Mrs. O'Neal."

Johanna hesitated, took a breath, licked her lips and headed into forbidding territory. "Sheriff, I am wondering if you can tell me about the men you pursued and killed."

Nathan cleared his throat and began by saying, "We followed all three of them, but could only find two, on the second day, and we killed them. Unfortunately, one of them got away, I'm sorry to say."

Johanna was quiet for a moment, trying to think of how to word her next question. "Sheriff, can you describe the two you killed?"

"Yes," Nathan said thoughtfully, as he was sure he knew what information Johanna was looking for. "One was in his mid twenties and had reddish, kind of blond hair, and went by the name of Joe. The other one was also probably in his twenties, slight of build, and darker hair. His name was Nelson."

"The dark haired man, was his hair long or short?"

"It was fairly short."

Johanna could not hide a look of disappointment. "I see."

"Mrs. O'Neal, can you describe the man who attacked you?"

Johanna looked at the Sheriff and then looked back toward the window and painfully nodded her head. She sat for some time without speaking.

Her words to Nathan, were calm and almost detached, as if she was talking about something else entirely, not describing the man who had beaten and raped her. The only indication to Nathan that this was a most painful and disturbing subject was the fact that tears began running down her face. As she spoke she twisted a piece of the bed sheet between the fingers of her right hand.

"He was tall and he had long dark hair, which was pulled back and tied behind his neck. His eyes were very dark...they were very dark brown...he had thick eyebrows. His face was long and somewhat thin. He was extremely strong and he... he threw me around my house... like...like I was nothing...*nothing*. The last word was the only one she emphasized.

"His name is Stiles, Mrs. O'Neal. Does that name mean anything to you?"

Johanna looked back at Nathan, meeting his gaze and shook her head thoughtfully, "No, I've never heard that name and I've never seen any of those men before. Do you know where they came from?"

"Up north, one from Ohio...Chicago, a couple of them. They met and came our direction, I'm sad to say."

Johanna nodded and wiped her face with the sheet she had been twisting.

"Do you think he'll be caught...Stiles? I would hate

to think that he could do this to someone else, to another family."

Nathan waited a few moments to answer and then said, lamely he thought, but he had no other answer: "It's my hope that eventually he'll be caught and brought to justice. I'll do everything I can within my power. I've already sent a letter by stage today to the Sheriff in Culver. There is a telegraph there and they can send inquiries out to gather information about these three men. It may take awhile... I have no idea how long...to get information back. But we will try our best. Also, I must tell you, Emily sends her best wishes. She and I are both very sorry about your brother James and Hernando." He paused and asked, "Do you have any other questions for me?"

Johanna shook her head and said, "No, not right now. Thank you for coming to talk to me. Please tell Emily thank you for her thoughts. "

Nathan stood up and said, "I'm going to be here until Daniel comes home. You try to rest now." Then he left the room.

Johanna couldn't take a truly deep breath without pain, but she attempted it, to try and relax her body and her mind. She wanted to see Daniel more than anything, but she dreaded it, because she would have to watch him bear the most difficult news he had ever heard.

Downstairs, Nathan went out on the porch and sat in the swing. He figured Daniel and his men would be home sometime tonight or by midday tomorrow if all had gone well on the drive. He had left Wilf in charge of things in Fergus and Wilf was glad to take that duty. Now there was nothing left for Nathan to do but wait.

CHAPTER 20

COMING HOME

CALVIN AND SAM HAD THE mules hitched early on the morning of departure from Culver. The mules and horses were rested and as the other drovers showed up at the livery to collect their mounts and head out, there was a jovial exchange of greetings and good natured kidding. Purchases made in Culver were stashed in the back of the wagon and everyone had bought something. Daniel noticed that both Swifty and Ellis were wearing new boots and as he saddled up Zeb, he had a pang of regret for not going ahead and buying boots for himself.

Soon, it was time to go and the group set off for home with only Jack and Ben glancing back at Culver. Traveling home would be easier since they were able to travel by road most of the way, rather than cross country. At some points, the road was little more than a trail, and other places it was wide and fairly smooth. The extra mounts were herded along by Swifty and Ellis mostly staying north of the road. The first day went quickly and they passed quite a few houses built back from the road, some with large corrals and barns. Fields of hay had been mown earlier in the summer and breeds of cattle the men had never seen before grazed in some of the fenced pastures. There were more farms and ranches than there had been two years ago. They also encountered a number of fences, where the horses had to be brought onto the road. The weather continued to be beautiful, although both Daniel and Calvin made note of the fact that there was a nip of autumn in the air and it was noticeably cooler than it had been the previous week. They were in the last days of August.

Camp wasn't set the first night until almost dark and they knew they were over one third of the way home. Since they were carrying so much cash and wanted no dangerous encounters, they decided to maintain a large fire and keep sentries during the night. Ellis and Swifty were first up and they kept the fire burning and sat in the darkness, listening to every sound, staying vigilant. Calvin and Daniel's turn followed, and they finished a quiet night.

Early in the morning they were again on the road after breakfast. There was a feeling of rain in the air and before noon they began to feel a mist which turned to a steady drizzle by early afternoon. By then, everyone had donned their slickers, gritting their teeth in consternation about the fact that they just couldn't get home without getting rained on. The wagon slowed as the road became somewhat muddy but didn't degenerate to mire, for which everyone was thankful.

By late afternoon they came to the only river crossing they would have, with a large bridge made with sturdy logs, more than wide enough to accommodate the wagon. Since they had crossed the bridge two years ago, it had been rebuilt and reinforced to handle the increased population in the area. After crossing the bridge the drovers watered all of their animals and let them rest for a while. Then they pushed on hoping the rain would quit before they made camp for the night.

The men ate supper around a campfire in the rain that had again become a fine mist. They hadn't made as many miles that day as they'd hoped, but Daniel and Calvin calculated they would make it home in late afternoon the next day if it didn't rain any harder.

Daniel checked his packages in the wagon to make sure they were still dry. The treated canvas of the wagon cover was holding back the rain, allowing only some moisture into the interior. However, to further protect the precious cargo he'd found in Culver, he took his slicker off and wrapped it around the packages. He was taking no chances, especially with the books for Sarah. He'd stay by the fire tonight since the Hanson boys were up for sentry duty, followed by Ellis and Swifty.

Calvin and Daniel tightened the canvas on the wagon to encourage additional shedding of rain, then joined the men at the fire for a supper of venison, beans, and welcome hot coffee.

The night passed slowly, rather miserably for Daniel, and in the early morning before dawn, the rain stopped. Daniel stoked the fire, grateful for its warmth, and tried to get dry.

Once everyone was up the next morning, Daniel and Calvin both urged an early start. The sun came out and began drying the road, making it possible to hasten the pace. By noon, they were coming into familiar territory. Ellis commented on this when they stopped for a rest: "Daniel, I think that ridge to the north is where we each got an elk, was it two years ago?"

Daniel looked to where Ellis was indicating and said, "You're right Ellis, that was the place. That was the year we each got a bull within an hour of each other. Our pack horses were so weighed down it took all day to get home. Remember? Filled the meat house."

"Yup, maybe we can do that again this winter. I'm ready." Ellis had looked tired earlier, but now, talking about hunting, he looked revived. It was what he lived for year round.

"Me too," Daniel said, "Why don't we try going back up there - maybe November? Weather will be moving the elk down out of the mountains if we get some early snow. I look for there to be more hunters coming from further away as time goes by."

"Afraid you're right," Ellis said, with a sad tone to his voice. He gave his horse a jab with his heels, once again moving west.

In mid afternoon the entourage reached the place where they would split up, each group going its own direction. Calvin and Sam would head for the Syme Ranch; by distance, the Hanson boys would probably reach home first.

Daniel told Ben and Jack it had been good to have them along and requested they ask their father to come to the O'Neal ranch in a day or two to receive his share of the payout for the cattle. Daniel was smiling as he said this, because he knew that Robert Hanson would be at his front door, bright and early the next morning.

The two boys took off immediately, driving their extra horses ahead of them at a full gallop, something they'd wanted to do since they'd left Culver. Riding behind the wagon for miles had been boring after the trip herding cattle to the rail head.

Calvin and Daniel took their time saying good-bye and Ellis and Swifty told Calvin that they had enjoyed their adventure with both he and Daniel. The four quickly discussed work they would be doing in the next month and after retrieving their treasures from the back of the wagon they split up, heading for home. Daniel stashed Sarah's books in his saddle bag and tied Johanna's precious package, still wrapped in his rain gear, carefully behind his saddle.

Daniel, Ellis and Swifty traveled fairly quickly and when they knew they were on O'Neal land, Daniel could feel the tiredness lifting from him, replaced by anticipation of soon being embraced by his wife and daughter. He could hardly wait to see their faces when he presented them with his gifts. It would be better than Christmas. The sun was now low in the sky and late afternoon was upon them and the air was cooling rapidly.

As they rode into the yard, Daniel noticed a single horse tied to the house hitching rail and a figure sitting in the swing on the front porch. Ellis and Swifty split off, driving the riderless horses to the large horse pasture, intending to head for the bunk house afterward.

As Daniel pulled his horse down to a walk and came close enough to see who was on the porch, the waiting man stood up and came to the railing.

Daniel immediately recognized Nathan Westphal,

Sheriff, friend, and occasional fishing partner. He knew instinctively that something was wrong to bring the Sheriff to his house this time of day.

Daniel rode up to the hitching rail and dismounted slowly, never taking his eyes off Nathan, hoping for some hint of what to expect. He untied the package from behind his saddle and lifted the saddlebags from the back of his horse and placed them over his left shoulder before turning to climb the front steps. He removed his gloves and tucked them into his belt. If there had been anything else he could have done to delay actually speaking to Nathan, he would have done it, because he knew he was about to hear bad news, and he didn't want to hear it.

"Nathan."

"Daniel."

Daniel climbed the steps slowly and stepped up onto the porch. "What brings you to my house Nathan?"

"I need to talk to you."

Daniel placed the saddlebags, parcel and his hat on the swing and walked to the end of the porch, as far away from Nathan as he could possibly get and then turned and sat down on the side porch rail.

Nathan watched him and then slowly walked over and sat on the railing running parallel to the front of the house, so he could face Daniel at an angle, rather than sit beside him. He waited a moment before speaking and Daniel asked no question.

"Daniel, there was something that happened here a few days ago and I don't know how to tell you, except to just tell you."

Daniel felt fear just below his heart, a panic feeling he had felt only a few times in his life. He swallowed hard, nodding at Nathan. "Go on," he said, even though that was the last thing he wanted Nathan to do.

"There were three men, who came onto your land, and they ambushed James, while he was fishing down by the river…and they shot and killed him."

Daniel could feel himself go weak and he continued to look at Nathan without responding. He somehow knew there was more.

"They came to the house and shot and killed Hernando in the yard just behind where I'm sitting." Nathan paused, knowing that each thing he added would need time to register with Daniel.

"They tied Rosa up here on the porch above the swing and then went inside."

Daniel could feel compression in his chest and it was difficult to breathe.

"Daniel, one of the men attacked Johanna and beat her very badly, causing…"

Daniel interrupted, "Is she alive Nathan?"

"Yes, she's alive but she has broken bones and a head injury. It's going to take some time for her to recover." There was a long pause and Nathan was about to resume when Daniel spoke.

"Was she…..did he,"…..there was a long pause……..

Nathan nodded and said, "Yes… she was raped."

Daniel felt everything inside of him give way and he slid down the porch rail until he was sitting on the rough boards of the floor. He lowered his head and put his arms across his knees, which were propped up in front of him. He sat there for some time, saying nothing. Nathan kept silent, knowing that Daniel was trying to absorb the reality of what had just been said.

Daniel looked up at Nathan and asked, "What about my daughter, did they hurt Sarah?"

"No, she hid and Ove Johanson and Rosa found her."

"Ove was here?"

"He and Henry came by to check on your family and found them an hour or two after it happened and Henry came to town and got us."

"Where are the men now who did this, Nathan?"

"Wilf and I took a posse after them and we were able to find two of them and we killed them. Wilf did a hell of a job tracking, but we lost the trail of the third. Had a bad rainstorm...could not backtrack and find him."

"Did you kill the man who harmed Johanna?"

Nathan took a deep breath and shook his head, "No, Daniel, I'm sorry, he's the one who slipped us. He got away. I'm very sorry."

"Jesus Christ." There was another long moment of silence. "Are my wife and daughter here now?"

"They are upstairs. This is the first day that neither the doctor nor his wife have been here for the whole day. They left about noon. Doc will be back in a couple of days to check on Johanna. Says she is improving well. It's just going to take time."

"James and Hernando...are they...did someone bury them?"

"Yes, several neighbors and people from town came. I had the posse wait until they were buried to leave."

"Thank you for that."

Daniel slowly turned and reached up to the porch rail to pull himself up and then sat back down on the rail.

"I want to see my wife and daughter now. I'm going inside." He paused and then asked, " Are you staying or heading back to town?"

"I think I'll head back to town, if that's alright. Do you have any other questions for me now?"

"Do you know who the men are?"

"Don't know much about them. Have names…questioned one of the men before he died…only know they were from up north. I've got inquiries out on them. Hope to get some information back, but it will be slow, I think."

Daniel nodded, "Okay Nathan, thank you, I know I'll want to talk again later, maybe in a day or two. Right now, I just want to be with my family."

The two men stood up and Daniel reached out to shake Nathan's hand, but then changed his mind and embraced Nathan and the two men stood together for a few moments.

"I'm very sorry Daniel. Nobody deserves something like this, but for sure your family didn't."

They stepped back from one another and Nathan turned and left the porch. Daniel waited until Nathan mounted his horse and turned to leave the yard before picking up his hat, saddlebags and the parcel he'd been so eager to present to Johanna and Sarah. Now the packages he'd so carefully brought home seemed strange and totally foreign in his hands. What did it matter now? He dropped the items on the sofa as he entered and went around the corner of the kitchen. Rosa was sitting at the table, well aware that Daniel was home, but not wishing to intrude on the conversation that had taken place on the porch. She stood as Daniel entered the kitchen and the two embraced silently. "I'm so sorry Rosa. So sorry about Hernando."

"I know, Daniel and I am sorry for you. It was a terrible day."

"Are you all right?"

"I am as good as I can be right now."

They parted and Daniel told Rosa he was going upstairs to be with Johanna and Sarah. He turned, took off his boots and left them by the front door and quietly climbed the stairs. His chest felt like it was in a vise and his legs felt weak beneath him.

The door to their bedroom was partly closed and he gently pushed it open, revealing his wife and daughter lying on the bed, both sound asleep. He stood there, motionless, watching them. He could see that Johanna's left arm was in a splint-and-sling and that her face was badly bruised. Sarah was curled up against her mother's right side, barely touching her.

The feelings that swept through Daniel were like none he'd ever known. He felt a tenderness that went deeper than anything he'd ever experienced and at the same time, there was another feeling that came up under that. It was unrecognizable and Daniel could not put a name to it. It was more than anger. He'd felt anger in his life. This dwarfed any anger he'd ever experienced. He reached out and gripped the doorframe on both sides with his hands, trying to calm himself. It took several moments, but slowly the feeling began to subside and he took a deep breath, exhaled, removed his gunbelt, wrapped the belt around the holstered Colt, and placed it on top of the dresser, turned and walked over to the bed and quietly sat down in the straight back chair.

The people he loved most slept on and Daniel sat silently beside them, not wanting to disturb the peace in the room. He wanted it to last as long as possible.

CHAPTER 21

DANIEL AND JOHANNA

SARAH WAS THE FIRST TO awaken and immediately saw her father sitting in the chair next to the bed. The sun was setting outside and the there was just enough light in the room to see him.

"Daddy? Is that you?" the little girl asked in a sleepy voice.

"Yes it is, Sarah Girl."

He straightened up in the chair and Sarah carefully stood up on the bed and stepped over onto his lap, wrapping her arms around his neck. Daniel held her close, feeling his throat tighten. He swallowed hard several times, not wanting to weep in front of his daughter. That couldn't happen.

Hearing them, Johanna woke and the first thing she saw in the near darkness was her husband holding their daughter. "Daniel?"

"I'm here, Jo."

He reached beyond Sarah, opened the small drawer in

the bedside table and pulled a match from its container, struck it and lit the kerosene hurricane lamp next to the bed. He turned the flame down, to keep the light in the room soft.

Johanna struggled to sit up and winced several times in pain, but managed to get into a sitting position. Daniel, realizing that embracing her would be painful, stood up and sat on the very edge of the bed. Still holding Sarah, he reached his right hand over and touched the right side of Johanna's face and neck. He leaned his face to hers and kissed her very gently on the mouth. "I love you," he said softly.

"Daniel, I'm *so* glad you are home." Their eyes met and held and there were tears that began escaping Johanna's eyes, making slow tracks down her face. Daniel brought his forehead to hers, but could not speak.

The three of them sat there in quiet for several moments and then Sarah broke the silence, "Mommy said you were going to bring me a surprise when you came home. Did you bring one?"

"Umm hum. Yes I did and in the morning I'll give it to you. Right now, we need to get you to bed so we can all rest. I know I am very tired from the long trip with the cows."

"Can't I see it now?"

Daniel hugged his daughter and then said, "Remember how we do Christmas, always opening presents in the morning? Well, that is how we're going to do these presents."

"Presents? Is there more than one? Sarah was keenly

interested now and Daniel couldn't help but smile. The fact that his daughter could bring some normalcy into the room at this moment amazed him. How wonderful it must be to be a child, he thought. He couldn't remember it.

"There might be more than one ...Now say goodnight to your Mom, 'cause I'm putting you to bed."

Sarah turned her head toward her mother and said, "Goodnight Mommy, I'll see you in the morning." Johanna told her daughter goodnight and that she loved her.

Daniel carried his daughter to her bed, covered her with her warm quilt and listened as she said her prayers, and then said the words he spoke to her every night: "Okay now I need a hug, a kiss, and a nose rub." Sarah obliged him with their nightly ritual, and then said, "I sure missed you Daddy."

"I missed you too, Sarah Girl, now you have to go to sleep so Mommy and I can rest."

Closing her door, all but a crack, he reentered the bedroom across the hall and closed the door. Johanna had continued crying while they were gone and was trying to get control of herself as Daniel came and sat down on the bed next to her . They sat in silence for a moment and then Johanna spoke.

"I know Sheriff Westphal has been waiting for you. Did he see you and tell you everything...about what happened?"

Daniel sighed and looked into her eyes and said, his voice breaking, "Yes he did ... and I am so sorry I wasn't here to protect you and our family. I should have been here."

"Daniel don't."

"If Ellis, Swifty and I had been here...these men wouldn't have done this. They would never have come onto our land. They wouldn't have *dared*. Daniel again felt the rage he'd felt earlier begin to overcome him.

Johanna touched his face and his hair and again implored him not to say these things, "It isn't your fault. No one knew this would happen. No one could have known."

Daniel continued, "James would still be alive if I'd let him go on the drive. I should have let him ...it was an easy trip. He would have handled himself well and been safe from this, if I'd only let him come with us."

This regret brought the tears from Daniel and that broke Johanna's heart. The two of them sat on the bed, gently holding one another. Daniel afraid of inflicting more pain; Johanna wounded and unable to embrace her husband. The sobs from both of them came in waves. They gently rocked, each trying to comfort the other.

Daniel cradled Johanna, stroking her hair and neck. " "God, I am so sorry... For what happened to you, I am so sorry."

Johanna tried to soothe him. "Shhhhh Daniel, Shhhhh, I'll be all right, I'm going to be all right."

Gradually, after some time the tears abated and they each tried to gain control of their breathing.

Daniel kissed her again, through tears that had come from each of them. There were long sighs as they both began to calm.

"Can you lie down beside me?" Johanna asked gently.

"Yes, but I don't want to hurt you."

"You won't Daniel, you couldn't possibly hurt me."

Daniel helped her find a comfortable position in the bed and then he carefully laid down next to her, reached back behind him and turned out the lamp. The two exhausted souls lay together for some time before going to sleep. Downstairs, Rosa went to bed in the pantry bedroom. She hadn't slept in the house next door since her husband had been killed. She didn't want to be alone. She felt it better to be in a house where there were people who needed her.

CHAPTER 22

THE DECISION

THE FIRST THREE DAYS AFTER Daniel returned home were very eventful. Robert Hanson, with sons Ben and Jack, came by early morning of the first day. Robert had been one of the men who had helped bury Hernando and James and he was not his usual brusque self. Ben and Jack were both very subdued, feeling somewhat ashamed about how they had behaved toward James the last time they'd been at the O'Neal ranch. They humbly asked Daniel if there was anything they could do; and Daniel said that no, there really wasn't, but thanked them for their offer. He gave Robert the envelope of money from the cattle sale and they left soon after that, with Robert saying that he was available to help in any way and Daniel knew he was sincere.

A devastated Calvin came to the ranch the first morning as well. His wife had told him what had happened when he got home. It had been all he could do to wait until the next morning to go to the O'Neal ranch. It was the first time Daniel had ever seen the man weep and it was Daniel who comforted Calvin, not the other way around. Calvin was at a loss for words and he too offered to do anything Daniel needed. Again, Daniel had to tell his best friend that at the moment, there was nothing to be done.

Ellis had seen Nathan and Daniel on the porch the night they had returned from the drive. He could tell from their behavior that there was serious trouble. Hernando and James had been nowhere in sight and Sarah had not come from the house to greet her father. He'd watched as the Sheriff had ridden away, and when it turned dark and Daniel had not come out to put Zeb in the horse pasture, Ellis had silently done that.

The following morning, Daniel had met with Ellis and told him everything. Ellis had not been able to meet Daniel's eyes and didn't try to speak, but only nodded and touched Daniel's shoulder as he turned and walked away, headed for the bunk house to break the news to Swifty.

After being told, Swifty stayed away from the house and immediately picked up the responsibility of Hernando and James' chores. The young man had no idea what to say to his boss, but was determined to take as much worry off Daniel's mind as he could. He was a Godsend.

Daniel had Rosa help him do an inventory of what had actually been stolen from the house. The shotgun, James' Winchester, ammunition for both, some food items, the Sullivan money clip and money, and one of the Sullivan silver candlesticks had all been recovered when Joe and Nelson had been killed. What hadn't been recovered was Daniel's horse, Shadow, one silver candlestick and the fox pelt. It was so painful for the two of them to realize that the lives of James and Hernando had been lost for this meager amount of property.

Johanna began trying to extend her time out of bed. She was still fighting the dizziness and disorientation. Unable to wear a dress, because of the splint-and-sling, she wore a pair of Daniel's trousers and one of his shirts, with her left arm inside. It would have to be her attire until her arm healed completely and she could once again wear her own clothing. On the second day, with Daniel's help, she was able to slowly come downstairs and sit in the living room.

Sarah, of course, had received her books and new doll the morning of the first day Daniel was home. She was overjoyed and wanted Daniel to read aloud from her new books immediately. He had promised her they would read together in the evenings, but that he was too busy during the day. The little girl was content to browse through the books and tried, by looking at the illustrations, to figure out what the stories were about.

When Daniel opened the package for Johanna as she sat in the living room, he watched her face and she was so pleased with the selections he had made. He told her he'd had a lot of help from the clerk, but she ignored that completely and thanked him many times. It was difficult for both of them to look at the material he had purchased to make new shirts for James. Johanna had run her hands over it and had simply said she would find a use for it. There were more tears and she'd had to take time to rest after that. Daniel had taken everything upstairs and put it in the trunk at the foot of their bed. He knew it would all have to wait.

At the end of the second day, while Johanna was upstairs, Daniel brought James' box of fishing flies into the bedroom. He opened it gently on the bed and they discussed them together. Daniel had her select the five flies that were about to take a short journey and he gently attached them to a scrap of material he'd found in James' wooden box under his bed.

On the third morning, Daniel rode out of the yard carrying James' fly rod over the saddle horn, the flies carefully placed in his shirt pocket and Ove Johanson's envelope in one of his saddle bags.

When he arrived at the Johanson farm, Ove had come from the house and greeted Daniel in the yard. Daniel dismounted, took the envelope from his saddle bag and approached the tall Norwegian carrying the fishing rod and envelope in his left hand. He grasped Ove's outstretched right hand and shook it firmly.

"Ove, thank you for everything you and Hank did for my family. There is no way I can ever repay you."

Ove found it difficult to speak and when he did, his voice was quavering, "I wish there was more I could have done…how is Mrs. O'Neal?"

"She is recovering, but has a long way to go. There is progress each day and it's just going to take time." Daniel could see the relief in Ove's face. "I have something here for you," he said handing Ove the envelope. "We got a good price on the cattle and the drive went well. We didn't lose any along the way and got them all there safely. It went well for us."

Ove took the envelope, but didn't open it; there would

be time for that later. Now, he just wanted to focus on his time with Daniel. "Thank you, Daniel, thank you for taking my cows with yours to Culver. Will you come in and have some coffee?"

"Yes, I'd like that very much, thank you." The two men turned and walked toward the house with Daniel saying, "Is Hank around? I have something for him, as well."

"He's doing his morning chores, I will call him," Ove replied. He opened the door and Hilda warmly greeted Daniel, using her mixed vocabulary but Daniel knew what she was saying, even if he didn't understand everything she said.

Ove stepped outside and called for Henry to come from the barn, where he was cleaning the two stalls. Once outside the barn, the boy saw the horse in the yard and knew immediately who it belonged to. He washed his hands in the watering trough and walked slowly to the house, not knowing what would happen when he got there.

Entering the kitchen, Hank saw Daniel sitting at the table with his father. His mother was busying herself, pouring coffee and getting some biscuits onto a small plate. Hank's younger sister was shyly standing by the cupboard, looking around the corner, watching the scene, quietly.

Hank was greeted by his father, "Look Henry, we have company."

Hank nodded and stayed by the kitchen door. Daniel could see by the look on the boy's face that he was not quite sure what was expected of him so Daniel gently gestured him forward, saying, "Hank, I have something for you."

It was then that Hank noticed what Daniel was holding… James' flyrod. He looked from the rod to Daniel, who nodded and said, "Yes, Hank, Johanna and I want you to have this."

As he was speaking he reached inside his shirt pocket, where he'd been able to feel a fish hook scratching him all the way from the O'Neal ranch. Careful not to get a hook in his finger, he gingerly pulled the piece of material from his pocket, placed it on the table and opened it, revealing the five flies. James had tied three, the other two had been tied by William Sullivan. Daniel couldn't tell the difference between them and he knew Hank couldn't either. The next time they touched water, they would belong to a novice with dreams of one day fishing like James.

Hank was overwhelmed and didn't know what to say, so Daniel continued, "Hank, you are welcome to come and fish at our place anytime you want."

The boy slowly came toward Daniel and reached out with his right hand until his fingers closed around the rod. He carefully picked it up, feeling the full weight of it and said, "I will come and fish whenever I can. Thank you very much." At that moment, his eyes met Daniel's and held. "Will you be able to fish with me sometimes?"

"Yes, I'll fish with you, whenever I can. I kept a few of the flies, so we'll see which fly catches the most fish. How about that?"

Hank smiled and said, "I think James would like that."

Daniel extended his right hand and the two shook hands, sealing the bargain.

Daniel stayed for coffee and biscuits and then excused himself, saying he had another stop he had to make. Ove walked him out to Zeb and the two men paused before Daniel mounted his horse. "Ove, thank you again for all that you did for my family. If you ever need *anything*, I'll be there for you."

Ove nodded and said, "You would have done the same for my family, I know that Daniel. I know that."

Daniel mounted Zeb and turned the horse to leave, waving to Ove as he left the yard. Next, he rode to Fergus, heading for the office of Nathan Westphal. This part of the day would give him no joy. He was preparing himself for a difficult conversation and he'd spent a sleepless night, thinking about how it might go.

In town, there were a few people along the street who nodded in his direction and others who looked away, as soon as they realized who he was. He pulled up in front of the small Sheriff's Office. Wilf came outside, having seen Daniel through the window as he rode up. Nathan was out of the office and Wilf was apprehensive about any conversation he might have with Daniel.

"Good morning Wilf," Daniel said as he stepped onto the sidewalk.

"Morning Daniel, are you looking for Nathan?"

Daniel took off his gloves saying, "No, actually, I was hoping to speak to you, if I might. Can we go inside?"

Wilf took a deep breath and said, "Of course, come on in." Once inside he invited Daniel to sit down on the bench and dragged the desk chair over, so that he wouldn't be sitting behind the desk while speaking to Daniel.

"What can I help you with?"

"Well...first of all I want to thank you for finding two of the bastards who hurt my family...I talked to Nathan and he said you did most of the tracking work...and I'm extremely grateful to you for that."

Like Nathan, Wilf found taking compliments awkward and in this case he felt very uncomfortable, because in his mind the mission had not been completed. He lowered his head, nodded and said only, "We tried."

Daniel continued, "Wilf, I'm going after the one who hurt Johanna and what I need from you is to take me to the last place you tracked him if you think you can find it."

Wilf had not expected this and sat silent for a moment before answering, " I think I could find the approximate place I lost the trail, but there is no way to know where he went from there. He didn't backtrack east and he didn't continue west, but he could have gone either north or south and you could go either way and spend a lot of time going in the wrong direction."

"I won't go the wrong direction. You take me to the place and I'll go in the right direction."

"What I'd like to do is go with you, Daniel. I wanted to go after him while we were still out there... but I couldn't...I can't. I work for Nathan and I can't go against his orders." Wilf paused. What he was saying was painful for him. He resumed, speaking softly. "You know he's going to try and talk you out of this, don't you?"

Daniel knew Wilf was right – Nathan would be totally against his decision and he was prepared for it.

"How is Mrs. O'Neal?" Wilf asked hesitantly.

"She's better, Wilf, I think she's…"

At that moment, Nathan came through the door and both men stood up. Wilf went over and sat on the desk, his perch to stay out of the way so Nathan could sit down next to Daniel. Nathan could tell that the two men had been in serious conversation and wondered what he'd missed.

Nathan sat down, looked at Daniel and asked him how he was. Daniel sat back down on the bench before speaking.

"I'm okay, Nathan." He paused and shifted his weight on the bench, leaning forward, knowing he was about to go into territory he'd never been in before, arguing with the lawman who was his friend. "I was just telling Wilf that I intend to go after the man who is still out there and I was asking him if he would take me to the area where the trail was lost." He decided to leave it at that and see how Nathan would react.

The silence in the room was total. Nathan said nothing for some time.

"Daniel, you know this man you are talking about is a stone cold killer. He killed James…shot him in the back… and he'd do the same to you without batting an eye. No disrespect Daniel, but you're not a law man. You have no experience with men like this and you would be at a severe disadvantage."

Daniel glanced over at Wilf and saw the deputy had

crossed his arms and was looking at the floor, intending to stay out of this portion of the conversation.

"I understand what you are saying, but I'm going after him and I need to know everything you know about him before I leave. I'm hoping you'll let Wilf at least take me out there and then I'll go on alone...but I'm going, Nathan."

"Daniel, this man may no longer be alone. He was with two others when he got here. He may well have teamed up with other men like the two we killed, so you could be riding into a shit storm."

"Yes, I realize that."

Nathan took a deep breath and continued, "You know the weather is going to be moving in here. It'll be working against you. We're into September now, it's not summer."

Daniel merely nodded and said nothing. There was a long silence before Nathan spoke again.

"When would you be leaving?"

"In a few days. Three or four at the most. There are a few things I have to do before I go. I'll be leaving Ellis in charge of the ranch, and I'm hoping Calvin will be able to help cover it. It'll be tough, but it is something that has to be done."

"Does your wife know you are going to do this?"

"No. She doesn't know yet. I plan to tell her sometime tomorrow."

It was pretty clear to Nathan at this point that he was not going to win this argument. He ran his fingers through his hair and then put his arms out to his side in a gesture of surrender, "Okay, I guess that's the way it is then." He turned and looked at his deputy who was now looking in their direction.

The three men talked solemnly for nearly an hour, Wilf and Nathan telling Daniel everything they knew about Stiles. His appearance and what they knew of the relationship between Stiles and the men he'd abandoned in the chase. Daniel was already well aware of the fact that Stiles was riding Shadow, as he was the only O'Neal horse missing. By the end of the conversation they had decided that Wilf would ride to the ranch in three days, stay overnight at the bunkhouse and then leave with Daniel on the morning of the fourth day, headed west.

Daniel and Nathan stood and walked outside, Nathan was deeply saddened, realizing this might be the last time he would see his friend alive. As he said good-bye and watched Daniel ride down the street, he felt like he had somehow failed to convey just how dangerous his road ahead would be. He took a deep breath and walked back into the office, where Wilf was still sitting on the desk.

"Wilf, I'm going home now - need to take the rest of the day off. Can you take care of things here?"

"Yup, I can do that."

Nathan reached for his hat, put it on and turned to go. "I'm trusting you to come back, once you get him out there."

"You can trust me, Nathan."

"Okay, I'm gone for the day."

Nathan went out, closed the door and started home. "God damn it," he said to himself, "sometimes this job is a bitch."

Daniel rode home in the afternoon, stopping off first at Calvin's place. He wanted Calvin to hear from him first hand what he intended to do. His friend had much the same reaction as Nathan, except Calvin offered to go with him on this quest.

Daniel politely refused his offer, but asked if he could help Ellis keep the ranch going while he was away.

Calvin, as always, asked the hard questions.

"Daniel, how long will you be gone?"

"I don't know, as long as it takes...a month, two months...I don't know."

The two men were standing outside by the hitching rail near the house. Calvin had told his boys to stay inside and Daniel could see them over Calvin's shoulder, watching them through the front window. They had been told some of what had happened at the O'Neal ranch. Their father had been as upset as they had ever seen him since he'd returned from the cattle drive. Their mood had been subdued, taking their cues from their father, the man they loved and emulated.

Calvin scuffed the toe of his boot around in the dirt and kicked a small rock, then looked up directly at Daniel and said, "What if you don't come back, Daniel? What then? What will Johanna do? Have you even *thought* about that?"

Daniel had tried hard *not* to think about that, but knew it was possible. "I don't know. I guess I just have to do everything I can to come back alive."

Calvin finally resigned himself to the fact that Daniel was going to do this. Like Nathan, he felt helpless with the prospect. His only option was to assure Daniel that he would do everything he could to help Ellis.

"What does Ellis think about this?"

"I haven't told him yet. I'll do that when I get home."

Calvin could only shake his head and assure Daniel that he would be available to help Ellis run the ranch.

Daniel rode away from the Syme place and headed home, arriving in the twilight. It had been a long day. He'd covered a lot of difficult ground with people he trusted and cared about and he knew that tomorrow would be even more difficult than today. There were moments ahead of him that he dreaded immensely.

CHAPTER 23

READY TO LEAVE

THE NEXT MORNING, DANIEL WOKE up as the early morning sunlight came through the window of the bedroom. Johanna lay next to him, propped up so she would be less uncomfortable. Her breathing was steady and strong. Her face was still very bruised and Daniel had seen her left side while helping her change her clothing the day before. The deep purple bruises and tenderness in these areas would be there for some time. Daniel now had a name and a description of the man who had done this damage.

It was hard for him to believe that a little more than two weeks ago, he'd awakened in this room the morning he'd left for the cattle drive. Everything was so different now. At that time, it would have been inconceivable that he would even be contemplating the possibility of killing someone. Now, he was.

Johanna woke and saw him watching her. "Good morning, Daniel."

He brushed a strand of hair away from her face and said, "Good morning Jo, did you sleep well?"

"Yes, I did. I was awake a couple of times, but I slept pretty well."

Daniel kissed his wife gently and then spoke, beginning a conversation he never thought he would have to have.

"I need to tell you that I'm going to be leaving again in a couple of days, and I'll be gone for a while."

Johanna was instantly fully awake. "Where are you going?" Somewhere in her mind, in the part that had endured the worst day of her life, Johanna knew what the answer would be.

"I'm going after Stiles," His voice was quiet, but firm.

"Are you doing this because you think you *have* to, because you think I expect it?"

"Yes and no. Yes, I have to and no I don't think you expect it."

"I don't. I don't want you to risk your life. I don't want *you* to be hurt…or killed over what happened. I couldn't bear it."

Daniel sighed, sat up, and turned so he could meet her eyes directly. "Jo, listen to me. This is something I have to do, and if I don't…for the rest of my life I'll wish I had. Do you understand what I'm saying?"

Johanna did. She knew that Daniel's responsible nature and his love for his family would override any sense of danger. It always had. She might fear for his life every moment he was gone, but she would unquestionably support his decision. That was *her* nature.

She reached out touched his face and asked, "When are you leaving?"

"Couple of days."

"Will you promise me you'll be careful."

"Yes, I will."

There was quiet for some time and then Johanna said, "Daniel, I love you so much, you know that, don't you?"

"And I love you."

"What will you tell Sarah?"

Daniel took Johanna's hand into his, and then paused. "I'll tell her that I'm going on a longer than usual hunting trip and I'd like you to go along with that if you can." Neither Daniel nor Johanna had ever lied to Sarah about anything. Daniel knew this would be difficult for Jo.

"Of course," Johanna replied. "Where will you go to find him?"

"I don't know yet. Wilf will take me to the beginning of his trail and I'll go from there. I'll find him."

There was really nothing more to say about it. Daniel was leaving, Johanna knew it, and what would happen was totally unknown. Daniel and Johanna rose and began their day, knowing they would spend the next couple of days pretending that somehow this would all turn out right. It was what they had to do.

Daniel spent a great deal of the day with Ellis and Swifty, going over all that would need to be done while he was gone. At first Ellis was insistent that he go along. Daniel knew that his hired man would be a tremendous asset to him on this hunt, but he also knew he needed him at the ranch.

His conversation with Ellis reminded him of the talks he'd had with James about not going on the cattle drive, and this brought pain to his chest and made speaking difficult. Seeing this, Ellis reluctantly relented and agreed to stay behind and take care of things at home. Swifty was quiet and when Daniel asked him directly if he would be leaving for any length of time before he returned, the young man had assured Daniel he would not leave the ranch until Daniel came back. None of the men spoke of the possibility that he *wouldn't* be coming back. They left that alone. Daniel told them that Calvin would be coming by from time to time to assist them with anything they might need help with. He also told them that Johanna would pay them monthly, as was their usual arrangement.

Daniel spent part of that day and hours into the next getting things ready for leaving. He cleaned weapons, readied Zeb and packed a minimum of supplies. There would be no pack horse, as he wanted to be able to travel light and move quickly. It was a risk, he knew, to travel with so little, but he felt it was the right decision.

In the afternoon, Daniel did something he had put off since arriving home: he made a trip to the family cemetery. It was a pilgrimage of penance. He rode the mile and a half to the cemetery, which was on a rise but out of sight of the ranch. Both the Sullivan and O'Neal grandparents had decided they wanted the cemetery close, but not in constant view, so it was near the middle of the distance between the two homesteads.

Once there he dismounted and went inside the Caragana hedge, which was taller than his head and protected the cemetery from drifting snow in winter. Daniel had no trouble spotting the newly dug graves. He stopped immediately when he saw the placement of Hernando's grave in the southwest corner. It disturbed him. It was not what he'd expected. Somehow, he'd thought the two graves would be side by side. He walked over to Hernando's grave and stood looking down at the freshly turned earth. No marker had yet been made or placed and he knew that would be his responsibility once he returned from the journey upon which he was about to embark.

"This will not do, my friend," he said aloud, "This will not do. We'll have to move you. Can't have you way over here." He removed his gloves and reached down to touch the gray-brown earth that had been carefully mounded. Daniel's hand was trembling slightly. He stood up and looked down, filled with so many thoughts and emotions.

He spoke aloud: "You were always there for us. Always." Daniel had known this man since he'd been a ten year old boy. Hernando had been a part of his life - a part of the ranch. It was difficult for Daniel to realize that this kind, hard working man, who always had a smile for everyone was gone. He stood for some time, remembering the last conversation he'd had with Hernando, at the table the morning he'd left on the cattle drive. Again, he was struck by how it felt like yesterday, and at the same time, a lifetime ago. "I'll be back to move you in a while," Daniel said quietly. It was something he knew he had to do before he left.

He then turned and walked towards the grave of his brother-in-law, James, who had been placed appropriately next to his parents. Daniel knew that if they'd still been living at the time of their youngest son's death it would have broken their hearts, so he was glad they hadn't lived to see it. He approached the grave slowly and when he got there, he lowered himself to his knees next to the head of the grave. He removed his hat, laying it and his gloves next to him. Here, in this place, totally out of the wind, it was very quiet. Daniel heard no bird, insect or rustle of grass. Only silence.

He took a deep breath and said, "I don't know what to say to you James. I just don't." He leaned back and looked around the cemetery and then back at the grave. "I am so sorry I left you behind and I'm so sorry you were killed. I'm just sorry." Sitting there, the feeling returned that he'd experienced when he first returned home, the one that had started on the porch with Nathan and then had overtaken him in the doorway of his bedroom when he'd first seen Johanna and Sarah. He could feel it coming up from the bottom of his soul and the center of his body and this time he didn't try to stop it or repress it in any way. He let it come. Within moments his emotions completely overcame him.

"God damn it." It was barely a whisper at first and then gathered momentum and volume, until it was a shout. "God damn it… God damn it. JESUS… God *damn* it!"

The rage he felt was at everything he'd carried quietly for so long. The loss of the babies, whose graves were just feet away from where he knelt. He'd never been able to let Jo or anyone else see how he'd felt about *that*. The responsibility that he'd carried since his brothers had left the ranch and his father had died. All of it. What had happened to Johanna, and what he felt now with the loss of James.

"What a waste, GOD what a waste. He was so good… He never hurt anyone in his LIFE. Why?" Now Daniel was shouting as loud as he could and the words reverberated against the hedge and on the inside of his head. He continued venting his anger. Tears, snot and sweat covered his face. He was on all fours now next to the grave pounding the ground with his right fist. The rage continued for some time. It took awhile for the waves of emotion to subside and then Daniel felt nothing but complete exhaustion.

He sat back and wiped his face with the sleeves of his shirt. There had been no answering reply to his shouted questions from James or anyone else and again the silence of the place prevailed. Slowly he settled.

Daniel took a deep breath and said quietly, "I'm going after him, James. Going after the son of a bitch who did this." He hoped that somehow, James could hear him. He sighed deeply and again looked around the cemetery. At that moment, he heard movement near the opening of the hedge he'd come through. Daniel sat very still, suddenly realizing that he had no weapon with which to defend himself. His attention was totally focused on the opening and then a deer stepped into view.

It was a young buck with spike antlers who stopped, framed in the opening of the hedge. Daniel made no movement and the deer entered the cemetery cautiously. He sniffed in Daniel's direction, took several more steps and then stopped. Deer and man looked at each other for nearly a minute, neither moving. In that moment, Daniel felt that somehow the animal was speaking to him. He felt a peaceful calm come over his soul. In some odd way, he knew this was James, offering him solace. He didn't question that deduction then or anytime later. He simply knew it was true.

Suddenly the deer raised his head, listening as if sensing some danger to itself, and quickly turned and bounded out of the cemetery. Daniel remained quiet for a few moments and then once again turned his attention to the grave in front of him. He touched the earth and then spoke quietly, "Go in peace, James. Go in peace."

He stood and gathered his hat and gloves and walked toward the gate. Once through, he mounted Socks and rode back toward the ranch to tell Ellis and Swifty that in the morning they would have to help him dig a new grave next to James and move Hernando to his new resting place. When Wilf arrived, Daniel would ask him to come out and help them actually lift the coffin out of the earth and place it next to James. Somehow, he knew Wilf would be willing to help them do that.

CHAPTER 24

THE DEPARTURE

EVERYTHING THAT DANIEL COULD DO to ready the ranch and himself for departure had been done. He had told Wilf he wanted an early start, and the deputy who had slept very little the night before in the bunk house, was sitting on the porch in the subdued light of early morning, waiting for Daniel to appear. Johanna had come downstairs, and as much as possible, had helped Rosa prepare breakfast for the two men.

Rosa had been somewhat surprised but inwardly happy to learn that her husband was now resting beside James and she had thanked Daniel demonstratively, hugging the grown man she had helped take care of as a child. It was unspoken but understood that when Rosa died, she would be placed next to Hernando.

It was quiet in the house the morning of departure, as Daniel and Johanna did not want Sarah awakened before her father left. The night before when Daniel had explained to her that he was leaving on a hunting trip the scene had been tearful. The child was fearful that something bad would happen to her and her mother if Daniel were to leave again. Daniel had assured her that Ellis and Swifty would be there to protect them and that Calvin would be stopping by as well. It had taken quite awhile to get her to settle down and go to sleep.

Now, the two men ate hurriedly in silence. Wilf could see that Johanna was gamely attempting to make a recovery and that pleased him. After finishing his breakfast, he excused himself and after politely thanking the women for breakfast, he told Daniel he would be outside, giving the two women time to say good-bye privately to the man they would undoubtedly not see again for some time.

The good-byes were quiet and subdued and remarkably unemotional; Rosa, Daniel and Johanna all trying to make the moment of departure as easy as possible for all of them. Johanna held Daniel with her right arm, holding him as close to her as possible and Daniel hugged her, trying not to cause her any additional pain. They kissed and exchanged "I love yous." Daniel exited the house quickly, not looking back. If there were tears, he didn't want to see them.

Once outside, the two men mounted their horses and rode away, heading westward over the path the posse had taken days before. They rode silently for several miles, keeping a moderate pace, with Wilf watching for landmarks he'd passed earlier.

All during the day when they would stop to rest the horses or take a break from the saddle, Wilf tried to quietly educate the younger man in the difficult subject of hunting for Stiles. He opened with the most stark and difficult truth, "Daniel, you *cannot* let him get the drop on you. If he gets a weapon aimed at you before you can react, he'll kill you. No doubt about it. You have to make the first move, once you find him."

Daniel knew that everything Wilf told him would be of great value, so he listened intently and acknowledged each piece of information with a positive nod or comment.

"Wilf, my strongest link to him is Shadow. I'm hoping he hasn't ridden him into the ground or crippled him in some way and abandoned him. If I can find my horse, the odds of finding Stiles are pretty good, I think. And Shadow is tough…very strong. He'll give it all he's got to stay upright."

Wilf knew this was true. The description of Stiles they'd given Daniel had come from Nathan's questioning of Johanna and Rosa. There were probably many men Daniel would come in contact with who would loosely fit the given description, especially if Stiles cut his hair at some point. Daniel had not questioned Johanna for additional information about Stile's appearance. He had not been able to do that, and Wilf understood.

When they stopped for lunch in early afternoon, Wilf suggested that Daniel take his Sharps rifle, rather than the Winchester which was cradled in the scabbard aboard Zeb.

Wilf affectionately patted the stock of his rifle saying, "Daniel you should take my Sharps and leave the Winchester with me. "This one," he said, indicating the rifle on his saddle, "will take out a silver dollar at two hundred yards."

"Have you ever actually done that?" Daniel asked, eyeing Wilf skeptically, knowing it was impossible to even *see* a silver dollar at two hundred yards.

"Nope, would be a waste of good money, but I know she could do it. No doubt."

It was the only laugh they shared that day, but it was welcome.

They were still in territory Daniel had hunted over the years, so from time to time they would stop and discuss the terrain. Wilf, even though he'd spent most of the tracking time of the earlier hunt looking at the ground, had no trouble navigating his way, while observing the surrounding hills and draws.

They were having some prime weather, the last glimpse of summer, and the men were glad to have it. When evening came and they made camp, Wilf commented that they would probably reach their parting point sometime in mid morning of the next day, if they kept the same pace they had all day.

The evening air was cool and Wilf built a good fire with plenty of fuel on the side to add during the night, should either of them wake.

They began settling in for the night and Wilf again turned the conversation to the task at hand. He began by again offering the Sharps to Daniel.

Daniel hesitated and said something he knew would be true, regardless of how long it took to find Stiles and regardless of what the circumstances of the find would be. "Wilf, I don't intend to kill him with a long shot from a rifle. I intend to kill him as close as I can get to him. He is going to know who I am and *why* I'm killing him. He won't have to guess and it will be no surprise shot."

There was a long pause, the only sound heard being the steady crackle of the fire, hungrily consuming the wood.

Finally Wilf spoke, "That's hard to do. It isn't easy to kill someone close up, even if you've done it several times. I know. I have. You need to be sure about it and my advice is to not let him get close enough to do the same to you. It'll be a lot easier for him to pull the trigger than it will be for you."

Daniel nodded, knowing that Wilf was speaking the truth. "I know," was all he could offer in return.

"Wilf what do you suppose makes a man feel he can rob and kill innocent people and beat and rape women and torture people who have no way to defend themselves? How does that happen?"

"Don't know Daniel, I've never understood it. Never will, I guess. Just some people feel it is their right to do that. They're real brave when they're going after a woman or someone who can't defend themselves. They don't listen to reason and they feel no remorse. I do know that. Only way to stop them is to kill them, and that's the hell of it. You end up doing something you'd rather not, because you know you have no choice. That's why I understand you being out here. I just don't want to see you get killed in the process. That would be…a very sad thing."

"You ever have a family, Wilf?"

"Yes I did. Wife and baby girl, like you. They both died…and I miss them. Wish things could have been different, but they're not and I've had to learn to live with it."

"You ever think about getting married again? Starting over?"

"Nope, couldn't go through that again. Just don't have it in me. Can't have any more losses. Not in this lifetime."

Daniel understood what he was saying, sure that if he ever lost Johanna and Sarah it would be difficult or impossible to even imagine starting over.

Wilf put more wood on the fire and again the topic turned to the hunt Daniel was about to begin. "You know that even when you kill him, there will be things that will never be settled."

Daniel noticed Wilf had said, *when*, not *if* and replied, "I think that I have to take this one step at a time Wilf… and just work my way through it. I'm trying not to get too far ahead of myself."

"Good plan. I think that's wise. " Wilf knew that Daniel was as ready as he could possibly be for this mission. He seemed calm and determined, not looking for vengeance, but rather some form of justice and settlement of debt. There was a difference, Wilf knew, and now he was pretty sure that Daniel knew the difference as well.

Wilf had done things during the war that he was not proud of. Things that haunted him. He'd killed men who were not men…merely boys. He'd killed in anger and desperation to stay alive and in vengeance for friends he'd lost. It had changed him.

Now, watching the fire, trying not to let the memories come too close, he hoped that somehow Daniel would get through this without losing himself.

CHAPTER 25

LOOKING

THE MORNING DAWNED WITH A clear sky, no wind, and cool, crisp air that made getting up and moving easy. Daniel knew that if he weren't on this trek, this would be the weather that would prompt him and Ellis to do some deer hunting. They would begin the task of filling the meat house for the winter. As things were, that would have to be an assignment that Ellis tackled alone.

Wilf and Daniel made a fire, ate breakfast, quickly saddled their horses and moved westward as they had the day before. Time went quickly and half-way through the morning Wilf found a shotgun shell that he'd missed the first time over this ground. This one was covered with mud and barely visible in the meager brown grass. He dismounted and picked it up, explaining to Daniel that the shells formerly found had aided him in the earlier pursuit.

A while later they came to a familiar stretch of shale and Wilf pulled up and turned and looked in all directions. "This is about it, Daniel. This is the place I lost Stiles." He said the words in a way that Daniel knew was a painful admission for him. Wilf raised his right hand and stretched it out in front of them. "From here...he could have gone just about anywhere."

Daniel sat in his saddle and quietly looked around. On the trail yesterday, he had remembered the morning on the fourth day of the cattle drive, when he'd had the uncomfortable feeling that someone was watching or following them. From his conversation with Nathan and Wilf, he knew that was about the time his family was being attacked.

There had also been the episode with the deer in the cemetery. Daniel couldn't explain either event and didn't try to. All he knew was that something or someone had been speaking to him. He was hoping that when they got to this point, somehow he would know which way to go. Now this morning, Wilf could see that Daniel was thinking and trying to decide which direction to take, so he sat quietly and didn't offer any advice, because at this point he had none to give.

Daniel looked at the terrain both north and south and his intuition told him "south." He couldn't explain it, he just felt it. He looked both directions again and then felt sure he should head south. South from where they sat the terrain was easier. North meant climbing, working to get across a high ridge. Going south, Stiles would have been able to move more quickly, and the man was trying to get away, not only from the law, but also from his companions. "It's south, Wilf."

Nodding, Wilf replied, "That's what I'd do to get away quick." Taking a deep breath, he continued, "I guess this is as far as I go," He knew he must let Daniel go on alone and return to Fergus, as he had promised Nathan.

"Glad you got me this far, Wilf. I really appreciate it." Daniel turned Zeb and moved to Wilf's right and extended his hand.

"Take care out there," Wilf said, as they grasped hands. "We'll be waiting for you when you get home."

"I will," Daniel replied, withdrawing his hand and turning Zeb southward. He looked back as he moved away and waved, kicking his horse into a brisk trot and then a light canter. He knew he needed to distance himself quickly to make it easier for the deputy to turn towards home.

As Wilf sat and watched Daniel disappear into the distance, the urge to kick his horse and go after him was intense. He knew that alone, Daniel was in way over his head and might be killed. After about fifteen minutes he turned Champ east and said, "Let's go home boy."

Daniel let Zeb come back down to a trot and then a brisk walk and it was quite some time before he pulled up and let Zeb take a rest. He didn't look back in the direction he'd come from and by afternoon, he was well beyond territory he'd ever traveled before. Even though this was a place he'd never been, he didn't feel lost or fearful. In his mind he was sure he was going in the right direction and somehow, he believed, he would find Stiles. He had to believe that.

Nightfall found him in a long draw with a wide and well traveled path that he'd been on for about two hours. All day long he had traveled the path of least resistance, as he felt this is what Stiles would have done. Now, he pulled off the trail and headed up to the top of a ridge, so he could see ahead.

In the distance he could see lights that indicated human presence. It looked like a cluster of buildings, perhaps a small town or community of some kind. He decided to wait until daylight to ride towards it. He didn't want to get shot as an intruder or suspected rustler.

He went back over the crest of the ridge he'd just climbed, found a level spot and made camp. Heat from the fire felt good and he settled in for the night, realizing this would be the first of many nights he would camp on ground he didn't know. Daniel was tired, but he felt good about the day's travel. Wondering what the next day would bring, he fell asleep, listening to coyotes howling in the distance.

In the morning, Daniel rode toward the cluster of buildings, which was more of an encampment than a town. It consisted of several crudely-built shacks that housed rough people who eyed Daniel with suspicion, as he rode in. There were several men and Daniel saw two women and a few children. They identified themselves as the Oakleys, and Daniel spoke to two older men. He stayed mounted on Zeb, as he was not invited to step down. Taking his time, he questioned them about Shadow and the O'Neal/Sullivan brand and a man with dark hair riding the gray horse. He led them to believe he was chasing a horse thief, saying nothing about the damage Stiles had left in his wake.

They said they hadn't seen anybody like that recently and Daniel watched their reactions carefully, trying to decide if they were telling the truth or not. He was pretty sure they were. He knew for sure Stiles wasn't among them as he'd spent an hour up on the ridge in the early morning hours watching these people and their corrals through his field glasses. Shadow and Stiles were not there. After a few minutes of Daniel asking questions and the Oakleys eyeing his Winchester and Colt, Daniel departed. They hadn't asked him if he was a lawman, but he knew they suspected he was. Daniel didn't indicate that he wasn't. He left it at that. He thanked them for their time and moved on.

After leaving them, Daniel had ridden further south and then taken cover and watched his back trail, making sure none of them came after him to rob him of his horse, weapons, money, or his life. He knew he'd be doing a lot of this in the days ahead. This was part of Wilf's admonition to "be careful"… he could take no chances.

The rest of the week was more of the same: Encountering ranchers, miners, travelers, and entering a few ramshackle towns and encampments. Each person questioned, each ranch observed from a distance before approaching, each town patrolled and searched before asking anyone anything. There were a few friendly small ranchers, eager for visitors, who offered him a meal and visited with Daniel about how things were further north.

At no time did Daniel share his intentions in this search or the true nature of the man he was pursuing. He kept his voice calm and casual when asking questions. He never knew when he might encounter someone who knew or had traveled with Stiles. Daniel's ability to read people improved by leaps and bounds and after a few days on the trail he began to appreciate men like Wilf and Nathan, who made their living and bet their lives on this ability. When speaking to people, he kept his right hand near the grip of his Colt, not in a threatening way, but in a manner that he hoped looked relaxed, yet ready.

After two weeks Daniel was seasoned in this hunt and had traveled southwest out of Colorado and into Arizona. The look of the people changed. It was warmer, there was more sun, and the people began to look acclimated to that. The rims of the hats were wider, the clothing lighter, and the skin more tan. The houses were built differently: less fortified against cold weather, with chairs and tables outside under awnings of wood and canvas. For the most part the people were welcoming, friendly and curious about where he was from. He knew he looked different from them, a person of more northern climate.

Daniel's pace was steady but not hurried. Being his frugal self, he bought few supplies. He killed a deer, set up camp and converted most of the meat into jerky and filled up on fresh venison. He missed Johanna's bread and vegetables from the garden. He missed Johanna. He missed home.

After a month the trip was beginning to get long, carefully covering every small town and ranch in his path. Now moving in a switchback pattern rather than a straight line, he got directions wherever he could, learning about all of the surrounding towns, ranches and mining encampments.

Daniel sometimes had the feeling he was traveling in circles, but he continued the pattern, knowing it was the only way one man could cover the area he must. Zeb was slowing down and showing signs of being pushed.

Daniel had to tighten his belt as he'd lost weight and he was wearing down. He'd stopped shaving and the few articles of clothing he had were starting to look tough. He knew he'd have to find a place to rest himself and his horse soon. For now, he pushed on.

CHAPTER 26

RESTING PLACE AND CROSSROADS

Moving further into Arizona, Daniel's intention to slow down and rest had remained just that, merely an intention. During the seventh week of the hunt, late one afternoon, Daniel rode into a small ranch that was the most prosperous looking he'd seen for at least a couple of weeks. He was greeted by a man who came out onto his porch carrying a shotgun, verbally admonishing him not to come any closer well before Daniel had reached the front hitching post. Realizing he must look like a vagabond of some sort, he pulled Zeb up, slowly raised his arms and asked the man not to shoot, adding that he meant no harm. Out of the corner of his eye, he saw two additional men who looked much younger come out from behind the north side of the house. They were carrying rifles that were pointed in Daniel's general direction. Daniel repeated that he meant no harm, that he simply was seeking information.

Perhaps it was Daniel's calm voice or the way Zeb lowered his head that made the armed men relax just a bit. The older man on the porch identified himself as Max

Sims, the owner of the ranch and he demanded to know what Daniel wanted.

"I'm looking for a horse thief...a man who stole a horse of mine...up north in Colorado."

"Son, you rode all the way down here from Colorado, looking for a man who stole one horse?"

"Yes sir, I did."

"Must have been some horse," Sims replied, in a voice that said he wasn't quite sure he believed what he was hearing.

"Yes he is. My best stallion, wearing my brand...stolen over eight weeks ago."

"Who are you and what's your brand?"

"My name is Daniel O'Neal from up near Fergus, Colorado. Have a ranch in that area and my brand is the O bar S. "

One of the armed men to Daniel's right, stepped out from the side of the house and walked around behind Zeb so that he could see the brand on Zeb's left hindquarter.

The man walked to where he could see Daniel's face and said, "Big gray stallion, maybe about six - seven years old? That be the one?"

Daniel, who still had his hands above his shoulders could feel his heart begin to race. He had no idea if these men were friends of Stiles, or what their dealings with him had been. He only knew they had the drop on him and there was no way he could reach his pistol or rifle before they could shoot him.

"Yes, that's him," was all Daniel said cautiously in reply.

"Man who rode him was a real son of a bitch. Caught him a week ago in the pasture, trying to steal our best mare in broad daylight, had a rope on her and was heading out. Took a shot at him, missed, damn it, and chased him for three miles after he dropped the mare's rope. Damn that stallion can run! You can put your hands down now."

Daniel felt himself smile for the first time in weeks as he dropped his arms to his sides. "Yes, he can move."

"You're a sight for sore eyes man. Why don't you step down off that run down horse and take a load off."

Daniel dismounted and walked with the man carrying the rifle to the hitching post and looped Zeb's reins over the rail. Sims, with the now-lowered shotgun, invited him into the house. The home was clean and neat and Daniel immediately felt out of place in his filthy clothing. Mr. Sims was very hospitable, as was his wife, who was introduced as "my wife Rebecca." "These are my two sons, Jeb and Michael."

"I'm pleased to meet you," Daniel replied.

"Please join us for some supper, won't you?" Rebecca asked in a pleasant voice, and turned to finish cooking dinner in the kitchen with another younger woman, whom Daniel imagined was a daughter, or wife of one of the other men in the room.

"Jeb, take this man's horse to the barn and *feed* him something, double down on some oats and put some hay in front of him." Jeb left to do that.

"I'm really dirty, do you have a place where I can wash up?" Daniel asked.

"Not a problem," Sims replied, "just go through the

back door, there's some soap on the shelf and a pump out back.

Daniel followed the man's directions and was soon pumping water into a basin and scrubbing his face, hands and arms up to his elbows. It was the first time he'd washed anyplace other than in a stream for weeks and he took advantage of it. He brought the towel hanging next to the pump up to his face and the scent of home reached his nostrils. He held it there, smelling the clean towel and felt as close to Johanna as he had since he'd left the ranch. He turned to see Sims watching him. "Sorry, I just haven't been home for a while and this feels good."

Sims nodded knowingly. "Yup, I was away in the war for three years, so I know what you're talking about, Mr. O'Neal. Why don't we sit, while my wife finishes dinner." He indicated a couple of comfortable looking wooden chairs nearby, under an outside roofed area, which undoubtedly provided shade on hot summer days. Daniel gratefully sat down and thought of his swing at home, as he sank into the chair. He leaned back and took a long, deep breath, relaxing.

Sims sat down in a chair across from Daniel and said with real interest in his voice, "Now tell me about this horse thief from Colorado,"

"The man is not from Colorado, he's from somewhere up around Chicago, a city way up north."

"I've heard of it," Sims replied, "How did he come to your place?"

"Came in while my hired men and I were on a cattle drive with my neighbors. We took our cows east to the rail head, about eighty miles, so we were gone several days. This man, Stiles, and two of his friends, came onto my ranch and stole some horses. Sheriff and posse chased and killed the two friends, but Stiles got away…that's why I'm tracking him now." Daniel was looking down at his hands in front of him while he told the story.

Max Sims sat silently for a bit, digesting what Daniel had told him. He cleared his throat and said, "Mr. O'Neal, I get a strong feeling this is about more than a missing horse. Am I right?"

Daniel looked over at his host, meeting his gaze, nodded and said quietly, "Yes, this is about more than a missing horse."

"Anything else you want to tell me about this?"

"No. Only if Stiles ever comes back here, don't let him near your house or your family. Just kill him."

"I will, you can bet on it," Sims said in a sober tone.

"Dinner will be ready in just a few minutes now, if you boys want to wash up," Rebecca's voice carried out to them.

Sims and his sons made the trip to the basin and then everyone, including Daniel filed into the house and ate dinner. Daniel was offered additional helpings of everything and hunger overrode manners that evening.

Afterward the men sat and talked about cattle and horses, while the women, Rebecca and Jeb's wife Cora, washed dishes and put things away. Max asked about Daniel's family and their ranch in Colorado and Max told Daniel how they'd come here from Georgia after the war.

After conversing for about an hour, Daniel realized he was exhausted.

The weeks of travel and a stomach full of food caused his eyelids to begin to fall and Max gently touched his arm and offered a room upstairs where he could get some sleep. Daniel hesitated, saying he would gladly sleep in the barn, but everyone insisted, so he took them up on the offer. He slowly climbed the stairs and was directed to his room for the night, a small bedroom at the end of the hall. Once he hit the bed, he was asleep in moments.

The Sims family prevailed upon Daniel to stay for another day and night, giving him time to rest, shave, take a bath, have his clothes washed, clean his weapons, and eat. Daniel was torn, especially after hearing that Stiles had been on this ground a little over a week ago. His instinct was to get back on the trail immediately and track Stiles down. However, he knew it would be to his advantage to be rested when he confronted Stiles, so he had stayed with the Sims. Zeb benefitted too, grazing and resting in their pasture.

Daniel saddled up early on the second morning and the entire Sims family came out to see him off. Daniel realized how much he'd needed this rest and he thanked all of them profusely.

"Well, you looked like hell when you got here, but you look a little better now," Max said smiling broadly. "Besides, we don't get that much company. You are always welcome here, and I hope you catch Stiles. He's a bad one." Both of the boys agreed and wished Daniel well. Rebecca called out, "Now you be careful out there." He nodded and said that he would.

Daniel mounted Zeb and said, "If you're ever in Fergus, Colorado, look me up. My family and I would be glad to have you." They said they would, though Daniel was fairly sure he'd never see them again. "You're good people," he added, then turned and rode out of the yard, grateful that there *were* good people. More good than bad, he knew.

The following days were intense, as Daniel rode hard to cover as much ground as possible, ground that Stiles might have covered after being chased by Jeb Sims. Daniel went to the last place Jeb had reported seeing Stiles and quickly found a trail that he tracked for several hours until it merged onto well-traveled road leading straight south. While following the hoof prints that he was sure had been made by Shadow, Daniel felt excitement and anticipation. He felt as near to Stiles as the prints he saw on the ground ahead of him. Those feelings faded rapidly as he lost the trail onto the road that carried hoofprints of numerous horses, wagon tracks, and evidence of animals being driven ahead of riders. He was left with only feelings of frustration and disappointment.

As he urged Zeb south, Daniel tried to watch both sides of the road, looking for a place where Shadow might have been reined off to head in another direction. He found no such place, so he continued on the road. It led to dead end encampments and small towns that took up his time as he looked cautiously for a horse and rider that seemed to have disappeared.

October turned into November and Daniel was now in southern Arizona. He was rapidly running out of resources. The money he had allowed himself to take from his family's reserves was almost exhausted. Once again, he and Zeb were tired and needed rest. Daniel's careful questioning of people along the road had led to no new leads as to Stiles' whereabouts. One day, late in November, Daniel literally came to the end of the road.

The road he'd been following came to a T. Daniel stopped and looked in both directions. He knew if he headed east, he would ultimately enter New Mexico and then Texas, if he went right, he'd come to California. He felt no inclination, heard no inner voice that urged him either way. Knowing he had to go one way or the other, he reined Zeb to the right and after about an hour he saw a structure rising in the distance.

He first recognized a short steeple and as he got closer saw the church beneath it. People were exiting the church, mounting horses and climbing into wagons and carriages, most of them heading west. Daniel reined up and continued to watch the people as they visited with one another and departed the church.

"Must be Sunday, Zeb," Daniel said as he leaned forward and stroked the horse's neck. "Next, they'll be headed for home and Sunday dinner."

When everyone including the priest had departed, Daniel rode up to the steepled structure, dismounted and for no reason that he was consciously aware of, walked up the wooden sidewalk and tried the door of the church. It was unlocked and he entered, carrying his rifle and saddle bags, which he never left with Zeb when he dismounted and walked away from the animal.

The interior of the church was quiet and the only light came from small clear windows on either side of the church, the votive prayer candles which burned in their glass holders, near the front of the sanctuary and the red glow from the altar candle.

Daniel dipped his fingers into the container of Holy Water just inside the door and briefly dropped to one knee, crossed himself while facing the altar, then rose. He walked halfway down the aisle and stepped into a pew to the right. That was where he always sat with his family in the church at home.

He sat down, placing the Winchester and saddlebags on the pew beside him as quietly as possible and then sighed. He hadn't worshiped in church since Easter and had not been to confession since June. "Not much of a church going record lately," he thought to himself. He remembered that when his father had been alive, the entire O'Neal and Sullivan family group had made the trek to church at least twice a month regardless of the weather or what needed to be done at the ranch.

He relaxed in the pew and looked around at the interior of the cool quiet place. Daniel had been in only two other churches in his life, the Catholic and Protestant churches in Fergus. One he worshiped in with his family, and the other he occasionally entered to attend weddings or funerals of friends.

This church looked nothing like either. Both churches in Fergus had been built by European immigrants to Colorado, with steep steps leading up into a wood framed building. This one had no steps, was made of adobe and had a low beamed ceiling, dark wooden altar, and the crucifix above and behind the altar was the finest piece of wooden sculpture Daniel had ever seen. The crucifix in his home church was roughly carved in comparison to this one, and painted a shade of white with pale facial features. This one was made of richly colored tan wood, beautifully carved, and polished so that in the near darkness it almost looked like a real human being hanging on the cross.

Daniel studied the figure intently and then heard his own voice whisper the words, "Christ, what am I supposed to do?" He hadn't planned on saying anything, so was somewhat startled by the words coming from his mouth.

There was no answer to his question, just as there had been no answer to his question of "Why?" in the cemetery weeks before. This time, no deer appeared to give him comfort and he was left with his own thoughts. He must decide what to do next and he reckoned this was as good a place to do it as any.

Daniel let his thoughts wander to places that up to this point of the journey, he had not allowed his mind to go. He'd been gone from home a long time now, longer than he'd ever been away. In all of those days, there had been only one person he'd found who had seen Stiles and Shadow. He knew that sighting was reliable, but there had been nothing since. It was time to deal with the possibility that he'd never find them, never be able to administer what he regarded as justice, and never retrieve Shadow before going home.

He wondered if he could admit that the hunt had been unsuccessful and just leave it? He sat there for some time, trying to picture what that would be like. He imagined being back at his ranch, knowing Stiles was still alive and free. He didn't like how that felt. What was his alternative? To go on? He was no longer sure he was even headed in the right direction. He was nearly out of money, he and Zeb were exhausted, and the T in the road felt like it had been a sign, forcing him to make a decision.

Daniel again looked at the figure on the cross. Christ hung there silently, suffering. Or was He dead, Daniel wondered? There was no way to know. Daniel only knew that there had been a terrible miscarriage of justice to bring Christ to the moment he now witnessed. Would this dying or dead man before him understand Daniel's pursuit of justice, or would Christ, could He speak in this moment, ask Daniel to forgive Stiles, go home and leave the justice part to God, at some future time.

Again, Daniel heard himself asking aloud, "Christ, what am I supposed to do?"

At that moment, there was a sound of rustling and whirring behind Daniel. Quickly and instinctively, Daniel turned to his right and put his hand on the grip of his Colt. The sound came from above and behind him and it took Daniel only a moment to realize that what he was hearing was the sound of a bird, stirring on the rafter furthest from him in the rear of the church.

He relaxed and let his eyes search the dimly lit church to locate the creature. It lifted from the rafter and flew straight down the aisle above Daniel's head, and landed on the floor, directly in front of the altar. Rather like a pigeon, only smaller, it was a dove of some kind, Daniel surmised, a type he'd never seen before. Once more the bird took flight and landed awkwardly on the end piece of the pew just ahead of Daniel. As in the cemetery during his en-counter with the deer, Daniel sat motionless and looked at the bird, as it cocked its head from side to side and looked directly at him.

As slowly as possible, Daniel rose from the pew and backed down the aisle. He reached the door and opened it, and stepped outside, holding the edge of the door between his thumb and first finger. Within seconds, the bird flew past him and Daniel turned his head to observe the bird's path of flight; it flew west.

Daniel watched the small dove until it was no longer visible and then went back inside. He sat down again in the pew next to his saddlebags and Winchester. As with the deer, Daniel felt he'd been spoken to by this creature. He felt the deer's message was that James was safe, but what was he to make of this latest encounter?

Slowly, as he sat there looking at his dimly lit surroundings, a plan of what he was to do came into his mind. He was sure it was the right answer, if there could be a right answer to his dilemma. He would go west to the town the churchgoers had come from; he'd rest, resupply and then head home to Jo, Sarah and the ranch. It was really all he could see to do. Daniel told himself that he'd done all that was humanly possible; not finding Stiles was not because he hadn't given it everything he had. Somehow, he knew, he would have to live with this decision; it would have to be good enough.

In this peaceful place, he felt calm about the finality of his choice. He bowed his head and prayed the only prayer he'd offered on this mission. "Almighty God, help me get home safely to my family and keep them safe until I get there."

CHAPTER 27 *

JOHANNA AT HOME

A COLD NOVEMBER SKY GREETED Johanna as she stepped outside the back door of the house to gather eggs from the henhouse. There was a feeling of snow in the air and Johanna hoped it would hold off for awhile, as this was the day Ellis or Swifty would go to town for supplies. Still encumbered by the sling on her left arm, she awkwardly wrapped the shawl she was wearing more tightly around her shoulders, as she entered the warm, quiet house where the hens were nestled protectively over their eggs.

Using her unfettered right hand, she gently took the warm orbs from beneath the slightly riled birds and placed them into her basket which she had set on a shelf by the door. She wondered which of the men would be making the trek to Fergus today. She wasn't sure, as they alternated their departures from the ranch, never leaving the women and Sarah unprotected. Johanna hadn't been to town since the attack in August and she was sure that now she wouldn't be going in for quite some time.

Every hour of the first couple of weeks after Daniel's

departure she had anxiously watched westward for his return. When inside the house every sound she couldn't identify brought her to the front window. But as the days turned into weeks, she became less and less hopeful that the ordeal of waiting would end anytime soon.

She spent the days recovering from her injuries and working as much as she could, hoping to exhaust herself so she would quickly fall asleep at night, rather than pacing around in the darkness worrying about her husband. Sometimes it worked, sometimes it didn't. There had been many nights when Johanna had not slept at all, worried about what might be happening to Daniel and what she and Sarah would do should he not return to them.

She had tried to resume some sort of normal routine, but without the daily contact with Daniel and her brother James, she found it very difficult to feel normal at all. There were constant reminders all around her of what had happened that fateful morning in August, which sometimes seemed like only yesterday.

Dealing with her shattered china closet had been heartbreaking. Two days after the attack, Rosa had removed all of the broken shards and taken them to a place over 200 yards from the house and discreetly buried them, carefully disguising the burial site so Johanna would never find it. When she was recovered enough to sit at the dining room table, Johanna and Rosa had carefully inventoried the surviving pieces. She now owned only two complete, undamaged place settings and a motley array of odd pieces, some of which, though serviceable, were chipped and visibly damaged.

Johanna sighed, "There's no way we can use these few

pieces for anything. Let's wrap them up and put them in the chest upstairs. Someday I'll give them to Sarah as a keepsake from her great-grandmother. I can't bear to look at them anymore." Tears were descending her cheeks as she said these words and Rosa made no reply but went to the downstairs bedroom and retrieved a stack of crumpled brown paper. Johanna was badly hampered by her broken left arm, but together she and Rosa wrapped the china.

Rosa made the trip upstairs to put the salvaged china in the chest at the foot of Johanna and Daniel's bed. She carefully placed it beneath the winter clothing, blankets, and dress material Daniel had brought from Culver. It was a sad day for both of the women, as it was a sign of defeat of their attempt to make the ranch a more civilized and gracious place.

By the middle of October, when the weather had begun to get colder, a new anxiety overtook Johanna. She had begun to feel sick in the mornings and having gone through this a number of times, she knew what the queasy, dizzy feelings meant. She was quite sure she was pregnant. Rosa said nothing, but Johanna was sure she knew as well.

One morning, when Johanna had come downstairs later than usual, Rosa had asked her if she was alright. That was all it had taken for Johanna to break down and cry, "No, Rosa, I'm not alright, I'm pregnant." The two women had embraced and Johanna had sobbed, as she had when Daniel had come home from the cattle drive. Johanna didn't need to elaborate to Rosa her fear that the baby might be Stiles' because Rosa understood that completely.

Johanna knew full well the child might be Daniel's, but the uncertainty about who the father was, coupled with the fear that Daniel might not return home alive, caused Johanna more worry and anxiety than she had ever experienced in her life. She had difficulty eating, could not concentrate on daily tasks, and for the most part slept very little. She knew that soon Ellis and Swifty would be able to see that she was expecting a child and she knew they would speculate about who the father was.

And then there was faithful Calvin, who came by at least once a week to check on how things were going. Once he knew, his wife would know, and then everyone in the area would know. For the first time in her life, Johanna worried about what people would think of her. As long as she could remember, her reputation had been governed by her family ties and the integrity that came with it. She had never had concern about what people might think or say about her. Since August, all of that had changed and now it was of utmost concern. More than that, she had no idea how Daniel, should he survive and return home, would deal with the prospect of another man being the father of her child.

Even Sarah knew her mother was not acting the way she normally did and had asked Johanna one day, "Mommy are you mad at me?" Johanna had hugged her daughter and kissed and cuddled her, assuring her that, "No, Mommy's not mad at you. Mommy just misses Daddy." After that, Johanna had tried very hard not to show Sarah her concern and fear. But, concern and fear were her constant companions.

After gathering the eggs, as she was exiting the hen-house, she saw Ellis standing in front of the porch patiently waiting for Johanna to give him the list he would need in town that day. "Good morning, Mrs. O'Neal, do you have the list for town?"

"Yes I do, Ellis. Just wait one moment and I'll get it." She went into the kitchen, where Rosa was stoking the fire and preparing to make breakfast. The list was on the table where she had prepared it the night before. Picking it up, she hesitated a moment, wondering how she would word her request for the extra thing she would need Ellis to do that day in town. She must make it sound casual and routine.

Once on the porch and down the steps, she handed the list to Ellis, took a breath and said, "Ellis, I wonder if you would stop by Doctor Messinger's office and ask if he might come out to visit me in the next week. I need him to check my arm." She said this while gesturing to the splinted, bandaged left arm, which she still kept in a sling most of the time, to hasten its healing. "It's been nine weeks and I think it's nearly healed, but I want him to check it."

"Certainly, Mrs. O'Neal. I'll be glad to do that." He looked at the list, to see if there was anything he needed to clarify, but it was all very straightforward. There were just a few things on the list, but they were all important. "I'll be back as soon as I can." He said this reassuringly, so she would know he wouldn't be lingering in town after the errands had been completed.

"I appreciate that, Ellis. Please be careful."

"I will, Ma'am." He tipped his hat, placed the list in his pocket, turned and headed to the barn to saddle his horse and head for Fergus.

Johanna turned to go back into the house, grateful she had Ellis and Swifty to take care of the many tasks that needed doing each day. She had no idea how they would have made it all these weeks without them.

Johanna's feelings toward Daniel vacillated daily, sometimes hourly. She loved him deeply and feared for his safety but also sometimes felt angry at him for leaving her and Sarah to pursue Stiles. He was endangering everything they had for a chance at revenge and justice. It had taken Johanna several weeks after Daniel had left for her to go visit her brother's grave for the first time. That day all she could think of after returning to the house was, "I hope Daniel kills him!" Her emotions ran wildly from one point to the next, like a child first learning to walk, going from one thing to another.

Sometimes at night when all was quiet, Johanna tried to pray. It was difficult. She knew that praying that the baby was Daniel's was pointless. That had already been determined. She prayed that Daniel would return to them safely, but wondered if that had already been determined. What if he were dead? Would she ever know when or where he'd died? She knew her faith was being tested, as it had been when two of her babies had died. Since she'd been a young woman, she'd known this could happen... that it did happen to women all the time.

But, when it happened to her, it had seemed like some sort of punishment...perhaps by God. Punishment for what, Johanna had no idea. She had struggled for several years, trying to understand why two children had been lost to her and Daniel, and she had no answers. She had felt turmoil for a long time until the birth of Sarah. Then there had been a quieting of her doubts, her questioning. Now she could feel the turmoil returning, buffeting her soul. So, when she prayed, she prayed only for calm. If she had that, she reasoned, she would hopefully be able to face whatever happened next.

That afternoon when Ellis returned from town, he delivered the supplies and told Johanna that Doctor Messinger had said he would be out in a day or two. Johanna simply nodded and thanked him, feeling only dread with this news.

Two days later, Doctor Messinger and wife Ellen arrived midmorning. They shared coffee and cookies and the doctor examined Johanna's left arm and was very pleased with the way it had healed. He removed the splint and bandage which made Johanna's arm feel extremely light and easy to move, though stiff and somewhat sore. The doctor cautioned her about using the arm for a while, asking her to take it easy and not do any heavy lifting for at least another month. He gave her instructions about exercises to strengthen the muscles and praised her for being so patient and careful to bring the arm to this point of healing.

There was an awkward silence as Johanna looked to Rosa who quickly spoke to Sarah. She asked the girl to help her with something outside and the two of them put on their warm wraps and left by the back door.

Johanna cleared her throat, knowing she didn't have a lot of time before the woman and child would return. "Doctor, I believe I'm pregnant," was all Johanna could say before the tears began escaping her eyes. Ellen moved over to the chair next to Johanna and put her arm on her shoulder. "Oh my dear," was her quiet reply.

The Doctor questioned her about her last monthly cycle and when she'd had sexual relations with Daniel and then paused. It was clear to him that this child could belong to either Daniel or Stiles and he knew that Johanna was in a state of agony about this reality.

"The most important thing at this time is your health, Mrs. O'Neal," he began. "I remember during your last pregnancy we had you remain in bed a good deal of the time to help ensure a live birth."

"Yes, that's what we did," replied Johanna softly. The tears were still coming, streaking her face, and she wiped them away with a handkerchief Ellen handed her.

"I think that very soon, probably in the next month or month and a half, you'll need to begin spending most of your days resting in bed if you want this child to be born alive." Their eyes met as he said this and Johanna knew full well what he was saying.

"I do want this child," Johanna said, pausing, "but I'm afraid of the possibility… I don't know if it's Daniel's and I know there is no way to tell. I have to pray and hope that it is his. I can't risk losing it. Do you understand?"

Both the doctor and his wife nodded and the doctor replied, "Yes, we understand, Mrs. O'Neal." He paused and then added, "You are very brave."

"I don't feel at all brave, I only feel desperate," Johanna replied.

The room remained silent for a moment and then Doctor Messinger added, "I will come out at least once a month to check on you, as I'm sure you are not going to want to risk a wagon ride to town. The rough road is too dangerous, it might cause you to lose the child."

Johanna was grateful for this offer. She didn't want to risk a ride to town, not only because it would be dangerous for the baby; she didn't want to be gawked at by the people there. Even though many of them were friends and people she liked, she knew it was just too much to ask for them not to speculate about her condition.

After the Messingers left, Rosa and Sarah returned to the house. Johanna announced happily to Sarah that now that her arm was free they could begin the task of making two new dresses for her. Sarah, of course, was delighted at this prospect and so Johanna began the process of dressmaking for her daughter.

She would wait until after the baby was born to use the material Daniel had brought home to make two new dresses for herself. Johanna decided that the material that had been bought for shirts for James would be put to good use in making two new aprons for Rosa. Evenings, after Sarah had been put to bed, found Johanna and Rosa sitting together in the living room, silently sewing on their respective projects.

Rosa used colorful thread to adorn the aprons with bright flowers and birds. Johanna made the dresses for Sarah larger than her current size to give her room to grow into them.

Both women thought of their husbands and recent times past, when everything had been different, but neither spoke to the other about their private thoughts. Occasionally they would look up, meet each other's eyes and smile knowingly.

CHAPTER 28

THE FIND

AFTER COMING OUT OF THE church, Daniel approached Zeb, replaced the Winchester in the scabbard and tied on his saddlebags, talking to the horse as he did so.

"We're going home, Zeb. Gonna' go down the road, rest up a bit, get some supplies and in a day or two head north."

Daniel had been talking to the horse for weeks. There were days that the only words he spoke aloud were to this roan animal, and he had gotten to the point where he imagined Zeb understood every word he was speaking.

Zeb, used to reading Daniel's body language and touch, knew that something was about to change. Daniel was moving in a more deliberate way than he had for awhile. The horse responded by perking up his ears and snorting loudly, moving away from the hitching post briskly after Daniel mounted and turned his head to the west.

The town they entered a few minutes later was very quiet. It was Sunday and none of the few stores on the main street were open. Daniel dismounted and walked ahead of Zeb, looking for a livery stable and a place to bunk down and get some rest. The town saloon was ahead on his right and there were only two horses tied to the hitching post. Daniel automatically looked them over carefully, but neither horse looked remotely like Shadow.

Daniel remembered walking the street in Culver after the cattle drive. He recalled how clean the windows of the shops had been and how proudly the merchandise had been displayed. The windows of the shops here were quite dusty in comparison and the merchandise looked nothing like the stylish fare of Culver.

Daniel noticed he could barely see his own reflection but unconsciously straightened up when he saw it. What reflection he could see showed a much thinner and more ragged image than he had ever seen looking back at him.

Suddenly Daniel stopped. Something in the window of the store in front of him caught his eye. He moved closer, tied Zeb to the hitching post and stepped up onto the board sidewalk. He continued toward the window, until he was less than an arm's length from the glass. On a table, just inside the window lay a beautiful fox pelt. Daniel craned his neck to see the tail of the fox trailing to his right. It was black as far down as he could see. The end of the tail wasn't visible, but something about the pelt made the hair on the back of his neck stand on end and he could feel his pulse pick up. "Damn," he whispered, "that looks like the pelt James took last winter."

He shaded his eyes and looked deep into the store. Was it possible the owner was inside? He went to the door and rattled the handle, but there was no response and he saw no movement inside. He went back to the window and bent to one knee, so that he was as close as possible to the glass pane.

He examined the other items on the table resting on the pelt and his eyes fixed upon a silver candle stick. "Jesus Christ." The words escaped his lips in a gasp. It was one of the two candlesticks that had sat in his wife's china cupboard for all the years of their marriage. It had been brought to this country by the Sullivans. It was one of the two that were brought out and placed on their table, only at Christmas and Easter. Daniel was not the most observant person when it came to candlesticks and things of that nature, but he was sure this belonged to Johanna and the Sullivan family. There was only one way in the world it could have come to this place. Stiles had been here and might still be. Daniel rose and looked around the street, his right hand momentarily went to the butt of his Colt. He felt a heightened sense of awareness.

Slowly he untied Zeb, mounted and rode down the street to the livery stable. The door was open and he heard a hammering noise coming from the inside, as someone worked on a horseshoe.

"Afternoon," Daniel called out loudly as he entered.

"Howdy," came the reply, "can I help you?"

"Yes, I wonder if I could put my horse up for a night or two?"

"Sure could, no problem." Daniel noticed several horses in the corral behind the stable and casually walked out the back door to look at them. None were his missing horse.

"Who owns that store across and down, the one with the red and yellow sign?"

"That would be Maynard Mills. He buys and sells and has a pretty good line of hardware."

"What time does he open in the morning?" Daniel inquired.

"Oh, that varies, sometimes 8:30 in the morning, sometimes later. Whenever he gets up and at it. Mondays, usually earlier, rather than later."

"This town have a boarding house?"

"Well, my sister runs a little place down on the corner. White house with blue trim. Has a couple of rooms she rents on a regular basis, people goin' through. She'll feed you breakfast and dinner, too, if you throw in a little extra."

"Thanks, I'll walk down there and talk to her. What's her name?"

"Ruby...Ruby Metzker and I'm Tony Anderson."

"Pleased to know you, Tony," Daniel said, extending his right hand, " I'm Daniel Johnson." Daniel had decided he'd not use his correct last name if he ever got near where Stiles actually was. He didn't know if Stiles knew his last name, but he was not going to risk it.

"You gonna stay around here, or just goin' through?"

"Haven't decided yet. For now I just need a place to rest. I'll decide about stayin' or goin' in a day or two, probably."

"Fair enough. I'll take care of your horse. He's welcome here for as long as you stay."

Daniel unsaddled Zeb and put the saddle across a

saddle tree that Tony indicated he should use. He led Zeb outside and turned him loose into the corral with the other horses. "Give him some oats if you got 'em and some hay and rub him down good. He needs some care."

"Fine. Will do that."

The stable was clean and the horses in the corral looked well cared for. Zeb was in a good place. Now he must find a place to settle in himself.

He walked down the street, carrying rifle and saddle-bags until he came to the house on the corner Tony had indicated. It was as neat and well cared for as the stable. Must be a family trait, Daniel thought as he was ushered into the upstairs room to which Ruby assigned him. She was cheery, but wanted to know too much. Daniel was careful to reveal only that he was traveling through and didn't mention his mission or that he was from Colorado.

Ruby was disappointed not to get any useful information from her new boarder, so quickly left him to get settled. Daniel's first item of business was to go to the window overlooking the street and examine everything below very carefully. There were few people or horses in the street this quiet Sunday afternoon, and Daniel knew he'd have to explore it, looking for any sign of Stiles. In the meantime he wanted to clean his extra set of shabby clothing, take a bath and shave, so he spent the rest of the afternoon accomplishing that agenda. Afterward, he had dinner in the kitchen with Ruby, Tony and a fellow boarder named Bolton, who was as quiet about his intentions as Daniel.

By the end of the meal, it was obvious that Ruby was pretty frustrated with both of them for not revealing anything important about themselves, so each man took his leave. Daniel went to take a walk about the town and Bolton read a book on the front porch. Daniel explored the entire town, which didn't take long, looking at each house as casually as possible. There were a number of homes that had small barn sheds behind with fenced in areas for their small collections of livestock. Daniel looked at every horse he could visibly account for and saw none that resembled Shadow.

He thought about possibilities and realized that hoping Stiles was still there was an outside chance. More likely, Stiles had come through here, pawned the belongings he'd taken from the O'Neal ranch and moved on. The question was: How long ago had that occurred?

Daniel knew that the hours until morning would seem like a lifetime and he was right. Sleeping was almost impossible, even though the bed was relatively comfortable. Each time he dozed off, it wasn't long before he would wake and look at the amount of light coming through the thin curtains. He wanted this night to be over quickly, so he could find out what the storekeeper could tell him about how he'd come into possession of the pelt and candlestick.

A number of times, Daniel thought about how he would craft his inquiry. It was about an hour before dawn when Daniel, only because of exhaustion, finally fell into a deep sleep. He was awakened by Ruby tapping on his door to announce that his laundered clothing was being placed outside his door and that breakfast would be served shortly.

After dressing and descending the stairs, he was greeted with a hearty breakfast, which he had a difficult time eating as swallowing was nearly impossible. He wasn't hungry, only anxious for the next couple of hours to be over with. Daniel noticed that his hand was trembling when he raised his coffee cup to his lips.

"Mr. Johnson, are you alright?"

"Yes I am Mrs. Metzker," Daniel replied as firmly as possible, "Just need my morning coffee to steady myself for the day." Daniel thought how ridiculous that sounded, but it was the first thing he'd thought of. Ruby seemed satisfied with the answer, but he noticed a curious look from both Tony and Bolton. He smiled and tried to act as normal as possible, but still found it difficult to eat or carry on a conversation. He was as nervous as he remembered being for a long time and he thought about his conversations with Wilf about a possible confrontation with Stiles. Would he, he wondered, be able to keep the upper hand when dealing with the man he'd been tracking for months now? It was the first time that any doubt had entered his mind.

He tried to shake this off and focused on getting through the meal. He glanced at the clock. It was just before 8:00 A.M. and Tony had said it might be 8:30 or later before the owner of the hardware store arrived. Between now and the time he entered the shop he must find a way to restore some calm to his countenance. He forced himself to eat what was left on his plate and have a second cup of coffee, just to prove to himself that he could do it.

Tony and Ruby were talking about an estate sale she hoped to attend at the end of the coming week and Daniel tried to concentrate on what they were saying, just to divert his attention. He slowly sipped the last half of the cup of hot liquid and took a couple of deep breaths. He saw Ruby turn her head to look directly at him.

"And Mr. Johnson have you decided if you'll be staying with us for this evening?"

Daniel lowered his coffee cup, noticing that his hand was now steady. "I'll know by noon probably, Mrs. Metzker. I'll try to let you know as soon as possible, as I realize you may have other people wanting to stay here." With that, Daniel pushed his chair back from the table, stood up, retrieved his hat from the shelf by the door and exited the house.

He turned left and headed down the street, noting that there were people out and about this Monday morning. He hoped the shop would be open within a few minutes, because he knew it would determine what he did next. He thought of the decision he'd made about going home, yesterday in the church. Now, he was sure that whatever he learned in the shop would alter his plan considerably.

In preparation for what might happen today, Daniel had spent about an hour during the previous sleepless night cleaning both the Colt and Winchester. The Colt was on his hip and the Winchester in the room he'd slept in the night before. He thought carrying the rifle around town this morning might attract too much attention, but he knew that no one here would think it suspicious to be wearing a sidearm.

Daniel took up a post on the front porch of the saloon, sliding down onto a beat-up straight back chair that had undoubtedly been sitting there since the saloon was built. It creaked under his weight and wobbled unsteadily. Daniel sat very still, so as not to make any noise or risk the chair collapsing. His entire attention was focused on the store just a little down and across the street. The morning sun warmed his face and he tried to take deep breaths to relax. No one walking in the street or on the wooden sidewalks seemed to notice him, which helped him feel a bit more calm.

A man wearing a brown shirt and pants and a worn bowler hat was walking quickly past Daniel's position across the street. He was fumbling in his trouser pocket for something, and Daniel saw him withdraw what could only be a key. The brown clad man walked directly to the shambled-looking hardware store, inserted the key and pushed the door open. It took a great deal of self control for Daniel to wait ten more minutes to let the proprietor complete his opening ritual. Daniel pushed himself up out of the pitiful chair and casually walked across the street and entered the store. He knew he must appear to be calm and clear headed.

The interior of the store was as much a shambles as its outside appearance. Things were very disorganized and not well dusted. The few aisles in the business were crowded and very narrow. Daniel walked to the window display and moved so that he could see the entire fox pelt, including the end of the tail, which was as Daniel remembered: a few brilliant white hairs in stark contrast to the remainder of the tail which was coal black. Daniel felt his knees trembling as he picked up the candlestick, the most dustless item in the display, turned it over and saw Johanna's grandparents initials engraved on either side of the now long-dead silversmith's trademark. Slowly, Daniel sat the precious item back down onto the hair of the pelt.

Daniel turned to find the store owner eyeing him curiously. "Can I help you with something this morning, sir?"

Daniel walked over and met the mans eyes directly, "Are you Mr. Maynard Mills?"

"Why, yes I am," the man answered smiling, wondering how this unknown ruffian knew his name.

"The fox pelt and the candlestick in the window," Daniel said, pointing towards the window with his right index finger, "brought in here by a dark haired man, dark eyes, about six foot tall?" Daniel made it a question to be answered.

"Yes…yes, he was dark haired, had it pulled back, went long down past his shoulders."

"How long ago did he come in here?" Daniel could feel his own heartbeat in his neck as he spoke, trying to be calm.

"Hummm, well now let me see," Mills said, looking towards the ceiling, tapping the fingers of his right hand on the counter. "It was about a week ago…ten days at the outside."

Daniel took hold of the counter, to steady himself. "Have you seen him since then?"

"Nope, only seen him that one time. Just came in here to hock the pelt and the candlestick."

The word "hock" brought a flash of anger to Daniel's voice. "They weren't his to do anything with. They were stolen from my house, several hundred miles north of here."

Mills obviously didn't like where this conversation was going. He took a step back from the counter and crossed his arms at the elbow defensively. "Well now, that's something you'll have to take up with the local sheriff, which might be difficult at the moment, as I understand he has gone looking for some horse thieves."

Daniel nodded, "I can understand that. I'm taking this up with you, Mr. Mills. How much did you give him for the pelt and the candlestick?" Daniel dreaded the reply, as he was afraid it might take all the cash he still had to get these items back.

"Let me check." Mills was now perspiring heavily and Daniel noticed as he took his ledger book down from the shelf behind the counter, it was Mills' hands that were shaking as he turned a page or two back in the ledger. "Now let me see. Yes here it is. Yes, it was eight days ago and it was just those two items…hmm, it looks like I gave him three dollars for both items, and he wasn't very happy about that. However, as I explained to him, I just don't have much call for those sorts of things. Thought mainly they would look nice in the window." The small brown clad man said these words without any understanding of what "those sort of things" had cost Daniel and his family. The two men spent several moments, just staring at each other.

Daniel spoke first. "Do you have any idea which direction the man went, after he left your store?"

"No, can't say that I noticed." Maynard Mills didn't add that he hadn't noticed which direction the dirty, sleazy looking man had ridden after leaving the store because he'd been too busy looking at the candlestick and the initials stamped on the bottom of the fine silver piece, knowing he'd made quite a deal for himself.

Mills continued, "You have to understand, Mister… I'm sorry, what did you say your name was?"

"Johnson, Daniel Johnson."

"Well you must understand, Mr. Johnson, that I had no idea these items were stolen from you, or anyone else."

Daniel took a deep breath, reached into his back pocket and pulled his remaining money out and counted his last, precious cash. He had seven dollars left to his name. "I will give you your three dollars back."

Mills eyed the other bills in Daniel's hand hungrily, but knew he dared not ask for more than he had paid the thief for the items Daniel was trying to retrieve. The idea of making a profit on the candlestick evaporated.

"Of course, I want to be fair about this, as I am a law abiding man myself, you understand."

Daniel didn't reply to this, but asked if the store owner could wrap the candlestick in some brown paper to protect it on the coming journey, which Daniel now realized would not be towards home.

Wordlessly, the proprietor retrieved the pelt and candlestick from the window, feeling a pang of loss as he did so. He took the items to the counter and tore off a meager piece of brown paper from a large roll and wrapped the candlestick in it. He was about to hand the item to Daniel when he again spoke.

"You know, Mr. Johnson, if I were going to speculate about the direction the man you are seeking took, I would guess west to the next town of Rimrock. It's not much of a town, but there's an ongoing poker game at the Crown Saloon. Sometimes when players run out of money they bring things here to pawn so they can stay in the game. Can't say as I help them out much because the items they bring in are usually not worth much, but it's cash money and that's what they're looking for."

Daniel was grateful for this information, as it was the closest thing to a lead he had. As he picked up the wrapped candlestick and draped the fox pelt over his arm and prepared to exit the store, he thanked Maynard Mills in as polite a manner as he could. Once out of the store, he walked back to the livery stable where he paid Tony and thanked him for taking such good care of his horse. He saddled Zeb as quickly as possible, collected his things at the boarding house, told Ruby how much he'd enjoyed his stay and made a hasty exit. Ruby was left to wonder what was in the brown paper package and what this odd man was doing with a beautiful fox pelt? She followed him out of the house, stood on the porch and watched him ride west.

CHAPTER 29

RIMROCK

DANIEL COVERED THE TWENTY-FIVE MILES to Rimrock, Arizona quickly. When he arrived, he found a town that was smaller than Fergus, and not nearly as prosperous. It looked run down and beat up. He quickly located the Crown Saloon and looked over the few horses tied at the hitching posts in front of the establishment. Not finding Shadow, he moved on to the livery stable and examined the corral and then patrolled the streets, up and down to no avail. He knew he had to find a place to settle to investigate further. Once he had Zeb stabled, and had found the cheaper of the two boarding houses in town, he set out on foot to see if he could find either his horse or Stiles.

Walking into the Crown Saloon was a nervous proposition, even though he was sure Stiles wasn't there at the moment. The place was a dive, there was no other way to describe it. The light was dim, the smell was of tobacco spit, urine, and Daniel was pretty sure someone had vomited somewhere on the premises recently. The bartender was short, nearly toothless and there was a stubby cigar jammed into one side of his unshaven face.

"What'll it be?" was his greeting.

"Whiskey," Daniel responded.

While the bartender poured his drink, Daniel looked around the place which was possibly Stiles' territory. In the corner nearest the bar, four men sat around a fairly large round table playing poker and goading one of the players about the time it was taking him to play his cards. Not much else was happening in the saloon at the moment.

Daniel casually questioned the bartender about the poker game and found that it was open and ran all the time. The bar opened at ten o'clock in the morning and closed at midnight, unless there was an all-night poker game going. The bartender wanted to know if Daniel was interested in joining the game and Daniel answered that "No, he was just curious." There were rooms upstairs, the bartender continued and a "couple of girls were available," if Daniel was interested.

"No, I'll pass,," Daniel replied. He carefully framed his next question. "Do some guys come and go here, look-ing for a game?"

"Oh yeah," the bartender replied, "Some guys are around here all the time, some you'll only see once a week, once a month, or a few times a year. Depends on whether or not they have money to burn."

"I see," Daniel said, trying not to show any emotion. "Thanks." He tossed back his drink, which was the worst whiskey he'd ever tasted in his life. He walked back out into the sunlight, wondering what kind of player Stiles was. Would he see him in a day, a week, a month, or had he moved on? If he had lost his meager three dollars, maybe he'd moved on down the road. Or, if he'd won, maybe he was somewhere in the area, waiting to play again.

Daniel absently walked along the street, his mind turning all of this over. If he was going to wait around here for Stiles to re-show, he'd have to find a way to earn money so that he could afford the wait. Where could he find employment here, he wondered?

The question was answered by a sign in the mercantile store window, across the street and two doors down from the saloon. "Help Wanted," the roughly written sign said and Daniel took a deep breath and walked into the place. He was greeted by a fairly large room, stacked floor to ceiling, wall to wall. The place was dirty and had a stale, overbaked smell to it. The man behind the counter wore an apron and was waiting on a woman who couldn't decide how much flour she wanted, one sack or two. The man in the apron had obviously dealt with her before and was exasperated. "Mrs. Madsen, if you buy two sacks, you know you'll use it eventually, whereas if you only buy one, you'll run out more quickly." The woman continued to hem and haw and the man looked over her shoulder in Daniel's direction and nodded to him, to let him know he'd be with him as soon as possible. Daniel waited patiently until the woman had left the store, having decided to buy one sack of flour.

"Can I help you, sir?" the man said, wiping flour from his hands, as he sized Daniel up, deciding this would be a small sale.

"I hope so," Daniel replied, giving the man his best

smile. "I saw your sign in the window and am looking for work, so I thought I would inquire."

"Have you ever worked at a store like this before?"

"No sir, I have not, but I've been in a few of them in my lifetime. Bought a lot of goods in stores like this," he said, eyeing the place closely and thinking of Emily Westphal who made sure that her family's store was always impeccable. She would no doubt shake her head in disbelief at this place.

"Are you good with numbers and working with people?"

"I have some education, if that's what you mean. Worked on ranches, had a family once and covered a lot of ground between here and Wyoming."

"What happened to your family?"

Daniel looked at the floor and then up at the man, hoping he looked truthful. "They died...drank bad water...my wife and daughter. I don't like to talk about it much. Been moving around a lot since then. Now just want to settle for awhile and decide what to do next." Daniel added no more, hoping it would be enough to prevent more questions.

"Well, I need help, that's for damned sure. Last man who worked here left about a week ago and took some of my merchandise with him. Lousy Texan. Have no use for them."

"Well, sir I am a hard worker and I'll learn anything I need to know and I've never been to Texas."

The man with the apron laughed, extended his hand and said, "I'm Conrad French."

"I'm Daniel Johnson, pleased to meet you. When do I start?"

"How about right now?"

So, that's how it began. Daniel became an employee of a mercantile store in a small backwater town in Arizona. He passed his days in the store, selling dry goods and hardware; always keeping his eyes on the hitching posts in front of the saloon, hoping Shadow would show up. At night, he'd leave his room in the boarding house which was two blocks over, to check and see if Stiles was in the saloon. About a week into his employment, he noticed a bedframe in the very back of the storeroom, a cot frame really, and asked Conrad about it.

"Sometimes things in town get rowdy, and I sleep in the back to protect the store from thieves and vandals."

Daniel turned this over in his mind. If he could sleep at night in the store, he wouldn't have to pay rent at the boarding house. Maybe by the time he got ready to go home he would have saved enough to replenish some of the family finances he'd spent on the trip. He suggested a plan to Conrad, saying that if he was in the store at night, Conrad could sleep at home and not have to worry about his business.

Leaving a relative stranger in his store at night would ordinarily have been something that Conrad French would have turned down in a heartbeat. There was something about Daniel Johnson that he trusted completely, and although he couldn't explain it, without hesitation he took Daniel up on his offer.

That night, Daniel took up residence in the back of the

store. He stored his belongings on an unoccupied shelf, unrolled the cot's mattress he'd found in a corner and laid down to sleep. Sleep did not come, only thoughts of Johanna and home. He rose from the cot and went into the store. He pulled the ladder used to access upper shelves over to the north corner of the building, then gathered a bucket, rags, soap and water from the pump out in back of the store. Daniel began cleaning every shelf, every can, every cannister and container in the store. Finally, when it was nearly dawn, Daniel finished the job by cleaning the counter which was covered with years of fingerprints and oil from the hands of hundreds of customers.

The entire store was spotless when Conrad came through the door at 8:30. He made no mention of how the store looked and neither did Daniel. But Conrad put extra cash in Daniel's pay envelope at the end of the week. During the next week, customers, especially the women, noticed the change in the place and commented to Conrad "how much more pleasant it was to come into his store nowadays."

Days blended into weeks and soon it was late December. On Christmas Day, Daniel ate at the boarding house with several of the residents and missed his family horribly. It was the first Christmas he had ever been away from the ranch and the ache he felt for home was all-consuming. He wanted nothing more than to just go home and be with Johanna and Sarah again. Something inside told him to wait. Wait at least a little longer. At least once a week, Daniel would go into the saloon to observe who was sitting at the poker table. There were some regulars, but often Daniel would see men he'd never seen before. It gave him hope.

His only refuge from the pain of missing home was to visit Zeb. Every few days, he'd saddle him and ride out of town for an hour or two. The horse had recovered well from the weeks on the trail and had put on some weight. So had Daniel; he could let out his belt a notch. In the store he found a shelf containing three pair of used boots. He tried each pair on and found one that fit perfectly. When he asked Conrad about the boots, Conrad hesitated and then told him they were the boots of men who had died in violent ways the last couple of years and had been too good to bury with the men who had last worn them.

Somehow, because he didn't know the man who had worn the boots, it seemed acceptable in Daniel's mind for him to wear them. At long last, he could finally deposit his old boots in the garbage pile out back. He found new clothing in the store, and as the weeks passed he bought a couple of new shirts and a pair of trousers. It felt good not to look and feel like a vagabond any more.

Conrad didn't ask him any questions about his past, but one day when Daniel was out of the store doing an errand he'd been sent on, the store manager went through Daniel's belongings and noticed how clean his clerk kept his weapons. He wondered about the candlestick, which he carefully re-wrapped once he'd examined it closely. What was this man doing with a valuable silver candle stick, and what was the meaning of the fox pelt? They were the only items of value Daniel owned. He kept his cash in the other saddlebag, along with his knife, flint and other personal items. Conrad knew this man had a story he wasn't telling, but he couldn't imagine what it was.

The first week in January, Daniel began to question the wisdom of staying in Rimrock any longer. He had already decided he would not go any further West. This was it. He would either find Stiles here, or he wouldn't find him at all. He told himself he would stay one more week and then head for home. He had made this pledge before and each time, he'd stayed on. This time, he told himself he meant it. Daniel had begun to feel detached from the reality that had been his life for thirty years and he didn't like how that felt. He was constantly aware of the fact that his absence was causing anxiety for Johanna and a strain on the manpower available at the ranch. He was coming to the end of his rope here and he knew it.

CHAPTER 30

STILES

IT WAS A DAY LIKE so many others Daniel had spent in the store. A customer came in and after paying for her box of supplies, said she needed help carrying her purchases to her small wagon parked out in front. Daniel obliged, visiting with her as he did so. He fit in well here with these people and the regular customers who came to Conrad's store liked Daniel; the conversations he had with them covered a wide range of topics, especially the current weather, horses and the rising cost of canned goods.

Daniel offered his arm to the woman as they crossed the sidewalk. He shifted the weight of the box of supplies he was carrying and together they walked to the back of the wagon where Daniel deposited the box. He turned and said good day to the woman who was chattering on about how she was looking forward to a visit from her daughter.

Daniel's field of vision was down the street to the east and as he turned to go back into the store he saw two riders approaching. He hadn't seen either of the men before. The horse on the side nearest the street was a deep gray color and larger than most horses in the area. Daniel froze in his tracks. As the two riders neared him, the gray raised his head and turned to look directly at Daniel. It was Shadow. There was no doubt. Daniel's gaze raised to take in the gray's rider.

He was tall, had long dark hair that was tied by a strip of leather at the back of his neck. He was rough looking, unshaven and unkempt. He turned to look at Daniel and it was then that Daniel realized he was staring. Quickly he lowered his gaze, turned and walked back into the store and immediately moved to the window where he could watch the man dismount Shadow and with the other man, enter the saloon. "It's him," Daniel whispered.

"Everything alright?" It was Conrad, who was watching Daniel closely.

"Yup, everything's fine. I just need to take a few minutes away from the store."

"Fine, take your time. Since things are slow today I'm thinking of maybe closing early."

Daniel removed his apron, went out the back door of the store and turned the corner to approach the saloon. He came up behind the horses shielded from the windows so he wouldn't be seen. He edged up to Shadow's left rear flank so he could observe the brand on the animals rump. He was sure this was his horse, but needed absolute confirmation.

The O'Neal/Sullivan brand was there, although it was not distinct because the horse was filthy and badly needed to be groomed. Shadow had lost weight, but looked sound. Daniel touched the brand and then worked his way toward

Shadow's head. The horse, turned his head and snorted, nodding his head up and down. It was obvious to Daniel the horse recognized him.

"Easy boy, easy," Daniel said softly. "Gonna get you home soon, you just have to be patient." He rubbed Shadow's neck and muzzle and stepped up onto the sidewalk.

He was unarmed. The bartender had never seen him wear a sidearm except the day he arrived, and Daniel knew that if he walked into the saloon wearing his Colt, the surly man would call attention to that fact. At this critical moment Daniel didn't want to stir any undue attention. His presence in the establishment would not be unusual as he had been in the bar at this time of day before.

Taking a deep breath he walked into the dim saloon and took a seat at the bar so that he had a very good view of the poker table. As calmly as possible he ordered a shot of whiskey and laid his money on the bar. The drink came and Daniel's total attention was directed toward the conversation that had begun in the corner.

A man Daniel had seen at the table many times came downstairs and shouted at the dark haired man sitting at the table, "Stiles, where the hell have you been?"

"None of your damned business," Stiles replied.

Stiles. There it was. The name. Daniel knew this was the man who had been on his land and in his house five months before; the man who had killed James, raped Johanna, and had been the companion of the men who had killed Hernando and ransacked his home. His heart was pounding, but he tried to remain calm and observe Stiles carefully. The dark haired man at the poker table had a

Colt pistol, worn on his right side. A large sheathed knife was attached to the back of his belt. Daniel had noticed there was no rifle scabbard attached to Shadow's saddle.

"Are you ready for a game, Stiles? Bring your money?"

"I got money, Asshole, so just deal the cards."

The man who had ridden into town with Stiles was seated in the opposite corner of the bar talking to another customer and did not seem to be interested in joining the game.

Daniel had no idea how long this game would take and he had things he needed to do as quickly as possible, so without waiting to listen to any more of this less-than-cordial conversation, Daniel downed his whiskey and left the saloon as quietly as possible.

Back at the store, he approached Conrad French and told him that he was leaving Rimrock.

His employer's face registered his deep disappointment. "Why Daniel? Why are you leaving now?"

"I'm sorry, Conrad, I really am. I have enjoyed working for you, but something's come up and I have to leave right now. I'm sorry." Daniel moved his hands outward in a contrite gesture. "You don't owe me anything more than you've already paid me."

"Nonsense Daniel, I will pay you the wages you are due through today, but I'm very sorry to see you go. You are the best employee I've ever had." As he spoke, he went to the small office just behind the counter and came out carrying some cash which he gave to Daniel. Accepting it, he shook Conrad's hand, went into the back room and organized his personal belongings, leaving them on the shelf. He went back into the store and picked up several things he knew he would need. Conrad didn't want to take his money, but Daniel insisted. He thanked Conrad for giving him a job and again apologized for leaving so abruptly and left through the back door.

After paying the liveryman for Zeb's care he saddled the horse, then led him to the back door of the hardware store and loaded his rifle, saddlebags and the rest of his belongings onto the waiting animal.

From his many trips to the livery stable, Daniel had learned that from the upstairs loft, he could see the front of the saloon and the hitching posts. That's where he headed, tying Zeb at the back door of the livery stable, near a bucket of water he could reach. The liveryman and Daniel had become well acquainted over the previous weeks, so he had no problem letting Daniel take a perch in the loft and asked him no questions about why he wanted to do that or why he was armed. He had learned long ago to keep his head down and his mouth shut in this sometimes volatile town.

In the loft, Daniel settled near the street-side opening, out of sight, and waited for Stiles to leave the saloon. It was his intention to follow, ambush, and kill him. If the man who rode in with Stiles left with him, Daniel would just have to deal with him when the time came.

Within the hour, Daniel watched Conrad French come out of the mercantile store, lock it up, and go home. Daniel knew he would forever be grateful to this man who had trusted him and given him a way to stay in Rimrock and wait for Stiles to appear.

About four hours later, in mid afternoon, Stiles and the

man he'd ridden in with came out the door of the saloon and stood near the hitching rail and talked. Daniel couldn't hear what they were saying, but Stiles' companion was agitated and gestured emphatically; their disagreement was obviously major. After several minutes, the second man threw up his hands, got on his horse and rode out of town in the direction they'd come from. Stiles rolled and smoked a cigarette and went back into the saloon.

It began to grow dark and Daniel alternately paced, sat and crouched near the loft window. He could not afford to lose sight of Stiles now that the man was within reach. Daniel had often thought about what his plan of action would be once he confronted Stiles. He knew his best chance of killing the man and getting away with it was to ambush him in a place where he would not be seen or easily found. The last thing Daniel wanted or needed was for one of Stiles companions to come after him. He must simply make Stiles disappear.

Night fell and there was just enough light coming through the saloon windows for Daniel to see Shadow at the hitching rail. A couple of other men arrived and entered the saloon and Daniel could hear occasional loud laughter and swearing, no doubt coming from the poker table. Daniel relieved himself in the corner of the loft a couple of times as the night wore on. He sat down near the loft opening and focused on Shadow while trying to stay awake.

It reminded him of the night watches he and Calvin had shared, while riding on the cattle drive. Daniel dozed off occasionally and he wished he'd brought some jerky into the loft with him. He didn't think he dared leave for even a moment, because that would invariably be the time Stiles would leave. God only knew when he'd come back to Rimrock, so Daniel knew he must stay the course. It was a long night and by the time light began to show in the east, Daniel had drifted off to sleep out of sheer exhaustion.

Something, Daniel never knew what, startled him awake. Was it the sound of Stiles striking the match to light his freshly rolled cigarette? Or, was it Shadow snorting at the smell of the ignited tobacco? Daniel wasn't sure, but he was suddenly wide awake. Below him in the dimness of early daylight, Daniel saw Stiles walk off the wooden sidewalk, untie Shadow from the hitching post and mount the horse. He turned Shadow and headed down the street in the direction from which he'd ridden into town the day before.

Daniel carefully moved back from the loft opening and quickly moved to the ladder leading down into the stable below. He quietly exited the back door of the livery stable and mounted Zeb, who was dozing, as Daniel had been doing only moments before. "Come on guy, it's time to go."

Carefully, Daniel guided Zeb down a parallel street, heading east as Stiles had done. He continued until he was nearly out of town and then held up for a bit before turning and heading for the main street. As he turned east again, the sky began to lighten noticeably, and Daniel saw Stiles and Shadow just leaving town at a trot.

Keeping Stiles in sight without being detected was not easy. Daniel left the road to the left side, thinking that because Stiles wore his gun on the right side, he was most likely right handed. Holding the reins in his left hand, if he turned to look behind him, he would be most probably turn right in the saddle. With Daniel riding behind and to the left, he was less likely to be in Stiles' line of vision. Daniel dropped back further, barely keeping Stiles in sight on the road.

From his weekly rides with Zeb, Daniel knew there were a number of side roads that led in directions north and south off the road Stiles was following. He knew these roads led to small ranches, many owned by people who did not want their privacy invaded. Daniel had never ventured off the main road, not wanting to ride up to a place where he would have to explain his presence. He had never asked any of the Rimrock area residents about Stiles because he knew the danger of word getting back to Stiles about a stranger looking for him was too great. He'd merely waited for Stiles to come to Rimrock and to him.

Light was rapidly filling the sky and the air was warming. Ahead, Stiles kept moving at a very steady pace. Whenever possible, Daniel used the rolling landscape to keep himself hidden.

Daniel calculated they had ridden approximately two miles, when Stiles turned off the main road. He headed north on a small, barely visible trail. This meant that Stiles was going to ride across the ground in front of Daniel, about 300 yards out. Daniel pulled up and used a sandy sidehill to shield himself completely from Stiles.

After passing in front of Daniel, Stiles kicked Shadow into a quick canter and Daniel urged Zeb into a trot to keep Stiles in view. Ahead, Daniel could see smoke coming up from behind a rather steep hill and suddenly Stiles rode to the top of the rise and then disappeared behind it. Daniel slowed and carefully worked his way up to the rim of the bluff. He dismounted, dropped Zeb's reins, and worked his way on foot up to the top of the abrupt ridge and looked over.

Below was a small shack, probably not more than twenty feet square with a corral and a small shed behind it. The horse Stile's companion had ridden to Rimrock the day before was in the corral, along with two other horses. Daniel watched as Stiles unsaddled Shadow and turned him loose into the company of the other mounts.

"Shit," was all Daniel could think of to say that fit the situation. He knew he was in for another vigil. He worked his way back to Zeb, found some jerky and water and then reclimbed the hill to the top overlooking the shack. There was no use second guessing what he'd done. He felt that shooting Stiles on the way out here would have been a mistake. He'd have to just wait and see what would happen next.

Chewing on some jerky and drinking some much needed water, Daniel looked at Shadow in the corral. It angered him that after leaving the horse all night at a hitching rail, Stiles had made no effort to feed or water the animal. Shadow went to the watering trough, where a rusty pump stood. There was no water in the trough and after a few moments, Shadow wandered away, nibbling at meager grass along the fence line. One by one, the other horses made the trip to the empty trough and they too wandered aimlessly about the corral. Daniel knew that whoever was in the shack with Stiles, was worthless. He wondered if the other animals were stolen, and if so where they had come from.

Daniel imagined that Stiles was sleeping it off after playing poker and drinking whiskey for much of a day and an entire night. Daniel wished he could just lie down and sleep for a couple of hours himself, but he knew that was a luxury he could not afford.

An hour stretched into two and then two more. As the sun began dropping in the sky into late afternoon, things began happening in the compound below. At first, it was just an argument. From 100 yards away and through a closed door, Daniel could hear it. It was loud. There were three distinct voices escalating in volume by the moment. Suddenly everything spilled outside, when the door burst open and Stiles and his earlier companion came through the doorway, tearing at each other. It was a fist fight with the potential of becoming lethal, as both men were wearing sidearms. Daniel held his breath.

A third man who was bigger than either of the other two came roaring through the door as well, carrying a leather satchel in one hand and a canvas bag in the other, shouting at the top of his lungs. "God damn it Stiles, we've had enough! Now take your shit and get out! You've been nothing but trouble since you got here. I've had enough and I know my brother has too." The large man hurled Stiles' belongings into the yard.

At about this moment, the man's brother landed a tremendous blow to Stiles' midsection and Stiles sat down abruptly on the ground. His right hand moved as if to reach for his Colt and the brothers in unison drew their weapons. "Don't even think about it Stiles," the big man roared. "It wouldn't take much for me to shoot you right here."

There was silence and Daniel prayed to God that Stiles

would make no further move for his pistol. Stiles made some reply, but Daniel couldn't make out what it was. Slowly, because the wind had been knocked out of him, Stiles got to his feet, collected the two items on the ground, and walked to the corral. Daniel watched as Stiles saddled and mounted Shadow. During the entire process, neither of the disgruntled brothers holstered their weapons. They were too familiar with Stiles to take that chance. As Stiles rode out of the yard, the big man yelled, "Don't ever come back here Stiles, or I WILL kill your ass."

Daniel watched intently as Stiles and Shadow set out - not back to the road to town, which is what Daniel assumed they would do - but rather cross country away from the shack headed north. Daniel wondered if he was heading toward another small ranch or hideout that might be secluded somewhere in the hills beyond. Maybe he had other acquaintances in the area who would take him in. Obviously, over the past weeks Stiles had been "laying low" somewhere, because Daniel knew he had not visited the town of Rimrock until yesterday. There was no way to know the destination of this dangerous, unpredictable man. Daniel would simply have to follow him.

CHAPTER 31

ENCOUNTER

THE RIDE AWAY FROM THE small shack was slow and Daniel surmised that wherever Stiles was going he was in no hurry to get there. Daniel rode Zeb away from the overlook in such a way that neither of the men below would see him. He found himself totally focused and any exhaustion he had felt earlier melted away completely. Trailing Stiles at a distance, as he had earlier in the day, Daniel kept well behind and to the left of his prey. Zeb, too, was intent. Daniel could feel the alertness of the horse beneath him. As when herding cows or hunting elk, Zeb sensed that whatever they were doing now was important and that he must be aware of his footing, being careful not to trip or stumble.

Stiles turned a bit East and Daniel was glad not to be looking into the sun which was rapidly dropping toward the horizon. After nearly half an hour Daniel watched as Stiles headed Shadow into a narrow stream and pulled the horse up, allowing him to drop his head and drink deeply. Daniel knew this might be a place where Stiles would do a 360 degree look around, so he used a large clutch of bushes to conceal himself. Stiles did turn completely around in the saddle and look back. Daniel and Zeb remained motionless. "That's it, Shadow, drink big, it's been awhile," Daniel thought, "Take your time."

He watched Stiles and Shadow leave the stream and ride over a small hill some distance away. Daniel waited a moment and then urged Zeb into the stream in the spot where Stiles had been and let his own mount refresh himself. Daniel felt they were far enough away from both the compound they'd left earlier and the road, that the sound of shots would not bring anyone to the site of what was about to happen. He had a definite plan and he wanted it carried out in private with no fear of interruption.

"It's time Zeb," Daniel whispered. "Time we got this done and head home."

Zeb nodded, shook his head and then left the stream and they headed to the base of the hill where Stiles had disappeared a few minutes before. Daniel dismounted and went forward to look over the crest, so as not to skyline himself. Looking north and east, Daniel saw nothing moving. No horse, no man. Nothing.

"I don't believe this," Daniel thought, "He couldn't have gotten away from me that quickly." In the fading light, Daniel realized that what he'd feared most was happening. Stiles was apparently evading him.

"God damn it," Daniel said under his breath. Hurriedly he went back to Zeb and rode north just below the crest of the hill. He crossed it about 200 yards north of where Stiles had so that if the man was looking back he would be less likely to spot Daniel coming over the crest.

Finding some cover, Daniel pulled Zeb up and tried to calm himself and think about what he should do. It would soon be full dark and hours before moonrise. Stiles might suspect or know he was being followed and could be waiting out in the darkness to ambush Daniel. Daniel's only hope was that Stiles had no suspicion he was being followed and would soon build a fire. He had to pray for that. Meanwhile, all he could do was inch himself forward as quietly as possible, relying on Zeb's innate ability to do that without falling into a hole or off a cliff. Daniel leaned forward in the saddle and spoke quietly, "Zeb, I am counting on you to help me find this bastard in the dark." Zeb made no answering sound, but without any urging, moved forward into the gathering darkness.

Puzzled by how Stiles had slipped away from him, Daniel rode in a slow switchback pattern, not wanting to get ahead of him. After what he estimated to be half an hour the unmistakable odor of burning wood reached him. Daniel pulled up and let his face feel the direction of any breeze. What breeze he felt was coming to him generally from the north, to his left.

Daniel turned in that direction and after a few minutes, he could see the source of the smoke. It was orange in color and quite small, but it was a fire, burning in the distant darkness. Daniel pulled Zeb to a stop, breathed a sigh of relief and just sat there for a bit. That fire was the most welcome sight he had seen in a long time.

Slowly he dismounted and felt the soft, sandy, loose soil beneath his boots. He estimated the fire was about 800 yards away, and he would have to cover that distance very carefully. He'd lead Zeb about halfway in and then go on alone. He knew this still could be an ambush. If Stiles had any idea someone was in his wake, he might have built the fire for the sole purpose of pulling his pursuer into its light to kill him. Daniel had to move fairly quickly, as he had no idea how long Stiles would let the fire burn before going to sleep if this was a legitimate overnight campsite.

Silently Daniel removed his Winchester from its scabbard and as quietly as possible checked the chamber and confirmed that the hammer was at half cock. Leading Zeb through the darkness, conscious of every sound he made with every step, he finally reached a point where he knew he must leave his horse and go on alone. Wrapping the reins around the saddle horn, he put his mouth close to Zeb's ear and quietly spoke three words, "Stay here, Zeb." He removed his gloves, put them into his saddle bag and moved away from the horse without looking back, knowing Zeb would obey.

Stiles was keeping the fire alive and that gave Daniel hope that he was unaware he was being followed. Fifty yards from the fire, Daniel could easily see that Shadow had been unsaddled and was tethered. Stiles was lying on the ground near the fire, his head propped up on his saddle. From now on, Daniel knew his approach must be silent. Small, scrubby bushes and stunted trees gave him a somewhat concealed approach, but the vegetation had also shed leaves and small twigs which could make sound underfoot. He moved forward stealthily.

At ten yards Daniel stopped, took a deep breath, brought his rifle to his shoulder, cocked it and in the loudest, most commanding voice he'd ever used, shouted, "Stiles…sit up and put your hands on your head."

Stiles visibly jolted to a sitting position, his back to Daniel. Daniel shouted again, "Hands on your head Stiles, or I will shoot you right now."

Slowly Stiles raised his hands to his head and yelled back, "Who's there?"

"It's Joe and Nelson and we're coming into your camp." Daniel used the names of the two men who had been with Stiles at his ranch. Hopefully, this would confuse Stiles and help keep him temporarily immobile.

Quickly, before Stiles could think too much about what he'd just heard, Daniel walked into the camp, coming up behind Stiles to his right. Walking around Stiles, keeping him about five yards from the end of his rifle, Daniel watched Stiles' face intently. As Daniel moved into his line of vision, Stiles' face visibly relaxed, as he saw the man approaching him was neither of the men Daniel had mentioned.

Very aware that Stiles was still wearing his revolver Daniel said sternly, "Keep your hands on your head and if you move at all, I will shoot you."

Stiles asked in a voice of genuine curiosity, "Who the hell are you? I've never seen you before in my life." Daniel could see that Stiles' mind was racing, trying to connect Daniel with some place or event from his past, and his expression showed he was coming up blank.

Daniel now stood directly in front of Stiles the fire to his right, the Winchester aimed at Stiles' chest. "My name is Daniel O'Neal."

Stiles shrugged, saying, "That name means nothin' to me."

"The horse you are riding has the O'Neal Sullivan brand. I'm the O'Neal part, my wife is the Sullivan part." Daniel said no more, letting what he'd just said sink into Stiles' mind.

The look of realization was discernable. Stiles tried to cover it by saying, "I bought that horse last fall, near the Texas border. I don't know where he came from. Don't know nothin' about no brand on that horse."

Daniel didn't hesitate. Stiles had played his hand and now Daniel played his. He said the words slowly, quietly, and distinctly so Stiles would understand them perfectly: "Before Nelson died, he told the Sheriff and his deputy who you were. My wife described you. I've been tracking you since the first of September, Stiles. You killed my wife's sixteen year old brother while he was *fishing* and Joe shot my good friend while he was unarmed in my yard. You *are* the man who was in my house."

There was silence, and only the sound of the fire was heard.

Stiles knew he'd played his last hand, but he was not going to beg for his life. Until the end, he would try to do harm. "You left your wife alone," he said, beginning to smile, "She was just waiting for…"

Daniel was not aware that he'd pulled the trigger of the Winchester but he was aware of walking forward and looking down at the man who was slumped back against his saddle, taking his last breaths. "Go to *Hell* Stiles," he said quietly as he drew his Colt and placed his second shot between the eyes of the man lying on the ground.

Daniel stood silently for about a minute, not moving,

watching the last of the light go out of the dark eyes as the body below them became completely relaxed.

He holstered his Colt and stepped back, feeling his knees begin to tremble and he was barely able to maintain his grip on the rifle. He turned his back to Stiles and took several deep breaths, feeling he might vomit.

After a few moments, he raised his head, wet his lips, and issued a loud whistle which quickly summoned Zeb out of the darkness.

Daniel walked to Shadow, followed by Zeb, and stood at the edge of the firelight between the two horses and wept quietly.

The next half hour went quickly. Daniel carefully went through Stiles' belongings, looking for anything that might have come from the O'Neal ranch. He found nothing familiar. There was an ornate pocketwatch in Stiles' pants pocket that had a picture of a woman on the inside left of the watch face. It was engraved on the back "Love to you James. Charlotte. 1864." It was obviously expensive and Daniel had no way of knowing if it had been stolen from someone or won in a poker game. He would take it to Nathan and let the lawman decide what to do with it.

In the satchel and leather bag, Daniel found only clothing that was dirty and worn. He piled that on top of Stile's body, along with the few cash bills and coins. He placed Stiles' saddle and blankets next to the body and then carefully poured the two large canteens full of lamp oil he'd brought from the hardware store over the body, clothing, saddle and blankets. He scoured the surrounding area, looking for small, loose pieces of wood and twigs and found an abundance. This he stacked around Stiles in a makeshift funeral pyre, until the body was no longer visible.

The lead rope and halter he'd purchased from Conrad French's store went on Shadow. Daniel put the bridle and reins Shadow had been wearing onto the growing pile of brush, blankets and human remains. Daniel wanted nothing that had belonged to Stiles to find its way back to the ranch. Next, there was the matter of wrapping the end of a piece of dried wood with a rag Daniel had brought along with him. He tied Shadow's lead rope to his saddle horn, mounted Zeb and walked the horse over to the campfire, which was dying rapidly. Leaning down and touching the rag to a remaining flame, he paused a moment, while the rag caught fire and then flipped it over onto the waiting pyre.

Within moments the dry brush, oil soaked blankets and clothing caught fire in a rush of flame. Quickly Daniel turned the horses and they trotted away from the blazing campsight. Under no circumstances did Daniel want the smell of Stiles' burning corpse to reach his nostrils. Several hundred yards away he turned to look back at the fire, which was now raging. One look back was all he needed.

Daniel turned Zeb's head north and they rode carefully through the darkness for several miles before pulling up. He found a place on a rise, near a substantial tree and tied the horses to it. Daniel then pulled the saddle off Zeb, drug it a few feet, lay down on the ground, wrapped himself in his blanket, and within minutes, the exhausted man was asleep.

CHAPTER 32

HOMECOMING

THE TRIP NORTH, EXCEPT FOR weather near the end, was much less difficult than the trip south had been. Daniel found the road he had traveled on so many miles south and used it to expedite his trip north. He stopped at the first town and bought supplies. He wanted to avoid other small towns and encampments that he had visited during the previous months so he could be as invisible as possible on the trip home. The fear of being tracked north was always in his thoughts and he circled and bypassed as many people as possible.

He thought of going back to the Sims homestead to let them know he had been successful in his mission but then decided against it. It would mean giving details, and Daniel had no intention of divulging them to anyone except maybe Nathan and Wilf, should they press him.

Traveling during daylight and camping at night beside ever larger fires as the weather turned colder, Daniel's thoughts were filled with Johanna, Sarah and the ranch. He ached to be home with them, hold them and try to pick up their lives where they had left off before the cattle drive. Some part of him doubted if this would be possible. There had been so much damage. He continually longed for the comfort of his family, his ranch, and his own bed.

A hundred miles from home, it began to snow. Even though it made travel more difficult it meant that Zeb and Shadow's hoof prints disappeared minutes after they'd been made. By this time he had left roads and trails and was traveling cross country and for the first time since leaving Arizona, Daniel felt "safe." The only people he would meet now would be game hunters.

The very last of January Daniel rode over a rise and saw a familiar ridgeline in the distance. He felt his heart rise in his throat, as he knew he was a day's ride from home. "Yes!" he shouted and then began to laugh out loud. Shadow, who was beneath him that day startled at the shout and Daniel patted the horse's neck to settle him. "It's okay boy. It's okay, we're nearly home." Again he shouted, so that any creature listening within the sound of his voice might know of his joy. He turned to look at Zeb on the lead rope. The horse was looking at him attentively, as he hadn't heard this many words from the man in over a week. "Zeb, God damn it, we made it. Can you believe it?" Zeb, with his usual good nature, snorted and bobbed his head.

At this point, the two horses and the man looked quite tough. They were on the ragged edge of hunger all the time because of the pace of the last month. The horses had been made to depend on grass they could reach by pawing the ground and Daniel's diet the last two weeks had been game he'd shot during the day and cooked in the evening.

He was running low on ammunition, had run out of coffee and other staples, and was down to one meal a day. A couple of days ago he had decided that when he reached his home territory, he would first go to Fergus, clean up, and get some clean clothing before going to the ranch. He had become accustomed to his appearance but did not want his wife and daughter to see him in this condition. He would postpone his homecoming for just a bit longer.

Early the next morning Daniel rode away from his last campsight. The night before had been cold with a bitter north wind. He had spent much of the night feeding the fire to keep from freezing, and trying to deal with the feelings of anticipation and anxiety about the next day's homecoming.

He'd thought about it often in the previous weeks. He knew this ride into his yard would be far different from any he had experienced in his lifetime. He'd finally decided not to think about what he would say or anticipate what those greeting him might say. Daniel knew he would simply have to experience it as it happened. The last five months had been spent dealing with unknowns every day and he was looking forward to falling back into a routine of familiar activities and everyday responsibilities. Every part of him yeaned for his earlier, simpler life.

In mid afternoon Daniel spotted the smoking chimneys of Fergus. The wind coming in his direction brought smells of cooking as well as burning wood. Daniel picked up the pace and was soon trotting down the main street to the livery stable and sheriff's office.

The snow that had fallen here a week ago was now brown and more mud than snow along the street and up against the wooden sidewalks. Few people were out and about this time of day and the ones who saw him didn't seem to recognize him. He wondered if Nathan and Wilf would still be in the office or would have gone home for the night. Through the window, he saw light from a kerosene lamp as he pulled up to the hitching post. He brought his right leg over Zeb's neck and slid off onto the ground, tied the reins to the rail, stepped up to the door and slowly opened it.

Nathan and Wilf were sitting in their usual positions, Nathan behind the desk and Wilf on the bench near the door. Both men looked up and it took a moment for them to recognize the road-weary man.

Wilf spoke first, "Oh my God, I don't believe it," he said with disbelief as he stood to face Daniel. "Oh my God," this time louder. He took one step, embraced Daniel and pounding him on the back said, "I'd given you up for dead, kid."

When he pulled back and looked Daniel in the eye, Wilf's eyes were brimmed with tears. He quickly brought his hand up to his face to brush them away and then turned to see Nathan next to them. The embrace Nathan gave Daniel was wordless - one that warriors exchange, knowing without speaking what has happened to the other. While embracing Daniel, through the window he saw the large gray horse on the lead rope next to Daniel's mount. Stepping back, Nathan finally spoke, his voice breaking with emotion: "You got him," was all he said. Daniel nodded and said, "Yes I did."

There was quiet laughter shared then by the three men, the kind that is only about relief, not celebration.

"Glad you're home," Nathan offered. "Have you been to the ranch?"

"No I haven't yet. Thought I would stop by here first and then I want to clean up some before I head home. Don't want my family to see me like this."

Daniel's first question was to ask if either of them had been out to see his family and he noticed that Nathan looked away, before answering. "Yes, I've been getting out there every couple of weeks just to check and see how they are doing."

"How are they?"

Nathan paused for a moment before answering and then said, "They're fine and I'm sure they're all going to be glad that you're home. "

Daniel noticed that Nathan looked away before again meeting his gaze. He continued, "Why don't we all go on over to the house. You can clean up there and Emily's going to be very glad to see you, too."

Before they left the office Daniel gave Nathan the pocket watch he'd retrieved from Stiles' body. Nathan mused, "You wonder where this came from, don't you? I'll keep it here, though I have no idea who it might belong to or how to get it back to them. The man cut quite a swath."

As they went out the door, Wilf volunteered to take care of the horses and meet them at Nathan's in a bit.

At the Westphal home Daniel felt like he'd walked into an oven as they entered the house. He'd noticed how warm the Sheriff's office had seemed, as well. He had become so accustomed to living outdoors in the cold, that a normally warm enclosure seemed stifling.

Emily was overjoyed to see him and began bustling about, heating water and preparing a place in the back bedroom for him to wash, shave, and change clothing.

She headed for the store to find Daniel some "decent clothing" and soon returned with a pair of heavy trousers and a warm woolen shirt.

When she'd first seen him, Emily had asked if he'd been home yet and Daniel noticed she'd glanced at Nathan, when he'd said he had not.

After he washed, shaved, and put on the new clothing, Emily tried to get Daniel to stay and have an early supper with them. He begged off, saying that he wanted to get home as soon as possible.

Wilf arrived and reported that the horses had been fed and watered and that he'd brushed them down a bit.

Daniel tried to pay Emily for the clothing she'd provided but she wouldn't hear of it, so he merely thanked her and told her how much he appreciated what she'd done for him. She asked Daniel to let Johanna know she was thinking of her and would be out to visit when it got a bit warmer. Nathan and Emily exchanged good-byes with Daniel as he left for home.

Nathan stayed behind with his wife and Wilf walked with Daniel to the livery stable.

"Y'all look a lot better than you did when you first rode in," Wilf said smiling, as Daniel brought his fed and curried horses out of the livery.

Daniel paused, and before mounting Zeb, looked Wilf in the eyes and asked, "Is everything okay at my place, Wilf?"

Wilf put his hand on the younger man's shoulder reassuringly. "Yup, everything is okay. Your wife and little girl are going to be damned glad to see you."

At that, Wilf removed his hand from Daniel's shoulder and stepped away. The image of the injured Johanna and dead boy in his arms coming home from the river had not left him and he knew he dared not say any more to Daniel about what awaited him. The entire town knew and he only hoped that the man before him would be able to cope with it. "Take care of yourself Daniel. You've got some resting up to do."

Daniel smiled, "I'm looking forward to that. Tired of sleeping on the ground and eating dead rabbit." At that both men laughed, Daniel mounted Zeb and Wilf watched the man and the two horses disappear into the distance. Only then did he turn and walk back up the street. Tonight he'd stop at the saloon on his way home to the boarding house.

CHAPTER 33

REUNION

LIGHT WAS NEARLY GONE FROM the sky when Daniel rode into the yard. Ellis had put the hogs to bed for the night and was the first to see him, as he came around the end of the barn. At first look, he wasn't sure of what he was seeing...then suddenly he was.

"Daniel," he shouted, "Is that you?"

"Yes it is," Daniel answered as he watched Ellis run to greet him. Swifty came out of the bunk house at the sound of voices and shortly the three men were laughing and pounding each other in greeting.

"*Damn*, it's good to see you Daniel," Ellis said with such conviction, that it conveyed to the arriving man all of the worry and anxiety that the ranch hands had experienced for months. Swifty didn't say much, but Daniel had never seen the young man smile the way he was smiling now. He too was obviously overjoyed at Daniel's return.

Ellis ran his fingers along the top of the gray stallion's mane, asking, "Did you kill the man who stole this horse?"

The question sobered the three of them immediately. "Yes. He won't be stealing any more horses." It was the only crime they would mention.

There was quiet for a moment, then Ellis offered to take the horses to the barn and said that he and Swifty would be eating in the bunkhouse that evening, so Daniel could be alone with his family. Daniel answered quietly, saying that "Yes, it would be good if you take care of Shadow and Zeb," then he added that he "would see both of them tomorrow."

Ellis and Swifty led the animals away and Daniel turned to enter the house. Everything was as he remembered it. It seemed so long ago since he'd climbed the front steps. Once on the porch, he ran his hand along the back of the swing and stood at the door a moment before he turned the knob and stepped inside. It was quiet. Rosa, who had been working in the kitchen when she heard the shouting and laughter in the yard was standing in the middle of the living room. Her apron, with colorful birds adorning it was pulled up to her eyes, to wipe the tears that were streaming down her face.

Wordlessly they embraced and her crying turned to sobs as she held the closest thing to a son she'd ever had. She softly spoke in her native Spanish the prayers she had said over and over every night, since he'd left in late August. Daniel held her, patting her shoulders reassuringly and let her finish. After she had regained control of herself he said, "Rosa where are Sarah and Johanna?"

Still patting her eyes with the tear soaked bottom edge of her apron, Rosa said, "They are upstairs." Daniel nodded, took off his dead man's boots, placed them next to the stairway and said simply, "I'm going up."

Rosa nodded and said, "I am fixing some supper that will be ready soon."

"Smells good." He turned and quietly climbed the stairs.

It was just like when he'd come home from the cattle drive. His wife and daughter were sleeping, nestled together, this time more closely. He looked at them and listened to their breathing. The old soft quilt covered both of them and even in the growing darkness Daniel could read by the curve of Johanna's body that she was pregnant. "My God," he whispered and then sat down on the edge of the bed. "My God," he whispered again and the combination of his voice and the movement of the bed awakened Johanna.

At first she startled, and then immediately recognized his familiar, but changed appearance. "Daniel!" was all she said. She rose to her knees and moved around Sarah to reach him. Her injuries were healed now so he could embrace her with everything within him.

"Jo. My God, Jo. I've missed you so much."

At first, the only word she could speak was the word, "Daniel," over and over. After a few moments, Daniel felt Johanna sigh deeply and then whisper quietly, "Is he dead?"

"Yes." It was the only word he needed to say. He knew she would never ask him anything about the five months he had been away and he intended to never speak about it.

Their kisses were intense, tender and the most meaningful and loving they had ever shared.

Tears came for both and Daniel nestled his head into her shoulder and neck, saying, "You smell so damned good."

"Your hair smells like a campfire," was her reply.

He laughed then and said, "Oh, I'm sure it does."

"And you need a haircut!"

They pulled back and looked at each other and then became aware that Sarah was awake. She was silent. There was no boisterous greeting for her father. She just lay there looking at the two of them.

Johanna reached for her daughter, saying, "Sarah, your Daddy is home."

Sarah said nothing, but pulled her old, battered doll to her cheek and covered her head with the quilt. Daniel and Johanna looked at each other and Jo leaned close and whispered into Daniel's ear. "It may take some time for her to get used to you again but she's missed you terribly." Daniel nodded, but felt a strange sadness. That his daughter might turn away from him was something he had never considered

Daniel touched Johanna's belly and mouthed the words "A baby," to Jo. She nodded. Her tears came again and their eyes met. Daniel leaned forward and kissed her very softly on the mouth. "I love you Jo," was all he said. He knew there was nothing else he could say in this moment. Asking her how long she'd been pregnant would have to wait for a later time, when they were alone and he could summon the courage to ask.

"The doctor says I must stay in bed, like before."

Daniel nodded his understanding.

There was just silence then, and Daniel let his hand move up her arm and then touch her face. The gesture spoke for him.

Rosa brought them food. There was a tray that Jo put across her with a towel to minimize the mess. Sarah sat up then and ate off the tray with her mother and avoided looking at Daniel altogether. She didn't ask if he'd brought her a gift. Daniel felt embarrassment that he hadn't even thought to bring her one, his only thought had been to return home. Now watching her, he doubted she would have accepted a gift with the exuberance that she had shown with the books and doll that Daniel had brought from Culver. She was a changed child. As changed as the rest of them.

That night Daniel learned that Sarah had been sleeping with her mother for months, saying she was afraid to sleep by herself. Johanna, lonely herself, had indulged Sarah's wish to be with her. There really wasn't room for the three of them comfortably in the bed, so Daniel went to sleep in James' room. He was exhausted and lying on this bed that was less comfortable than his own, his mind was churning with the realities he had been forced to deal with in the past few hours.

His wife was pregnant, and he didn't know if he was the father of the child she carried. His daughter, who had adored him for the first five years of her life, now seemed to want nothing to do with him. He realized that in the coming days he'd have a lot to cope with. Tonight, his body and mind were exhausted and sleep overtook him in a way it hadn't since the night he'd killed Stiles.

The next morning he encountered another reality he had not expected. Swifty, Ellis and Rosa had developed a routine that was like clockwork. The three of them were indefatigable. From early morning until dark they made the ranch run smoothly. Every detail was taken care of. Without Hernando, James and Daniel, they had found a way to make it work.

Ellis had been able, even in the midst of all the winter chores, to fill the meat house with elk and deer. Swifty had become a wood cutter without equal and the triple stacked wood pile next to the house and around the smoke house would last them through the winter and well into spring.

The young man had filled out and become muscular with the additional chores and responsibilities and the pride of accomplishment shone in his eyes. He was part of something now, like he hadn't been before. Daniel was very glad for all of it. He needn't have worried about how things were going at home in his absence. But now, he felt as though he had lost his place at the ranch. Completely.

Over the next week the three men worked together. Checking the cows in the lower pastures, they found the herd in good condition. There had been little pressure from weather and Ellis had kept wolves and coyotes pretty much at bay. The cows that were pregnant would begin to calve in another six weeks or so and Daniel could tell it would be a busy calving season. His domain was in the best shape it could possibly be.

Soon after he arrived home, Daniel made the trip to Calvin's ranch. His best friend, who like Wilf and Nathan had given him up for dead, heartily welcomed him home. Again, there were no overt questions about what had happened. Calvin had only needed assurance that Stiles was indeed dead. Calvin's lack of help from Swifty and Ellis was apparent, so they decided that the two hired hands would spend the majority of their time at the Syme ranch for a while. This would accomplish two things - Calvin would have some help and Daniel could step back into his role as the owner of his place.

Daniel could not continue to pay the two hands for their full-time service. After helping Calvin, they would do some work in town. In the early summer, they would again return to the two ranches and help with branding and other major summer work.

Now carrying the full load of the outside tasks kept Daniel busy and he worked long hours, coming to the house in late evening, tired.

After a couple of nights, Sarah had relinquished her place in her mother's bed at night, but spent long hours with Johanna during the day, providing good company and giving Johanna a chance to read to her daughter. Since being confined to bed, Johanna had begun teaching the little girl, who would soon be six, how to read her storybooks. With precious paper and the stub of a pencil, she was instructing Sarah how to form letters and educating her about the sound that each letter made. This delighted both of them, as Sarah was a quick learner. Johanna encouraged Sarah to let her father read to her or to show him how much she knew about reading herself. The girl wanted no part of it but she would not communicate to Johanna why.

Being in the middle of the two people she loved most was difficult for Johanna.

The first night they spent alone in their room together, Johanna told him how at a loss she was to explain Sarah's behavior."I was gone a long time, Jo. I think we have to give her time to come around. After I've been home for a while, maybe she'll warm up to me again."

Daniel said nothing to Jo about how painful it was for him to lose the contact he'd always had with his daughter. He didn't want to add any stress to his wife, as he knew from experience how difficult it was for Johanna to endure her confinement.

Earlier in the evening, when Daniel had taken his daughter to her bed, she had not wanted to do their nightly hug, kiss or nose rub. He wondered if being almost six meant that she was now too old for this favorite thing of theirs, or was this just one more part of her rejection of him. Daniel had no way of knowing.

As he covered her with her quilt, he asked her where her dollie was and she held up the ragged, now almost un-recognizable old doll. "No," Daniel said, "I mean the one I brought you from Culver, when I brought you the books. Remember?"

"She's in there," Sarah had replied, pointing to the closet. "I don't like her and I want her to go away."

Daniel had stood up and walked to the closet and in the near darkness had seen the small doll in the blue checked dress sitting on the floor, deep in the closet, against the back wall. Daniel had reached down, picked the doll up and brought her back to Sarah's bed.

"Why don't you like her?" Daniel asked.

"I don't like the way she smiles," Sarah had replied, not looking at her father.

"Okay," Daniel had replied, "I'll take her away."

Sarah said nothing.

At the hallway door, Daniel had turned before leaving and said, "I love you Sarah girl."

Again there had been no reply and Daniel had gone out into the hallway and down the stairs. Rosa had retired to her own house, where she had been sleeping since Daniel had returned home, so Daniel had the downstairs area to himself.

He carried the small doll that he had so carefully picked out for his daughter to the stove. There was still a significant fire in the firebox and he opened the door, thinking to drop the doll inside. He stopped and looked at the small figure in his hand. Why, he wondered should this creature be punished for something she had not done? He let the firebox door go closed.

"This is crazy. This makes no sense at all," he said out loud. He couldn't believe he was behaving as though this human looking object was a real person.

He opened the firebox door again, but he could not put the doll to the coals.

Closing the firebox door a second time, he turned and determined he would put the doll somewhere out of the way, where his daughter could not find it. But where? His eyes wandered the downstairs area. There was no place he could determine that Sarah couldn't see the doll or find it.

He aimlessly walked to the back hallway and the

broom closet then turned left into the downstairs bedroom/ pantry. His eyes were drawn upward and he decided to put the doll on the very top shelf next to what was left of the applesauce. Sarah couldn't see onto that shelf and the doll would be safe there. Sometime later he'd figure out what to do with it. For now, this solution would have to do. He decided he wouldn't worry Jo with this latest chapter of his relationship with his daughter.

Now in their room together, Johanna and Daniel were sharing the first truly private moment they'd had since Daniel had returned. It was quiet in the bedroom as Daniel undressed and slipped into the bed beneath the blankets next to his wife. He lay so he could see her face clearly, and let his hand caress her through her cotton nightgown. It felt so good to finally be next to her.

The lamp was still on and he wanted the light so he could read his wife's face when she replied to the questions he knew he must ask. He lay there for a moment, wondering how to begin. Johanna spoke first.

"Daniel, we have to talk about this."

"I know. How do we start?"

There was a long silence and Johanna said softly, "There is only one way to start and that is by saying I'm going to have a baby and I'm not certain if you are the father."

Daniel knew that neither of them would say Stiles' name. That was a given. They must somehow discuss this, without naming the other principal character involved, who had caused them both so much heartache.

"Jo, how far along are you and when is the baby due?"

"I'm just over five months pregnant and the baby is due in May," Jo replied. Daniel noticed the quaver in her voice and he paused. Silently, he did the math in his head. There was no way around it. This baby could be either his or Stiles'. Something told him that whatever he said next was going to mean the success or failure of his continued relationship with this woman he loved.

He couldn't tell her it didn't matter, because it did. To both of them. He couldn't tell her he loved her no matter what, because she already knew that.

Daniel took a deep breath and said the thing he felt most. "Johanna, this is my child. This is our child. It just is."

Quiet again filled the room and Johanna said in a voice barely above a whisper, "But we don't know that."

"*I* know that. I know that this is my child. I'm it's father. It's mine." His voice was quiet, but emphatic. He didn't add the words, "No matter what," because that entertained the possibility that Stiles had fathered the child inside her. He would not let that thought into his mind or into their conversation. He waited for any reply she might have and none came. He waited a long minute. Both of them were very aware of the breathing of the other.

Daniel's right hand rested on the curve of her belly. Beneath his hand he felt faint movement. The baby was there - it was responding to his touch. "I can feel the baby moving," he whispered to Johanna and kissed her mouth. Johanna's only reply was, "I feel it too."

Daniel took another deep breath and said firmly but

gently, "Now is there anything else you think we need to discuss about this?"

"I love you so much Daniel. So much."

Daniel reached over and turned off the lamp. "I love you too and I'm really glad we're sleeping in the same bed again because James' bed isn't that great." He heard Jo's chuckle.

In the darkness Johanna realized that the conversation she'd been dreading for months was over. She knew Daniel meant every word he'd said and that from this moment on, her part of the bargain was to believe and to behave as though this child was Daniel's, even if it wasn't. She wondered if either of them could maintain this attitude indefinitely. She knew Daniel would try, and so she must.

Holding Johanna, his right leg across her thighs and right arm protectively across her body, Daniel hoped he had sounded as convincing as he wanted to be. He knew it was vital that he stand by Jo now. He had accomplished what he'd needed to do. He'd killed the man who had invaded his world, his house, his wife. Now, he needed to prove to Jo that it had all been worth it. That it had real meaning. He loved her and the fact that she had endured the ordeal of the previous months meant everything. Daniel prayed to God that the baby would survive the full nine months, and that Johanna would survive its delivery in May. Her loss was what he feared most. He knew without her, he would become Wilf, a man without the heart or will to ever enter such a venture again.

CHAPTER 34

THE ARRIVAL

DAYS EVOLVED INTO WEEKS AND the weeks into months. It seemed that every day brought a new revelation to Daniel. He had never realized how much of the conversation within his household James had initiated. The boy's enthusiasm for life in his daily tasks and adventures had been shared with a sense of humor and energy that was now gone. Everyone missed him. Hernando had carried the load of all the "simple tasks" that were now additional work for Daniel. Rosa was more quiet and Daniel realized that her grieving for her life's mate was profound. He made a special effort every day to embrace her when he left for his morning chores and to do the same in the evening, after supper as she departed for her house. He daily thanked her for everything she did to keep the house running without the help and companionship of his wife.

Daniel's relationship with Sarah continued to be tenuous. She would occasionally allow Daniel to read to her and he was sure it was due to some stern prodding by her mother, but he welcomed the time he got to spend with his daughter, whatever the terms. Sarah would from time to time venture out to the barn with her father to check on a newborn calf that needed extra attention, but she would quickly insist she wanted to return to her mother.

Daniel felt that he and Johanna were closer than they had ever been - each of them so grateful for the love of the other, a feeling that had been intensified by their long separation, and a realization during the absence that they might never see each other again.

Calving had begun in earnest in early April and much of Daniel's time was spent outside, caring for the newborn additions to the herd. Ellis came back to help him. The two men sometimes worked tirelessly into the night, and Daniel would return to the house before dawn to lie down and rest next to Johanna for a few hours before again venturing out to see if more calves had been born.

Although she was terribly uncomfortable now, Johanna's pregnancy was progressing well and every couple of weeks Dr. Messinger would stop by to check on her. His concern for her was apparent and his kind words and assurances were always welcome to Daniel, who knew that every week that passed meant the baby's chances for survival increased.

James' horse Red was now rarely seen near the barn or the fence. She spent her time deep in the large horse pasture, as she had learned that no amount of time spent by the gate would bring the boy out of the house. She'd matured and her color had deepened to a rich dark red. Daniel kept an eye on her and would weekly ride Zeb out to get as close to her as possible, so she could remain somewhat accustomed to him and not go wild altogether.

She would let him get to within a few yards of her and then back away. Daniel had no intention of trying to rope or ride her, but intended to soon put Shadow into the main horse pasture and his hope was that the two would breed, as he knew that had been James' intention. He knew it would be a strong bloodline, if Red's wildness wasn't too dominant.

While Johanna watched, Rosa and Daniel had readied the crib that had been stored on the back porch since Sarah's infancy. It now silently stood at the foot of the bed, ready to receive the child soon to be born. Sarah seemed quite interested in the prospect of having a brother or sister. She had many questions for her mother: How soon would the baby be able to play with her? How soon would it walk, talk and read?

Both of her parents were happy and encouraged to see Sarah so animated about the upcoming birth, because it was a rarity now to see their daughter interested in the happenings of their lives.

During the nights that were spent with Johanna and not in the barn, Daniel slept with his right hand on top of Johanna's now large belly, waiting patiently for movement beneath. It didn't matter what time of night the baby moved, Daniel would waken and marvel. Johanna's gentle breathing in sleep was the only sound Daniel strained to hear.

At the end of the first week in May all of the calves had been born. Spring was upon them now and there were more warm days than cold ones. Grass in the lower pastures was greening and upper elevation snow run off caused the river to swell and roar. Hank rode by to see them and to examine the water level at the Aspen grove; he and Daniel rode out together. There was so much about the boy that reminded Daniel of James at that age and he encouraged Hank to come back in mid-June so that they could get in some fishing, even though Daniel knew he would be in the middle of rounding up the calves for branding at that time. Fishing with the boy was a promise he intended to keep at all costs.

Two days later, mid afternoon, Johanna went into labor; earlier in the month than she had thought it would happen. There was no doubt in her mind that this was not a false alarm, however, and she sent Sarah downstairs to find Daniel, who was with Ellis making some repairs to the smoke house door. Daniel came bounding up the stairs and was greeted by Johanna's words, "It's time."

Ellis saddled a horse and headed for town to get the doctor, while Rosa readied the things he would need once he arrived. Johanna seemed very calm, Daniel thought as he walked in circles, upstairs and down and intermittently sat on the bed, watching his wife warily. Every few minutes, he would ask her if anything had changed and if she was all right. Finally, Johanna had suggested he take Sarah outside for a bit or feed her some lunch. He was reluctant to leave Johanna, but the look his wife was giving him said, "Please do this, Daniel," so he gathered up Sarah who was insisting Johanna read to her and took the little girl out of the room. "I'll read to you, Sarah, but downstairs."

Thus began the hours that for all of them seemed to move slowly, with waiting being the only thing that could be done. Daniel walked in the yard with Sarah, took her to the barn to see a new colt that had been born two days earlier, read to her on the swing and fed her lunch. He tried to answer his daughter's many questions about how babies are born in a way he thought a father should answer these questions when asked by a nearly six year old girl. He tried to distract her with the subject of her upcoming birthday in June and what it would be like to go to a real school, beginning in August. Sarah would have none of it. It was babies being born she wanted to talk about.

Over an hour later, Ellis returned with the doctor. Dr. Messinger rode his horse rather than drive his carriage, which told Daniel he thought it was important to be with Johanna as quickly as possible. Ellis reported he'd run into Calvin Syme and Swifty in town, and that Swifty would be out later in the day to help with chores that needed to be done for the next couple of days or so. Calvin had asked to be contacted if there was anything he could do.

After Daniel was able to get Sarah to lie down for a nap, he again checked on Johanna, who was in obvious labor now. He wanted to stay with her, but was told it would be best if he didn't. It had been the same when Sarah had been born, so after kissing Johanna on the forehead and telling her he loved her and would be downstairs if she needed him, he left her to the doctor and Rosa and retreated downstairs.

It began to get dark, and when Sarah woke from her nap and tried to see her mother, she too was admonished to go downstairs where her father waited. By lamplight the two exiles ate a cold supper and then retired to the sofa, where Daniel proceeded to read every book Sarah stacked in front of him. Finally, when he was hoarse from reading the last book, he simply sat with her and stroked her hair, something she had not allowed him to do for months. After a few minutes she asked, "Daddy, where is my dollie?" Daniel quietly went upstairs and retrieved the threadbare doll from Sarah's bed, stopping for a minute to listen outside his bedroom door to the sounds coming from within. Quiet voices came through the wooden boards of the door, but no hint of how close they might be to the baby's arrival.

Descending the stairs and holding the doll out to Sarah, he was surprised to hear her say, "No, not that one, the one you brought me last summer."

Daniel paused, then asked, "The one with the blue checked dress?"

"Yes, that one."

Daniel felt something welling inside of him that he had not felt for a long time and realized it was a combination of joy and humor. He last recalled experiencing it with James, when he'd realized he'd been wrong about the boy's choice in a horse. He'd begun to think he would never experience this feeling again in his life.

He cleared his throat, which was tight with emotion. "Well, I don't know, maybe she's here someplace in the house. It's been a while since I've seen her. Should we try and find her?"

The smile on his daughter's face was one that Daniel had not seen since before he'd left on the cattle drive and it nearly brought him to his knees. He held her right hand in his left and picked up the lamp with his right and together they began exploring the house. Upon reaching the downstairs bedroom pantry, after a few moments of superficial searching he had suggested they check up on the top shelf next to the applesauce. He picked her up so her small hand could feel along the top, rough board shelf. He watched her face as her fingers reached the doll and lifted it in surprised discovery. "She's here," the little girl exclaimed and she first hugged the doll and then her father.

Daniel was transfixed at that moment and the two of them just stood there, while Sarah examined the heretofore unlikeable doll with new eyes. "I like her now," was all she said as they ventured back into the living room to reseat themselves on the sofa.

Very shortly thereafter the space of the house was filled with a new sound. Sounds Sarah had never heard before and Daniel had not heard for over five years. Johanna was giving birth in the room above their heads. Daniel could tell that Jo was trying not to loudly cry out, as that was her nature, but he knew she was in pain and it was difficult for him to try to remain totally calm for Sarah. She asked numerous times, "Is Mommy was going to be okay." Daniel held his daughter and assured her that "Yes, Mommy will be okay in a little while, the baby is coming now."

At the baby's first cry, Sarah wanted to go upstairs. Daniel, whose relief was beyond words, gently told his daughter they must wait just a little longer. About twenty minutes later, Dr. Messinger came downstairs, looking tired but it was obvious he shared Daniel's relief. "Everything went very well and you can go upstairs now," was all he said.

The two of them made their way upstairs and quietly, as if entering a church for worship, opened the bedroom door where Johanna and the newborn were resting. Rosa was finishing the gathering of soiled bedclothes which she was about to take downstairs, along with the basin containing the afterbirth. They exchanged smiles and Rosa said only, "You have a beautiful child," and then offered that she would see that the doctor had something to eat. He had agreed to sleep in the downstairs bedroom for the remaining hours of darkness and then would head back to town. Daniel was glad of that.

After Rosa left the room Daniel turned his full attention to Jo and the baby she held in her arms, wrapped and peaceful. Johanna looked exhausted but extremely happy and relieved that the ordeal of the delivery was over. Sarah climbed up on the bed and crawled over to her mother and asked to see the baby while Daniel stood beside the bed watching. Johanna turned the baby so Sarah could see it and met Daniel's eyes with her own and said, "It's a boy. Here Daniel, take him."

Daniel felt himself sit down on the edge of the bed and the baby being put into his arms. He folded the edge of the blanket back, so he could look this new child in the face. The features of the baby looked exactly as he remembered Sarah the first time he'd seen her. "He looks like his sister," Daniel said softly.

Johanna nodded, "That was my first thought too."

The baby's fair, soft hair was as blond as his sister's had been. Daniel ran his fingers over the soft down. The nose and ears had the same curves and coloring as his older sister had at birth. The weight of the baby was substantial and Daniel knew he weighed more than Sarah had. "He's a big guy," Daniel commented as he opened the blanket to look at the baby more closely.

Johanna spoke, "He has your hands, Daniel." And it was true. Daniel saw his own hands at the end of the baby's chubby arms. He couldn't help but laugh at this and the sound of Daniel's laughter caused the baby to startle and open his eyes. They were slate blue and the lashes surrounding them were the color of Johanna's and James'.

Daniel had not imagined how he might feel at this moment. He had secretly feared it and somehow dreaded it, but now he rejoiced in it. This was without any doubt his son. The tears that came from his eyes and ran down his cheeks matched Johanna's, which prompted Sarah to ask softly, as if still in church, "Why are you two crying?" which brought laughter from them both. It was the laughter of relief and celebration and it filled the room. The tiny human in Daniel's arms looked about him in wonderment as he heard the voices of the people he would spend years of his life with for the first time.

An hour later Sarah was settled into her bed and Doctor Messinger had retired to get what sleep he might before dawn. Rosa had put the birthing bedclothes in cold water to soak and had gone to her house to rest. Johanna and the baby dozed with some much needed sleep. Daniel left the house and went into the front yard. The deep night sounds surrounded him and it was peaceful. No wind stirred. Skyward, there was an abundance of stars visible and Daniel went down to his knees, and sat down on the ground and took them all in.

His world had drastically changed in the last twelve hours. There was much to rejoice about. He had his daughter back. She was his again and he knew the bond he'd shared with her in the previous hours was unbreakable. He would not allow it to ever be broken again.

He had a son. My God what a beautiful child he was. Healthy, alert and vigorous. After putting Sarah to bed, Daniel had spent time with Johanna and the baby and watched him nurse hungrily for the first time. Afterward they had decided to name the baby James Daniel. It had been Johanna's choice and Daniel felt that if it were not too painful for her to have a son named after her murdered brother then it would be an honor to call him James.

Now, under the stars Daniel could only pray that the baby would survive his first, most vulnerable years and live to grow up. He had no idea if his son would decide to stay and continue their fragile legacy in this hard to live in place. He might leave it at the first opportunity as had his own brothers, but Daniel knew at least there was a chance it would continue.

For the first time in his life Daniel realized that he did not own the land he was sitting on. It owned him. One day in the future it would claim him and he would lie beneath it, as did his grandparents, his parents, his babies who'd died, his brother-in-law James and all of Johanna's relatives. He would eventually become part of the earth that he now labored so intently upon. He felt no fear or sorrow about this. He embraced it. He silently thanked God for his family now asleep in the house behind him and for the privilege he felt of just being here, and prayed that he would always be worthy of this place he called home.

EPILOGUE

PRESENT DAY

JACK HOLLISTER ROLLED HIS SUV'S driver side window down and let the cool early September air hit his face. It felt good to be "out from under" for awhile and he intended to make the most of the next two weeks.

He and his wife Michelle owned and operated an outfitting operation in Jackson Hole, Wyoming, catering to white-water rafters in the summer and skiers in winter. Dudes who came from places like Houston, New York and Chicago looking for the *outdoor experience*, before going back to their work a day world. He had obliged them for over fifteen years now and the wear and tear was finally getting to him. He'd go back and do it again, when the ski crowd started arriving, but he needed a break from college students who were careless and people who felt they were entitled to treat his crews badly because they'd paid him a bundle to provide a good time.

Jack was now in his "off season" mode and it took him to what he loved doing most - moving cemeteries. He'd grown up in a family of third generation funeral directors and while his brother David had decided to take the plunge into the profession, Jack had opted out. However, he discovered that by osmosis he had absorbed the love of cemeteries that most funeral directors share and it was one part of the profession that he had not been able to let go of. The histories that were written on gravestones, especially the old ones, held a fascination for him. Every cemetery told a story of families and their lives, especially the small family cemeteries that were scattered all over the country. Modern day progress sometimes dictated that these final places of rest be moved to allow for highways, housing developments, schools and "the better good" of growing communities. Jack had found his niche. He was among a small group of people that loved to exhume dead human beings to be moved and put elsewhere.

The task at hand was one state over in Colorado. A developer was building houses on a tract of land that contained a small family cemetery and Jack and the crew he'd put together were being contracted to move approximately twenty graves to a county cemetery within the city limits of Fergus, Colorado. He was supposed to have arrived there today, but last minute business had detained him and now he was trying to make up time. He'd get into Fergus late tonight and get to the cemetery site in the morning. For now, he just set the cruise control at 70 mph and cranked up the music volume. He'd made sure his stick containing the best of The Oak Ridge Boys was the one plugged in and he rocked into the night.

Early the next morning, just after 6:00 a.m. Jack rolled out of bed in the small but clean Fergus Arms Motel. He grabbed a doughnut and coffee in the lobby, then headed for the excavation site, guided by directions he'd received from the backhoe operator. This was not a site he'd be able to find on GPS, the man had advised him, and it took him nearly thirty minutes, but Jack finally spotted the large yellow backhoe in the distance and steered in that direction.

Pulling up to the cemetery, Jack was struck by the view he had from this vantage point. He could understand why people would want to build in this location, as it had everything. He could see the river snaking through the valley, an Aspen grove in the near distance and beyond that, the foothills of the Rockies. It was beautiful.

Pulling up next to a large gray pickup, he could see that the backhoe was already at work. The operator had his work cut out for him. The first order of business would be to clear away the monstrous caragana hedge. It had been unkept and untrimmed for decades and there was no gate, only a path recently cut through with large clippers on the north side so that the graves to be removed could be examined. The large backhoe was tearing into the hedge on the south side and the uprooted caragana was being haphazardly stacked on a pile that would have to be hauled away later to a land fill west of Fergus.

Noting Jack's arrival the operator shut down the backhoe and came over to greet the man who would be supervising the operation. He removed the glove from his right hand and stuck it out toward Jack saying, "Morning. You Jack Hollister?" Jack nodded.

"Well I'm William Overgaard - your backhoe man. Hope you don't mind I went ahead and started pulling the hedge. It's a bear."

Again Jack nodded and said he'd like to take a look at the graves they'd be moving.

After the two men got through the cut out area of the hedge, Jack could see what they would be dealing with. There were two upright stones on either side of what looked like had once been a pathway. The name Sullivan was on the stone to the left and O'Neal was the name on the stone to Jack's right. Both were cut from the same gray flecked Minnesota granite that Jack had seen many times before.

All but one of the graves were marked with slant face markers made of the same gray granite as the upright stones. The weeds were high, but the summer sun had dried and bent them over, so the tops of the stones were visible.

"Looks like somebody back in the forties got all of these graves marked at the same time," Jack remarked. He'd seen this style of lettering and raised engraving on a lot of graves from that era.

He walked along the row of graves on the O'Neal side. There were five generations of family here. A Patrick and Catherine, husband and wife no doubt, then a Mary and John, who had died several years apart; a Maxwell, who had died at the age of thirteen, two small stones that each read only Baby O'Neal; then a Daniel and Johanna, with Johanna dying five years before her husband. Then a James Daniel O'Neal with a wife named Olivia Christine. James had died in 1952, with his wife following four years later. The only remaining stone in that row was an upright marble military marker for a Marcus Daniel O'Neal who had been born November 4, 1919 and had died June 6,

1944. Beneath the date of death it read, 101 ABD U S Army and below that WWII. Jack felt the hair rise on the back of his neck. The only member of this family's fifth generation to be buried here had been a paratrooper who had died in Normandy on the first day of the Allied invasion. "Wow," was all he could whisper.

On the Sullivan side there were fewer graves. A Thomas and Mary Sullivan, followed by a William and Sarah, both dying in their sixties, followed by a Thomas who had died at age four and a James who had died at the age of sixteen, then a Hernando and Rosa Garcia, with Rosa dying thirty years after her husband. Jack noticed that both James and Hernando had died in August 1883. Only the month and year were noted. "There's a story there," Jack thought, "I wonder what it is?"

Jack paused and looked around the entire enclosure. It spoke of great care for decades and then decades of neglect. Jack spoke, "Once we get this hedge down and out of the way, we'll get started on taking them out of the ground one at a time."

"Yeah, I left my smaller backhoe back at the house. It's gonna take all day to get this hedge out and I'll need to bring in the smaller rig tomorrow on my flatbed."

"That will work out well," Jack replied, "My recovery team is coming in tonight and we'll get started early, say 7:00 tomorrow morning?" The big man in coveralls nodded, shook Jack's hand again, spit a load of tobacco juice downwind and walked back to his machine.

For years, Jack had been working with the same four guys, who had the same bug he did about cemeteries, all connected directly with funeral home families. They lived as far away as Jackson, Mississippi and Knoxville, Tennessee and they had grown close and worked together well, although they only saw each other sporadically, as Jack received contracts. They were scheduled to work for the next fourteen days and time would be of the essence. They would remove each body and keep the stones organized with each removal before getting them placed in the county cemetery in Fergus.

William Overgaard would be the one to do the initial digging down to the bodies and then it would be Jack and his four crew members who would have to get down in the graves with shovels and small hand tools to find out what kind of containers the people had been buried in. Sometimes they came out, container more or less intact, and sometimes they'd be sifting through earth to make sure that every bone possible was accounted for. It was tough, meticulous work, but Jack felt it was the most rewarding thing he did for a living.

His next task was to go to the cemetery in Fergus and connect with the sexton and get the low down on where the bodies uncovered would be placed. He'd had numerous phone calls with the man, and he sounded like he knew what he was doing.

Before going to Fergus, Jack drove his Jeep around the property. He wanted to see what was left of the places where the people he'd be moving had lived. Already there were survey stakes in all directions of the cemetery. The owner of the land and the contractors who would be building the development had big plans here.

Following a very faint trail for about a mile and a half west, Jack came to what was left of a wood frame house.

This, he'd been informed by the contractor on the phone was the Sullivan place. There wasn't much left. The roof was completely gone and only two walls were left standing. Vines on the west side of the house had taken over the porch that had collapsed on one end. There were piles of fallen down structures that had been small outbuildings. All that was left of the barn was a pile of boards that looked like it had been hit by scavengers, as there were saw marks on many of the boards. It looked like artsy people who made picture frames and nick knack shelves and did all sorts of things with aged barn wood had been having a field day.

Jack backtracked to the cemetery and then drove in the opposite direction, along the same faint trail that had been recently traveled by pickups carrying survey crews and contractors. After a few minutes Jack came to another wood framed house, which had obviously been lived in more recently, as the condition was less severe. This was where the O'Neals had lived. Jack parked, turned off the engine, and got out of his vehicle. There was an older more dilapidated house a few yards from the main house that was completely overgrown with weeds and vines. Behind Jack stood a barn, which although still on its feet looked like it might fold up any day now. Survey stakes with orange tape on the tops lined the barn on the east side and Jack knew that within weeks, this whole place would be leveled and the outline of streets and houses would begin to take shape.

Jack couldn't resist climbing the front steps of the house. The steps had been rebuilt in some previous decade so were still usable. The porch was the width of the house and looking up to the ceiling of the porch, Jack could see two O-shaped rings where a porch swing had no doubt at one time been hung. The front door of the house was ajar about two inches and with some effort, Jack managed to work the door open.

The inside of the house was dusty with cobwebs in every corner and hanging from the ceiling. No furniture remained but an open staircase was visible. Carefully testing the floor and finding it still solid, Jack ventured across the front room and looked to his left into the kitchen. The place was small, but had a cozy feel. A back door off the kitchen stood open and a falling down back porch was visible. Turning his attention to the stairway, he mounted the steps, testing each one which creaked under his weight.

"I'm gonna get killed doing this some day," Jack said under his breath as he turned the corner at the top of the stairway. Three small rooms, one on his left and two on his right were also without any furniture but Jack looked into each room. All the windows were still intact, except in the room to his left, the largest bedroom. Tattered curtains of the fifties vintage softly fluttered with the slight breeze.

As always, when in these old houses, Jack could sense the presence of the people who'd lived there. It was a strong feeling that always filled him with wonder and reverence. With a sigh, he turned and left. He wanted to get to town to see the final destination of his charges. He made a call to his in-town cemetery contact who said he would meet Jack there in half an hour.

Fergus was a thriving town of about eight thousand people who depended on agriculture as the backbone of the economy, but with some off road tourist trade and a small complex of computer technology industry. The look was "Denver Trendy," as a lot of people who lived here had moved in this direction to get out of Denver, but had brought a great deal of the culture of the place with them. Jack always had to smile at this phenomena. It was the same in Jackson Hole. There was no place more trendy now, though in the beginning it had been a place to get away from all of that. There were parts of downtown Fergus that were still "old Colorado" which pleased Jack.

The designated cemetery went way back to the beginning of the settlement of the territory. There was an old section and a new section. A Catholic section and a Protestant section. Old school. Again, Jack was greeted by raw wood survey stakes and short orange streamers. It was easy to find where he would be working.

The cemetery sexton turned out to be a man of about thirty-five years of age who had his ducks in a row. All the paperwork had been done and he was Mr. Efficient. Jack was glad of this, because over the years he'd run into some real headaches at this end of the operation. After about a twenty minute conversation about how the graves would be laid out and how important it was to set the gravestones squarely, instructions about where the heavy equipment was to enter and exit and what care must be taken of the grass as much as possible, Jack knew the drill. The young man climbed into his Prius and left and Jack decided to explore the rest of the cemetery a bit.

The old cemetery was closest to him. Jack began walking the rows. The part of his job he loved the most was reading the stones and reading between the lines where the story was really told. Certain family names stood out. Certain stones stood out.

Jack noticed the tallest, most ornate and prominent stone stood near the middle of the old section. Jack walked to it. It was a slate gray, white streaked beauty that stood almost five feet tall. Four sided, square, larger at the bottom with a sleek edifice rising with a six inch solid granite cross at the top. Jack leaned forward to read the name, which was weathered. It read James Wilfred Bennington III, and underneath the full name was the word "Wilf". There was no date of birth, only a date of death October 12, 1892. Below the date were the letters CSA, which Jack knew from experience stood for Confederate States of America. So, this man had been a Confederate soldier. Below this was the simple epitaph "Soldier, Protector, Friend." Jack looked at the stones on either side of the monument and saw there were no other Benningtons. To its left were stones for a William and Hazel Montgomery. William had died forty years before his wife Hazel and she had died ten years after Bennington. Jack moved on.

In the next row he found graves for several Symes, a Calvin and Emma, a Matthew, who Jack saw had died when he was twenty-two, and then a Luke Syme, buried next to a Sarah O'Neal Syme. Jack wondered if this Sarah was connected to the O'Neals he had visited earlier in the day. There was no way for him to know.

A row further over he encountered the name Westphal. There were only two stones bearing that name, a Nathan and an Emily. He noticed the words "Loving husband and Sheriff" under Nathan's name and the date of death was, October 12, 1892. It rang a bell and he turned and walked back to the gray monument to confirm what he thought he already knew. Nathan Westphal and the Confederate soldier had died on the same day. Another story, Jack mused.

He continued to walk the rows a bit, noting the number of people who had died in the flu epidemic just after WWI. There was a small veterans section and the usual flag pole, where the old and new cemeteries came together.

Jack walked back to the designated new resting place for the people he would be bringing here over the next two weeks. He made notes in his ever present notebook about how they would be placed in what he hoped would be their final destination. It would be tough to get this all done in two weeks he knew, but felt confident he and his crew could do it.

He looked at his watch. The doughnut he'd eaten for breakfast wasn't going to last him much longer. He needed some lunch and then he'd touch base with Michelle and each of his incoming crew then head back to see how Overgaard was doing with the hedge. Reaching his vehicle he turned for one last look at the cemetery, then got in, started the engine and drove away.

ACKNOWLEDGMENTS

First and foremost I'd like to thank the very good men and women I have known and loved in my lifetime! They have had a tremendous influence on my life. When it came to creating characters like Daniel, Johanna, Nathan and Emily, Wilf, Hazel, Ove, Hank and the others, I had a wealth of material to draw from. I am forever in their debt.

Secondly, I'd like to thank my husband David, who was my editor. It seems I have a penchant for commas. In our first reading together, I think he took about seven hundred of these elements of punctuation out of the book. He added about three, I think. Also, initially some of my paragraphs were three-quarters of a page long. That needed fixing. Having a second pair of eyes, looking at sentence structure and inflection was so important. He helped me out a lot in that regard. Thank you darlin' for your patience and the many hours you put into this project.

In addition, David was my "go to" person, when it came to questions I had about firearms.

Dr. Robert Kane, our local Veterinarian, answered some questions I had about horses and cattle. I appreciate his input.

There are five people I used as Beta Readers – people I asked to read the book and give me feedback. Thank you to my son Jess and his wife Sarah, my brother Frank Cable, and friends Christine Bassett and Joyce Kane. As a first time author it was difficult for me to let anyone read this book after it was first completed. When I began writing I had no idea how emotionally involved or protective of my characters I would become. I so appreciate the insights and suggestions my Readers gave me. You were a big help in this process.

A special Thank You to Andrew Joyce, author, who gave me some much needed guidance, when it came to the publishing of this effort. He gave me some very valuable advice and took a lot of stress out of a complicated process.

Lastly, like Daniel, I'm very thankful for my family and the privilege of just being here. It's been quite a trip! I wouldn't have missed it for anything!